# THE FISH AND CHIP SHOP DETECTIVES

From the corner of a café in Devon, former archaeologist and historian, Jenny Kane, is currently having a wonderful time writing a brand new, cosy crime series: *The Fish and Chip Shop Detectives*, for Hodder & Stoughton.

Jenny Kane has been writing professionally for the past 20 years. With over 40 novels published to date (including *Misty Mornings at The Potting Shed*, *Midsummer Dreams at Mill Grange* and *A Cornish Escape* as Jenny Kane, and *The Folville Chronicle* series as Jennifer Ash), she has also written 20 plus audio scripts and novellas for ITV's popular 1980's television show, *Robin of Sherwood*. (Released by AUK Ltd and Spiteful Puppet from 2017 to 2025.)

Jenny teaches creative writing via her tutoring business, Imagine.

All Jenny Kane's news can be found at www.jennykane.co.uk

# THE FISH AND CHIP SHOP DETECTIVES

## JENNY KANE

HODDER &
STOUGHTON

First published in Great Britain in 2026 by Hodder & Stoughton Limited
An Hachette UK company

The authorised representative in the EEA is Hachette Ireland,
8 Castlecourt Centre, Dublin 15, D15 XTP3, Ireland (email: info@hbgi.ie)

1

Copyright © Jenny Kane 2026

The right of Jenny Kane to be identified as the Author of the Work has been asserted by her in accordance with the Copyright, Designs and Patents Act 1988.

All rights reserved. No part of this publication may be reproduced, stored in a retrieval system, or transmitted, in any form or by any means without the prior written permission of the publisher, nor be otherwise circulated in any form of binding or cover other than that in which it is published and without a similar condition being imposed on the subsequent purchaser.

All characters in this publication are fictitious and any resemblance to real persons, living or dead, is purely coincidental.

A CIP catalogue record for this title is available from the British Library

Paperback ISBN 9781399754491
ebook ISBN 9781399754507

Typeset in Monotype Plantin by Manipal Technologies Limited

Printed and bound in Great Britain by Clays Ltd, Elcograf S.p.A.

Hodder & Stoughton policy is to use papers that are natural, renewable and recyclable products and made from wood grown in sustainable forests. The logging and manufacturing processes are expected to conform to the environmental regulations of the country of origin.

Hodder & Stoughton Limited
Carmelite House
50 Victoria Embankment
London EC4Y 0DZ

www.hodder.co.uk

*To my wonderful dad.*
*Cornish to the core.*

# Chapter One
## Monday 2nd June

Maggie wrapped a serving of fish and chips in paper and passed the aromatic package across the counter. There was something about her latest customer that made her give him an encouraging smile. He seemed lost.

'Here you go, me 'ansum. Best fish and chips for miles.'

'Thanks.'

Offering up the card machine so that he could pay, Maggie nodded towards the rucksack at his feet. 'On your holidays?'

'No. Well, sort of.' He shrugged, the movement giving him the air of a scarecrow swaying in the wind.

Judging the lad to be of a similar age to her daughter, Izzie, Maggie experienced a maternal pang. 'Sort of?'

'Yeah.' He threw her a shy grin as he turned away, giving the shop door a firm tug as he closed it behind him.

As soon as he'd left the warm environment of Robbins' Fish and Chip Shop, Maggie found herself speculating about her latest customer.

*Student maybe . . . Here on holiday with his mates after his exams, but they've had a row and he's taking some time out . . .* Picking up a cloth and a bottle of sterilising spray, she wiped droplets of vinegar off the counter. *Or he's fallen out with his girlfriend and he's after a bit of headspace.*

Smiling to herself, Maggie pictured her daughter joining in her musings. She and Izzie had always enjoyed people watching, guessing what others were like as they sipped coffee in the local café or sat on the harbour wall, observing Mousehole's non-stop supply of tourists as they meandered by.

Checking the time on the large, fish-shaped wall clock above the counter, Maggie headed to the front door and turned the open sign to closed, before calling through to the office beyond the serving counter. 'Mr Robbins, I'm closing up.'

The short grunt that greeted this news was all she needed to remove her apron, unpin the white boater from her head and hang them both on a hook inside the office door.

'I'll see you at six.' Maggie waited for the second grunt of acknowledgement she knew her boss would give her before she left.

Eric Robbins – known to everyone as *Mr* Robbins (with an emphasis on the *mister*, as though he felt very protective of the title) – was seated in his usual position at a square table in the centre of his office. Hunched forward, his palatial buttocks wedged into an orange plastic chair, a pair of black-rimmed designer glasses hooked over his cauliflower ears. The 1960s design of the spectacles served to emphasise, rather than diminish, the line of his repeatedly broken nose. One hand rubbed continuously at his stubbly chin, while the other scrolled through whatever it was he was studying on the tablet propped up in front of him. He wore a crisp white apron and a white fabric boater, despite only rarely stirring himself to interact with the frying of anything, let alone to engage in conversation with a customer.

In ten years of working as Mr Robbins' assistant in Mousehole's one and only chippy, Maggie had never discovered what it was he read so diligently every day.

Her daughter, who had a variety of interesting and increasingly unlikely theories as to how Mr Robbins came to have a boxer's face, was convinced he was a gangster. He certainly looked like one – at least, he looked like how a gangster ought to look if you took the media's word for it.

Maggie suppressed a chuckle as she recalled Izzie's observation that her employer looked like Ray Winstone in a pinny.

Once the expected grunt had escaped from Mr Robbins' taciturn lips, Maggie stepped into the June sunshine and relocked the chip shop's door behind her.

Inhaling the fresh air, emptying her lungs of the scent of chip fat, Maggie waited for a steady stream of tourist traffic to trundle along the narrow road which ran directly in front of the shop. Glancing towards the village to the right and then to the harbour before her, she was about to stride towards home, when she hesitated.

The lad she'd served ten minutes ago was perched on the lowest end of the harbour wall, staring at his phone. His package of fish and chips sat, untouched, beside him. Maggie almost went to see if he was alright but stopped herself.

*I'm just missing Izzie. If she was here she'd tell me that the last thing he'd want is me interfering.*

Turning in the opposite direction, Maggie strode into the heart of Mousehole, ruffling her hands through her hair as she went in an attempt to dislodge some of the chip shop's greasy scent from her unruly chestnut curls. She had arranged a phone call with Izzie for an hour's time, and that was something she didn't want to be late for.

\*

Ryan's stomach growled, but not even the delicious aroma of fish and chips coming from the wrap of food beside him tempted his appetite. He wasn't sure if he'd bought something to eat out of habit or simply for something to do.

Temporarily oblivious to the beauty of the seaside village behind him or the lapping of the sea before him, Ryan sat on the edge of the grey harbour wall, his legs hanging down, his phone held out before him. The row of tethered fishing boats, the beauty of the clear blue sky and the caws of the seagulls that gathered, each waiting expectantly for their chance to strike once his dinner was opened, was lost on him. He only had eyes for the message on the screen before him.

**I'm in Portugal!! Was very last minute. Exploring the whole country with friends. Only 3 months. Let's put things on hold. I'll see you when I get back. B. x**

*She couldn't even be bothered to phone to tell me in person.*

A mix of anger, hurt and humiliation churned in his stomach as an unwanted tear came to his eye. Wiping it away, Ryan peered around him, making sure no one had seen his brief burst of emotion.

*I get why Bea would want to explore the country; after all, her mother is Portuguese, but why didn't she call before she left? There's nothing 'only' about disappearing for three months.*

Shaking his head, he lowered the phone and absent-mindedly unfolded the paper from his late lunch, his slim fingers selecting and eating a chip without engaging his brain in the process.

As he chewed, he considered his options. Should he stay in the area and wait for Bea to come home, or should he go straight back to Penzance and get a train home to Birmingham?

*Go back to Birmingham for what?*

His family had cautioned him against going to Cornwall with Bea, convinced he'd never be happy there after being a city boy for the first twenty-two years of his life. Since leaving university the previous September, his friends had scattered to various places of work across the UK. There was no one left at home to spend time with beyond the walls of his parents' small terrace. And, if he was brutally honest, he knew they didn't really want him there.

Try as he might – and he had tried – he'd yet to find a job, his second-class sociology degree not quite hitting the mark with any of the employers he'd approached.

*It doesn't help that I don't know what I want to do.*

Ryan looked along the wall, just in time to see a young seagull hopping hopefully in his direction. He shooed it away. 'If I was more like Bea, it'd be alright. She can just zip off, pleasing herself, knowing that her first-class degree has already secured her a job with a legal firm in Penzance. *Plus*, she has a home in Mousehole already lined up for her, thanks to her family's property rental business.'

The seagull appeared as unimpressed by this information as his own parents had been. Ryan could hear his father's gruff voice now: 'No pride in something you haven't worked for, son.' He squirmed at the thought of having to tell them that Bea was travelling across Portugal for the next three months, without him, and that their life together was on hold.

'On hold, *not* over.' Ryan looked the seagull in the beak. 'That's what the text said. So, that means she's coming back to me, right?'

The gull gave an encouraging squawk as Ryan reached for another chip.

The lady in the chippy had been right. They really were very good chips.

# Chapter Two

'Hello, sweetheart.'

'Hey, Mum.' Izzie's voice sang down the phone.

'How come you're always so lively when it's the middle of the night for you?' Maggie beamed into the video call as her daughter's freckled face and bright purple hair came into focus.

'Because I'm young and spritely,' Izzie teased, 'and I'm talking to my wonderful Mum.'

'Thanks, sweetheart.'

'How many murders have you solved before the detectives this week, then?'

Maggie chuckled; her habit of turning every crime show she watched into a personal challenge, to see if she could beat Poirot and his cohorts to it, was something she loved to share with her daughter. 'Just two; one on *Dalgliesh* and one on *Death in Paradise*. But—'

'But *Death in Paradise* doesn't really count because the killer is always the most famous of the guest actors?' Izzie interrupted with a laugh.

'You got it! Actually, I've not had the chance to watch much television lately. I've been volunteering at the library a bit more, and the shop's gone onto summer opening hours now the season's picking up, so I'm working every day.'

'Gangster man not hired anyone for the summer yet, then?'

'Not yet. He'll have to soon, though. By the time the school holidays start, we'll be rushed off our feet.'

'He's probably not sold enough stolen diamonds to pay for this year's temp.'

Maggie giggled. 'Quite possibly not.'

Tucking a spiral of hair behind her ear, Izzie asked, 'What are you doing at the library, then? Helping the Silver Surfers with their computer skills again?'

'Yep. Via word puzzles this time. I've started a Crossword Club.'

'Fab! Just crosswords or puzzles in general?'

'Puzzles in general – but word puzzles. I was going to call it Puzzle Club, but there's one of those already for the jigsaw fans, so . . .'

'Crossword Club it had to be.'

'Precisely, love. The idea being to research answers they don't know on the internet. Mind you, there's one old chap, Harry – you remember him?'

'The old guy who lives on The Wharf?'

'That's him! He will insist on bringing his Sudoku along, and no matter how many times I tell him I can't help as I don't know one number from another if I don't have a calculator to help me, he won't have it.'

Izzie raised a mug to her smiling lips. 'I bet he's hell-bent on converting you to number puzzles.'

'You've got it. He's a nice chap, mind, Harry. Ex-sailor. Has many a story to tell in-between researching crossword clues online while telling the rest of us that we ought to be searching for answers in the books first, as it's a library.'

'He has a point.'

'Normally I'd agree, but as this is a club designed to help the computer-shy learn how to use Google . . .'

'Ah, I see.'

'Anyway, enough about my life. What adventures have you had this week?'

'Loads!' Izzie shuffled closer to the screen. 'And the best bit of it is that they've led to a new adventure. A big one!'

A sense of unease stirred in Maggie's chest. 'An even bigger adventure than starting uni in September and swimming with sharks?' She shuddered. 'I can't believe you did that. I'm glad you told me after you'd already done it, or I'd have been worried sick.'

'I was completely safe. It was totally epic.'

'I will take your word for it.' Maggie pictured the cuddly toy shark she'd bought for her daughter, which waited on her recently made-up bed, ready for Izzie's return in a fortnight's time. 'And while I'd love to visit New Zealand after hearing all the wonderful things you've said about it, there is no way I'm going to stop being afraid of sharks, epic or not.'

'Fair enough, Mum.'

'I'm looking forward to hearing more about it and seeing all your photos when you're back, though.'

'And I'm looking forward to showing you, but . . .'

For the next few minutes Maggie barely took in what her daughter was saying, beyond the fact that she'd been offered a temporary job at an Outward Bound activity centre for the next six months, had already sorted out her visa to cover her extended stay, and had spoken to Bath University about delaying her entry for a year.

'Mum?' Izzie's face had taken on a concerned edge. 'Mum, are you okay? You don't mind me staying longer, do you?'

'Of course I don't. It's a wonderful opportunity for you.'

'And we did say, didn't we – before I left – that if an opportunity came, taking a year out before university would be okay.'

Maggie knew she had said that, but only because she hadn't thought Izzie would want to be so far away for so long. Muzzling her emotions, she said, 'You won't be coming home until Christmas, then?'

'Twentieth of December.' Izzie's enthusiasm faded a touch. 'It's okay, Mum. I *am* coming back, it's just . . .'

Maggie hastily reassured her daughter. 'You'll love every minute of it. If you don't have the adventure of a lifetime when you're nineteen, when will you have it?' Hoping she sounded convincing as a raft of disappointment threatened to consume her, Maggie gripped the handle of her tea mug and plastered a smile on her face. 'And just think how much we'll have to chat about over Christmas dinner.'

★

Ryan's phone screen went from being crystal clear, to grainy, to scrambled and back to clear, on a repeating cycle, as he tried to speak to Bea.

'It's just three months, Ryan. I'm sorry it was so last minute. I tried to call, but I had no signal. I knew you'd already be on your way south, so I sent the text and thought I'd wait until I had arrived here before I spoke to you.'

Biting back the temptation to ask why she hadn't phoned him the moment she'd been invited to go, or while she was packing, or from the airport, he said, 'So, Portugal, then?'

'Yes!' She positively squeaked with excitement. 'It's sooo amazing! You'd love it. I can't help wondering why my mother ever left.'

*If it's so amazing, why didn't you ask me to come too?* He knew the answer to his unspoken question. *Because she knows I could never have afforded to go.*

'I'm glad you're happy, Bea, really I am – but what about me? *Us*?'

'We're fine, silly. I'll be back in twelve weeks, then we'll be together, just as we planned.'

'And right now? I have nowhere to go.' Hating that he sounded desperate, Ryan held his breath as the line froze for a second, building the tension before Bea spoke.

'Yes, you do. The flat is all yours. I've told my parents to expect you.'

'Are you sure? I mean, they've never met me.'

'I've told them about you. They're dead happy for me.'

Ryan let out a rush of air. 'That's such a relief. I wasn't—'

Shaking her head, Bea interrupted. 'You didn't think I'd leave you high and dry, did you?'

'No . . . no, of course not. I was just all geared up to start our life together and get a job and . . . everything. You know.'

Blowing him a kiss down the line, Bea gave Ryan one of her killer smiles – the sort of smile that had made him fall for her in the first place. 'You know the address. I'll text Mum to remind her to be there to hand over the keys, but I'm sure she'd have remembered anyway.'

'Thanks, Bea. I'm really looking forward to . . .' His voice trailed to nothing as the screen froze. Then the line went dead.

\*

Maggie leant over the bathroom sink and washed her tear-stained face with a brusque scrub of her hands. Then, patting her face dry with her towel, she pushed her shoulders back and scowled at herself in the mirror.

'If you were Izzie, you'd have done exactly the same. It's no good telling your daughter to grab every opportunity that comes her way if you begrudge it when she does just that.'

Abandoning her plan to spend an hour or so weeding her small garden, Maggie clicked on the kettle. 'In situations like this, only one thing will do.' She opened the fridge and pulled out a block of cheddar. 'Cheese and biscuits, strong coffee, a cryptic crossword and an episode of *Inspector Morse*.'

By the time she had watched Morse and Lewis apprehend the murderer, she'd finished two crosswords, eaten her pre-evening-shift tea and had shared her analysis of how the onscreen crime must have been committed with Morse before congratulating him for his logical, if somewhat prosaic, reasoning.

'Nothing like a bit of crime solving to make us feel better, isn't that right, Izzie.' Maggie tapped a finger on top of a photo of her daughter that sat in the corner of the room, before readying herself to face Mr Robbins and four and a half more hours at the fish and chip shop.

\*

Smarting with embarrassment, Ryan hooked his rucksack onto his shoulder and marched away, as fast as possible, from the Edwardian house that had been converted into flats. He hadn't even been invited to cross the threshold to see the inside of the place in which he and Bea had planned to live.

With no idea where he was going, Ryan found himself wandering back towards the harbour.

*They more or less laughed in my face when I told them who I was and why I was there.*

'Move in while you wait for Beatrice to come home?' Bea's mother's high-pitched voice had cut him like glass. 'Oh, that's totally impossible. You must have completely misunderstood my daughter. We will need to let it out until she's home. Unless you can afford the rent here alone? I assume you *are* working.'

As she'd asked the question, her thin brown eyes had blatantly sized him up, wordlessly dismissing him as worthless as he'd admitted that no, he wasn't currently employed. There had been no chance to tell her that his intention was to find work as soon as possible. Ryan had found himself listening for a trace of a Portuguese accent – but there was none. Bea's mother could have sprung straight from the Home Counties, twinset, pearls and all. Reining in his thoughts, Ryan had turned his attention to the equally hostile but considerably taller man who stood behind his wife with a proprietorial hand on her shoulder.

'What about Bea's job? She was supposed to start work on Monday.'

'I've arranged things so that she can have a sabbatical before she starts.'

Ryan was given no chance to comment on this, for Bea's mother was intent on ending their encounter.

'I suggest—' her haughty expression focused on the end of the street beyond them, a direction she wished him to take '—that you go back to . . . where was it? *Birmingham*. And look for a life there.'

Having made the word 'Birmingham' sound like an unpleasant rash, Bea's mother had closed the door in his face. For a second or two he'd stood statue-still, in shock. His girlfriend had decided to go travelling for three months without telling him, her mother had just slammed in his face the door to the home he thought he'd be living in, and if he went back to the Midlands, there was nothing to look forward to but a load of *I-told-you-so*'s.

Now, perched back on the harbour wall, Ryan released a long shuddering breath as the seagull he'd chatted to earlier came to join him.

'Go away. I've got no food this time.'

The young gull sidled closer, giving him a beady stare.

'Don't you start.' Ryan fixed his eyes on the bird. 'I need a job. I need to find a roof over my head for tonight, and I need to accept that my girlfriend's parents think I'm a pointless oik. At least Bea was sure we'd be together after her trip.'

*Bea looks a lot like her mum. Dark hair, clear, easily tanned skin* . . . His thoughts dissolved into a sigh.

Readjusting his position against the harbour wall, Ryan peered along the narrow road to where he'd noticed a taxi rank. 'I'll go into Penzance, see if there's a hostel I can kip in, and hunt for a job here to keep me going until Bea comes home.'

He was not ready to listen to the little voice telling him that, whatever Bea had claimed, there was a good chance she might not be coming back for him.

# Chapter Three

Maggie's usual optimism had reasserted itself by the time she'd walked the one hundred and thirty metres that separated her home on Duck Street and the chip shop on the corner of South Cliff and North Cliff roads.

She might be sad that her daughter was going to be away for longer than planned, but at least Izzie would be home for Christmas.

*And she* will *come home. She won't get a permanent job out there.*

As the prospect of Izzie emigrating tore at her heart, Maggie peered upwards. Wisps of clouds came and went across the vivid blue sky as the spring breeze blew in off the sea. She couldn't help but smile. While the village held limited excitement for the local teenagers, she knew she couldn't live anywhere else in the world.

*I could visit Izzie every year if she did stay over there.* Maggie's smile faltered. *Every other year, once I'd saved up for the flights.*

She told herself off, knowing that she was lucky to have a daughter who she got on with, and who enjoyed her company in return. Their twice-weekly video calls had been a standard part of their lives since Izzie had gone abroad three months ago and would – Izzie had promised – keep going once she went to university.

As she turned onto North Cliff, Maggie slowed her pace. The young man she'd served chips to, prior to closing up that afternoon, was still seated on the harbour wall.

Checking her wristwatch, seeing she had ten minutes before it was time to don her hat and make sure the chippy was ready for the arrival of their first customer, Maggie increased her sedate pace. She loudly cleared her throat as she got closer so that he had time to come out of whatever introspection was holding him hostage against the grey wall.

'Hello again.' Maggie came to a halt a few paces away, not wanting to invade his personal space.

'Oh, hello.'

'Did you enjoy the fish and chips?'

'Yes. Very nice.' He looked back at the sea view, while adding a belated, 'Thanks.'

Despite the closed-off expression on his face, Maggie kept talking. 'Tell me if I'm being a nosy old bat, but are you okay? I couldn't help noticing that you were here when I left work at half-two, and now it's approaching five.'

He flashed a forced smile in her direction, before returning to his study of the horizon. 'I haven't been here the whole time.'

'Mousehole is so beautiful. Lots to explore.'

'Yeah.'

*He sounds just like Izzie. Nice village, but nothing much in it.* 'Great view here too.'

'Nice boats.'

'Yes.' Maggie started to struggle. 'So, you're okay, then?'

'Uh-huh.'

Maggie hoisted her handbag further up her shoulder and gestured towards the chippy. 'Well, if you need anything, you know where I'll be.'

The offer of assistance seemed to surprise the young man. 'Why would you want to help me?'

'You do need help, then?' She cocked her head to one side, an action that brought an unexpected smile to the lad's lips.

'For a second, you looked like the seagull I've been chatting to.'

Her eyebrows rose. 'You talk to seagulls?'

Instantly self-conscious again, he mumbled, 'Yeah, well, sometimes.'

'I often talk to them. Helps order the thoughts now I'm on my own; the advantage being they don't answer back.' She took a step closer. 'I'm Maggie, by the way.'

'Ryan.'

'From the Midlands?'

'Birmingham.'

'I had a great day in Birmingham the December before last. Christmas shopping with my daughter in that huge shopping centre place.'

'The Bullring.'

'That's it. You know it?'

'Had a Saturday job in a bakery there.'

'On your hols, then?'

'Yes. No . . . I'm just staying here for a while . . . maybe longer.' Ryan flushed.

Experiencing what she always called a 'lightbulb moment' when she was working out who the felon was in whichever work of detective fiction she happened to be reading, Maggie asked, 'You wouldn't be after a job, would you? It would be temporary, and I'm not sure how many hours, but . . .'

Ryan's head shot around to face her so fast Maggie found herself taking a step backwards. 'A job?'

Wondering if she'd been rash in more or less offering him a position without asking Mr Robbins first, Maggie ploughed on regardless. 'With me at the chippy. The owner should have advertised for temporary staff already for the season, but as ever, he's forgotten. My daughter, Izzie, did the job last year, but she's travelling in New Zealand for a while.'

'Travelling.' A cloud passed over Ryan's face. 'There's a lot of it about.'

'I'm sorry?'

'It doesn't matter.' Ryan shrugged.

Deciding not to press the point, Maggie added, 'Izzie is convinced Mr Robbins – that's the chip shop's owner – is in the mafia or something.'

'Seriously?'

Maggie chuckled. 'He has that look, but he's a total lamb. Tends to leave me to it customer-wise, though, so an extra pair of hands is vital for the summer months.'

'It's very kind of you, and I am after work, as it happens, but I also need a place to live. I doubt a part-time job serving fish and chips is going to pay the rent.'

Maggie almost offered him Izzie's bedroom there and then, but common sense kicked in. *Hold on, you know nothing about this lad.* 'You've nowhere to live?'

'No, I was supposed to . . .' Ryan trailed off. 'It doesn't matter.'

Maggie waved a hand towards the shop. 'Come on, let's see if Mr Robbins is hiring yet, and if so, you could try out. You might even have a job by bedtime.'

'But . . .'

Guessing what he was going to say, Maggie continued, 'I've several friends who own bed and breakfast places in the village. Most of them owe me a favour. I'll find you a bed tonight, and then you can worry about reality tomorrow. How does that sound?'

Ryan studied the woman next to him, her mad mound of curls blowing haphazardly in the wind that was now cutting in off the coast and getting trapped in the U-shaped harbour, making the fishing boats tethered below them bob erratically on the waves. 'Why are you helping me?'

'Because I'm annoyingly nice.' *And I miss my daughter, and something about you reminds me of her.* Ignoring the thought at the back of her mind, Maggie gave him a firm smile. 'I'm also late for work. Are you coming, or not?'

*

Ryan wasn't sure why he was following the woman from the chip shop, but as he had no better plan, he decided he'd worry about telling her he couldn't afford a night in a bed and breakfast later. His phone had already informed him there were two youth hostels within taxi or walking distance, and both had room for him – but only for one night.

*If I get this job, I'll need a place for the whole summer.*

Ryan dismissed the notion. He'd been singularly unsuccessful with every job he'd applied for, from teaching assistant posts to being a counter assistant in Greggs; getting not one interview in the past six months, therefore, the chances of him having a job by bedtime were so small, the situation wasn't worth worrying about.

Dragging himself out of his introspection, Ryan realised he was lagging behind Maggie. He was used to his friends – and Bea in particular – telling him he walked too fast, and ought to slow down for them, but now he was having to hurry to keep up with the woman who he'd assumed was his mum's age.

*

Approaching the chippy for the second time that day, Ryan looked up at the building. Facing out towards the harbour, placed at the corner of two roads, its large picture window gave it a welcoming feel, as did the brightly painted sign above the door proclaiming him to be on the threshold of *Robbins' Fish and Chip Shop*. He smiled to see that the 'i' in the word 'fish' had been replaced with a drawing of a small fish, balancing on its tail.

Following Maggie as she pushed open the front door with a flourish, he was surprised to find himself smiling.

'Welcome to Mr Robbins' fish and chip shop.'

Ryan's grin expanded as Maggie announced their arrival as if they'd just stepped off a plane into paradise, rather than walked into a stark white chippy, which smelt of non-stop frying, salt and vinegar, and cleaning agents.

'If you wait here, I'll go and see the boss.'

As Maggie disappeared through a door, which was wedged slightly ajar with a ship-shaped doorstop, Ryan suddenly felt nervous. A feeling that intensified when he heard a monosyllabic, 'Suppose so,' from the depths of the next room.

Emerging, now wearing a plain white apron and a matching boater, and holding out a similar get-up to him, Maggie said, 'If you want to pop your rucksack into the office and put these on, I'll show you the ropes.'

Ryan took a step forward but then stopped. 'Are you sure? I mean, does your boss want me here?'

Maggie chuckled. 'Mr Robbins knows he needs to employ a helper for me, but he'll always put off paying another wage until he has to.'

'That doesn't exactly reassure me.'

'Mr Robbins trusts my judgement. Don't worry. Now then, let me introduce you to the wonderful world of health and safety instructions and hygiene protocols.'

# Chapter Four

Maggie watched as Ryan funnelled a helping of chips into a cone and passed it to their latest customer. Despite being anxious to begin with, he was a quick learner and was already using the till like a seasoned professional.

As the daylight dimmed to night, and the customer numbers dwindled, Maggie suggested they take a coffee break. 'If you go into the office, you'll see a tray near the window, complete with mugs, kettle, tea, coffee and sugar. Mr Robbins will probably stay quiet or grunt at you. He has tea – leave the bag in the mug. He takes it white with three sugars. I'll have tea, but black with no sugar. The milk is in the fridge under the office window.'

Not particularly keen on meeting his so-far-anonymous potential employer, Ryan asked, 'Why do you call him Mr Robbins and not by his first name? Is he terribly formal?'

Maggie laughed. 'Everyone calls him Mr Robbins. In all the time I've worked here, I've never heard anyone address him in any other way. I only know his name is Eric because sometimes post is addressed to Mr Eric Robbins, but he stubbornly insists on the full use of his surname and title.'

Ryan glanced towards the office door. 'And he'll be alright with me just walking in?'

'I promise.' Maggie moved nearer the counter as the shop door swung open and a teenager came in. 'Go on, me 'ansum. I'll serve this lass; you get the drinks.'

Already uncomfortably warm in his jeans and sweatshirt beneath his apron, he felt horribly self-conscious as he went into the office. Mr Robbins was seated at a table in the very centre of the room, peering at a tablet screen.

'I'm Ryan. Maggie said to come in and make us all a drink. Is that okay?'

A large hand, with incredibly thick fingers, pointed towards the tray Maggie had described.

As conversation was obviously not going to be forthcoming, Ryan hurried past the large man and, relieved to find the kettle already full of water, clicked it on, before fumbling some teabags out of a pot marked 'Cookies'.

Feeling the pressure of Mr Robbins' presence, even though the man's gaze had not wavered from the tablet screen, Ryan willed the kettle to boil faster.

The sound of Maggie chatting to a customer, the tapping of the till, and the hum of the kettle as it built up to the boil, wasn't enough to fill the awkward semi-silence. Ryan knew he'd have made mindless chatter in any other circumstances. He'd always found silence in the company of another person uncomfortable and felt a desperate need to fill it.

Opening the little fridge, which contained nothing but two cartons of milk, Ryan couldn't stand it anymore. 'Thank you for letting me try out for a job here.'

A slight squeak from the seat beneath Mr Robbins' bulk informed Ryan that he'd been heard and that, perhaps, his attention had been diverted from the screen he studied so diligently.

'Maggie's been very kind to me and . . .'

The voice that cut through his gratitude took Ryan by surprise. Not because it was gruff and gravelly, but because his companion had actually responded.

'Three sugars.'

'Yes. Maggie said.' Ryan dug a teaspoon into a bag of slightly damp granulated sugar.

'She said you had nowhere to stay.'

'Oh, umm. There's a hostel in Penzance, so . . .'

'There's a bedsit.'

'Bedsit?' Ryan silently cursed as he spilt some sugar across the tray.

'You deaf, boy?'

'No. Sorry, I didn't know Maggie had told you that I needed somewhere to . . .'

'She's a good girl.'

Wondering if he'd ever finish a complete sentence in the chip shop owner's presence, Ryan poured some milk into his own mug, before adding some to the one he'd used for Mr Robbins.

'I've a bedsit here.'

Ryan turned, mug of tea in hand, to see Mr Robbins jabbing a single finger towards the ceiling.

'You want to see?'

'Well, I . . . the rent might be a bit much in Mousehole, and . . .'

'Go and see.' A single key had appeared in Mr Robbins' hand.

Feeling unable to argue, Ryan took the key and placed the tea mug on the table. Wondering if that meant that he had got the job at the chippy or if he was about to view a bedsit with no income to pay the rent, he followed Mr Robbins' line of sight.

A white door, which would have been almost invisible in the white wall if it hadn't been for the black handle that opened it, awaited his attention in the corner of the room.

Not asking why there was no keyhole, Ryan glanced towards the shop. 'I should check Maggie is . . .'

'Maggie is always alright. Go and look now.'

\*

Behind the white door, Ryan found a set of steep, narrow, uncarpeted stairs, which ran straight upwards, leading into total darkness. Fumbling for a switch, he eventually found one and bathed the staircase in a dim but appreciable light.

Hearing the creak of wood beneath his black trainers, Ryan found his pulse had quickened as he ascended. Trying to dismiss the notion that literally anything could be awaiting him at the top, he kept going. The alternative being to dash back down and explain to Mr Robbins why he wasn't doing as he was told.

A second white door awaited him at the top. This one did have a keyhole, and Ryan slotted the key into the lock. Tasting the ever-present hint of fish and chips in the air, he pushed open the door.

Before him was a surprisingly spacious, recently painted bedroom with a single bed beneath a picture window which, Ryan saw as he hastened towards it, faced out to the harbour and the sea beyond. He found himself holding his breath, amazed by the beauty of the moonlight as it twinkled on the waves.

After a few seconds, Ryan tore his eyes from the scene and viewed the rest of the room. A small chest of drawers by the bed was butted up to a single wardrobe, both of which were made from pine. A table with a folding wooden chair sat opposite the bed, adjacent to the door he'd just come through. Following the curved wall of the room around, only now did Ryan register that the chip shop was on the corner of two roads, and the bedsit took up the entire attic space.

A sink sat next to another table, on which sat a microwave oven and a portable hot plate. A small fridge-freezer was on the floor next to it. The lack of hum told Ryan it was off.

'At least that means there won't be a human head in there or anything.'

Wishing Maggie hadn't told him about her daughter's theory that Mr Robbins was in the mafia, Ryan opened a free-standing larder-style cupboard which stood slightly out from the curved wall, next to the fridge. It contained two shelves, stuffed with plates, mugs, saucepans and so on, as well as three empty shelves which, presumably, awaited any future tenant's food.

At the deepest part of the curved wall, a square block had been built out. It had the appearance of a built-in wardrobe that hadn't quite worked against the shape of the room. Opening the door, after a couple of tugs at the stiff hinges, Ryan was confronted with a toilet, mini sink and a narrow shower unit.

His first thought was that Mr Robbins couldn't have had the shower room built with any intention of using it himself. At least, not if he'd ever wanted to take a shower. *He'd never fit in here.*

Backing out of the bathroom, Ryan returned to the window. There was no denying that it was a perfect hideaway. 'I could wake up looking at that view.' He was surprised to find himself smiling.

Not worrying about the fact there was no bed linen or any sign of towels because he'd never be able to afford the rent here anyway, and had no idea if he'd got the job downstairs, Ryan remembered that he hadn't taken Maggie her cup of tea yet.

\*

'Six months tenancy. Low rent if you take the job in the shop.'

Ryan's jaw dropped open as Mr Robbins announced that both a home and employment were his for the taking.

'Thank you, but I . . .'

'Minimum wage, but only fifty quid a week rent. Yes?'

As his mouth opened and closed in shock, Ryan mumbled, 'Thank you. Yes, please.'

'Good. Maggie needs you.'

Recognising this as the dismissal it was, Ryan picked up the two mugs that were cooling fast and hurried out to the shop.

Perhaps his luck was finally improving.

# Chapter Five
## Monday 9th June

Maggie peered at the puzzle book. Its pages were being propped open on the shop counter with a box of tomato ketchup sachets on one side and a roll of blue wipe-up cloth on the other. 'Here's a nice easy one.'

'Every time you say it's an easy one, it isn't.' Ryan swept up the remnants of a chicken and mushroom pie from the shop floor.

'Trust me – this time it is easy. In fact,' Maggie tapped her ballpoint pen against the clue, 'it's a bit of a classic. I've seen this question more times than I care to mention.'

'Go on then, hit me.'

'Musical anagram: Carthorse. Nine letters.'

'Oh, that one! That is a classic. Orchestra.' Ryan smiled. 'Have you always enjoyed puzzles?'

'Ever since I was small. I did them with my grandad. My fondest childhood memories involve sitting on his knee, being allowed to fill in the answers to the clues for him. Or watching whodunnits on the tele. I got so good at solving puzzles of all sorts that he'd joke I'd be the next Jessica Fletcher.'

'Who?'

'*Murder, She Wrote.*'

'Of course!'

'Do you like crosswords?'

'Not crosswords really,' Ryan smiled as he gestured to the one they were doing, 'although they're growing on me.

I've always liked logic problems. The ones with the weird, stair-shaped grids.'

'Oh, I love those! Real mind benders sometimes. Izzie and I can spend hours on just one.'

Propping the broom up against the wall, Ryan collected a dustpan and brush. 'Is the old guy at the library still trying to convert you to Sudoku?'

'Yes. Harry's a lovely chap, but I can't see him ever getting to grips with modern technology. Mind you, he is eighty-one, so why should he?'

'I think it's brilliant that you do that.' Ryan crouched down, sweeping the pie debris into the dustpan. 'I can't imagine my mum taking time out from her life to help others like you do. Or wanting to do a puzzle with me, come to that.'

Maggie wasn't sure what to say. In the week they'd been working together, Ryan had become more at ease in her presence. They'd chatted about all manner of things, and, despite their age gap, a friendship was growing. This, however, was the first time he'd mentioned his family. She kept her eyes on the crossword as she ventured, 'What's your mum like?'

'Old-school.'

'You mean she's a housewife?'

'Yeah. Dad likes it that way.'

'Oh.' Not sure how to interpret Ryan's closed tone, and telling herself she shouldn't jump to conclusions, Maggie read out the next crossword clue. 'Moulin red. Five letters.'

'Rouge.'

'You're getting better at this.'

'Hardly surprising, as we do three a day!' Ryan adjusted the boater on his head. 'And this crossword is fairly easy.'

'So far.' Maggie scanned the rest of the clues. 'Izzie and I always have a crossword or codeword on the go.'

'You two seem really close.'

'We are. Probably because it's always been just us.'

'You're not married?'

'No.'

Maggie instantly regretted her blunt answer as Ryan stuttered, 'I wasn't being nosy, I . . .'

'It's fine.' Seeing Ryan colour, Maggie hastily gave him a potted history. 'I was going out with someone, fell pregnant, he didn't want to know and scarpered. End of. So it's just Izzie and me, and I wouldn't change a thing.' Maggie watched as Ryan unfolded his gangly frame from where he'd been sweeping up. 'How about you? You get on okay with your folks?'

'My parents are fine and everything, but I came along rather late in the day. I've always had the impression that I was an unplanned surprise.'

'They must be very proud of you, though.'

'Not that you'd notice. Dad's a brickie. He and Mum expected me to be the same, or be a carpenter or something that could be called "a solid profession", rather than wasting time with "airy-fairy thinking".' The memory of his mum proclaiming that she supposed 'being a chip server was better than nothing' and 'what can you do with a sociology degree anyway?' was eclipsed by an image of Bea's parents. He wondered what they'd make of him working in Mr Robbins' shop. *Very little, probably.* Looking back up at Maggie, he said, 'They're glad I've got somewhere to live, though.'

'I'm sure.'

'As satisfied as they sounded about being right about me and Bea, they'll be glad not to have me under their feet.'

'Oh, Ryan, I'm sure that . . .'

Ryan raised his hand to stem the flow of reassurances he knew were about to come from Maggie's mouth. 'I know my parents love me; they just prefer it when I'm not there. The bedsit is perfect for me. I can't understand why Mr Robbins isn't renting it out for a fortune or living there himself. It's been recently redecorated, so why was it empty?'

The memory of Izzie suggesting her boss used it as a place to store his loot flashed through Maggie's mind, but she said nothing.

Ryan answered his own question. 'The smell of the chip shop would probably put a lot of people off living here. I've only been here a week, and already I don't have a single item of clothing that doesn't have a whiff of fat about it.'

'I can believe it.' Maggie returned them to the safer subject of puzzles. 'When I watch crime shows on TV, I try and work out who did it before the detective. Izzie and I have an unofficial competition when she's with me. We both write down who we think "did it" before it's announced. The winner has supper made for them.'

Ryan smiled. 'I love detective shows too. I used to watch them with my gran when she was alive.'

'A woman of taste.'

'She was great.' Ryan rejoined Maggie behind the counter. 'Her favourite was *Sherlock*.'

'One of the classic versions: Jeremy Brett, Basil Rathbone, Peter Cushing?'

'No, although she did love those. She preferred the modern one; had a real thing for Benedict Cumberbatch.' Ryan grinned. 'It didn't bother her that she was old enough to be his mother – grandmother, even. She was a bit like you.'

Not sure how to react, Maggie said, 'You think I'm the sort of woman that falls for actors a fraction of my age?'

'Nah. I meant, she was full of fun and took no notice of how old she was.'

'Implying I'm ancient.'

'Only a little bit.' Ryan laughed as Maggie stuck her tongue out at him. He was about to offer to make them a drink when his mobile vibrated in his pocket. 'Oh.'

Seeing two points of red appear on Ryan's cheeks, Maggie frowned. 'Bea?'

'Yeah. Do you mind if I take it?'

'Not at all, but be quick. It'd be sod's law that Mr Robbins picks this moment to see how we're getting on. Go outside. I'll tell him you're emptying the bins if he comes through.'

*

Ryan had been gone almost half an hour. Maggie had been managing without him, while trying not to dwell on the fact that Ryan's parents appeared to think him a disappointment. Hoping he was mistaken, and telling herself it was none of her business anyway, she served a handful of customers in his absence, but now there was a queue of five people waiting, and if Ryan didn't reappear soon, she'd be forced to call Mr Robbins to come and help her.

She was halfway through wrapping a round of scampi and chips, while having a conversation about a recent episode of *CSI: Miami* with one of their regulars, when Ryan hurried back inside. His put-out expression would have to be dealt with later.

It was another hour before the stream of customers had calmed to a trickle and they had the chance to make a drink. Maggie waited until they each had a cup of tea in their hands before asking Ryan if he was alright.

'I'm fine.'

'That's what my daughter says when she's far from fine.'

'I'm not your daughter,' Ryan snapped, before immediately backtracking. 'Sorry.'

'It's okay.' Maggie glanced up at the clock. 'It's almost half-eight. Why don't you head off? It's gone quiet, and I can't think we'll have many more folk through the door before we shut at nine. Take yourself to The Mariner or something. See if you can find some people of your own age to chat to.'

Ryan flipped over the chips cooking in the fryer. 'I can't. I'm not supposed to finish until half-nine. And we have to tidy up after closing.'

'I'll do it. You can do it for me tomorrow night.'

'Thanks, Maggie. I think I will. ' Ryan felt a stab of guilt. 'It isn't that I don't enjoy your company, it's just that . . .'

'I totally understand. Most folk who come in here are either over forty or under eighteen and you miss your old friends.' Maggie bent to the cupboard that was built in under the sink, and pulled out a stack of cardboard chip trays. 'Although, speaking as a friend, if you want to tell me how that little madam has upset you this time, I'm all ears.'

'I wish you wouldn't call Bea that. She isn't that bad.'

Maggie gave him a rueful smile. 'Ryan, me 'ansum, she disappeared to another country without warning, and that was the first time she's called you since – unless she has called, and you've not said.'

'That was the first time.'

'I take it she's having fun.'

'Time of her life, she said.'

'Without you. That was a bit thoughtless.' Maggie spoke softly, seeing the hurt in her young friend's eyes. 'Did she ask how you were doing?'

'No. No, she didn't.'

# Chapter Six

The pub was packed. A mix of tourists and locals occupied every spare inch. As Ryan hunkered down at the small round table he'd managed to snag after purchasing his second pint, he covertly scanned his fellow customers.

While a few people of his own age had been and gone over the last hour, they'd all been in established groups. He'd known that Maggie's suggestion that he find someone of his own age to speak to wasn't something he'd find easy to do. Friendships in the past had always developed via set situations: classrooms, lecture halls and so on. Casually striking up conversations with strangers was Maggie's thing, not his. On this occasion, however, Ryan was surprised by how disappointed he felt. Part of him had hoped that maybe there'd be someone to talk to. Every now and then, he'd cast a semi-envious glance towards the restaurant part of the pub. Several couples sat together, chatting happily in the candle-enhanced light, sharing a meal and displaying the sort of public intimacy he'd imagined he and Bea would have.

*And you will – when she's home. She said she was coming back.*

Finding himself wishing that Maggie – or at least one of her puzzle books – was with him, Ryan was about to leave when his eyes were drawn back to the restaurant. The couple at the table nearest to him had been all undivided attention and hand-holding a few minutes ago, but now the mood had changed.

Amidst the hubbub of chatter and laughter, not to mention the occasional bark of a dog from beneath the regulars' bar stools and the background music coming from a series of speakers fixed at intervals around the stone walls, Ryan became aware of an argument.

The woman had her back to him, so he couldn't see the expression on her face, but the man she was with, who Ryan judged to have been in his mid-twenties, looked furious. His hand was clenched into a fist around the spoon he'd been using to eat his pudding.

Lowering his eyes, Ryan strained to listen to what was becoming a loudly hissed row. He found himself thinking that Maggie would have come up with an excuse to get closer to the table by now, so she could work out what was going on. Ryan smiled for the first time since he'd left the chippy. Everything about Maggie suggested that she had missed her calling. She'd have made a great detective.

He was abruptly pulled from his thoughts by the scraping sound of a chair being sharply dragged backwards across the terracotta tiles that formed the dining area's floor, and the man was storming out of the pub, his face red.

Silence blanketed the pub as everyone turned to witness the unfolding drama; then, as if nothing had happened, the drinkers returned to their pints, glasses of wine and meals – all except for the young woman who, Ryan guessed, was mortified with embarrassment as she sat alone at the dinner table.

Uncomfortable on her behalf, Ryan stared into his pint. *I can't go and check on her, it would look weird. Anyway, who the hell would want me interfering? It's not like I'm in any position to give relationship advice.*

He took refuge in his lager, while occasionally flicking his gaze in her direction. She hadn't moved. Trying to work out if she was crying, staring at the back of her blonde hair and examining her shoulders to see if they were heaving up and down, he was relieved to see she was still.

*Unless she's doing that silent crying thing women do sometimes.*

Suddenly she stood up, unhooked her bag from the back of her chair and walked – not to the exit – but to the bar.

He watched her slender figure weave through the crowd. Her jeans were black and slim-fitting; her shirt, semi-low-cut, sexy but not sexual.

A couple of minutes later, Ryan spotted her blonde bob reappearing from the direction of the bar. She was actively searching for somewhere to sit. But there wasn't anywhere – not a single seat – except for at the small table where he sat.

\*

'Hey, Mum!'

'Izzie! To what do I owe the pleasure so soon?' Maggie grinned into the WhatsApp video call, while her insides did a backflip. *Something's wrong.*

'Thing is, Mum, I've had a brilliant couple of days.'

'Why does your tone make that sound like a bad thing?' Maggie's parental radar notched up to full-on problem mode.

'It got me thinking, that's all.'

'Thinking, or overthinking?'

'Possibly both.' Izzie pulled a face. 'That's why I called. You'll know what I should do.'

Maggie leant in closer to the screen while grabbing a cushion from the sofa seat beside her and giving it a cuddle in lieu of her daughter. 'Do about what?'

'They've offered me a full-time job.'

A wave of cold washed over Maggie as she heard the words she'd been dreading since Izzie had first told her she'd saved enough to go to New Zealand for a pre-university adventure.

'Mum? Say something.'

Hugging the cushion tighter, Maggie did her best to disguise how gutted she felt about the prospect of her child being so far away forever. 'You mean, what do I think about you working there instead of coming back to England and getting a degree?'

'Yes.' Izzie began to chew at a fingernail. A sign Maggie knew to mean that her daughter was undecided.

Taking this as a positive, Maggie said, 'All I can advise, love, is that you don't make any decisions in a hurry. Investigate the situation properly, re visas and so on. Find out *exactly* what the Outward Bound folk you're working for are offering, and for how long. Then, ask yourself if you'd be sorry, in a few years' time, not to have done a degree.'

'I will.' Izzie beamed. 'You're the best mum in the world, you know that, don't you?'

'I doubt that, but thanks.'

'You are. Everyone else's mum would have demanded they come home and begged them not to live so far away.'

Maggie smiled. 'I don't want you to live so far away, but I do want you to be happy. Just take some time to think before you commit to anything, okay?'

'Okay, Mum. Love you.'

\*

The woman sitting opposite Ryan had almost finished her large glass of Merlot. The wine, he noted, was almost the same shade of dark red as the varnish on her nails.

She hadn't spoken since she'd asked if he minded her sharing the table. It had felt fine to start with, but after a while, with everyone around them engrossed in chatter, the localised silence had become too much for Ryan.

'Are you alright? Hope you don't mind me asking, but I couldn't help seeing your . . . friend walk out.'

'Fiancé.' She took a gulp of wine. 'Toby. Former fiancé, maybe. I don't know.'

'Oh. Sorry.'

'There's no need for you to be sorry. You didn't upset me.' She looked up at him. 'I'm Tania.'

'Ryan.'

Scanning the room, as if to check there was no one she knew to overhear her, Tania muttered, 'Well, you know why I'm drinking in here on my own, but why are you?'

Thrown off guard by the bluntness of the question, Ryan found himself telling her everything about his girlfriend's abrupt departure, how Maggie had found him a job and a home at the chip shop, and how he was surprised by how much he was enjoying the work but was missing having company between shifts.

Tilting her head to one side, Tania's bright blue eyes radiated concern as she asked, 'You're convinced your girlfriend is coming back, then?'

'Yes.' Ryan took a mouthful of lager. 'She says she is, so I have to believe that.'

Tania sighed. 'Toby tells me I must believe him too.'

As Tania's sentence trailed into thin air, Ryan asked, 'Is that why he left, because you told him you didn't believe him about something?'

Her eyes strayed to the pub doorway. 'He accused me of not trusting him.'

Ryan followed her line of sight. 'You're hoping he's going to walk back in and say sorry for storming off.'

'Yeah.' Tania swivelled her position on the stool so she was facing away from the doorway. 'Pathetic, isn't it.'

'No, it's human.'

Tania knocked back the last mouthful of wine. 'We're getting married in the local church at the weekend. This is our – was supposed to be our – hen and stag time.'

'Hen and stag *time*? More than just one night of celebration, then?'

'Yeah.' Her shoulders slumped. 'We're staying in a local hotel to have a few days of fun. It's our wedding gift from my parents. They're travelling at the moment, but will be back on Friday in time for me to stay with them the night before the wedding, but the others will stay here. Toby and his best mate, Hugh, are going surfing tomorrow, and two of my friends are joining me for a hot tub and spa break thing. I picked up Daisy from the station earlier. She came in from Oxford this morning – there were supposed to be three of us, but Bea has gone travelling at the last minute.'

Ryan's pulse stilled for a second before it accelerated at an increased pace. 'Bea.'

'Yeah. Bea is somewhere in Portugal.' Tania rolled her eyes. 'Typical of her. She's lovely and all that, but if she wants to do something, she does it, and hang how it makes anyone else feel. She said she'd be back for the wedding, next week, but I can't see it myself.'

Feeling more of a fool by the moment, Ryan whispered, 'Three months.'

'Pardon?'

'Bea is travelling around Portugal for three months. At least, that's what she told me.'

Tania's neatly lipsticked lips opened wide as the penny dropped. 'My friend Bea is your girlfriend?'

'So it seems.' Ryan tried to avoid the stunned expression plastered across Tania's pretty face. *She doesn't think I'm good enough for the likes of Bea either.* 'I think we both need another drink.'

# Chapter Seven
## Tuesday 10th June

After a semi-sleepless night, during which she had veered from lying awake and worrying about never seeing Izzie in person again, to short bursts of sleep that had thrown her into nightmarish dreams about faulty Outward Bound equipment endangering her only child, Maggie knew that sea air and a dose of Agatha Christie would be the only way she'd get through the day.

With a flask of coffee, a croissant and her latest library book in her bag, Maggie locked her front door and headed towards the harbour. The early morning sky was shrouded in cloud, but there was a suggestion of sunshine building towards the east.

She had only taken a few steps when she came to an abrupt halt. The sound of a siren pierced the air, its persistent shrill out-screaming the seagulls that swooped overhead.

*Police, fire or ambulance?*

The question was answered as the sound crescendoed and a police car and an ambulance swung around the nearest corner and swept past Maggie towards the harbour.

Quickening her pace, Maggie's imagination went into overdrive. *An accident? Someone having trouble out at sea? An assault . . . a murder?*

Telling herself off for being ghoulish, she kept walking. *I was going to the harbour anyway; I'm not going there to be nosy.*

Ashamed of the excitement that filled her, blaming it on her obsession with detective fiction, Maggie listened as she strolled forward. The sirens were still blaring, but the sound wasn't fading, telling her that the ambulance and police car had stopped moving.

Skirting the edge of South Cliff, Maggie wasn't surprised to see several of the locals opening their front doors to find out what was going on. She paused as she spotted 'Sudoku Harry' (as Ryan had started to refer to him) in the distance, standing in his front doorway.

Heading towards the row of houses that made up The Wharf, Maggie hailed him, 'Morning, Harry.' She lowered her voice as she reached his side. 'Any idea what's happening?'

'Dead body.'

'Her next door says it's been washed in on the tide.' Harry jabbed a finger towards the terrace to his right.

'That's so sad.'

'Probably one of them refugees fallen off a boat.'

Looking directly at Harry, Maggie bit back her annoyance at his comment. 'If it is, then I hope their family is alright. I can't even begin to imagine what it must be like to be so afraid that you would risk your life coming—'

Harry cut in, 'It must be bloody awful. Poor sods.'

Ashamed that she'd jumped to the wrong conclusion about Harry's views on the matter, Maggie agreed, 'Heartbreaking. I was heading down to the harbour for some air before work, but as the police have cordoned off the area, perhaps I'd better change my mind.'

'Or you could go and find out what's going on and come and tell me later.' Harry winked. 'Don't pretend that puzzler's brain of yours isn't curious.'

It was strange to see the blue and white tapes that formed a police cordon around the far end of the harbour. Feeling as if she was on the edge of a film set, Maggie joined a gaggle of other onlookers. As she stood there, staring across and down to where a white awning had been erected in the wet sand below the highest point of the harbour wall, her sense of sadness returned.

Whoever was being tended to by the professionals, all kitted out in blue all-in-one forensic outfits, was certainly dead.

Her skin prickled as the whispered gossip around her suggested numerous theories.

*Heart attack ...*
*Pub fight ...*
*Washed-in body ...*

Maggie scrutinised the area around the harbour wall. The tent the police had assembled was directly below it. *As if someone had fallen off ...* She gulped back the bile that settled in her throat as she imagined the fear they must have experienced as they fell – the ground rushing up, the ending resulting in unavoidable pain and probable death ... *Would you think about it? Would there have been time to consider the chance of a life in a wheelchair or no life at all once you hit the ground?*

Swallowing hard, she found herself speculating. *Depends on when they fell ... if the tide was in, then they could have drowned ... then again, if the tide was in, they might not have fallen after all. Harry could be right; the victim may have been washed in.*

Telling herself off for letting her imagination run away with her, Maggie pulled away from the growing crowd and edged around the harbour wall, following the road towards the chip shop.

Passing the occasional group of people standing around, also watching the activity below, Maggie kept moving until she reached the point directly above the tent below. Another police cordon was in place, the blue and white tape blocking access to the pavement and adjoining part of the road.

*Do they think the person fell too? Unless they were pushed ...*

A police constable was standing, tablet in hand, just behind the tape barrier. As Maggie approached, he called her forward.

'Good morning, madam, would you mind if I asked you a couple of questions?'

Taken aback, Maggie moved towards the constable. 'Certainly. Can I ask what's happened?'

'A young woman's body has been found.'

'How awful.' Maggie shuddered, 'And you are?'

'Constable Harker.'

Maggie's mind raced. 'Do you know who it was?'

'Such details need to remain confidential for now, madam.'

Feeling foolish for asking, Maggie mumbled, 'Of course. How can I help?'

'I'm asking anyone passing if they were in the area last night, and if so, whether they saw anything that might pertain to the incident.' Harker tapped on the screen he held in front of him. 'Can I start by asking your name and address, please?'

'Maggie Tyson, 4 Duck Street. I work at . . .'

'Robbins' Fish and Chip Shop. Yes.' The constable's smile lit up his round face. 'I used to collect a portion of chips every other Friday for my grandad when I was a kid.'

Maggie suddenly felt about two hundred years old. *It's true what they say about policemen getting younger.* 'Sorry, I don't remember. So many people come and go.'

'It's been at least five years since I've been here. I moved away once I left school to do my police training.'

'I've been serving chips a frighteningly long time.'

'What time did your shift finish last night?'

'Shop closed at nine. I did the clean-up, and at half-nine I said goodnight to Mr Robbins and was out by nine-forty, maybe just before.'

'Mr Robbins stayed put?'

'As ever.'

'Still rarely leaving the confines of the chippy, then?'

Intrigued that the policeman knew her employer's aversion to fresh air, Maggie found herself looking forward to telling Izzie about this conversation. 'He's an indoor man, that's for sure.'

'Do you know what time he headed to his campervan for the night?'

Maggie's eyes widened. 'You know he has a van in Newlyn?'

'I do.' The constable gave her a knowing smile.

Her mind raced; *Mr Robbins is really private ... why would the police know about his campervan? Perhaps Izzie is right about—*

'Miss Tyson?'

'Sorry.' Maggie forced herself to focus. 'No, I don't know what time he leaves the shop in the evenings.'

The constable typed something into his tablet and then asked, 'And did you have any reason to come down to the harbour after work?'

'No. I might have glanced towards it. I often do – you know, to make sure there's no traffic before I cross the road to the pavement.'

'You don't walk along the pavement on the shop side of the road?'

'It's too narrow. It's a really short walk home, and I like to stay near the sea for as long as I can. The breeze helps get rid of the chip shop aroma.'

Without raising his eyes from his tablet, the young policeman asked, 'And you saw nothing unusual?'

'No. There was the usual handful of tourists propped up against the wall, but nothing that made me stop and think.'

'You went straight home?'

'I did.' Beginning to wish she had lingered after work, Maggie ventured, 'These questions, they don't suggest an accident.'

Keeping his eyes on his notes, the constable said, 'It's just routine.'

'I'm sorry I couldn't be more helpful.'

'Not at all.' He lowered the tablet. 'That's all. Thank you.'

Resisting the urge to ask questions, and accepting her dismissal, Maggie resumed her walk. Pondering the conversation she'd just had, she settled herself onto a bench on the far side of the harbour and stared out to sea.

*A young woman's body.*

*Could have been an accident.*

She looked back the way she'd come, in time to see Constable Harker speaking to Mrs Drake, the manager of the village shop.

*Police cordons, questions in the street, an awning over the body to study it in situ.*

*They aren't convinced this was an accident.*

# Chapter Eight

Ryan rubbed the sleep from his eyes as the alarm on his phone announced that it was eleven o'clock in the morning. Rolling over, he winced as the familiar thud of a hangover reminded him that he'd had a night out at the pub.

Getting up slowly, glad the world wasn't spinning, Ryan knew he'd need coffee and a dose of headache tablets before he could even contemplate a day working with deep-fried goods.

The revelation that Tania had known Bea had shaken Ryan more than, logically, it should have done. Bea had grown up here, Tania had grown up here – therefore, it wasn't strange that, in such a small place, they knew each other. The only real coincidence was that they'd gone to the same private school in Truro rather than the local primary and secondary schools.

*Why did Bea let Tania believe she could make the wedding when she told me she'd be away three months?*

Ryan lay back again, his head hitting the pillow that Maggie had lent him with a gentle thump, which nonetheless made his brain rattle in his skull. He closed his eyes, ignoring the swirl in his stomach that told him that he needed food while, conversely, warning him that food might not be wise.

\*

Half an hour later, Ryan had struggled through a hot shower and gingerly eaten some dry toast. He winced as he downed two cups of extra strong black coffee and a pint of water before crawling into his jeans and a crumpled T-shirt, and heading towards the stairs, bracing himself to pass Mr Robbins on the way to his lunchtime shift. The bedsit may have been perfect for him – but the prospect of perpetually sidling past the ever-present fixture of his enigmatic boss made Ryan uncomfortable.

On opening the door at the bottom of the staircase, he was surprised to find Mr Robbins wasn't there. His absence was somehow more alarming than his presence would have been.

*Where is he? What's he doing?*

Both questions were immediately answered as he heard Mr Robbins' growly voice through the interconnecting door with the chip shop.

'It's been a while, Constable Peters. How are you?'

*Police? Was Maggie's daughter right about him?* Creeping forwards, Ryan hesitated, peering through the semi-open doorway as he heard the policeman reply.

'I'm well, Mr Robbins. And it's Sergeant Peters now.' He tapped the epaulette on his left shoulder. 'Got my promotion a while back.'

The grunt Ryan heard his boss give could either have been positive or negative; it was hard to tell.

'You working back here, then? Maggie never said.'

'Because I didn't know!'

Surprised at the indignation in Maggie's voice, Ryan listened harder as the sergeant responded.

'As of six months ago. Transferred.'

'Six months!'

Ryan frowned. *Why's Maggie so shocked?*

'Forgive me, Maggie, I should have let you know, but until today, I've had no reason to come out to Mousehole.'

'I see.'

Ryan didn't have time to consider Maggie's reaction to the sergeant's statement, for Mr Robbins was clearly set on getting to the point of Peters' visit.

'What do you want, then?'

'Just doing the rounds after last night's incident. Maggie has already spoken to Constable Harker, but we're asking everyone local if they saw anything out of the ordinary.' Through the gap in the door, Ryan saw him open a tablet. 'Maggie said she left here at just gone half-nine last night. That means you were here on your own after that, Mr Robbins. Did you see or hear anything?'

'Nothing. I left for the van before the lad came home.'

'The lad?'

Ryan felt himself tense as the sergeant scribbled something on the tablet. *Why are the police here? What van?*

'Got meself a lodger in the bedsit.'

'Have you now, and what would this lodger's name be?'

Ryan froze as he heard Maggie say, 'Ryan. He's our seasonal assistant. He's a nice lad, David.'

'And where can I find this nice lad?'

*David? Does Maggie know the policeman personally?* Feeling guilty, even though he had no idea what wrong had been done, Ryan shuffled silently backwards a few steps, before taking a deep breath and striding into the room, hoping they'd assume he'd just come from upstairs. 'Morning, Maggie, where's Mr . . . Oh.'

Maggie gave him an 'it's okay' smile as she introduced him to their visitor. 'Sergeant Peters, this is Ryan Stepney.'

'Mr Stepney.' The policeman gave a friendly nod, which did nothing to calm the anxiety rising in Ryan's stomach. 'Can I ask you – we are asking everyone locally – where you were last night, and if you had heard or seen anything out of the ordinary?'

'Nothing out of the ordinary. I was here until about half-eight, then I went to the pub.'

'The Mariner?'

'Yes.' Ryan looked at Maggie. 'Is there another pub?'

'Not in Mousehole, no, but it's not a long walk to the next village.' Answering on Maggie's behalf, the sergeant tapped on his tablet's screen but kept his eyes on Ryan. 'You're from the Midlands.'

'I know.' Realising he'd sounded sarcastic, Ryan hastily added, 'Birmingham. Umm, what's happened?'

Sergeant Peters ignored the enquiry. 'What time did you leave The Mariner?'

'About eleven.' Ryan pressed a hand against his forehead as his hangover continued to make its presence felt.

'You had a drop too much of the hard stuff?'

'Five pints of Tribute,' Ryan muttered. 'It's been a while since I had more than two at a time.'

Mr Robbins broke his silence. 'Good stuff, that.'

'Yeah,' Ryan mumbled, feeling the policeman's interest in him crank up a notch.

'And who were you drinking with, Mr Stepney? Or were you drowning your sorrows alone?'

Maggie spoke before Ryan had the chance to reply. 'Can I interrupt a moment? We're opening soon, and I don't have everything ready yet. Do you mind if I get things going?'

'Not at all.' Peters gestured towards Mr Robbins' office. 'Let's go through there, shall we, Mr Stepney.'

'Well, um . . .' Ryan didn't dare look at Mr Robbins in case his employer was about to blame him for having to have a policeman in his inner sanctum.

'Get on with it, then,' Mr Robbins growled.

Leading Sergeant Peters into the office, Ryan asked again, 'What's happened? What incident is it you are enquiring about?'

'All in good time.' The sergeant pulled out Mr Robbins' orange chair and sat down. 'Take a seat.'

Doing as he was told, Ryan said, 'I went to the pub on my own. I've not been here long, and I don't know anyone apart from Maggie, so . . .'

'You know Mr Robbins.'

*Ah, so maybe that's what this is about; he wants to see if I know anything about my boss.*

'I don't think anyone knows Mr Robbins. Not really.' Ryan darted his gaze towards the door to the chip shop and back again. 'That's the impression Maggie's given me anyway.'

'And she'd be right. He's an enigma that one, and no mistake.' Peters placed his tablet on the table. 'You were saying, about the pub.'

'I got there about quarter to nine. It was busy, but I got a table on the restaurant side of the bar area. I had a couple of pints and played a few games on my phone. I was on my own until about nine-thirty, when a woman joined me.'

'A young woman?'

'Twenty-ish, I'd guess.' Ryan wasn't sure if he'd imagined the edge of interest in the policeman's tone, or not. 'She'd had a row with her fiancé. He left, and she stayed. There was nowhere else to sit, so she asked if she could have the spare stool at my table and sat with me.'

'Did you know this woman beforehand?'

'No. As I said, I'm new here.'

'So you did. Did this woman tell you her name? Did you have a conversation, or did you simply share a table and get lost in your mobiles?'

'She was quiet for a while, but then it felt weird not speaking, so I said hello, and we started talking.' Ryan massaged his temples. 'I think she needed to offload. Sometimes it's easier to talk to a stranger, isn't it?'

'It can be. Like on a train or a bus – it's easy to share a confidence with someone you'll never see again.'

'Yes.' Relieved that the policeman understood, Ryan let a little of the tension he'd been holding escape in a puff of exhaled air.

'And her name, lad?'

'Tania.'

'Tania Stevens?' Sergeant Peters picked up his tablet and slowly rose to his feet.

'I don't know – she never gave me her surname.'

'I think you'd better come with me, Mr Stepney.'

'Come with you? Why?' Ryan's shoulders stiffened, and he wasn't sure he could remember how to breathe properly.

'Because the body of a young woman was discovered in the harbour this morning, and her driving licence gives her name as Tania Stevens.'

# Chapter Nine

Maggie had been restless all afternoon. While she'd been at work, every few minutes she'd found herself glancing towards the door of the chip shop, expecting Ryan to come walking back through it.

It had been a long time since an excess of trade had forced Mr Robbins to help her at the counter, and it hadn't been lost on the regulars that he was the one battering the cod and shuffling the chips. Maggie was grateful that Ryan hadn't been there long enough to be missed by most of their customers. Those who had asked after him were informed that it wasn't his shift.

Only one subject of conversation had featured as orders for chip-based lunches had been made. The body in the harbour.

Now, her lunchtime shift over, Maggie stood outside the police station in Penzance, hoping she'd guessed right about which local station Ryan would've been taken to. Pacing up and down, she felt both restless and useless at the same time.

*Why do they want to talk to Ryan?*

Wishing they'd had time to talk before Sergeant Peters had arrived, Maggie decided she'd give it five more minutes, then she'd go inside and ask if Ryan was there.

*He must have met the victim in the pub . . . unless . . . Bea?* Maggie stopped dead and shook her head. *No, it couldn't have been Bea's body; she's abroad.*

Lowering herself onto a nearby bench, Maggie felt the prickle of an idea tapping at her brain.

*Unless she's only been pretending to be away. Unless ...*

The memory of a television show she'd once seen came back to her. The plot had centred around a woman who'd claimed to be abroad on holiday with friends but was actually staying locally, shacked up with a lover – something that had gone undetected until her body had been discovered in a local swimming pool. Maggie tutted under her breath. 'You've seen the photos Bea's sent Ryan, showing off where she is. If they're fake, then that's one hell of a film set.'

Aware she was in danger of allowing her love of detective fiction to take over from common sense, Maggie focused on the police station and willed Ryan to be alright.

Trying not to think about how much she'd come to care for the boy in such a short space of time, and knowing it was probably displacement due to her fear of Izzie never coming home again, Maggie found herself thinking about David.

*Why didn't he tell me he was back from pounding Bath's Georgian streets?* She closed her eyes. *He said he had no reason to come to Mousehole ...*

Reining in her imagination before it got out of control, Maggie opened her eyes again and muttered to the nearest seagull, 'What was it Marlowe wrote? "... *but that was in another country* ..."'

Giving a humourless grunt at the seagull's answering squawk, Maggie exhaled slowly and resigned herself to a long wait.

Two minutes later, however, one of the stiff doors which formed part of the station's run-down entranceway was pushed open, and Ryan came out. She saw him blink against the brightness of the afternoon sunshine.

'Ryan!' Maggie called, raising a hand from the other side of the narrow road. 'Over here.'

The sag of his shoulders sent her hurrying forward in full mother hen mode. 'Are you alright?'

'Hungry.' Ryan wiped a hand over his eyes.

Not commenting on the fact that he appeared to have been crying, Maggie pointed to a café a few doors down on the opposite side of the road. 'Let's get some coffee and a late lunch down you.'

Ryan fell into step next to Maggie. 'Mr Robbins . . . is he cross? Have I lost my job?'

Surprised that this was his first concern, Maggie was happy to reassure him. 'Of course not. Mr Robbins is not a natural customer-service type; he'll not give your help up lightly.'

'Did he serve with you today? There were already people coming in as I left. I bet it was busy.'

'It was, and yes, he did help me.'

'I'm sorry I just left.'

Maggie placed a hand on his arm. 'Ryan love, you hardly walked out on me. The police asked you to go with them. In that situation there isn't an option. They ask, you go.'

'Tell me about it.' A yawn escaped Ryan's lips.

'You need coffee and cake.'

'And possibly a solicitor.'

'What?' Maggie looked shocked. 'Why?'

Ryan gave a full body shrug. 'Because I'm not a local, because I sound different, because I'm young and because I was the last person seen talking to Tania before she died. Take your pick.'

\*

The slab of coffee and walnut cake Maggie had bought Ryan hadn't touched the sides. She waited until he'd downed his coffee before asking, 'So, the woman they found is called Tania, and you met her last night?'

'Yeah. Tania Stevens: although I didn't know that was her surname until just now. Do you know her?'

'I don't. At least, not by name. I suppose I might have known her by sight if she used the chippy.' Maggie let a moment's silence pass before asking, 'What do they think happened to her?'

'It might've been an accident. They aren't sure. Keeping their options open, apparently.' He added an extra spoonful of sugar to his mug. 'Sergeant Peters was joined by a Detective Inspector Diane Houseman when they spoke to me.'

Maggie wrapped her hands around her cup, glad of the coffee's warmth despite the heat of the day. 'You were formally interviewed?'

'It felt like it, although they mentioned several times that we were just having an informal chat, and I could go if I wanted to.'

'I see.'

'It wasn't very nice. The room smelt as if it had never experienced fresh air, and there was a half-empty coffee cup on the table. It had that weird cold coffee smell.' Ryan held his mug to his lips and inhaled an altogether more pleasant coffee aroma. 'It was more like an episode of *The Bill* than *Agatha Raisin*.'

'You're way too young to have seen *The Bill*.'

'Repeats on the Drama channel with Gran.'

'Of course.' Curiosity vied with not wanting to be seen as nosy or interfering as Maggie tentatively asked, 'Do you want to talk about it?'

Ryan kept his eyes on his almost empty mug. 'Inspector Houseman suggested that Tania was drunk and had fallen off the harbour wall. I told them she hadn't had that much to drink, but because I had, they don't see me as a reliable witness.'

Refraining from saying that, objectively, she could see their point, Maggie asked, 'What do you think happened?'

'There's no way she fell. Tania was upset, angry even, but not drunk. I can't imagine why she'd have suddenly lost her balance.'

'Umm.' Maggie felt a flicker of unease laced with excitement. 'So, if she didn't fall . . .'

'Then someone pushed her, or she jumped. I can't imagine her jumping, so . . .' Ryan paused. 'Why does Mr Robbins sleep in a campervan if he has a bedsit above the shop?'

Maggie was surprised by the abrupt change in subject. 'You've just been released from a police station, and you're asking me that?'

'It struck me as odd – and I've had a lot of sitting around thinking time. It was over an hour between me being taken in for "a friendly chat", as Sergeant Peters called it, and any chat happening.'

Suspecting this meant that the police had taken their time because they were checking to see if Ryan had a criminal record, Maggie said, 'All I know about the campervan is that Mr Robbins likes the view in Newlyn where it's parked up.'

'It isn't so he has a vehicle permanently pre-packed in case he needs to make a hasty getaway, then?'

'That's exactly the sort of thing Izzie would say.'

Ryan noted the unusually dull edge to Maggie's voice when she mentioned her daughter's name. 'Are you okay?'

'She's thinking of staying in New Zealand long term.'

'Oh. I'm sorry.'

'Thanks.' Maggie fiddled with some of the crumbs on her plate. 'As long as she's happy, it's okay.'

'For Izzie, it's okay. For you, it stinks.'

Taken aback by his astute observation, Maggie kept her eyes on the spattering of cake crumbs. 'Why did you say you might need a solicitor? What happened in the pub last night?'

'I'll get another coffee first. Do you want one?'

'Best not, or I'll be having to dip out of serving chips all evening to have a pee.'

\*

A glass of water and a fresh coffee, along with two packets of crisps, joined the empty mugs and cake plates that littered the table between Ryan and Maggie as he explained how Tania had come to join him at his table in The Mariner.

'You didn't overhear the row she had with her boyfriend?'

'No, but the body language was clear enough. He was not happy with her questioning him about something. Later, Tania told me that she'd asked him about what he'd been up to lately. He'd been taking secret phone calls and what have you.'

'Secrets connected to wanting to surprise her on their wedding day, perhaps?'

'Apparently it happened too often for that.' Ryan plucked a crisp from the open packet. 'Basically, we spent the evening sharing relationship woes. I told her about Bea leaving me high and dry, and she told me about her concerns over Toby.'

Wishing she had a notebook on her so she could jot things down, Maggie asked, 'Toby is the boyfriend's name?'

'Yeah. The police told me his name was Toby Marrell. Tania is – was – only twenty-two. Same age as me.' Ryan crunched another crisp. 'We only got chatting because it would have been weird not to as we were sharing a table in a packed pub.'

'If you were talking about your partners, it was more medium-sized talk than small talk.'

'Suppose so. She said she hadn't seen me around before and assumed I was a tourist, so I told her about the Bea situation.' He sighed. 'Tania was quite helpful actually. Told me that at least having some time here without Bea will help me decide if I like living in Cornwall and allow me to work out what to do with my degree'

'Sounds like Tania was a sensible woman.'

'I think she was.' Ryan lowered his voice, aware that they might be overheard. 'She knew Bea.'

'What?' Maggie sat forward. 'How?'

'They were friends from school. Bea was supposed to be here for Tania's hen party today.'

'Small world.'

'Isn't it. I didn't tell the police in case they thought so too. It could be seen as a bit too much of a coincidence.'

'I see.' Hoping withholding this information wouldn't prove to be a mistake, Maggie went on. 'And Tania was expecting to see Bea, just as you were?'

'Yes. She cried off at the last minute. I mean, she could hardly nip back from Portugal just for a day in a hot tub.'

Not commenting on Bea's casual carelessness when it came to other people's feelings, Maggie asked, 'And this row Tania had with Toby?'

Ryan scrubbed his hands through his short hair, leaving it standing up in haphazard spikes. 'Like I told the police, everything had been wonderful between Tania and Toby until a couple of weeks ago, when Toby started to become evasive about where he'd been and who he had been with. He'd been telling Tania not to worry and, as you suggested, that he'd been planning secret things for the wedding.'

'But she wasn't buying it?'

'No. Something wasn't sitting right with her, and she asked him when her secret surprise was going to happen.'

'Let me guess, there was no surprise.' Maggie shook her head.

'Spot on. Toby told her that his plans hadn't worked out and that the surprise was off. When she asked him what it had been, he declined to answer, saying he wanted to use the same surprise another time. But something about his reply made her doubt him, which led to the row and Toby storming off.'

'Trust issues?'

'Big time.'

'Did Tania have any idea what he was doing, if he wasn't planning something for her?'

'Another woman was her first theory, but she'd already discounted that. She couldn't think of anyone who he might have been seeing, nor when he'd have time for an affair, as he worked long hours.'

'A workplace affair, then?'

'I don't think so . . . Apparently he has one assistant, who is good at their job but who he doesn't like very much.'

'Male or female?'

'She didn't say. She did say it was Toby's own business, importing and exporting goods. Profitable but small-scale.'

'What else did Tania say?'

'Not a lot beyond that the main part of her hen party was today, with two friends and a spa date, while Toby was having his stag do with his best friend . . . Hugh, I think she said. They were planning to go off to do something – I know she told me, but I can't for the life of me remember what it was.'

'Did she say anything else?' Maggie helped herself to a crisp.

'That was it. I offered to walk her back to her holiday accommodation, but Tania didn't think Toby would be impressed if we were spotted together. She didn't want to risk making matters worse.'

'She wasn't thinking of calling the wedding off, then?'

'She didn't say so. I think she really loved him.'

'Love can be unbelievably stupid.'

Ryan stared at the open crisp packet but said nothing.

'Sorry, Ryan, I didn't mean you and Bea.'

'I suspect I'm being stupid, though. She might not come back.'

'Bea'll come back.' Maggie didn't add that she doubted she'd come back for a boy that her parents didn't approve of – especially if her family's money was as important to Bea as Maggie suspected it was. 'She has a job all lined up for her, doesn't she?'

'Yeah.' Ryan opened a packet of crisps. 'Anyway, Tania left the pub about half-ten. I stayed and drank more than I ought to have done while I overthought about Bea, life and stuff. I didn't see Tania again.'

As a cloud passed over his already pale face, Maggie coaxed, 'There's something else, isn't there?'

'Yeah.'

'Go on.'

'At eleven I left the pub, but I couldn't face going back to the bedsit and the smell of chip fat, so I went for a walk along the harbour.'

'Oh.'

'That's what the police said.'

# Chapter Ten

As they wandered along Penzance's Market Jew Street, Maggie asked him for the second time, 'And you definitely didn't see anyone when you walked along the harbour?'

Ryan shook his head. 'As I said to you and to the police *three* times, I passed a few tourists and a dog walker near the pub itself, but otherwise it was quiet. There was no sign of Tania. Most people that left the pub at the same time as me went in the opposite direction.'

'Fair enough. Sorry to ask again.'

'It's okay.' Pausing in the shadow of a large statue of Sir Humphry Davy, Ryan mumbled, 'The problem for the police was that I can't say exactly what time I got back to the chippy. I'm pretty sure it was before midnight, but I'd had too much to drink, and I have no recollection of checking my phone to see the time.'

'Awkward.'

'Yeah.' Ryan blew out a puff of air. 'The police are going to want to talk to me again, aren't they? To see if I remember more later.'

'Very probably.'

Ryan dug his hands into his pockets. 'Maggie, do you know Sergeant Peters, then? You called him David?'

'Went to school with him. He was in the same year as me.' Maggie peered up at a seagull that had perched on Humphry Davy's stone head. 'I can't say I know him anymore.'

Suspecting that Maggie knew more about the sergeant than she was letting on, Ryan asked, 'Do you think I should tell them that I have a vague connection to Tania via Bea? If they found out later . . .'

'I know what you mean, but is it relevant? I was thinking, you had never heard of Tania until last night, and you have never met any of Bea's school friends before. Or have you?'

'No.'

'Then maybe it's best not to muddy the waters. If they ask you outright about any personal connection to the victim, then tell them; otherwise I'd leave it alone. It's not like you're a suspect.'

'I felt like a suspect.'

'I can imagine. But think about it – you told the police about the row with Toby – about the secret phone calls and the non-surprise surprise. Toby's going to be top of their watch-list, not you.'

'Thanks, Maggie.' As they resumed their walk towards the nearest bus stop serving the route to Mousehole, Ryan repeated his early claim. 'I swear Tania wasn't drunk. Why would she have fallen? And why would she sit at the highest part of the harbour wall when it's so much easier to sit at the lower end – and why was she there anyway? She was heading back to her hotel – at least, that's what she said.'

'You think someone killed her?'

'Yeah. And so do you.'

As they reached the bus stop, Maggie lowered her voice. 'It crossed my mind. You suspect Toby?'

'I think there's a good chance, but if he went back to the hotel as he said, then it could have been anyone.'

'Bus is coming,' Maggie said as they weaved around a lady blocking the pavement with her bicycle so they could get to the bus stop. 'Anyone encompasses a lot of people.'

'Well then.'

'Well then, what?'

Ryan gave her a knowing look. 'Come on, Maggie, I can see you're dying to get to the bottom of this. It's written all over your face.'

'Are you suggesting we investigate Tania's death?'

'Yes. No. Maybe.' He let out a heavy sigh. 'I'm saying that I'm worried the police won't.' Nodding in the direction of the oncoming bus, Ryan waited until they were seated before he went on. 'They could just write this off as an accident, or worse, they could decide it wasn't an accident and that I was responsible.'

Maggie muttered, 'Once the pathologist has finished, they'll know more.'

'But can they tell the difference between being pushed and falling? All it would have taken was a gentle shove if she hadn't heard anyone coming.'

Maggie shivered. 'No bruising from a punch or anything, you mean.'

'Yeah. If that's how it was. And you can bet whoever did it won't have left a helpful clue like they do on the telly.'

'No flower or insect that can only be found in one place telling us where either Tania or the killer had been earlier in the day.' Maggie gave a rueful smile.

'And no handy CCTV, or eyewitnesses that aren't brave enough to come forward until the last minute.' Ryan watched the distant shape of St Michael's Mount out of the window as they moved along.

'I suppose we *could* make a few enquiries.'

Ryan looked sharply at Maggie. 'I wasn't actually serious.'

'Why not? I'm not suggesting we go full Sherlock, just that we ask a few questions. Friendly-like.'

Despite himself, Ryan grinned. 'You're already in your element, aren't you? Did you ever consider joining the police?'

'It crossed my mind when I was at school, but not seriously. Working as a private investigator always appealed. In my teens I was keen to be my own boss, set up an agency, even.'

'Did you go to university?'

'No.' She hesitated, before explaining, 'I lived with my grandad after my A levels. He was ill and couldn't afford a decent care home, and I couldn't stand the thought of him being alone, so I looked after him. Only a few weeks after he died, I discovered I was expecting Izzie. And now it's now.'

'Do you ever wish that—'

Maggie interrupted. 'It wouldn't hurt to ask a few questions about what happened to Tania. Anything we learn, we'd tell the police.'

Accepting that the issue of Maggie's past was closed, Ryan asked, 'But how? Where would we start?'

'Her friends. The ones she mentioned when you chatted last night. Can you remember their names? It shouldn't be that hard to find them. Mousehole's a tiny place, and I know pretty much everyone in it.'

Suspecting they were crazy for even contemplating the idea, Ryan muttered, 'I suppose, sooner or later, everyone buys fish and chips.'

'Exactly.'

\*

'I've told you everything I told the police and everything Tania said to me, but I'm sorry, apart from Bea, I can't remember if she mentioned the names of the girls invited to her hen do.' Ryan pinched the bridge of his nose.

'Lots has happened to you in the last few hours.' Maggie gave a side of cod an extra firm swipe through the batter mix. 'Try and work backwards. Think back to the last thing she said to you and see if remembering events in reverse triggers something.'

'I went through it all with the police. Honestly, Maggie.'

'I know, but you're in a safe place now, with no pressures other than whether to have more coffee today or not. Just try.'

Closing his eyes, Ryan did as Maggie asked. Working slowly, he pictured Tania getting up to leave and ran their conversation through his mind in reverse. 'Daisy. One of them was called Daisy – but I swear she didn't mention the other one. Tania only mentioned that name because she said she had been to fetch her from the station.'

Maggie paused in the act of checking the temperature of the frying oil. 'Oh, well done!'

'Thanks.' Ryan let out a puff of air to release his tension. 'Yeah, Daisy wasn't from here. She got the train in from Oxford.'

'Ah.' Maggie deflated slightly. 'Then I'm not going to have a clue who she is, am I. Although tracking someone down just by the name Daisy wouldn't have been easy, even in a place this small.'

'Sorry.'

Maggie quickly reassured, 'No need to worry, we just need a new angle. How about Toby? You said his surname was . . .'

'Marrell.'

'That's it. So, we find him – or people that know about him. It would be good to establish where he was between half-ten and eleven. As her partner, he has to be chief suspect.'

'And the fact they rowed does make him appear guilty.' Ryan chewed his bottom lip. 'But, I don't know . . . if we killed everyone we rowed with, there'd be no one left.'

'You said he had an import and export business. We could find that.'

'But we don't know where it is. I assumed local, but it might not be. It might not even be in Cornwall.'

'Less of the defeatist attitude, young man.' Maggie pulled an ancient copy of the Yellow Pages out from under the counter. 'Time to let your fingers do the walking.'

'What?'

Maggie tutted. 'Youth of today! Not enough time watching television adverts!'

Ryan chuckled. 'That's a novel twist on an old argument.'

'Flick through the book and see if there is a Marrell's listed as a business name. Check under exporters, importers and furniture suppliers.'

Picking up the tattered book, which was so faded that it qualified more as beige pages, Ryan did as he was told. He'd got halfway down the short list of importers local to the region when he was struck by the obvious. 'Toby didn't look much older than me, which means any business he started would be since he left university, so not that old. Which means it most definitely will not be in here.'

'Ah.'

Ryan closed the book and showed the cover to Maggie. 'This book is dated 2010, and . . .'

'Alright, I get it. He was a child when that volume was printed.'

'If we're going to find Toby, it'll be more likely via Google.' He fished his mobile from his apron pocket. 'Or Facebook.'

Maggie tilted her head to one side. 'Do young folk use that? Aren't you all on TikTok and Snapchat, leaving FB to us oldies?'

'I'll scroll through all of them, but I'd be surprised if Tania wasn't on Facebook, especially with a wedding coming up. Bea likes to use it to show off her holiday photos. Plus, if Toby owns a business, I bet it has an associated Facebook business page.'

Maggie said, 'Let's hope he's made it simple for us by naming his business Marrell's.'

'Ummm . . .' Ryan began a Google search.

'Bea might be able to help.'

'Bea?' Ryan felt conflicted between wanting to grab hold of an excuse to contact his girlfriend and never wanting to talk to her again – well, almost never.

'You said she was a friend of Tania's.' Maggie paused to serve a portion of battered sausage and chips. 'Not just a friend, but someone who she was close enough to that she was invited to both the hen party and wedding.'

'The wedding.' Ryan felt the muscles in his shoulders tense.

'Ryan?'

'Bea would have been invited to the wedding, wouldn't she?'

'I assume so.' Maggie paused. 'She didn't tell you about being invited to a wedding, did she?'

He shook his head. 'Wedding invites are usually to someone and their partner, aren't they?'

'Sometimes. Usually. I'm sorry, Ryan.'

'She didn't ask me to go with her.'

'No.'

'You don't like Bea, do you?'

'I've never met her, so I couldn't say.'

Ryan gave her a firm stare. 'Come off it, Maggie.'

'Let's just say I dislike how she's treated you. You don't deserve to be messed about like this.'

'Oh.' Not sure where to look, his cheeks blushed with a red warmth; unaccustomed to being cared for in this fashion, Ryan was relieved when the door to the shop opened, and a family came in to buy their supper.

★

A steady stream of customers meant they didn't get the chance to return to the subject of Tania's death for another hour. During that time, while shovelling chips and applying salt and vinegar with a heavy hand, Maggie wrestled with her conscience.

*I shouldn't have mentioned Bea.*

She watched Ryan out of the corner of her eye. He was ultra-focused on what he was doing, making her suspect that he was trying to do anything but think – not about Tania or Bea or his recent experience at the police station.

*But if we're going to find out what's going on, then we will need Bea . . . I can't ask Ryan to call her after all she's done to him.*

Telling herself she should forget the whole idea and leave things to the police, Maggie was shocked at her level of disappointment. The prospect of investigating what had happened to Tania had given her a buzz that she wasn't sure she wanted to analyse.

Nor did she want to think too much about the surge of excitement she experienced when, as the final customer of the evening left, Ryan pulled his phone back out of his pocket and announced he'd call Bea.

'Are you sure?'

'If it turns out that the police can easily prove what happened to Tania, then we should back off and leave it to them. But if things are less clear-cut, and there is a chance that we can help find out what happened, then we should.'

Maggie smiled. 'You're a good lad.'

'I know. It's so annoying.' Ryan grimaced. 'I'll call her now. There's no time difference between here and Portugal.'

'Bea ought to be told about Tania, even if she can't help us.' Maggie headed to the shop door and flipped the sign from open to closed.

'I'll see how that goes. If it feels okay to ask questions once I've told her the bad news, I will, but if not . . .'

'Understood.' Maggie removed her hat.

'Do you want me to clean the counter first?'

'I'll do it while you talk to Bea.'

'So you'll be around to hear about it afterwards to find out what I've learnt?' Ryan teased.

'Maybe.' Picking up the wiping-down cloth, Maggie stuck her tongue out at him. 'Go on, call her. And Ryan . . .?'

'Yes?'

'Don't be too forgiving; she hasn't behaved well towards you.'

As Ryan disappeared into the office, Maggie heard him shout a 'hello' to Mr Robbins, before the sound of his trainers bounding up the wooden stairs to his bedsit echoed through the shop.

# Chapter Eleven

The sound of Bea sniffling as she wiped away her tears had quickly faded after Ryan had told her about Tania's death. He decided not to think about this, just as he'd decided not to ask her why she hadn't told him about the wedding or why she hadn't asked him to go with her.

'How come you knew Tania anyway?'

Not caring for the suspicion in Bea's voice, Ryan tucked his knees up under his chin as he perched on his bed. 'I got talking to her in the pub last night. I mentioned your name and she said she knew you.'

'You weren't chatting her up, were you?'

Suddenly angry, Ryan barked, 'No, I wasn't! She'd been there with her future husband – until they had a row. She stayed after he stormed out, and now she's dead. And, if you recall, I'm with you!'

The moment of silence lasted just too long down the phone line.

'Ah.' Ryan closed his eyes and concentrated on breathing. 'So, I'm not with you. Well, that would explain why . . .'

'Of course you are!' Bea broke in. 'Sorry, it's just a shock. Tania was my friend, and you're calling out of the blue, and . . .'

'Bea, I'm your boyfriend, allegedly; I'm allowed to call you whenever I like.'

'What do you mean, *allegedly*?'

Hearing the high-pitched edge to her voice, which meant an argument was imminent, Ryan was struck by how similar the sound was to the one her mother had made while peering down her nose at him. Ignoring his natural inclination to just accept things, Ryan said, 'You left me here, with nowhere to live and no work, without any warning whatsoever. If I'd done that to you, you'd have dropped me like a stone.'

'But . . .'

Ryan's pulse beat faster as adrenalin lent wings to his tongue. 'Your parents turned me away. I'm not living in your flat.'

'What?' The shriek was more piercing this time.

A mental image of Maggie cheering him on took Ryan by surprise as he continued, 'If you'd asked me about my life during the last week or so, you would have known that. But on the one occasion you made time for me, all you did was talk about yourself.'

He heard Bea swallow before she said, 'I must have asked about . . .'

'No, Bea. You haven't asked how I am, if I'm okay with you disappearing with no warning, or what I'm doing to earn money in your absence. All you've done is tell me what you're doing. Did it ever occur to you that I might mind you flitting off and holding up my life?'

Bea's response shot out in a hectoring whine. 'It was such a good opportunity. I assumed you'd be pleased for me.'

'It is a good opportunity, and I am pleased for you, but I'm a bit fed up with you assuming I'd be okay. If you'd told me beforehand, I'd have had time to sort out alternative arrangements and not come down to Cornwall until you were back. Your parents treated me as if I was something unpleasant on the sole of their shoes.' Now he'd started to speak, Ryan found he couldn't stop. 'In fact, I'm beginning to doubt that your mum and dad had any idea of my existence. If it hadn't been for Maggie, I would be homeless and jobless, or worse.

I'd have to go back to my parents and face all their *I-told-you-so*'s.'

'*I-told-you-so*'s?'

Although he couldn't see her face, Ryan could easily picture Bea's expression. Her perfectly made-up face would have a small V-shaped furrow in the middle of her forehead. *She's probably twirling a strand of hair in her fingers too*. 'My mum and dad didn't think I'd last five minutes with someone like you. They'll be delighted to have been proved right.'

'They've never even met me! How dare they judge me like that!'

Ryan snorted. 'They were right, though, weren't they! And before you get all offended about *my* parents, *your* mum was pretty quick to slam the door in my face.'

There was a stunned silence down the line, before Bea mumbled, 'I'm sorry. I should have told you the minute I was asked to go away. I didn't think.'

'Thank you.' Stunned to get an apology, and finding himself wondering if it was an all-time first for Bea, Ryan asked more gently, 'Are you interested in what I'm doing in your absence?'

'Obviously!' Bea took a deep breath, before going on more calmly. 'I know you're still in Cornwall, or you wouldn't have met Tania.'

'Talking of Tania, why did you tell her you weren't going to make the hen night but would be there for wedding – which was obviously a lie?'

'It was no such thing! It was . . .'

'A lie.'

Deflated by Ryan's sternness, Bea sighed. 'Okay, so it was. I was just being nice. Letting her down gently, one disappointment at a time.'

'So you'd let her down over the hen night and then later let her know you weren't going to be a bridesmaid – *after* she'd done all the final preparation on the bridesmaid dresses, so she spends money on an outfit you're never going to wear.'

Ryan could almost hear Bea's mouth open and close as she stuttered, 'I didn't think about it like that. I was just being . . .'

'You were being Bea.' Ryan dragged himself back from the edge of anger, changing the subject back to their personal circumstances. 'Anyway, I'm not living in the flat like you assumed – you *did* assume I was there, didn't you?'

'I did, yes.' Bea whispered. 'I can't believe Mum and Dad turned you away. They promised me.'

'You hadn't told them much about me, though, had you?'

'Not a lot, no.'

'So they probably pictured a southerner with a posh accent and a first from Cambridge, not a Brummie in tatty jeans with a two-two from Birmingham.'

'*I* went to Birmingham.'

'Ah, but you're their little princess. The rules are different for you.'

There was a longer silence this time, before Bea audibly drew in a lungful of air. 'I'm sorry, Ryan. Can we start again? Will you forgive me?'

Hope surged in his chest as, sounding far more delighted than he intended to, he asked, 'You still want to be with me?'

'Absolutely I do!' Bea paused. 'Hang on, who is Maggie?'

*

One look at Ryan's face when he'd bounced back into the shop told Maggie he had a lot of news to impart. She had been instantly suspicious of how happy he looked and was worried that Bea had managed to rewrap him around her fingers during their conversation.

After telling herself off for jumping to conclusions, Maggie offered Ryan the chance to chat over a plate of cheese and biscuits and some decaf coffee, followed by a night on her sofa bed. An offer which had been quickly accepted.

\*

'Heidi Spenser-Davies and Daisy Makepeace!'

Maggie scribbled the names in a brand-new notebook. 'That's brilliant! Well done.'

Ryan picked up a cheese-laden cracker. 'That wouldn't be a new notebook purchased especially for this investigation, would it?'

'I happened to see it in the village shop and thought it might be useful.'

'Really?'

'Maybe.' Maggie grinned. 'What did Bea tell you about these two women, then?'

'That Tania met Daisy at university, and that Heidi is a mutual friend from here – Lamorna to be precise. Heidi, Tania and Bea went to school together. Heidi didn't go to uni.' Ryan took a crunch of cracker. 'She's set to inherit a heap of land and her parents' home, Lamorna Manor.'

'Not worth going, then.'

'She missed out, though, don't you think? The friendship, fun, learning to cope alone and stuff.'

Maggie shrugged. 'I don't know. Like I said, I never went.'

Ryan put the remains of his cracker and cheese back on his plate. 'What would you have studied if you'd gone? Law?'

'No, I was never clever enough to have gone, and certainly not clever enough to have studied law.'

Taken aback, Ryan said, 'What? But you're really clever! You'd be a great criminologist or something.'

'Thanks, but I'm not the right sort of clever, and back when I was young no university took anyone with the mediocre A level grades I scraped. Anyway, I had other stuff going on, and now – well, it's too late.'

'Of course it isn't.'

Surprised by the conviction in Ryan's voice, Maggie glanced at the open notebook in her hand. *Why am I doing this? Is this just me trying to prove to myself that I am clever enough to have done a degree? My family always said I was, but ...*

'You okay, Maggie?'

'Sorry, yes. Just thinking – I'm not sure we ought to be doing this.'

Picking up his cheese cracker again, Ryan asked, 'Are you having a change of heart because you think we should leave it to the police, or because, stupidly, you've decided you aren't clever enough?'

Maggie couldn't help but laugh. 'You're not as daft as you seem.'

Leaning forward, Ryan spoke fast. 'We won't investigate Tania's death; we're just trying to find some stuff out about the circumstances leading up to it. About her life. Then we can tell the police if we find anything useful.'

'And it might take the focus off you.'

'That too.'

Maggie gave a decisive nod. 'Okay then. But I'm relying on you, Ryan. I know what I'm like when I get the bit between my teeth. I can get a bit single-minded.'

'Is that a way of warning me you'll get obsessed, and I might need to tell you when enough is enough?'

'Something like that.' Maggie laughed as she picked her pen back up. 'So, what did Bea say was planned for Tania's hen do?'

'It was supposed to be four friends having a facial, massage and whatever else you women do on a spa day. Although, obviously it became three friends, with Bea going AWOL.'

'Less of the "you women" please.'

Polishing off the last of his supper, Ryan chuckled. 'Not a scented oil sort of person, Maggie?'

'Not even a scented candle sort of person.' Maggie scribbled *spa day* on her pad. 'Where was this booked to take place?'

'The Cabin Hotel. Toby, Tania and the others were staying there for the week.'

'I know it. You'll have seen it when the bus brought us into the village earlier. It's on The Parade; looks towards the Mousehole Rock Pool. I've heard that, if you're staying in one of the upper-floor bedrooms, you can see out towards St Clement's Isle.'

'Sounds nice.'

'Expensive.'

'Naturally,' Ryan acknowledged, 'it was for a special occasion, and I got the impression that Tania was well off.'

'Because she knew Heidi and Bea, who both have well-off families?'

'More because of what she wore and how she was.'

'Her manner?'

'She had the same sort of confidence as Bea – the type that comes with a private school education and knowing that she's unlikely to have to worry about money.' Ryan paused. 'I think I might've been a bit harsh with Bea when I told her about Tania.'

'I'm sure you were very kind.'

'Not really. I used it as an excuse to get cross with her – you know, about ditching me for travelling and stuff. I shouldn't have done that – not when her friend's just died.'

Maggie took her time to respond, choosing her words with care. 'What you maybe need to ask yourself, me'ansom, is if you want to spend your life with someone who makes you feel that way, even in such extreme circumstances?'

'Well . . .'

As Ryan lapsed into silence, Maggie returned them to the subject in hand. 'You were saying, about Tania. She was confident.'

'It wasn't what she wore or said; it was more the way she wore her clothes, the way she sat . . . upright yet relaxed.' Ryan frowned. 'I'm not making much sense, am I?'

'It's okay, I know what you mean.'

'She wasn't a snob or anything. I liked her.' Ryan whispered, 'I can't believe she's dead. I only knew her a minute, but . . .'

'It's okay. Sometimes you only need to be with someone for a few moments to know you get on. You'd made a friend, and then she was taken from you.' Maggie gently asked, 'What did she look like?'

'Slim. Blonde – her hair was in a bob.'

'Eye colour?'

'Blue, I think.'

'Height?'

Cradling his coffee, Ryan closed his eyes. 'I'd guess about five-five, but she wore heels, and most of the time she was sitting down, so I can't be certain.'

'Attractive?'

'Very.' Maggie caught Ryan blushing as she looked back up from her notebook. 'She wore black jeans, a light coat and a velvet cap that she took from her bag and put on before she left. Both blue.'

'What did Toby look like?'

'I didn't see him clearly. He had short brown hair, slightly spiked, like he'd gelled it. About six foot, I think; although he stalked out of the pub fast, so I could be wrong about that.'

'Anything else about him that struck you?'

'He was angry. The way he held his cutlery and his glass – like he was squeezing them so tight they might break. And, I'd say, from the glimpse I had of his expression, he was also a bit embarrassed.'

'Like he felt caught out, or because of the scene they were creating?'

'I'd guess the former, but I can't be sure. From what Tania said, I don't think Toby liked her questioning him. She told me she was worried she couldn't trust him.'

'Because of the lack of the promised surprise.'

'That was certainly part of it.' Ryan stretched his long legs out in front of him. 'It wasn't a case of her not loving Toby. I think she felt uncertain about him but was determined to talk to him and sort things out.'

'She was going to talk to Toby. Right then? Straight after she left you in The Mariner. That's what she said?'

'Yeah, that's what she said she intended to do.'

Maggie turned the page in her notebook. 'But she can't have.'

'How do you know?' Ryan leant towards the notebook where Maggie was fast adding points to her original scribbled map.

'Here's the pub.' She drew a little square on the paper. 'Here's The Cabin Hotel, and here—' Maggie added a broken oval to show the shape of the harbour '—is where Tania was found.'

'It's in the opposite direction to the hotel.'

'Exactly. So, unless Toby was at the harbour, or somewhere in that general direction, then . . .'

'Tania changed her mind about going to see him straight away.'

'Or she met someone who changed it for her.'

# Chapter Twelve

'Here's the chippy, and here are the main roads that run through the village.'

Ryan watched as Maggie continued to scribble before him. 'I think we need a bigger map – no offence, Maggie, your drawing is great and everything, but it's getting a bit crowded. And, ummm, I can't read your writing. Sorry.'

Wishing he was wrong, Maggie admitted defeat. 'I've never had the clearest handwriting. When he wasn't saying I should be a detective, Grandad joked I should have been a doctor.'

'You'd have been a good GP. You listen when people talk.'

'Oh. Thanks.' Maggie got up and went to a bookshelf where the books were topped with an array of randomly stuffed leaflets and things that might come in useful one day.

'What are you searching for?'

'A map.' Maggie extracted a handful of takeaway menus off the top of a row of Agatha Christie novels. 'You'd be surprised how often maps are shoved in with the post, advertising the local tourist haunts. Ah, here we are.'

She unfolded a shiny red and yellow flyer that had been designed to promote the various art galleries that occupied the myriads of studios between Mousehole, Newlyn and Penzance.

As Maggie smoothed the map over the coffee table that sat before the sofa, Ryan tapped a finger against the harbour. 'Tania was found here, at this end.'

Maggie drew a circle around the spot, before adding another one to The Mariner pub. 'The Cabin Hotel isn't marked on here, but I'll add it.' She penned a small rectangle near the Mousehole Rock Pool. 'This will do for now, but tomorrow I'll go into the library and see if I can borrow a decent map.'

Ryan looked at her like she was mad. 'Or you could download one from Google and print it out right now. That way it'll be black and white, so easy to read. Not to mention not shiny – much easier to write on. Where's your printer?'

'I don't have one. I always use the one at the library.'

'Surely Mr Robbins has one?'

'Do you want to be the one who explains to him why we want to borrow it?'

'Good point.'

Aware that Ryan was regarding her as if she was from another century, Maggie laid down her pen. 'I don't know what I'm doing, do I? Can you imagine Poirot making such a mistake?'

'You didn't make a mistake – you're just keen. Anyway, Poirot was pre-computer and had a dopy moustache.'

Maggie giggled. 'You realise such a comment is considered sacrilege in Christie aficionado circles.'

'Doesn't stop it being true.' Ryan gestured to the rucksack he'd grabbed from his bedsit before leaving the shop. 'I have a laptop. I'll find you a map now. We can go to Penzance library tomorrow and print it out so we can write on it.' He paused. 'You do have Wi-Fi?'

'Of course I do! I'm forty-seven, not ninety-seven! And I use the library because if we don't use them, we lose them!'

'Sorry. I didn't mean to imply . . . I mean, you're not old or anything, just older than . . .' He faltered, his sentence fading to nothing, before he hastily added, 'And I have nothing against libraries.'

'I'm sure you don't. I'm sorry too. I shouldn't have snapped. I have a bit of a thing about people not using libraries anymore.' Maggie gave herself a shake, her natural smile returning. 'I have Wi-Fi and a laptop – although it's a bit outdated and needs replacing – but I don't have a printer. Used to, but we fell out, and I never bothered to replace it.'

'Not much point if you hardly use it.' Ryan opened his computer. 'Mum almost threw her printer out of the window once. They can be quite frustrating when they won't play.'

'Glad it isn't just me.' Maggie moved around so that she was seated next to Ryan on the sofa. 'You're right, though, we're going to need a bigger, clearer map we can use to work out where everyone is and where they've been.'

'Like in a police incident room.'

'Just like that. Or, at least, like the ones we've seen on the telly. I've never been in a real one.'

Ryan pressed a few buttons on his keyboard. 'I'm not in a hurry to see any part of a police station again, to be honest.'

'If we find something useful out, we'll have to go and tell them, though.'

'I know, but at least we'll be there by choice.' Ryan opened Google, taking care to filter for copyright-free images, and typed in *Map of Mousehole*. 'Okay . . . we don't want a plan of a mousehole . . . ah . . . here we are.'

A minute later a crisp, uncluttered, black-and-white outline of Mousehole was displayed on the screen before them. 'Hang on, if I'm careful . . . yes!' Ryan copied and pasted the map onto a blank page on the screen. 'Now we can type and draw straight onto here. Although, I should say that I'm not the best graphic artist, so don't expect anything remotely approaching cartography.'

'As long as we understand what we are looking at, who cares. I think it's brilliant!' Maggie beamed as she watched Ryan at work. 'Let's start again. Whereabouts in the harbour was Tania found . . .?'

\*

It was only when the carriage clock on Maggie's fireplace mantel chimed midnight that they stopped what they were doing. The map was full of every detail they could think of, including annotations showing estimated times for how long it took to walk from the pub to the harbour, and from the pub to the hotel. Meanwhile, Maggie's notebook was filling up with neat pages of notes about Tania and Toby's situation as they understood it.

'Tomorrow we should go to the hotel to talk to Daisy and Heidi.' Maggie closed her notebook. 'I want to know where they were when Tania left the pub.'

'Are you sure they'll be there? Would you hang around at the hotel you were supposed to be staying at if your friend had been murdered?'

'Nope, but Daisy came over from Oxford, and the tourist season has started. Finding somewhere else to stay locally at short notice would be tricky. Although, I suppose she could simply have gone home.'

'Unless,' Ryan stifled a yawn, 'Heidi took her to the family pile.'

'Good point.' Maggie opened the notebook again and jotted down the contingency plan. 'If we have no luck at the hotel, we'll go to Lamorna.'

'Can we stroll up to the manor just like that?'

'I don't see why not.' Maggie put her notebook down more decisively this time. 'But first we will go to The Cabin, as Toby and his friend . . .'

'Hugh.'

'. . . should be there as well. Now though, we should get some sleep.' She gestured to the sofa. 'It's an easy pull-out. If you don't mind getting the bed open, I'll grab you a duvet and pillows.'

# Wednesday 11th June

Maggie hadn't needed to set an alarm clock in years. Ever since she'd inherited her parents' home on their untimely death due to a motorway pile-up, just prior to her sitting her A level exams, the sound of seagulls overhead had lulled her into wakefulness in the early hours. Often, she would doze for a while, cosy between the realm of sleep and wakefulness, before the need for caffeine peaked at around seven o'clock. Occasionally, she dropped back into a deep sleep, but those moments were rare, and she couldn't remember a time when she'd slept beyond eight o'clock in the morning.

Today, her eyes closed as she lay against her pillow; the squawking outside told Maggie that it was somewhere between five and six in the morning.

Wondering if Ryan had slept, she felt a sense of peace. It was nice having someone else in the house. Not allowing herself to dwell on why she hadn't offered him Izzie's bedroom, Maggie sat up, already knowing that this was one of those mornings where further sleep would elude her.

Resting against the wooden headboard and gazing around, Maggie's gaze fell upon her new notebook. The combination of guilt and excitement she felt when she'd bought it came back to her. Even as Maggie had tapped her bank card to pay for it, she'd told herself she was being silly; that there was no way she'd be using it to record her thoughts about the manner of Tania's death.

Maggie began to reread the notes they'd made, stumbling every now and then over her awful handwriting that sometimes even she couldn't read. *I really must write more slowly or in capitals . . .*

Tugging open the curtain that hung over the window, she felt the warmth of the early morning June sunshine tickle her cheek. Stifling the urge to get up and go outside, as that would involve walking through the living room and so risk waking Ryan, she turned her attention back to the notebook, muttering to the seagulls cawing to each other on the roof above.

'Tania rowed with Toby the night before their hen and stag dos. She was sure he was hiding something, but Toby denied it and stormed out. Tania stayed, and the only other place to sit was with Ryan. They talked and discovered they have Bea in common. Tania left about half an hour before Ryan. He then went to the harbour but saw no sign of Tania.'

A timely squawk from above made Maggie look upwards. 'It's good to know you're listening out there. So, my feathered friend, whatever happened to Tania either happened in the thirty-minute period between her leaving the pub and Ryan leaving the pub, or after Ryan had walked to the harbour and left again. I wish he wasn't so vague about when that was.'

Closing her eyes again, Maggie continued to share her thoughts with the birds outside. 'It must be a coincidence that Bea knew Tania . . . but it is weird. Everything Ryan has said about her makes it easy for me to believe that she'd leave him high and dry without flinching. But why would she leave an old school friend . . . a best friend presumably, otherwise why would Bea have been one of only three girls invited to Tania's hen do . . . and disappear to travel without a word to her?

'Unless . . . maybe Bea didn't think there'd be a wedding . . . Does Bea know something about Toby? Did she think there'd be no point in delaying her trip because the wedding was never going to take place?'

A shrill squawk from outside reeled in Maggie's musings. 'Okay, so I'm letting my imagination run away with itself.' She gave herself a shake and threw back the duvet. 'Ryan or no Ryan, I need a coffee.'

\*

'It's okay, you don't need to tiptoe.'

Maggie heard Ryan's pillow-muffled voice as she gently pulled back the living-room door. 'I hoped you'd be asleep.'

'What time is it?'

'Just gone six.'

A low groan escaped from the bundle of bedclothes on the sofa.

'You don't have to move. I just need coffee.'

'Me too.' Ryan rolled over.

'You sure you don't want to go back to sleep?'

'Not a hope. I've been awake for ages. I can't stop thinking about Tania.'

'Hardly surprising.' Maggie padded across the carpet towards the kitchen. 'I've been sat in bed talking things over with the seagulls.'

'Really? I thought you said you talked to the gulls when we first met just to make me feel less of an idiot.'

'Nope, I'm just as crazy as you are.' Maggie smiled.

'Only since I got to Cornwall.' Ryan slowly sat up. 'Do you and the seagulls really think we should go to the hotel, or should we leave things to the police?'

Maggie flicked the kitchen light on. 'Ask me that again after I've had a cup of coffee.'

# Chapter Thirteen

'They might not be up.' Despite her being almost a foot shorter than him, Ryan was having trouble keeping up with Maggie's purposeful pace. 'It's not quite nine, and they're on holiday.'

'Their friend is dead. We couldn't sleep, so what makes you think they could?'

Knowing she had a point, Ryan found himself glancing nervously over his shoulder, half-expecting a police car containing Sergeant Peters to draw up, telling them to butt out. 'But, what will we say? We can't just march up to the reception desk and demand to talk to the friends of a dead guest.'

'We can ask if they're still there.'

'But why would they talk to us? They'll probably assume we're journalists and tell us to get lost.'

Maggie brushed a handful of curls out of her eyes as she marched along. 'You'll explain to them that you were a friend of Tania's and want to find out what's going on.'

'But I only met her last night.'

'They aren't to know that.'

'They're her oldest friends,' Ryan protested. 'They'll know everyone who was due to come to the wedding.'

'You clearly haven't been to many weddings. They're always full of cousins no one's heard of.'

'So, you want me to pretend to be a cousin, not a friend?' Ryan stopped walking. 'Hang on a minute.'

83

Breaking her stride, Maggie paused and looked over at Ryan. 'Okay, so the pretending to be someone close to Tania is a bad idea. I was just thinking aloud, but if we want to find things out, then we need a way in. We can come clean to Daisy and Heidi once we get past the receptionist. If you've changed your mind about wanting to investigate, I'll totally understand.'

'It isn't that. I do want to know what happened, but what if they tell the police I've been asking questions? Won't that make me appear more guilty, even though I'm not? As if I'm worried about what they might say about me?'

Maggie looked at the notebook she was holding out before her like a shield. 'Or it could show that you're someone who cares that the truth is discovered.'

'Come on, Maggie, this isn't telly.' Ryan stared ahead of them, along the street. The Cabin Hotel was in sight. 'I think this is a good idea, but . . .'

'I get it. You've been through enough in the last twenty-four hours. I'm sorry. I was getting carried away.'

'You're going to leave this to the police, then?'

'No, I'm not. I'm going to see if I can get some answers.' Maggie gestured out before her. 'The police clearly aren't bothered. Not a police car in sight.'

'It's early yet.'

'They would already be here if they wanted to talk to her friends.'

'More likely, they spoke to them yesterday – or they are using an unmarked car.' Ryan shook his head.

'Even better, that means the police do care, and we can discover exactly what the girls told them.'

Sliding his hands into his jacket pocket, Ryan said, 'You aren't going to let this go, are you?'

'Not until I've spoken to Tania's friends. I can't shift the feeling that something isn't right.'

'But the police . . .'

'Ryan, if the police decide that Tania's death wasn't an accident, then you're a suspect.'

'I only . . .'

'It doesn't matter what you did or didn't do; the fact remains that you are the last known person to have spoken to Tania, and you went to the place she died late at night, after which no one saw her alive. *Worse*, you have no memory of exactly when you got home!'

'Oh God.' The remaining colour drained from Ryan's face.

'And I'm not having it! I'm not having the police accuse you of something you did not do!'

\*

Ryan sat on the bench near the bus stop. His head swam with conflicting emotions, the strangest of all being the realisation that someone cared enough about him to go into battle on his behalf. Staring out to sea, he tried to remember any previous time when someone had had his back. Apart from a brief occasion when his maths teacher had encouraged him to pursue his love of numbers and do the further maths A level, when his parents had both told him he shouldn't bother, as he was 'getting above himself by thinking he'd be able to cope with the work it involved', he couldn't think of a single time.

Ryan knew his parents loved him, but they had a habit of reminding him he hadn't been planned and was often an inconvenient presence in their lives. A part of their life that hadn't been planned and was often inconvenient. They'd been right about the further maths A level too – he'd managed half of the first year before his teacher had gently suggested that perhaps it wasn't for him after all, and he should swap to statistics instead.

'I suppose doing statistics was useful . . . it might even be useful now, to help Maggie investigate . . .' Even as he spoke the words beneath his breath, he couldn't see how being able to analyse crime stats or draw a mean graph would help them much.

After they'd decided it probably wasn't that wise for him to go to the hotel after all, Ryan had left Maggie to it. Instead, he'd decided to head into Penzance to get their map printed out.

As he watched the seagulls dive and soar as they patrolled the shore, ever on the lookout for a fish from the sea or an unwary tourist's ice cream cone, Ryan was joined on the bench by another passenger. It was only when his unknown companion spoke into his mobile phone that Ryan turned to take a glimpse of his fellow traveller.

*Toby!*

'Yes, the bus! I'd rather be getting a taxi, but according to the hotel receptionist, it would be quicker to wait for a bus than a cab at this time of day – no idea why, it's hardly the back of beyond . . . An Uber! Down here? As if! Come on. You know the area better than that . . . What? Oh . . .'

Ryan kept his eyes steadfastly on the sea view before him; his ears, however, were wide open. He knew Maggie would expect him to remember every word spoken, and probably develop some theories on who Toby could be talking to and why he was waiting for a bus at that time in the morning.

Wishing he'd had the foresight to bring a notebook with him too, he suddenly remembered the record feature on his mobile. With his heart thudding hard, sure he was probably infringing some right of privacy or other, he took out his phone and surreptitiously pressed record.

\*

Refusing to listen to the utterly unhelpful voice of doubt that niggled at the back of her head, telling her that Ryan was right, and they should leave things alone, Maggie had walked through the open double doors which led into The Cabin's reception area.

The young woman behind the counter had been polite but firm on the subject of whether Miss Makepeace and Miss Spenser-Davies were still in residence, stating that she wasn't able to give out such information. Disappointed, but not surprised, Maggie had thanked her and asked if it would be alright if she stayed for coffee. To which she was swiftly informed that the lounge was open to residents and non-residents alike.

Now, an overpriced black coffee set out in front of her, with a wonderfully aromatic side order of croissants and butter, she sat with her back to the sea, looking out across the hotel's coffee lounge. The majority of the tables were empty. Most guests, Maggie imagined, would either have been and gone by now – taking the chance to get out into the June sunshine to explore the local landmarks or make a start on their sandcastle while the good weather lasted – or be tucking into a giant English breakfast in the dining room.

Maggie surveyed the comfortable space. Dotted with a mix of circular and rectangular tables, each was adorned with a pale green tablecloth, matching place mats and silver cutlery. A wooden clipboard, showing the light breakfast delights on offer, was placed centre stage between stainless-steel cruet sets and a tea or coffee pot stand. The scent of freshly cooked bacon, sausages and baked goods wafted through from the dining room, filling the air with mouthwatering temptation.

Placing her notebook and pen open on the table before her, Maggie applied a smear of butter to the corner of her croissant as she continued to observe the scene.

Three tables were in use. Two held elderly couples, who were happily munching copious amounts of toast and butter while chatting or reading newspapers. The third table was occupied by a family of four, the children in their teens.

Rather than talking to their silent parents, they were deeply engaged in whatever they were watching on their phones.

There was no sign of anyone who could be Daisy or Heidi. Maggie buttered another section of the croissant, sipped some coffee and picked up her pen.

*9.17 a.m. No sign of Daisy or Heidi at breakfast in Cabin. Nor of anyone who might be Toby or Hugh. Have they already eaten, gone out for a while or have they checked out?*

Reading over her scribbles, Maggie pulled a face and mumbled, 'Not exactly detective-level thinking.'

As the waiter, whose nametag revealed him to be called Jack, came in her direction, a box of sugar cubes in his hands, she gave him a wide smile. 'This is lovely.'

'The pastries here are very popular.' Jack used a metal scoop to load some fresh sugar into a pot on the table next to Maggie.

'Nice and light, yet filling. A good alternative to a Full English.' She increased the wattage on her grin. 'I bet lots of your guests pick the continental option.'

'They do.'

'Especially the young ones?' She peered around her. 'Although, maybe you don't have that many younger guests?'

'This place mostly attracts older couples or families. We do get groups of young people sometimes, though. For the spa mostly.'

'Spa days.' An idea leapt into Maggie's mind. 'That's why I'm here, to see if a spa day is the sort of thing my daughter would like as a gift.'

Putting down his box of sugar, the waiter checked his wristwatch. 'The spa doesn't open until ten, but I'm sure they'll be able to help you.'

'There's a rather relaxing vibe in here, so I imagine it's even better in the spa.'

'I'm not sure how relaxed it'll feel today.' Putting the lid on the sugar pot he'd filled, the waiter lowered his voice. 'A hen party was booked in, but the bride met with an accident, so obviously . . .' He shrugged in lieu of finishing his sentence.

'How sad. I bet the bride is gutted.'

He shook his head. 'Dead.'

'No!' Maggie sucked in her breath. 'How awful! Are all her guests here? I mean . . . if they were staying?'

'Yes. They . . .' Jack abruptly stopped talking. 'Sorry, I'm not supposed to give away anything about our guests. Confidentiality and all that.'

Maggie held up a hand in understanding. 'Not at all. I shouldn't have asked. Just shocked, I suppose.' She picked up her coffee cup. 'Thank you for telling me about the spa. I shall go to see it as soon as I've finished my breakfast.'

# Chapter Fourteen

Plonking his white boater onto his head, Ryan tied his apron into place as he listened to Maggie tell him about her visit to the spa. He privately applauded Maggie's ability to get information out of people without confrontation.

'The spa is beautiful. I can see why it appeals to people who like sitting down while being cooked to within an inch of their lives.'

Ryan chuckled. 'I take it from that that a sauna is on a par with scented candles for you; not your thing?'

'Nor Izzie's. Neither of us would ever be able to sit still long enough to make paying for it worthwhile.'

'But you pretended to be looking into booking a session for Izzie?'

'The lass was very helpful. Talked me through how the spa days work. I asked if they had availability today, and she said not; that they were fully booked, apart from the swimming pool. I could have used that if I'd been willing to pay a tenner for an hour.'

'Steep!' Ryan stacked a pile of boxes up ready to be filled with fish and chip lunches onto the counter. 'She didn't mention any cancellations?'

'Nope. Which means that either the spa receptionist hadn't been informed of the situation, or that . . .'

'Heidi and Daisy intend to carry on with the spa break without Tania.'

'Precisely.' Maggie lifted two pieces of cod out of the fat, and placed them in the warming cupboard, ready to be served. 'I hung around for a while, asked about all the stuff they have going on down there, in the hope that Heidi and Daisy might appear, but after twenty minutes of mindless chatter about the benefits of seaweed wraps, I felt I'd pushed my luck far enough.'

'You did brilliantly. Thinking of the spa angle was inspired.' Ryan scooped a generous handful of tomato ketchup sachets out of a box under the counter and put them in a basket on the counter next to the till. He never ceased to be amazed that people would willingly pay fifty pence for the equivalent of a tablespoon of sauce.

'It was rather frustrating. According to Cindy – the lass I spoke to in the spa – the spa days start at half-ten and run until half-three. I would have liked to loiter so I could speak to the girls when they arrived to have their muscles knitted and purled, but I had to get back here for eleven.'

'At least we know they're still staying there.'

'We don't though – not really. All we know, or suspect, is that their spa session wasn't cancelled, so we've hardly taken a giant step forward.' Maggie paused as a customer came in. Two servings of fish and chips later, she said, 'I'd hoped I'd at least be able to see them, so we knew who they were by sight, or overhear a conversation, even.'

'Funny you should say that.'

'You've overheard something?'

The knowledge of his eavesdropping had been bubbling in Ryan's stomach ever since he'd slid his phone into record mode on the bench prior to his trip to the library.

'When I was at the bus stop waiting to go into Penzance, I wasn't alone. Toby was there.'

'What?!' Maggie ran a fresh side of cod through some batter mix. 'Why didn't you tell me before?'

'I didn't want to distract you. He was on the phone. I, ummm, I secretly recorded his conversation.'

'Oh my God! That's brilliant. I'd never have thought of using my mobile to record a conversation. Not that I had a conversation to record this time, but in the future I might.'

'You're enjoying this, aren't you?'

'I suppose I am.' Contrite, Maggie sounded determined, 'I won't stop looking into things until the police officially knock you off their "of interest" list. After that, I'll stop playing P.I. and get on with doing crosswords again.'

'Thanks, Maggie.' Ryan waved a hand upwards. 'The map is upstairs. I went for the A3 size so we could see everything more clearly.'

'That's great, we'll have a gander later. For now, can I hear the recording?' She glanced towards the door. 'Let's listen now, while it's quiet.'

Ryan extracted his phone from his jeans' back pocket and propped it up against the till. 'Just before I started recording, Toby had said to whoever was on the other end of his call that the hotel had advised him to get a bus rather than wait for a taxi – then he moaned about there being no Ubers here. Then there was a longish pause while he listened to whatever was being said. That's when I started to record the conversation.'

'I wonder why he didn't have a car with him?'

'Or, if he did have a car, why he wasn't driving it.'

Maggie grinned. 'You're getting as bad as me for asking questions. It's a good point, though. You'd think a successful businessman would have his own transport. I'm assuming Toby is successful.'

'Tania implied he was, so he'd have a car.'

'Unless he shared one with Tania, and she was due to use it today.'

'If that was the case, he'd have the use of it now that Tania isn't here anymore.' Ryan bit his lip as he recalled the vibrant, determined, heartbroken young woman he'd spoken to in the pub. 'A drink!'

'Sorry?'

'I bet, if they're local, they decided not to bother with cars so they could drink. It was supposed to be a week of celebrations, after all. They could have left their cars at home and got a cab to the hotel.'

'Good thinking. I bet it was as straightforward as that,' Maggie conceded. 'You've no idea who Toby was talking to?'

'Beyond that it felt like it might have been a work colleague, not a clue. I've listened to the recording three times now, and I can't even decide if they're male or female. When I spoke to Tania, she said he had one regular assistant at work.'

'Probably them, then.'

'Probably.' Ryan lowered his voice as he remembered the ever-present Mr Robbins only a few metres away in the adjoining office. 'Tania said she'd wondered if Toby was having an affair, but had decided not as she couldn't work out where he'd find time.'

Maggie muttered. 'There's always time for an affair if you want one.'

'Pardon?'

Ignoring him, she urged, 'Come on, play it. We don't have long.'

'Okay. I should warn you that the seagulls and occasional passing vehicles get in the way sometimes.'

Maggie came closer to the phone as Ryan pressed play. After a few seconds of silence and the rumble of a lorry passing close to the bus stop, an annoyed, educated male voice could be heard.

'...You said you could handle it! I wasn't planning on working today, as you well know. It's my stag do – at least it was! ...What a fucking nightmare. The police want to talk to me later. God knows why. I wasn't there when she fell. You said this was a simple operation. One I wanted nothing to do with, but you insisted! ...For goodness' sake! As if life wasn't complicated enough right now, and ... Hang on, the bus is here.

I'll be there in half an hour. Try not to let me down again before then!'

As the mobile clicked off, Maggie said, 'Play it again, please.'

This time she closed her eyes as she listened.

Ryan shut his eyes too but felt silly, so opened them again. 'Hear anything else?'

'Nothing new. But you never know.' Maggie opened her eyes. 'Toby said he'd see whoever he was talking to in half an hour, so they weren't far away.'

'At work, I suppose – wherever that is.'

'We need to find out.'

'He didn't sound upset, did he?' Ryan moved around to the front of the shop, unlocked the door and flipped the closed sign to open.

'He did not. The worst he sounded was inconvenienced.'

'Come to think of it, he wasn't giving off upset vibes when I saw him.' Ryan washed his hands before heading to the till, ready for the first customer of the day. 'I didn't look closely at him – didn't want Toby to wonder why I was staring – but he didn't seem sad.'

'No sign of tears?'

'Not that I saw. I was more thinking that he wasn't hunched or pale. If I'd lost the woman I'd been about to marry, I'd be hunched. Broken. I'd go sort of – inwards.'

'And you wouldn't be sat at a bus stop shouting at an employee.'

'I doubt I'd be thinking straight enough to get dressed, let alone anything else.' An image of Bea filled Ryan's mind. He couldn't help but wonder how he'd feel if he was in Toby's position.

'After work, let's study that map. We might not have got very far today, but looking at that might help us get our thoughts together.'

'Sure.' Ryan resolved to get up to the bedsit a few minutes before Maggie so he could make a token effort at tidying it up, at least managing to hide the pile of dirty washing and opening the window to let some fresh air in. 'Or do you want to scoot over to the hotel again between shifts to see if you can talk to Heidi and Daisy after their spa treatments?'

'I would, but if they don't finish until half-three, and we have to be back here by half-four to prep for opening at five, it'll be tight. Sometimes I really wish I could drive! It would make life so much easier.'

Ryan dug his hands into his pockets. 'I can drive.'

'Do you have a car?'

'Well, no.'

'Public transport it is then . . . which would mean a taxi if we wanted to see the girls today.'

'We?' Ryan shook his head. 'I'm not sure I should go. The police might not like it if . . .'

The door to the chip shop opened, and a family of tourists came in.

'Hold that thought, Ryan.' Maggie smiled at their customers. 'Right now, it's chip time.'

# Chapter Fifteen

'I've remembered something else Tania said in the pub.'

Maggie kept her eyes on the vinegar bottle she was refilling. 'Go on.'

'You know I said that Tania had wondered if Toby was having an affair but had dismissed the idea?'

'Yes.'

'After that, she talked about trust generally; she was sure he was up to something. What other things, apart from being unfaithful, could she catch him out at?'

'Lying generally?'

'But about what?' Ryan pulled a face. 'I can't decide if she was trying to convince herself he was faithful when she actually doubted that was the case, or if she really believed he was.' He paused. 'Do you think I should tell the police? They did ask me to let them know if I remembered anything else.'

'You should if the verdict isn't accidental death. Until then, I'd leave them alone if I were you.' Maggie glanced up at the fish-shaped clock. 'We haven't had a customer for twenty minutes.'

Ryan sucked on his bottom lip. 'Is that your way of saying you want to leave now, so you can be waiting for Heidi and Daisy?'

'Bit early for that, but I did wonder if you fancied heading to my place with the map as soon as we've closed up so we can look at it properly.'

Knowing that he had nothing else to do, Ryan agreed.

'Then, I wondered if you'd mind setting up for the next shift without me at half-four?'

Ryan grinned at Maggie. 'Because you'll be at The Cabin Hotel?'

'On my way back from it hopefully, but if I do get to talk to the women, I may be late.'

'Deal.' Ryan's palms prickled with nerves. 'You will be careful, though, won't you?'

'I'm only going to see if I can have a chat about Tania.'

'I know, but if it wasn't an accident, then someone killed her, and if that person finds out you're . . .'

'Poking my nose in?'

'I was going to say, making enquiries, but I suppose it depends on your point of view.'

★

Standing on the doorstep of Maggie's home at the top of Duck Street a few hours later, Ryan watched as she climbed into the taxi, before heading back inside. It felt strange being in her home without her. He weighed the spare front door key she'd just given him in his hand before putting it in his pocket and going into the dining room. Ryan smoothed a hand over the map they had been studying together.

When travelling on the same bus as Toby earlier that day, Ryan had alighted two stops later than he needed to, on Penzance's Market Jew Street, so he could find out where Toby'd been going, but luck had not been on his side. The stop had been a popular one, and Toby had got off before him and disappeared up the stairs that ran from Market Jew Street to Bread Street, while Ryan got held up helping a mum carry her pushchair down off the bus and onto the pavement.

That meant, Maggie had reasoned while they'd examined the map, that Toby worked somewhere in the Chyandour

Cliff district of Penzance, which was on the way out of town towards Marazion. Ryan's task now was to research any import and export traders operating in that area. Having drawn a blank the last time he hunted for such an enterprise, he wasn't sure where to start.

As he waited for his laptop to boot up, Ryan let his eyes stray around the room. The bookshelves that lined two walls were crammed full. The dominant feature was murder mystery fiction. Judging by the huge number of books, ranging from Ellis Peters' Brother Cadfael investigations to Colin Dexter's *Inspector Morse* and taking in Christie, Conan Doyle, McDermid and countless others, it seemed that Maggie was not just a voracious reader but a hoarder of books. Here and there, laid in a haphazard fashion on top of the shelved books, were puzzle books, maps of the area, bus timetables and cards showing taxi company numbers.

Feeling as if he was intruding, Ryan returned to the task he'd been given and tapped *Exporters based in Penzance* into his search engine.

\*

Maggie hooked her bag higher onto her shoulder, and, hoping a different person was on reception so she didn't have to explain why she was back again, she headed into The Cabin Hotel's lobby. Thankfully, there was no one behind the desk at all.

Rather than heading down the spiral stairs to her left, which wound down to the spa in the basement, Maggie made her way towards the coffee lounge.

*If I'd spent the day in a spa, I'd either want a drink at the bar or a large coffee and cake straight afterwards.*

Clutching her bag closer, feeling the reassuring presence of her notebook within, she ignored the nerves in her stomach. She hadn't told Ryan she'd packed her swimming costume, just in case she had to fall back on paying for an hour in the pool in order to get through the spa's doors if she had no luck in the coffee lounge. Moving forwards, Maggie exchanged a friendly smile with a man going in the other direction, hoping she looked as if she had every right to be there.

She was about to follow the path she'd taken at breakfast time when she heard the faint chink of glasses and female voices off to her right. Changing direction, she followed the noise and, turning a corner, found herself in a sparsely populated bar, just as two women moved from the bar to a table near the window. Both wore brightly coloured summer dresses, but their expressions were nowhere near as cheerful as their outfits or the orange, umbrella-spiked cocktails they were drinking.

*That must be them . . .*

Heading to the bar, ordering herself an apple juice, Maggie sat down two tables away from the women, her chair facing them. Rather than pull out her notebook, she produced a crossword puzzle book from her bag and proceeded to pretend to answer clues while she listened.

'. . . Daze, I want to check out. This doesn't feel right.'

*It's definitely them. That means the woman speaking is Heidi . . .*

'Me too.' Daisy sucked her drink through a spiral straw. 'Toby said we should stay and do what Tania wanted us to do, but . . .'

'I know. I felt okay about it this morning. Well, not okay, but sort of alright about doing what he wanted, but the more I think about it . . .'

'Yeah. It feels wrong.'

Heidi let out a long sigh. 'So much for spa days relaxing you. I've never been so tense in my life.'

'Maybe it would have been okay if Bea had been here too.' Daisy released a sigh that was even louder than Heidi's. 'All I did during my massage was overthink, cry a bit and generally mull over all the fun we've had with Tania over the years.'

'Me too. And I feel so bad that we're having her hen do without her. Plus, there's this guilt that I wasn't there to help her. She invited us to the pub to chat after their meal, but...'

'We didn't want to be gooseberries – yeah...' Daisy wiped a hand over her teary eyes. 'In normal circumstances, not getting in the way would have been the right thing to do.'

Maggie raised her eyes from her puzzle book as Heidi's voice faded into silence. Both women looked drawn.

Daisy plucked the umbrella from her cocktail glass. 'Then I started wondering: *was* there something wrong, or are we just thinking that something was wrong between her and Toby because the police won't say what happened? I mean, if it *wasn't* an accident...'

Heidi shook her head hard and fast. 'No. No way. Tania did *not* kill herself. No.'

Daisy cradled her glass against her chest. 'She was so happy – had so much to live for. She was about to get married, for heaven's sake!'

Silence descended over them. Maggie found herself holding her breath as she waited for the women to resume their conversation.

'I only kept going today because Toby made it clear that's what he wanted. Mid-massage I was so tense the woman with me gave up. Stuck some whale music on and told me to breathe deeply instead.'

'I'm surprised that didn't happen to me too.' Daisy took another suck from her straw. 'I wish Toby had come down to breakfast. When I sent a text to see if he wanted anything, he just said he wanted to be on his own.'

'Not surprising, I suppose. I hardly have an appetite, so I bet Toby doesn't either.' Heidi took a sip of her drink. 'Not knowing when the police will want to talk to us again is unnerving. Although I can't think of anything else to tell them.'

'Nor me.' Daisy grimaced. 'Even if they haven't got any more questions, they'll want to see Toby to tell him what the cause of death was. The pathologist will have done – well ... what they do, by now, won't they?'

'I don't want to think about Tania all cut up.' Heidi wiped a tear from her face. 'Why was she at the harbour without Toby anyway? They were supposed to be having one last night together as single people, before staying apart until the wedding.'

Maggie filled in the crossword clue in front of her. *They don't know about the row ... Toby didn't tell them ...*

'Probably had one of their rows.'

'Probably.'

Maggie jotted down: *Toby and Tania had lots of rows.*

Blowing her nose on a tissue, Heidi asked, 'You don't think Toby will expect us to have dinner with him and Hugh tonight, do you?'

'I'm not sure those two are talking to each other again yet.'

Maggie sat up a little straighter. *Why aren't Hugh and Toby talking?*

'I really want to go home.' Heidi put down her glass. 'I know the police aren't keen on us leaving here, but they didn't *actually* say we couldn't leave the hotel, just that they'd rather we didn't leave the area.'

Daisy twirled a strand of hair around her fingers. 'You sure it'll be alright?'

'I can't see why not. You can stay at mine if you like; my parents won't mind. We can tell the receptionist that we'll be at my place. Lamorna isn't far away. I'm sure that nice sergeant will understand, and the police do have our phone numbers. To my mind it's a cert Tania didn't kill herself, so all they'll be doing is coming to see us to confirm it was a horrid accident.'

'Suppose so.'

Heidi offered an arm out for Daisy to take as she stood up. 'Let's get out of here. Tomorrow we were supposed to be having a make-up and dress rehearsal with Tania. The thought of sitting here without her …'

'Enough said. I'll text Toby.' Daisy put a hand into her palatial bag and had a rummage. 'Oh damn, I must have left my phone in the spa. Can you text him while I go and fetch it? Probably best you do it anyway.'

'Sure.' Heidi pulled out her phone. 'You know, he's not that bad, Daze. And Tania loved him.'

'I know, but I still think he's shifty.' As they departed the bar, Maggie heard Daisy mutter, 'Toby … he doesn't seem that upset, does he …'

# Chapter Sixteen

Ryan was in the process of turning the closed sign to open when Maggie rushed through the chip shop's door. She grabbed her hat from its hook.

'You made good time.' Ryan picked up Maggie's apron, ready to pass it to her the moment she'd finished washing her hands.

'Did he notice I wasn't here on time?' She bobbed her head in the direction of the office door as she scrubbed soap between her fingers.

'If he did, he didn't say.'

'Sounds about right.' Maggie smiled. 'An enigma through and through.'

'That's what Sergeant Peters said.' Ryan glanced at the office door, lowering his voice as he added, 'Does anyone know *anything* about Mr Robbins?'

'Beyond that he's owned this place for almost fifteen years – nope.' Taking her apron from Ryan, Maggie looked around with approval. 'Any problems setting up?'

'Don't think so.' Ryan lowered two pieces of fish into the vat of fat before him. 'I've only prepped four pieces of cod so far. Last Wednesday evening was quiet, so I thought maybe we should put less through the batter mix upfront, so it keeps better.'

'How on earth did you remember that?'

103

'Don't know. I just do, you know, remember stuff like that.' He shrugged. 'I was going to prep a couple of haddock next.'

Opening the fridge, Maggie pulled out the rack of haddock. 'I'll do it.' She peered into the warming compartment of the counter. 'Sausages look good. Nice, even batter. Well done, that's not easy to get right.'

'Thanks. I don't think I've concentrated on anything so much since I did my exams.' Unaccustomed to praise, Ryan felt two points of warmth colour his cheeks as he changed the subject. 'How did it go? Did you see them?'

'I did.' Maggie slipped on some gloves and picked up the haddock. 'I forgot to record the conversation, but I've written it down.'

'Conversation? You spoke to them?'

'No, I sat near them in the hotel bar. They'd done the spa day to please Toby, but they weren't comfortable about it. And get this, they think the same as us; they don't think Toby seems upset either.'

'I get that he was hurt when Tania said she didn't trust him, but wouldn't that be wiped out by the shock of her loss?'

'We're all different, but yeah, it's odd. Cold, even.' Maggie lowered her voice. 'I've got a theory. I'm probably well off, but we have to start somewhere.'

'Go on.'

'Heidi and Daisy have checked out of the hotel. It was Heidi that pushed for it, although Daisy quickly agreed to go with her.'

'Guilty conscience? Fleeing the scene-ish. Is that what you're thinking?' Ryan knocked some paper napkins into a neat pile. 'Heidi's motive?'

'I wondered if she was jealous of Tania – wanted Toby for herself?'

'Go on.'

'It's a shot in the dark, really, but it was obvious that Daisy didn't like Toby. She said he was shifty. Heidi was very quick to defend him. Daisy implied that Heidi knew Toby a lot better than she did, which struck me as odd, as Heidi was the one who didn't go to university with Toby, Tania and Daisy . . . so how would she know Toby better?'

'Could be something as simple as Tania and Toby spending a lot of time in Cornwall since they graduated.'

'True.'

'And if Daisy didn't trust Toby, then it's hardly likely she'd want to spend much time with him.'

'Again, true.' Maggie wrinkled her nose. 'I'll put the "Heidi being jealous" theory on the back burner until we've learnt more about them all.'

'Probably best. I discovered something too; there's no trace of Toby's business online.' Ryan stopped talking as the shop door opened and the first customer of the evening came in.

Half an hour later, they were alone again, and Maggie continued their conversation as if they'd not been interrupted. 'No trace at all? Are you sure?'

'After you'd gone, I did some serious hunting. If a Toby Marrell does have a business in Penzance – whether it's on the side towards Marazion or anywhere else – then I can't find it.'

'How about import or export places in general?'

'I found no more than the three I'd already discovered. There are two in town and one out towards Sennen, and none of them have anyone called Toby Marrell there.'

Maggie frowned as she checked the amount of chips waiting to be fried. 'How do you know?'

'I phoned them.' Ryan's stomach clenched as he remembered how nervous he'd been and how he'd had to pep talk himself into making the calls. 'I hate using the phone.'

'You're on it all the time!'

'I meant that I hate talking to people on the phone.'

'Izzie's the same.' Maggie asked, 'What did you say so it didn't seem weird?'

Ryan grinned. 'I pretended I had a consignment of furniture I wanted bringing in from Morocco. Insisted on speaking to the owner or manager before committing myself to anything; asked for contact details and so on.'

Maggie looked at Ryan with a half-surprised, half-impressed expression on her face. 'What happened to not wanting to be involved in case the police find out?'

Keeping his eyes on the counter, Ryan said, 'I got to thinking, what if she was killed . . . I liked her.'

'I know you did. You're a good lad.'

'Thanks, but I'm not so sure Toby is. What if this business of his doesn't exist? Officially, I mean.'

'You think he lied to Tania about what he does for a living?' Maggie suddenly put a finger to her lips, silencing Ryan's forthcoming response as Harry hobbled through the door.

'Evening, Maggie.' The old man rested his weight on his walking stick as he reached the counter. 'And this must be your new helper.'

'Harry, meet Ryan. Ryan, this is Harry, a regular member of my puzzling club at the library.'

'Pleased to meet you, me 'ansum.'

Ryan nodded at the old man. 'Maggie tells me you like Sudoku.'

'You could say that,' Harry chuckled. 'I'll convert her to number puzzles yet, I hope.'

Maggie shook her head. 'Doubtful. Fish and chips? Or are you going to go mad and have a pie today?'

'It's a fish and chip shop, Maggie! I want fish!' Harry tutted. 'So, have you worked out what happened to that young lass yet?'

Ryan exchanged a *How did he know what we're doing?* look with Maggie as he shovelled a portion of chips into a box.

'Not really my area, Harry.' Maggie placed a piece of cod on top of the chips. 'You'll need to ask the police if you want a progress report.'

'If you say so, but I saw the glint in your eye when I told you a body had been found. The ultimate quiz – a whodunnit – and no numbers to be seen!'

Maggie rang Harry's purchase into the till. 'Nothing to investigate. Police think the poor girl fell.'

'Sad, that.' Harry passed over a ten-pound note. 'Such a waste. How she fell off, though, I can't imagine. Unless she was drunk or on drugs or something. With young people today, you can never tell.'

Ryan bit the inside of his cheek, stopping himself from commenting on this sweeping statement. He couldn't help being glad that Bea wasn't there, for she'd have had no qualms about saying something short and to the point about Harry's unconsidered generalisation about the young generation.

'I'm sure she was a perfectly nice woman.' Maggie wrapped the fish and chip box in paper and passed it across the counter. 'Will I see you at the library tomorrow, Harry?'

'You will. Can't miss my fortnightly session of being hopeless with modern technology.'

Ryan waited until Harry had gone before he asked, 'Why would he think you'd be investigating?'

'He was just being Harry. He's always been one for fishing for a bit of gossip.'

'But . . .'

'The poor man's all on his own with an overactive imagination. He wasn't being serious.'

\*

It was almost closing time before Ryan voiced a thought that had been building in his head since Harry's departure. 'Was it just the women you saw in the hotel? No sign of Toby or his friend?'

'Hugh. No, no sign. What was interesting, though, was that the girls said that he and Toby had rowed and weren't speaking.'

Ryan's eyes widened. 'A row about what?'

'They didn't say.'

'Perhaps—' Ryan's shoulders knotted with tension as his sentence was interrupted by the opening of the shop door.

Maggie found her voice before Ryan did. 'Sergeant Peters, Constable Harker, do you have news about Miss Stevens, or are you after some food?'

'No chips today, thank you, Maggie.' Sergeant Peters crooked his fingers and gestured for Ryan to come forward. 'I'd like to talk to your helper here.'

Ryan raised his batter-spotted gloves. 'I'll, um, just take these off and wash my hands.'

Maggie held the sergeant's gaze. 'I'll ask Mr Robbins to help me so you can use the office.'

'No need for that.' Peters raised a hand to his colleague, who walked around the counter to where Ryan was drying his hands.

'Mr Stepney, we would like you to come to the station with us, please.'

'The station again?' Ryan's voice sounded rather strangled. 'Why?'

'There's a few more things we need to know.' Constable Harker pointed to Ryan's boater. 'If you could take your work clothes off, please.'

His heart racing, Ryan looked helplessly at Maggie. 'But I don't know anything else.'

'Then this won't take long, will it, sir?'

The use of 'sir' made him instantly feel guilty despite his innocence, as Ryan muttered, 'Will you be okay here on your own, Maggie?'

'Don't worry about me. You get off with these gentlemen. I'm sure you won't be gone long.' Maggie gave the sergeant a steady stare. 'I take it then that the pathologist has found cause for you to investigate further, and you need Ryan to give a formal statement this time?'

'You know I can't answer that, Maggie.'

'I do, but I also know that, if it had been an accident, you'd have been able to say so.'

David gave her a half smile. 'You always were a clever girl.'

'From what I remember, you've always been pretty sharp yourself.' Maggie retorted. 'I don't suppose it's worth me asking how Tania died?'

'You suppose correctly.'

'Ryan didn't do anything. He just happens to have been the last person you've found who saw Tania alive.'

The sergeant stepped back to let Harker and Ryan out from behind the counter. 'We just need to speak to him.'

'But why? Surely her fiancé is your chief suspect. Statistics show that most suspicious deaths . . .'

'I know what the stats say about partners being the most likely suspects in a murder, Maggie. We just need to chat to Ryan a bit more, that's all.'

'At half-eight at night? What can't wait until the morning?'

Peters shook his head. 'Come on, Mr Stepney. Let's not keep Detective Inspector Houseman waiting.'

# Chapter Seventeen

Maggie flew through the office, paying no heed to Mr Robbins' enquiring glance as she pounded up the narrow wooden staircase. Relieved that Ryan hadn't locked the door to his bedsit, she was in the room in seconds.

Knowing her employer would have something to say about closing the shop half an hour early when he realised what she'd done, Maggie surveyed the scene.

The aroma of fish and chips fought with the scent of young adult male. Wrinkling her nose, she threw open the window and tried not to see the random piles of discarded clothing that dotted the bedroom side of the bedsit. In contrast, the bed, while unmade, was at least tidy, with the duvet neatly folded back and the pillow plumped, ready for him to climb back into it.

*Tonight, hopefully.*

A sense of urgency assailed her. She felt she ought to tell someone what had happened, but who? Ryan hardly spoke about his parents, and when he did, the impression wasn't one of a harmonious relationship.

*There's Bea, though . . .*

Knowing Ryan had his mobile on him, she wondered if the police would take it away to read his texts and examine his calls. Maggie briefly considered searching his room for an address book, then laughed at herself. People under thirty did not have address books; they had computers and mobiles instead.

*His laptop...*

Spinning around, Maggie turned her attention from the bed to the table and chair near the kitchen area. There it was. His laptop – open and, mercifully, already on and logged into his WhatsApp app.

*He probably keeps it like that.*

Taking some comfort from the fact that the police hadn't decided to take the laptop, but knowing if they had got it into their heads that Ryan was involved in Tania's death, they'd come back for it later, Maggie scrolled through his previous messages. 'There must be some from Bea ... there must be ... Ah ...'

Not sure if she was about to help or make things worse, she read the last message the couple had exchanged and, being very careful not to read it, began to type ...

*

'Has it been made clear to you that you can leave at any time, Mr Stepney?'

'Yes.' Ryan found himself seated at the same table, in the same stale-smelling room, with the same police personnel as before. He wouldn't have been surprised if the plastic cup of half-drunk coffee that sat on the edge of the table was the same one he'd seen there last time as well.

'Good.' Houseman shuffled some papers, before laying them on the table and putting her tablet on top of them. 'As my colleagues informed you, the examination of Miss Stevens' body has revealed that she did not fall from the harbour wall by accident.'

Ryan felt as if his tongue was stuck to his throat.

'We've invited you back to talk to us as, now that we know we have a murder investigation on our hands, we need to do things more formally.'

*Invited? Yeah, right ...*

Houseman patted the paperwork before her. 'This means we'd like to formally take your statement now that you've had time to think more carefully about the evening of Monday the ninth of June. Okay?'

Ryan madly tried to force his mouth to make enough saliva so he could speak without croaking.

'Perhaps you'd like some water?' Sergeant Peters suggested.

'Please.' Ryan gave a grateful nervous smile, as he reminded himself he'd done nothing wrong.

Having gestured to Constable Harker, who left his vigil by the door to fetch the water, Peters softened the atmosphere. 'How are you settling into working with Maggie?'

'It's okay. Maggie's nice.'

'She is. Robbins' Fish and Chip Shop is something of a landmark around here.'

Wishing the constable would hurry up, Ryan licked his lips, constantly aware of the inspector's sharp green eyes on his as Peters engaged him in small talk. 'It's popular. We were busy. I hope Maggie's alright on her own.'

'Mr Robbins will help her.' Peters paused as the door to the interview room reopened and Harker came in with a jug of water and three plastic cups.

Ryan glugged the wonderfully chilled water down his parched throat.

Houseman took off her suit jacket and hung it on the back of the chair. 'Better?'

'Thank you.' Ryan wiped a hand across his lips. 'Sorry. It's been a busy evening, and I hadn't had a drink since four.'

'Not a problem.' Diane Houseman sat forward, her angular expression softening a fraction as she smiled. 'Now then, before we go back to the beginning, is there anything else you can tell me about your chat with Miss Stevens in the pub, that you'd forgotten before?'

'Yes. I was only saying to Maggie before Sergeant Peters and Constable Hacker arrived that I remembered something Tania said about Toby.'

The detective pushed a stray black hair from her eyes. Her smile evaporated. 'I believe we asked you to contact us if anything came to you.'

'I was going to call you in the morning.'

'I'm sure.'

Houseman sounded far from sure, making Ryan feel thoroughly told off. 'I was. But I can't make you believe me.'

Sergeant Peters took a sip of his own water. 'Have you and Miss Tyson chatted much about what happened?'

'A bit.' Ryan wondered exactly how much to say about Maggie's intention of getting to the bottom of what was going on, while avoiding being caught lying to the police. 'She's the only person I really know here.'

'You knew Tania.'

'Only for the length of one conversation.' Ryan sighed. 'I liked her. I wouldn't have hurt her.' He closed his eyes for a second before adding, 'That's what you think, isn't it? That I'm the one who killed her.'

Not answering his question, the detective stated, 'Tania was about to marry someone else.'

The deadpan way Houseman spoke didn't make Ryan feel any better.

'If you're thinking that I did something in a fit of jealousy to stop her marrying Toby, then you need to think again. I knew the woman for the time it takes to drink a few pints of beer. That's it! Anyway, I've a girlfriend of my own. Christ!'

Peters looked up sharply. 'Calm down, Mr Stepney.'

Ryan took a deep breath. 'Tania was excited about getting married. She and Toby might have had a row, but she said nothing about them splitting up. If she had, I would have said so last time I was here.'

'Unless you'd forgotten.' Houseman's voice was devoid of emotion.

'I would not have forgotten that.' He looked from the detective to the sergeant. A nervous sweat broke out on his palms. 'Would you like to know what I *have* remembered? Although, it's nothing much.'

'Go ahead.'

'I told you last time that Tania and Toby's row was about trust, and that she'd dismissed the idea that he was having an affair because she couldn't work out when he'd have the time.'

Peters grunted in disbelief, reminding Ryan of Maggie's reaction to the same point.

'Yeah, well, that's what Tania said. I don't know if she was kidding herself or not.' He shifted in his seat. 'She said she didn't trust him – but she didn't say over what.'

'Is that all?' Houseman tapped her fingernails against the table.

'I told you it wasn't much.'

'Okay, Mr Stepney. We will look into that.'

Ryan took another drink of water, more to escape the detective's unsettling glare than to quench his thirst. 'Shall I redo my statement now?'

'In a minute. First of all, is there anything else you've forgotten to mention?'

An image of him sitting next to Toby at the bus stop, the recording on his phone and Maggie's trips to The Cabin Hotel loomed large in his mind. 'Ah, well, umm – actually there's one other thing I haven't told you.'

'You forgot something else?'

'Well, no – I just didn't say.'

Peters leant forward, his voice quiet but firm, 'Mr Stepney, I'm sure I don't need to remind you that withholding information from the police is—

'No, you don't need to.' Ryan rubbed his hands over his eyes. 'I just didn't want my own relationship dragged into this.'

Houseman's expression remained impassive as she said, 'The girlfriend you mentioned just now.'

'Yes. Bea.'

'Bea what?'

'Harper-Georgeson.'

Houseman sat up a little straighter as she exchanged a questioning glance with her colleague. 'As in, the daughter of former town councillor Victor Harper-Georgeson?'

Ryan shrugged. 'I've no idea, but it's not a common surname, so maybe.'

'You haven't met her mother and father?'

'Just once, but her father's job wasn't mentioned.'

His interviewers stared at him in silence. Ryan was sure they were thinking the same thing.

*What would the daughter of a man like that be doing with a scruffy bloke from Birmingham?*

Eventually, Peters broke the tension. 'If all you did was speak to a woman in a pub – Tania Stevens in this instance – then why would you worry about your relationship being dragged into things? You said you chatted to Tania after she sat with you, as it would have been rude not to. Does your girlfriend know about this conversation, Ryan?'

'Of course she does.'

'And where is Bea right now?' Inspector Houseman's eyes narrowed. 'You're living above the chippy, not somewhere I'd imagine Miss Harper-Georgeson is likely to want to reside.'

Ryan bristled, partly from the assumption the detective was making about his girlfriend and partly because he knew she was right. Bea would never live in a bedsit, let alone in one that stank of chip fat.

'She's exploring Portugal with a group of friends.'

Peters' eyebrows rose. 'That was not the answer I was expecting.'

Houseman gave an unexpectedly sympathetic smile. 'You must miss her. Hard to settle into a place like Mousehole as an outsider. Is that why you went to the pub alone, to find someone of your own age to talk to?'

'You know it was. I said so last time. I wasn't there with the intention of picking someone up.'

'But you spoke to Tania.'

'I'm speaking to you, but that's not because I fancy you!' Ryan felt like screaming. Why were they making him feel like the bad guy? Worse, he was pretty sure Houseman was enjoying it.

'Come on . . .' Peters' voice took on a warning tone. 'We're trying to find out who killed your friend.'

Ryan scrubbed a hand through his hair. 'I know. And I'll help you, but please stop treating me like a criminal. And I'd hardly describe her as "my friend". I just happen to be the last person you can find who spoke to her.'

Houseman placed both her palms flat on the table. 'Okay, let's call a truce, shall we? You tell us what you decided we didn't need to know about Bea, and anything else that you might have decided wasn't of interest to us before, and we will hold off on the inquisition. Deal?'

'Deal.' Ryan's stomach gave a growl. 'And I'll do that statement. But can it wait a bit? I've not eaten yet, and I'm famished.'

Peters turned to Harker. 'Three coffees, please, Constable. And see if the canteen has anything edible left, will you?'

As the constable disappeared, Peters faced Ryan again. 'What was it that you didn't tell us before?'

'Bea knew Tania.'

'Your girlfriend knew the deceased?' Houseman's eyes narrowed.

'Yeah, but I didn't know that until I chatted to Tania in the pub. Bea and Tania went to school together.'

Peters leant back in his chair. 'What a coincidence.'

'Yes.'

'Was Bea coming back for the wedding on Saturday?'

'No. Bea was invited to that, and the hen do as well, but she was offered the chance to go travelling and decided to do that instead.'

'She was close enough a friend to be invited to what I gather was a small hen do for only Tania's closest friends, but went abroad instead?'

'Yeah.' Ryan sighed.

'I wonder why?'

'It was a once-in-a-lifetime offer.' Ryan spoke the words he'd been telling himself on and off since Bea's abrupt disappearance.

Houseman shook her head. 'Not to someone from a family with that sort of money, it wasn't.'

Ryan felt sick, and for a moment he stopped hearing what the police were saying to him from across the opposite side of the old grey table.

*They're right, Bea's loaded. She could have gone travelling anytime, but she chose the week we were supposed to move in together. Was that to avoid going to Tania's wedding, or to avoid living with me?*

The buzz of Houseman's phone broke through Ryan's thoughts just as Harker returned with some food and a mug of coffee.

'Ah, if you'll excuse us, Mr Stepney, I need to deal with this.' She waved her mobile as if in explanation as she got to her feet. She gestured to Peters to go with her. 'You eat up some of these sandwiches, and we'll be back as soon as possible.'

'Can't I just come back tomorrow?'

Houseman's face gave nothing away as they disappeared through the door, repeating her half-hearted reassurance. 'We'll be back shortly.'

*

Despite having left a note on his pillow and messaging his phone, Maggie had heard nothing from Ryan for hours.

Now, as the clock ticked around to midnight, Maggie pulled on a jumper against the evening chill as she sat at her dining table. The map they'd been working on together lay to her left, her notebook was open before her, and an ever-growing list of questions she wanted answers to had been scrawled onto the page before her.

Maggie was tempted to call Izzie to talk things through, but she resisted the urge. They might start talking about what was happening here, but they were bound to end up discussing Izzie's life choices, and Maggie didn't feel strong enough to have her daughter's long-term absence confirmed yet.

She checked the time again. Three minutes past midnight. 'They can't still be talking to him . . . can they?'

# Chapter Eighteen
## Thursday 12th June

The door reopened, temporarily moving the taciturn Constable Harker from his vigil.

Ryan wasn't sure if he was relieved or alarmed to see Detective Inspector Houseman come back into the room.

'Sorry to keep you, Mr Stepney. As you can appreciate, these things take time.'

Not appreciating this at all, Ryan rubbed a hand over his tired eyes. 'It's gone midnight. I'm happy to do a statement, but couldn't I come back in the morning?'

Ignoring his repeated question, Houseman explained, 'The reason I was so long was that the toxicology report for Miss Stevens came in while we were talking. Naturally I needed to study it, time being of the essence in such cases. We can now conclusively say that she hadn't taken drugs, nor had she had an excessive amount to drink.'

'I know she hadn't.' Ryan sat forward. 'So, are you saying Tania was poisoned?' His palms glistened with nervous perspiration as he wondered what the detective was thinking about his role in all this. A vision of Maggie sitting at her table with her map and notebook came to mind. *I bet she's there now, trying to work out what happened.* 'How? I was with her, and no one passed her a drink, and she didn't eat anything while with me.'

'No, I said we are waiting for a report to see if she *might* have been poisoned. That part of the test was inconclusive, so needs to be run again.'

'Inconclusive?'

'That's what I said. In the meantime, we have to consider poison as a possibility.' The detective wrote something down, before asking, 'Tania appeared to be in good health when she was with you, Ryan? Not showing any sign of being unwell after eating her meal?'

'No. Nothing like that.' Ryan's mind went into overdrive. *Surely there are clear signs of poison that the pathologist would spot, tests or no tests.*

Houseman's eyes flicked up from her tablet. 'When you were in the pub, did you buy Tania a drink?'

'No. She got her own.'

'And were you alone at any time with her drink?'

Ryan's apprehension levels rose even higher than they already were. 'No . . . yes . . . she popped to the toilet once.'

'Ah.'

'Ah? What does "Ah" mean?' Ryan looked from the detective to Sergeant Peters and back again.

Houseman laid both her palms against the table. 'It means, Mr Stepney, that I have enough evidence to hold you for further questioning regarding the murder of Tania Stevens.'

Shock robbed Ryan of speech for a few precious seconds, before he managed to stammer, 'But I didn't . . . why would I?'

'The pathologist has confirmed that Tania died roughly between nine and eleven in the evening, and as you were with her until half-past ten . . .'

'I see.' Ryan gulped. 'She was killed before I walked to the harbour.'

'Or while you were at the harbour.'

Ryan went cold. 'But I didn't . . . I . . .'

Houseman got back to her feet. 'We'll talk about it all in the morning. Would you like us to get you a solicitor?'

'A solicitor?' Ryan repeated as he struggled to comprehend the situation he was in.

'It's a good idea to have someone who has legal know-how to talk things over with you.'

'But I didn't do anything.'

'All the more reason to have legal representation. Try and get some sleep; as I said, we'll talk again tomorrow.'

★

Ryan was surprised he'd slept. He could only conclude that sheer exhaustion, with an accompanying helping of fear and disbelief, had caused him to relax enough to drop off. As he lifted his head off the plastic padded square that claimed to be a pillow, however, he felt a million miles from rested and totally disorientated. He wasn't sure what time it was, but he'd guess it was early.

When Houseman had left the interview room the evening before, Ryan had assumed he'd be going home, with a request to return that morning. It was only when Sergeant Peters had escorted him, not to the station's exit, but to the custody suite, that the reality of it all had sunk in. A reality that took on an even more frightening edge when they took his mobile phone from him.

*They're going to find the recording I made at the bus stop.*

★

Hopping onto the bus, Maggie wished she didn't have her library group that morning. Not only did it mean she wouldn't be able to check that Ryan was back safely, but that she didn't have time to embark on her plan to interview Tania's friends and Hugh until after her lunchtime shift at the chippy.

Watching the seagulls soaring over the sea, she whispered, 'He must be home. He just wouldn't have wanted to message and risk waking me up.'

As the cream and blue Mousehole Minibus ambled through the narrow lanes, Maggie ordered her thoughts. *If they found out that Bea knew Tania, they're going to wonder why Ryan didn't mention that before – on top of already knowing that he was the last one to see Tania alive – and if they've found that recording . . .* She closed her eyes. *He's going to have to tell them we've been investigating, isn't he . . .*

As the bus slowed to a stop, Maggie opened her eyes again. A teenage boy was getting on. His faded black jeans and oversized jacket were so like Ryan's that Maggie felt a pang of something entirely maternal.

*Just because I'm not his mum, doesn't mean I can't look out for him. I know he's innocent. And if necessary, I'll prove it.*

\*

Harry was the first to deliver the news that the goddess Rumour had leapt upon her winged chariot. He'd barely reached the side room in the library where Maggie was setting out a series of crossword puzzles next to four computers, each ready and waiting to be used as research tools, when he shared the news.

'Someone's been arrested for killing that lass!'

'Arrested!' Maggie's insides did a backflip.

'Talk of the town. A man was taken in for questioning last night.'

'Taken in for questioning is not the same as being arrested.'

'Yeah, yeah. I know.' Harry waved a hand as though batting away that minor point. 'Helping the police with their enquiries! We all know that's just another way of being arrested. I mean, why invite someone to the station if you don't think there's a good chance they did it?'

Flustered, Maggie began doodling on the edge of a crossword sheet with her ballpoint pen. 'You can't make assumptions like that.'

'Stands to reason.' The old man was untroubled. 'Anyway, it isn't just me. I heard people were talking about it on the bus trip in.'

Maggie hooked her mobile from her pocket, willing a message from Ryan to appear on the screen. There was nothing.

'You okay? You seem a bit peaky.' Harry lowered himself into the nearest chair.

Maggie grabbed her bag. 'Feeling a bit queasy. Sorry, Harry . . .' Heading to the door, intent on finding the nearest library assistant, she added, 'I have to go. See how you get on with the puzzles without me today.'

'But, I can't use . . .'

'Of course you can, Harry. The others will be here soon, and I'll get one of the library staff to check on you all now and then. I'm sure they'll help if you get stuck.' Maggie called over her shoulder as she fled, 'I look forward to hearing about how much you managed next time.'

Not entirely sure where she was going, Maggie ignored the guilt she felt at leaving the Crossword Club before it had even got started.

Having told the nearest library assistant that she felt unwell – not entirely untrue – Maggie was consumed with the desire to do something to help Ryan. *He can't have been arrested, surely?*

She hurried outside. *If it wasn't for me, Ryan wouldn't be in this mess. I encouraged him to go to the pub, and to investigate.*

She stopped dead.

*What if the police find the recording he made?!*

Torn between going to the police station to ask what was going on and heading to Lamorna to talk to Tania's friends, Maggie dropped both ideas and jumped on the first minibus back to Mousehole.

\*

Walking the few metres from the bus stop to the chippy, Maggie was met with the sight of a police car outside the shop. Quickening her pace, she pushed her shoulders back as she saw Sergeant Peters coming out of the front door with a laptop in a see-through bag in his hands and a furious Mr Robbins on his heels.

'David? That's Ryan's computer.'

'I am aware of that.' He passed the laptop to Constable Harker, who was waiting by the car.

'You haven't arrested him, have you?'

'He's just being kept in for questioning. So far.'

'But that is ridiculous. Ryan's as straight as a beanpole.'

David crossed his arms over his chest. 'You know better than to expect me to comment on that.'

'You'll have checked him out; you'll know he has no record.' Maggie could feel Mr Robbins hovering behind her. 'The only thing Ryan is guilty of is talking to the victim of a terrible crime.'

David tilted his head to one side. 'How long have you known him?'

'It doesn't matter how long I've known him. He's a good man who wouldn't hurt anyone.'

'You can't know that for sure.'

'Ryan is someone more likely to be bullied than to bully. Why have you taken his laptop?'

'And searched my bedsit?' Mr Robbins grunted from behind.

'Standard procedure.'

Maggie wondered if they already knew she'd used the laptop to contact Bea. 'So, you'll have taken his phone from him as well, then?'

Peters gave her a long stare. 'What makes you ask that?'

'I've sent him messages asking if he's alright, and he's not replied.' Unable to read David's expression, Maggie tried again. 'You must have seen them?'

'Not my job. That's what we have detectives and a tech unit for. I saw the handwritten note you'd left him upstairs, though.' He regarded Maggie thoughtfully, before adding, 'You care for the young lad.'

'Ryan's here all alone. Someone has to watch out for him.'

'I know you like 'em young, Maggie, but this one's a bit young, even for you.'

Seething, Maggie took a step closer to David, speaking through gritted teeth. 'I am choosing to believe you did not just say that.'

Peters' smirk disappeared from his face. 'Sorry.'

'So you damn well ought to be. He's Izzie's age, for God's sake.'

He pulled off his peaked cap and ran a hand through his hair. 'Yeah, like I said . . .'

'You're sorry. Fine. Let's leave that there, shall we?'

'I must be getting back.'

'Talking of which,' Maggie whispered, 'why did you come back? To Cornwall, I mean.'

'I missed the scenery, I missed the people, but mostly, I missed—'

Not sure she wanted to hear the full answer to her question after all, Maggie broke in, 'Ryan's a good lad.'

'So you keep saying.' Peters looked back up at Mr Robbins behind her. 'I suggest you keep this place going between you today. I'll make sure Mr Stepney knows you were asking after him.'

Before Maggie had the chance to say anything else, Sergeant David Peters was back in the car, and the constable was driving them away. Maggie didn't have to turn round to know that all the neighbours would have been watching the show. Never had the term 'twitching curtains' been more accurate.

'I don't like the police coming here. I don't like people seeing them come here.' Mr Robbins' eyes met Maggie's and remained there, unblinking. 'Do something about it.'

'What can I do?'

'You're my assistant, aren't you? If word gets around that I've employed a murderer, the business will fold, and that's my livelihood and your job out the window.'

Thinking that, in fact, the opposite would be true – that the locals and tourists alike would be flocking in to taste fish and chips that might have been prepared by a killer – Maggie repeated her question. 'What can I actually do?'

'You were investigating.'

'You knew about that?'

'Just do something about this.'

'Right, I will.' Maggie felt the weight of her notebook in her bag. 'I might be a bit late for lunch opening.'

'I'll set things up.' Mr Robbins held her gaze for a fraction longer. 'Don't get back here later than twelve.'

# Chapter Nineteen

By the time she marched back up the steps into The Cabin Hotel, Maggie had assembled a plan. It was only a rough plan, and was beset with potential pitfalls, but that – and a determination to prove Ryan innocent – drove her past the reception desk and into the coffee lounge without stopping.

*If things had gone to plan when I was younger, I'd have got good A levels, gone to university and become a criminologist or trained to be a private detective ... Mr Robbins thinks I can do this, and he's not known as Mr Encouraging, so perhaps this is my chance to find out if I have a touch of the Madame Blanc in me ...*

As she'd travelled to the hotel, in a cab ordered by her employer, she'd taken the time to flick through her notebook and calm her racing pulse.

*I'll stick to the plan.* She sat back at the same coffee table she'd occupied last time, and thanked Cornwall's patron saint, St Piran himself, that the same waiter was on duty as before.

'Can I get you a drink, madam?'

'Thank you. A coffee, please.'

'And one of our croissants today?'

Maggie agreed to the order and began to rehearse what she'd say to Jack when he got back. She was halfway through wondering how to make the waiter believe that she was there on behalf of her daughter to enquire into Toby's wellbeing after the death of his fiancée – sure that Izzie would not mind the lie and might, in fact, encourage her sleuthing – when a man in his early twenties came into the lounge.

Maggie watched as he slouched onto one of the wicker-backed seats. She'd put money on him being totally unaware of his surroundings.

*Ryan said Toby had dark hair, so that can't be him.*

The waiter returned and placed a coffee cup, complete with complimentary biscuit, and a warm croissant with butter pot on the table before her.

'Thank you.' Seizing her chance, with one eye on the newcomer, Maggie asked, 'Is that gentleman alright?'

Jack pulled a face as he whispered, 'You know I told you that a bride had died; well, that chap would've been the best man at the wedding.'

Realising she was only three tables apart from Toby's best friend, Maggie watched the blond-headed man continue to stare into space. 'I think he needs a coffee. Could you get him one from me, please, Jack?'

'Well, that's very kind of you, madam, but everything he orders while he's here goes on his friend's slate anyway.'

'Nonetheless, I think he should have something. He looks like he needs someone to talk to, and his friend is probably otherwise occupied if he's just lost his future wife.'

The waiter's eyebrows rose, but he didn't argue, going off to make up another coffee, leaving Maggie to think fast. *How can I make the best of this situation without coming across as totally heartless?*

Hoping Hugh didn't leave before the waiter came back, Maggie refused to let the doubts that were crowding into the back of her mind take hold. Reasoning that the worst that could happen would be for him to accuse her of being nosy and have her thrown out of the hotel, she took a mouthful of croissant.

A couple of minutes later, Maggie saw Jack return to the lounge, a tall latte glass in his hand. She lowered her eyes to the puzzle book she'd pulled from her bag as she heard him telling Hugh that she had bought the latte for him. Not sure whether to remain deeply engrossed in the consumption of her croissant and crossword or look up, the decision was taken out of Maggie's hands as she heard trainered feet padding across the soft carpet towards her.

'Jack said the coffee was from you.' The young man gave her a wry smile. 'It's kind of you, but if you're a journalist expecting a scoop for the price of a latte, then I'm afraid . . .'

'I'm not from the press.' Maggie held out a hand. 'You looked in need of caffeine, and well . . . I'll be honest, I know what's happened, and I felt a bit sorry for you. That's all.'

'I see.' He stared past Maggie and out to the seascape beyond the large picture window. 'They were saying at breakfast that someone's being questioned by the police, but that could mean anything, couldn't it?'

Glad her companion hadn't jumped to the same conclusion as Harry, she said, 'It's early days yet. It probably means they've found someone who spoke to Tania before she died.'

'Tania?' His sorrowful demeanour was abruptly wary and defensive. 'You knew her? Is that why you're here, so you can accuse me as well?'

'Accuse you? I don't even know you.'

'Sorry.' He sighed slowly. 'As you can imagine, we've all been a little bit under the microscope.'

Maggie picked up her cup. 'Surely the police don't think you . . .'

'Not the police, no.' He slumped into the seat opposite Maggie, running his palms over the legs of his jeans. His defiance vanished as fast as it had arrived.

Watching him closely, Maggie ventured, 'I never had the pleasure of meeting Tania. A friend at work knew her a little bit, and her name has been on everyone's lips since her identity was released. The police asked me if I'd seen anything, just like they did the rest of the village.'

'Of course. Sorry. It's all too horrid.'

Maggie got up and fetched his latte from where he'd left it, bringing it back to the table. 'Here, this will help. At least, coffee always helps me. I'm Maggie, by the way.'

'Hugh.' He took the tall, slim glass and sat down. 'Thank you.'

'How well did you know Tania? If you don't mind me asking.'

Hugh took a gulp of his drink. 'We'd met a few times when she was with Toby at uni, but I wouldn't say we were friends. She did a different course, and our paths didn't cross that often. I had hoped to get to know her better.'

'You were her fiancé's friend, then.'

'I'm the . . . I *was* the best man.'

'I see. Her fiancé must be in a terrible state.'

'You could say that.' Hugh took another drink. 'The last time I saw Toby, he wasn't thinking terribly clearly.'

'Hardly surprising.' Maggie sliced a corner of croissant off with her knife. 'When was that?'

'Not since he and Tania left for the pub before she died. Toby's made it clear by text that he wants to keep himself to himself for the time being.'

Pushing her plate towards Hugh, Maggie asked, 'Would you like some croissant?'

'No. Thank you.' Hugh looked as if the idea of food was beyond him.

'You should eat. Keep your strength up.'

A smile broke through, knocking away Hugh's solemn expression. 'You sounded like my mum then.'

'That's an improvement.'

'Sorry?'

'Usually people say I sound like their gran.'

'You aren't old enough.' Holding his latte glass tightly, Hugh's smile met his blue eyes, showing Maggie just how attractive this man was. *Tall, blond, obviously well-educated and, if his clothes are anything to go by, well off . . .* Not commenting on his compliment, but pleased to hear it anyway, Maggie almost held her breath as she asked, 'Is Toby still staying here?'

'Yeah. The police asked us to stay put for the time being.'

'How come you were all here in the first place?'

'It was a present from Tania's parents. A week here for them before they got married, and we – me and Tania's friends – were staying too, for the hen and stag dos.'

'Which never happened.'

'No. No, they didn't.'

Wondering how to get more information out of Hugh without it being too obvious, Maggie surveyed the otherwise empty room. 'At least you're staying somewhere nice. I'm sure Toby and Tania's friends are glad of your support.'

'The girls have gone.'

'Oh.' Maggie feigned surprise. 'I thought you said the police asked you to stay.'

'They didn't tell the police. Didn't tell me for that matter.' Hugh's sullen demeanour returned. 'Just left a note with reception that they'd gone to Heidi's parents' place in Lamorna.'

'Lamorna? Nice place to live. Expensive.'

'Yeah. The manor house, no less.'

'Wow.' *I'm already getting accomplished at pretending I don't know things – is that good or not?* Maggie settled further back into her chair. 'It's a shame you didn't see Toby after he got back to the hotel, after his argument with Tania in the pub.'

'You know about that?'

'It's a gossipy village.'

Hugh grunted in a way that reminded Maggie of Mr Robbins. 'You think Toby needs an alibi?'

'I have no idea, but the police will probably want to know where you all were, and if anyone can vouch for you.'

'They've already asked that. I was in bed. Had an early night as I thought I'd be surfing the next day, and it always takes it out of me more than I like to admit to.' He paused. 'I was alone, alas. I might have been seen by a member of staff heading to my room, but I can't say for sure.'

Maggie nodded towards the corner of the room. 'There's CCTV in here, so there probably is in the corridors as well.'

Hugh kept his eyes on the view as he said, 'I expect you're right.'

'How about Tania's friends? Where were they?'

'No idea. Having cocktails in the bar, probably. We had no plans as a group that night.'

'Don't answer if you think I'm being nosy, but have you and Toby fallen out?'

Hugh pushed his fringe away from his eyes. 'He's not always the easiest person to be friends with.'

She nibbled a little more croissant. 'You said just now that you'd been accused of something – was that Toby? Did he accuse you of hurting Tania?'

Hugh's already pale complexion went ashen. 'He did. Lashing out, of course. There's no way I would, or could, hurt anyone like that, but once he gets an idea into his head . . .'

'Can't be easy, having your best friend turn on you like that.'

Hugh picked his glass cup up again. 'I reckon he'd had a skinful. Hard to tell down the phone line, but he certainly wasn't thinking straight.'

'Even so.' Maggie cocked her head to one side as she studied the tired man opposite her. 'You want to tell me about it? Sometimes it's easier to speak to a stranger.'

Hugh peered up at her, reminding Maggie of the way Ryan looked at her when they first met. 'Why would you want to listen to me?'

'Because I think you need to talk to someone, and because, frankly, I'm here, on my own, killing time before I go to work. The alternative is this crossword, which I've been stuck on for weeks.'

'Why don't you look up the answers on Google?'

'It's cryptic, no idea what to look up. And anyway, the point of doing them is to work it out yourself, not just look things up.'

'Oh, right.' Hugh lounged back in his seat.

'I like puzzles, and I don't like them to defeat me.' Maggie dabbed a fingertip across her plate, capturing some croissant flakes. 'You known Toby long?'

'Since birth. Our mothers are best friends.'

'Long time.'

'Twenty-five years.'

'And you grew up around here?'

'Yeah. Well, Sennen actually.'

'Are you still living there?'

'No.' Hugh gave a sharp shake of the head. 'I got out as soon as I could.' He glanced back towards the window. 'I mean, it's lovely here, but there's not much going on if you don't want to serve the tourists.'

'So you left?'

'London. Went to university there, same one as Toby and Tania actually, but I stayed, and they came back. I'm a computer software manager.'

Maggie couldn't think of anything worse but said, 'Good for you. Expanding your horizons. Toby wasn't tempted to stay with you in the capital?'

'I think he'd have liked to, but his time at university was rather different from mine.'

'Different?'

'I went to study so I could escape from here; Toby went to have a good time.'

'I see.' Maggie drained the remainder of her coffee. 'Discos and what have you.'

Hugh threw her a stare that consigned her to the era of the dinosaurs. 'Nightclubs, wine bars, and weed. I've always suspected he dabbled in cocaine as well. It's rife in London in lots of circles – although Toby always maintained that he never went that far.'

'Drugs?' Maggie leant forward; her interest clear despite herself. 'He doesn't still do them, does he?'

'Nah. Tania would kill him for a start . . .' Hugh's words petered out. 'Would have, killed him. Oh hell.'

'Wouldn't she have been against him being that wild at uni?'

'I doubt she'd have been that keen, but Tania did a difference course, and they had separate friends and lives at uni, as well as spending time together.' Hugh sighed. 'This is too awful.'

'I'm sorry.' Maggie felt the press of time as she added, 'I didn't mean to make things worse.'

'How much worse can it be?' Hugh threw his hands up in despair. 'My best friend's bride is dead in suspicious circumstances. Toby accused me of pushing her off the harbour wall – which I most certainly did not – and Toby himself has gone AWOL. Meanwhile, Tania's friends have buggered off and left me here on my own, and I can't go back to London because the police said we have to stay here, although I'm the only one who's listened to that!'

'Gone AWOL? You said he was keeping himself to himself. I assumed you meant Toby was in his hotel room and not coming out.'

'Nah. I've knocked on his door a few times and he hasn't answered. I was getting worried, so asked one of the chambermaids to go in. The room was empty, although the receptionist tells me he hasn't checked out yet.'

'Had the bed been slept in?'

'Yes – well, it was unmade when she went in, but apparently he and Tania had asked them not to bother with the daily housekeeping service. I guess they imagined they wouldn't be getting out of bed for more than meals and to do the spa thing and a bit of surfing.'

'Oh, what it is to be young and in love.'

'Yeah, well, I wouldn't know about that.'

Feeling increasingly sorry for her companion, Maggie remembered the recording Ryan had made. 'Could Toby have gone to work?'

'Probably.' Hugh picked his empty latte glass back up and rolled it between his palms.

'You could go and see him there. You did say he was local.'

'Yeah. He's got an office in Marazion.' He pulled a face.

'There's nothing wrong with Marazion.'

'It's not the place, it's just his . . . I'm not keen on seeing his business partner. Rachel. She and I had a thing when we were students.'

'I see. That would have been awkward for you at the wedding. I'm assuming she'd have been there.'

'Actually, no. Toby did me a favour there and didn't invite her.'

'That can't have been easy for him, as they work together.'

'I'm his best friend.' Hugh shrugged. 'Rachel was . . . and probably still is . . . a bit of a player when it comes to relationships. I doubt she'd have wanted to come anyway. She and Toby always got on in a work capacity – they were on the same course at uni – but I'd be hard pressed to call them friends.'

Maggie frowned. 'How did Rachel get on with Tania?'

'No idea. I have kept my distance from Rachel ever since.'

'She broke your heart?'

'You could say that.' Hugh circled the signet ring on his left index finger around and around. 'I fell for her, hook, line and sinker, as the saying goes. She wasn't so devoted.'

'Someone else?'

'Yep. No idea who, but whoever they were, they clearly had more to offer her than I did.'

'Love?'

Hugh laughed. 'Rachel doesn't know the meaning of the word. Money and influence, that's what works for her and . . .'

Hugh's words faltered as a movement in the doorway to the coffee lounge made them turn round.

'Ah, I think I should leave you in peace. Looks like you might be needed.'

Gathering up her bag, Maggie was on her feet as Hugh mumbled, 'Oh shit . . . Thank you for the coffee and . . .'

Maggie didn't hear the full extent of Hugh's thanks. She was already heading out of the side exit before Sergeant David Peters had the chance to spot her.

# Chapter Twenty

Ryan had refused a solicitor. A solicitor would mean this was real. That this was *actually* happening. That he was in a real interview room waiting for a real detective to come and take a real statement from him about a real murder.

No one had mentioned the recording on his phone yet. For a while Ryan had clung onto the hope that they wouldn't find it. That the real killer would be found before they got that far, and he'd be out by lunchtime. But as the clock on the interview room wall clicked closer towards eleven-thirty, he'd given up on that faint hope.

His mind wouldn't settle. It raced between picturing courtroom scenarios of him being convicted of a crime he hadn't committed, to him trying to survive in prison, to the reaction of his parents. He could see them shaking their heads, their disappointment in him confirmed beyond question. Even though he knew he was letting his imagination run away with itself and that there was no evidence against him, Ryan found himself visualising the reaction of Bea's parents all too clearly: self-righteously telling all their friends how they'd turned him away from their daughter's home, and how narrow an escape Bea – who'd been having a moment of rebellion – had had.

Closing his eyes, Ryan wondered if Maggie was still intent on investigating, or if, now the police had been to the bedsit to fetch his laptop, she'd given up – believing him guilty too.

Ryan didn't want to consider Mr Robbins' reaction to having the police visiting his bedsit.

*Poison.*

He took a deep breath.

*I don't know anything about poison. I have no idea where to find it or what different poisons do.*

Suddenly he imagined he could hear Maggie's voice in his mind. *They have your laptop. They'll be checking your search history – there'll be nothing about poisons and no evidence of you ordering any online. It'll be okay. Hang in there.*

Ryan found he could breathe a little deeper. He hadn't done this – they had to prove he had, and they wouldn't be able to.

*And anyway, Tania might not have been poisoned – the first tox test wasn't conclusive . . . I could be worrying over nothing.* But then . . . Ryan hugged his arms around his chest for comfort . . . *if she wasn't poisoned, but was still murdered . . .*

Deciding he'd be better off spending his time thinking about who might have hurt Tania rather than worrying about himself, he asked the constable on the door, 'Would it be possible to have some paper and a pen?'

★

Maggie hopped impatiently from one foot to the other. A police car was parked on the road by the hotel. She felt exposed as she willed the quarter-to-twelve bus to hurry up. If David spotted her, he'd want to know what she was doing there.

*Hugh might tell him about our chat anyway, and Ryan's probably had to tell the police I'm investigating.*

Resolving that she'd far rather put off a conversation with David about what she was doing until she had some useful information to share, Maggie perched on the bench by the bus stop, hiding behind an advertising board.

She was musing over what Hugh had told her, when the sound of the bus approaching brought her to her feet.

Turning, ready to embark, she found herself face to face with Sergeant David Peters.

'Oh.'

'Oh, indeed, Maggie.' David gave her an incisive look. 'Not a coincidence, I think.'

'I came out for a coffee. Change of scene.'

He checked his watch. 'It's two minutes to twelve. You should have been at the chippy at eleven-thirty.'

'Mr Robbins is opening today.'

He took a step away from the kerb as the bus pulled up. 'Wonders will never cease.'

'This is my bus.'

'I'll drive you back.'

Maggie moved closer to the bus's entrance, where an old lady was currently negotiating her way down the step to the pavement. 'I'm fine, thanks. Anyway, you've got work to do. Ryan is innocent, and you should be going after the person who really did it.'

Sergeant Peters offered a hand to the old lady, who gratefully took it, and, walking stick in hand, made her way along the path. 'And that's what you've been trying to prove, isn't it – that he didn't do it?'

Heat rose in Maggie's cheeks. 'I have no idea what you mean. Now, if you don't mind, I've got chips to cook.'

Taking no notice of her, Sergeant Peters gave the impatient bus driver a thumbs up, and he immediately drove off.

'David!'

'Just get in my car, Maggie. We'll talk as I drive you to work.'

Defeated, Maggie climbed into the passenger seat. 'Is Ryan alright?'

'He was fine when I last saw him. Nervous and a bit shaken, but he's holding his own. Refused a solicitor, mind, which wasn't the brightest idea.'

'A solicitor! Why does he need one?'

David kept his eyes on the road. 'Don't ask daft questions. Why were you talking to Mr Parkinson?'

Deciding it was pointless to pretend she hadn't been talking to someone in the coffee lounge, especially as it was probably covered by CCTV, Maggie said, 'I didn't know that was Hugh's surname.'

'The waiter said you bought him a coffee.'

'A latte. He looked lost and lonely.'

'Like Ryan did.' David blew out a ragged breath. 'You do like your waifs and strays, don't you, Maggie?'

Bristling, she adjusted her safety belt. 'If, by that, you mean I care about other people, then yes, I do.'

Snorting, David said, 'Hang on a minute, it's Thursday. Weren't you supposed to be at the library this morning helping educate the elderly in the ways of the world wide web?'

'And how would you know that?'

'There are posters up advertising it in Tesco.'

'Oh yeah. Well, I took the morning off.'

'To help Ryan.'

'Why do you make that sound like a criminal offence?' Twisting in her seat so she could see his face clearly, Maggie found herself thinking he needed a haircut. His once brown hair, now largely grey, with just an occasional hint of its former colour, was beginning to tuft at the nape of his neck.

'Because interfering in police business is a criminal offence.'

'I've not been interfering, I've been helping.'

'Maggie . . .'

'You need a new shirt, that collar is fraying.' Not waiting for his response, she added, 'I spoke to Hugh, that's all. I went to the hotel in the hope of talking to Tania's friends – the ones that know Bea – so that I could find out if they knew what was going on. I wanted to be able to find something out that might help Ryan. I would have told you if I had discovered anything useful.'

'Maggie, I get it – I do. You're one of life's helpers. But someone's been killed. What if the person responsible finds out you've been asking questions?'

Maggie swallowed slowly as the implication of what he was saying sank in. 'Ryan is innocent.'

'That's it. That's all you have to say.'

Hearing the frustration in David's voice, Maggie found herself smiling. 'Careful, or I might accidentally start to think you care.'

The sergeant slowed the patrol car and turned onto North Cliff. 'Before I let you go and serve chips, tell me what Hugh told you.'

'Okay, it'll save me popping into the station later.'

A crease formed on David's forehead. 'You were going to come to the station?'

'To share what I'd discovered, yes. Although, whether your boss would've listened to me is another matter.'

'She'd have listened, but she's not a big fan of people interfering.'

'I'm not interf—'

'Just tell me, Maggie. Please.'

Maggie rested her head back against her seat. 'Hugh said that he and Toby had a row, and that he hadn't seen him in person since before the murder, although they'd spoken on the phone. Hugh was in his room when Tania was meeting her fate in the harbour.'

'And you believed him, just like that, without knowing anything about him.' The sergeant shook his head.

Maggie chose to ignore the incredulity in his voice. 'I have an open mind, but I suspect that the hotel's security system will confirm who was in the rooms.'

'Ummm.'

'That was a loaded "ummm".'

'There is CCTV in reception, the bar, spa, stairways and lift . . .'

'But not in the corridors?'

'You've got it.' David slowed as he drove past a pair of cyclists. 'There's a back entrance that isn't covered either. Nor is the exit that the staff use through the kitchen or the garden.'

'Oh.'

'Quite.'

'Any point in me asking if you found anything of interest on the CCTV coverage?'

'It's not been analysed yet.' He threw her a look of acceptance and asked, 'Did you learn anything else?'

'Hugh told me that Heidi and Daisy have checked out. He is feeling rather abandoned.'

'Damn! We asked them to stay put.' He sighed. 'Anything else?'

Deciding not to tell him that she knew where the women had gone until she'd had the chance to speak to them herself, Maggie said, 'That was it.'

'You didn't tell Mr Parkinson that Ryan was in custody?'

'Of course not!' Maggie paused. 'When you first spoke to Hugh, did he tell you about his row with Toby?'

'Maggie!'

'Okay, worth a try.' Maggie stared out of the passenger window. 'Row or not, it's odd that Toby's disappeared so soon after his future wife was killed.'

'You think he's disappeared?'

'Hugh led me to believe he'd gone to ground somewhere.'

'Thank God you didn't start knocking on hotel doors searching for him! I wouldn't have put that past you!'

Maggie knew that if David hadn't turned up, she'd have done just that. 'Did you look for him in his room just now?'

'Obviously.' David scowled. 'He wasn't in.'

'So you'll be trying his home or the office in Marazion next, then?'

'Marazion?' David banged his hand on the steering wheel in frustration. 'Hell, Maggie! You said you hadn't learnt anything else.'

'I thought you meant new stuff. You must have already known that.'

'Of course we knew, but that is beside the point.' David shifted uncomfortably, making Maggie wonder if the police had really known about the office's whereabouts. 'You have to butt out of this.'

Ignoring his bluster, Maggie said, 'Toby could have done a runner.'

David drew the car to a halt outside Mr Robbins' shop. 'Do you know something about where he is? If you do—'

'I promise, I have no idea where Toby is, but I can't help speculating that—'

'I know where you are going with this, and that's the second time you've tried to give me some statistic you got off *Murder, She Wrote* or some blasted podcast that's told you most murders are committed by partners.'

'Well, they *are*.'

David blew out a sigh. 'We're investigating everyone concerned in this case, not just Ryan. We do know what we are doing.'

As she undid her seat belt, Maggie swivelled around to face him again. 'There is something else I've just remembered.'

'Or you've just decided you'll tell me.'

'Do you want to hear it or not?'

'Just tell me, Maggie.'

'Hugh said he didn't know Tania that well, but he'd have known her a bit – she dated his oldest friend. I got the impression he liked her, but that she was just part of the group he socialised with– not someone he spoke to alone very often. Whereas Toby he has known since birth – literally since birth – and yet the more I think about it, I can't help wondering if they were friends out of habit – that Toby had drifted apart from Hugh.'

David said nothing as he regarded Maggie, his expression carefully blank.

Unclipping her belt, Maggie found herself justifying what she'd said. 'This isn't knowledge, this is a feeling. A hunch. Women's intuition, if you like such an outdated concept.'

'I know better than to be baited by arguments like that. Go on, tell me what else you've hunched.'

Ignoring the twinkle in David's eyes, Maggie went on. 'Hugh mentioned that Toby did drugs at uni, and—'

'Did he, now? Funny, he didn't say that to me.'

'Would you have done in his shoes?'

David raked a hand through his hair in frustration. 'And once again, this is something you should have told me straight away.'

'I *am* telling you straight away. And, like I said, I'd have told you later today anyway, but I wanted to think before I came to the station.' Maggie maintained his gaze. 'I'm not suggesting Toby is still into drugs, or was ever into them big time, just that that's the moment when the boys could have grown apart. Hugh wanted to work hard to get out of Cornwall, and Toby was out for a good time.'

'Right.'

'And Ryan told me that Tania and Toby had argued about her lack of trust. Why, that's what I want to know. Perhaps it was a drug thing; could Tania have suspected he was dabbling with narcotics?'

Ignoring her question, David abruptly leant across Maggie and opened the passenger car door. 'I have to get back, and you need to rescue the customers from Mr Robbins' charms.'

Maggie climbed out of the car. 'You know where to find me if you want to hear more hunches. You'll take care of Ryan, won't you?'

Not answering her question, David switched on the indicator, ready to pull back out into the traffic. 'Please, promise me you won't carry on with this.'

As he drove off, not wasting his time by waiting for her to respond, Maggie's eyes followed the squad car's progress until it was out of sight. She had to admit, despite needing a haircut, her ex-boyfriend was looking extremely well for his age.

# Chapter Twenty-one

Mr Robbins stared pointedly at the fish-shaped clock on the wall and back again as Maggie arrived in time to see him serving a portion of chips to a lone teenager. He didn't need to say anything for her to understand his reproach.

'The bus was late.' Hanging up her bag, Maggie went to the sink to clean her hands as her employer finished serving the customer. 'It's only half-past twelve.'

'There's bin three customers.'

'I'm surprised there's only been three. It's June and the weather is stunning. Perfect sit-in-the-harbour-with-a-cone-of-chips weather.'

'Harbour's sealed off.'

'So it is.'

As soon as Maggie had donned her apron and hat, Mr Robbins scuttled towards the sanctuary of his office doorway. 'Learn anything?'

'Yes, but I can't tell you now.' Maggie headed to the till as another customer came through the door. 'Unless you want to help me serve.'

'Later.'

*

'Looks like you've been busy.' Detective Inspector Houseman gestured to the paper on the table as she came into the room. Behind her, Constable Harker carried a tray holding two cups and a pile of plastic-wrapped sandwiches, similar to the ones Ryan had seen the day before.

'I was ordering my thoughts.'

'Always helpful.' Houseman sat down as Harker took his position by the door. 'How are you doing, Ryan?'

'Alright, considering.' He took the coffee that was being pushed across the table towards him. 'Thank you.'

'Let's get that statement down now. Then, when Sergeant Peters gets here, we can chat about these thoughts of yours.'

Ryan yawned, the motion reminding him of just how heavy and tired his entire body felt. 'I didn't kill her.'

Clicking the lid off her coffee cup, the inspector said, 'You can understand why we had to keep you here, though?'

'Suppose so. I was the last person seen talking to Tania, and I was alone with her drink in the pub for a few minutes. If you are saying she might have been poisoned, then . . .' Ryan found he couldn't finish the sentence.

'Exactly.' Houseman gave him an approximation of a smile.

'I don't know anything about poison.'

'I'm pleased to say that we can rule that out.'

'Then why did you tell me that—'

Shuffling through a few tabs on her tablet screen, Houseman interrupted Ryan's question. 'There was a delay in the new toxicology report getting back to us – it was rather late yesterday when it was noticed that one of the tests hadn't been done properly. Human error and all that.'

Ryan said nothing.

'Although there were no visual signs of poisoning, until we could definitively rule any sort of intoxication out, we needed to be careful. I'm sure you can understand how negligent we would have been to let you go if it had turned out to be a poisoning.'

'And do you now believe I was telling you the truth when I said she wasn't intoxicated in any way?'

'It isn't a question of believing you or disbelieving you. It's what can be proved.'

'But her stomach contents will have shown that—'

'Let's just get on, shall we? Once again, I can offer you the duty solicitor if you want him.' Houseman put a hand on the tape recorder and opened a new tab on her tablet.

'No thanks.' Ryan slumped back in his chair.

'Okay.' The detective clicked on the recording device. 'So, Mr Ryan Stepney . . .'

'Hang on . . . if she wasn't poisoned, then how did Tania die?'

\*

As soon as she'd turned the open sign to closed, Maggie sent a brief email to the library, apologising again for her hasty exit and thanking them for overseeing the Crossword Club on top of all their other duties.

All lunchtime Maggie had felt rather disconnected from events, swapping her usual banter with the customers for internal musings. Musings which had culminated in her formulating a plan of campaign for the afternoon – one which would mean forgoing her habitual late lunch on her lap, while viewing whichever television detective took her fancy that day.

With a promise to Mr Robbins that she'd be back in time to set up for the evening shift, Maggie dashed out of the door and, with a second promise – this time to her rumbling stomach to grab a sandwich from the first suitable shop she came to – Maggie made her way to the bus stop.

\*

The fan that whirred in the corner of the interview room sounded like an angry, trapped fly. The room was hot and sticky, and with three people in its grey confines, it had a claustrophobic atmosphere which was giving Ryan a splitting headache. As he leant forward, his black T-shirt unpeeled from the grey plastic chair with an unpleasant sucking sound. He could smell how badly he needed a shower.

'Are you sure there is nothing else you wish to add to your statement?'

'Nothing else, Inspector.'

Houseman clicked off the recording device. 'Thank you, Ryan.'

'Does that mean I can go now?'

'Not quite yet.' She pushed Ryan's untouched sandwich nearer to him. 'You should eat.'

'I should wash too.' Ryan wrinkled his nose. 'And change my clothes.'

'We'll see what we can do.' Houseman got to her feet. 'The technology team will have finished their initial search through your laptop and phone soon. We'll have another chat once that's done.'

A flush of colour came to Ryan's face.

'Ryan?' The detective gave him a shrewd look. 'Something you want to tell me?'

Memories of the texts and emails he and Bea had shared when they'd first got together crowded his mind. He'd kept them, relived them. Memories of a happier time when he'd never doubted that Bea accepted him for who he was. There'd been no suggestion then that she might be embarrassed by him once they were out of the university environment.

'A few of the messages between me and my girlfriend . . . they're personal.'

Houseman didn't look up. 'We'll have seen worse, I promise you.'

Ryan swigged back the last of the coffee in his cup. It was stone cold and utterly revolting. 'There's something else on my phone.'

The inspector immediately sat back down. 'Something that should be in your statement?'

'No. Something that I should tell you before you find out yourselves.'

'Go on.'

'Maggie and me, we've sort of . . . sort of been investigating Tania's death. At least, we'd begun to.'

\*

The bus trip to Lamorna had been painfully slow, but Maggie had used the journey wisely – as far as her Wi-Fi signal had allowed.

She'd already been fairly sure that she was right in thinking that the police wouldn't be able to hold Ryan for more than twenty-four hours if they didn't charge him. Now, thanks to a visit to Google, she knew that was genuinely the case and not just a fiction invented for television. This meant Ryan would be released by the evening, as she couldn't conceive a situation in which they'd have enough evidence to arrest him.

Comforted by the thought, Maggie walked up the gravel-covered driveway towards Lamorna Manor. Torn between knocking on the front door and going around the back to try and find a kitchen door, the decision was taken out of her hands when she heard a shout.

'Can I help you?' Heidi was walking in Maggie's direction, an annoyed expression on her face. 'We aren't open to the public.'

'I'm sorry to bother you. I was wondering if you could help me.'

'Do you need directions?'

Having decided that honesty was the best policy, Maggie said, 'I'm here about Tania – she was your friend, I believe.'

'How did you—'

Quickly Maggie cut in, 'I'm not a journalist, nor am I the police.'

'Then who are you?' The woman sounded more exhausted than angry.

'My name's Maggie, and my friend was the last person to see Tania before she died. He's currently helping the police with their enquiries.'

The young woman took a backwards step. 'But if the police think he . . .'

'They just know he spoke to her before she died, that's all.' Maggie felt she was losing control of the conversation before it had even begun. 'I've spoken to Hugh. He told me that Tania's friends had checked out and come here.'

'Hugh did?' The woman's forehead creased, making the small collection of freckles on her forehead disappear.

'Apparently Toby accused him of hurting Tania.'

The woman nodded. 'Yeah. That was pretty horrible.'

A prickle of curiosity nudged at Maggie. 'You overheard them?'

'Only Hugh's end of things. It was a phone call.'

*So Hugh wasn't lying about the row being via the phone and not in person.* Already pleased she'd been able to confirm something she'd learnt, Maggie asked, 'Am I right in thinking you're Heidi?'

'Yes.' Her eyes narrowed a fraction. 'Hugh told you that too, did he?'

'That Tania's friends were called Heidi and Daisy, and that you lived here, yes. But I already knew your names. A work colleague knows Bea, and she told him a Heidi and a Daisy were going to the hen night.'

'Bea?' Heidi's demeanour softened slightly. 'Isn't she exploring across the back of beyond somewhere?'

'Portugal. So not really the back of beyond.'

Heidi gave Maggie an appraising stare. 'Why are you here?'

'To talk to you and Daisy so I can find out what happened.'

'That's the police's job.'

'I'm helping them.' Maggie mentally crossed her fingers. 'Passing on anything I learn. Although, I should say that I'm working on behalf of my friend too.'

'Like a private detective, you mean.'

'Very much like that, yes.'

'Okay, then.' Heidi gestured to a high, well-kempt hedge that ran off to the left of the house. 'Daisy and I are having tea in the garden. If you'd like to join us, I can grab another cup.'

'Thank you.'

As Maggie followed the tall woman's athletic stride, an anxious excitement flowed through her veins.

*I'm doing it, Grandad! I'm being a detective!*

# Chapter Twenty-two

'He wrote off Toby's car?' A surprised Maggie leant back on the well-padded garden chair, appreciating the immaculately mowed lawn that ran towards the slate-roofed manor house. It reminded her of Trerice House near Newquay, and she found herself wondering if it had been designed by the same person.

'Yep. Hugh's lucky to be alive.' Daisy offered Maggie the sugar bowl. 'He came away without even a scratch.'

'Unlike the car.' Heidi poured some tea into Maggie's newly provided cup. 'Toby was furious, and rightly so. By the time we'd found out what had happened, he'd had a drink or two, and things got a bit heated.'

'More like a drink or twelve.' Daisy tutted.

'I suppose it's not surprising, considering his future wife was in the vehicle.' Maggie frowned. 'When did you find out about the accident, Heidi?'

'Not until the evening of the day it had happened. Tania was shaken, and Toby was heartbroken.'

'And Hugh?'

'Was making himself scarce, and I can't blame him.'

Maggie asked, 'When was the crash, exactly?'

Daisy tucked a long red hair back up under the bandana from which it had escaped. 'The day before Tania was . . .'

A film of tears came to Daisy's eyes as Maggie extracted her notebook from her bag. 'Would you mind if I made notes?'

'If it'll help find out what happened to Tania, then you can do anything you like.' Heidi selected a shortbread biscuit from a painted bone china plate. 'Your friend – the one who you're helping – you are *sure* he didn't do this?'

'Completely sure. We aren't even certain what happened yet, are we? I can see why the police need to talk to him, though. He saw Tania in the pub and spent some time talking to her before she died. But they'd never met before then.'

Daisy sighed. 'I expect she had a good old moan about Toby to him.'

'It was more a mutual whinge about partners and life, I think.' Maggie picked up her cup from its matching saucer. 'Can I just confirm, the car crash, you said it was the day before, so that would have been the eighth of June – last Sunday?'

Heidi exchanged a look with Daisy. The women appeared to come to an unspoken decision to confide in Maggie, before Daisy ventured, 'Toby . . . he wasn't what we expected for Tania.'

'Why do you say that?'

The redhead dabbed up some biscuit crumbs with her fingertips. 'Tania was really kind, and Toby was a bit . . .'

'Manipulative,' Heidi chipped in. 'Everything was always someone else's fault, nothing was ever good enough, and he took offence at everything and anything.'

'Yeah,' Daisy added. 'He had a habit of twisting things so, if something went wrong, it was not his fault. Or if there was a situation he didn't like or agree with, he could make you feel really stupid.'

'You aren't selling him to me.' Maggie felt her tentative theory about Heidi being jealous of Tania marrying Toby evaporating.

Heidi shrugged. 'Tania adored him. Said everyone had flaws and that she loved him in spite of his.'

'Plus, he's a bit of a charmer.' Daisy had another pointless go at securing her hair behind her ears. 'Everyone likes him when they first meet him.'

'A regular Prince Charming.' Maggie jotted down 'manipulative' in her notebook.

'More like a frog.' Daisy grunted. 'But Tania was besotted, so what could we do but support her?'

'Would you say that Toby loved her in return? She was an attractive woman, I understand.'

'She was. Well off too. Both assets that would appeal to Toby. He acted like he loved her, so I suppose he did. I mean, they were getting married – not something you have to do these days, so when it does happen, it's sort of extra reassuring.' Daisy's rosy cheeks coloured up even more. 'Well, to me it is anyway.'

Heidi gave her friend a supportive squeeze of the wrist as Maggie said, 'The more I know about Tania and Toby's lives and the people involved in them, the easier it'll be to help the police. One thing I have discovered is that Toby's business partner, Rachel, had a thing with Hugh when they were at university.'

'That bitch!' Heidi snapped.

Daisy held Heidi's arm tighter. 'Rachel broke Hugh's heart.'

'So he led me to understand. He also said she had left him for someone else back then. I wondered if that someone might have been Toby?'

'Why Toby?' Heidi asked.

'In all honesty, it was just a thought based on the fact that he is the only other bloke I know to be connected to Tania right now.'

'There's just no way, Maggie.' Daisy shook her head, sending her red hair flying across her face. 'He would never have done that to Hugh.'

'Anyway,' Heidi added, 'he was already seeing Tania, and it was obvious he was smitten.'

Daisy muttered, 'Even if it was only with her money.'

Taking note of Daisy's clear distrust of the bridegroom, Maggie asked, 'Is that when you all met Toby?'

'I already knew him,' Heidi said. 'He and Tania met here, in Cornwall, when they were seventeen. Stayed together all through their university years. Daisy and Tania met at university, and . . .' She turned to her friend. 'I first met Toby when I went to London as Tania's guest for the end-of-first-year ball, didn't I, Daze'

'Yeah. That's when we first met too. When Tania invited Heidi to the ball.' Daisy smiled at Heidi before freeing her arm and picking up her teacup. '*And* when we first met Hugh – he was with Rachel then. I'll be honest, I've never really warmed to Toby. I tried to, for Tania's sake, but I always felt he had a dark side.'

Maggie focused her attention on Daisy. 'Dark side in what way?'

'A bit too secretive . . . I always wondered if he was up to something dodgy.'

'Daze, you're letting your imagination run away with you. He was a bit much sometimes, but he wasn't a crook or anything.' Heidi pushed the plate of biscuits closer to Maggie. 'Please, help yourself.'

'Thank you.' Maggie selected a cookie. 'You mentioned Hugh. I got the impression from him that he wasn't with Rachel long.'

'I'm not sure how long it was.' Daisy added a lump of sugar to her tea. 'But, by the time we visited London again, which must have been about three months later, she was seeing someone else. We never asked who.'

Heidi nodded. 'It wasn't Toby. In fact, now I think about it, I don't think we saw Rachel again until university finished, and Tania and Toby got back to Cornwall with degree certificates and a ring on Tania's finger.'

'I assume Rachel is running the business this week?'

The girls both shrugged, before Heidi volunteered, 'She could be abroad. From what Tania's said in the past, it's Rachel, not Toby, who does any required travelling.'

Mentally crossing off her list 'Rachel/jealousy' as a possible motive, adding 'check if Rachel was in the country' for completeness, Maggie returned to their previous line of enquiry. 'Can we go back to the car crash? You said Hugh wrote the car off, but was anyone else in the vehicle apart from Tania?'

'No.' Heidi shook her head. 'The car skidded and hit a brick wall. Crunched the front right up. Luckily it had a long nose to take most of the impact and excellent brakes, so they stopped before it crunched them too. Both had bruises where the seat belt caught them, but otherwise nothing – a miracle, really.'

'No airbag marks? Sometimes those things go off so hard and fast they can bruise you too.'

'No airbags. Vintage car. They're damn lucky to be alive.'

Daisy sniffed. 'I swear Toby was more upset about losing that stupid car than he was about losing Tania.'

Maggie took another sip of her tea. 'Why did Hugh have the car anyway?'

'Ironically, he was doing Toby a favour.' Heidi peered up at a rhododendron bush that was planted next to the table. Its purple flowers hung down over them, providing them with some much-needed shade. 'Toby had planned to go and pick up the hire suits for him and Hugh for the wedding, but he'd had a work thing come in that he couldn't miss, so he asked Hugh to fetch them.'

'Hugh couldn't go in his own car?'

'Doesn't have one. No point when you live in London.'

'Makes sense.' Maggie chewed the end of her pen. 'Do you know what Toby's work thing was?'

'No.'

The memory of the call Ryan covertly recorded echoed in Maggie's mind as she asked, 'Wasn't Toby on holiday? Hugh led me to believe that Tania's parents had paid for a week at the hotel?'

'What Toby is supposed to do and what he does aren't always the same thing.'

'I see.' Maggie looked back up at Heidi. 'Did you tell the police all this?'

'They only asked us about the day Tania died.' Heidi bit into her shortbread. 'They said they'd speak to us again, but we left the hotel, so that hasn't happened.'

Daisy twirled a strand of hair through her fingers. 'We shouldn't have just left without a word, but it felt so wrong being there.'

'I'm sure the police will understand. You've had a terrible shock. It's not like you've fled the country. But,' Maggie warned, 'they will track you down, so you might want to call them and tell them you're here.'

'I can't. Lost my phone somewhere in the spa.' Daisy pulled a face. 'So annoying. I must buy a new one.'

'We did leave a message at the hotel reception in case the police wanted to speak to us.' Heidi shifted in her chair. 'Is Hugh alright? I feel bad about leaving him behind.'

'Toby's there too,' Daisy reassured her friend. 'Hugh'll be okay.'

Keeping the knowledge that Toby hadn't been seen for a while to herself, Maggie said, 'I didn't think Toby and Hugh were talking.'

'The crash has put a dent in their friendship, but they've been close forever; they'll be alright.' Daisy brushed some crumbs from her lap. 'Having us out of the way will probably make it easier for them to make up. Swallow their male pride in private.'

Not convinced that Daisy was right about that, Maggie asked, 'Why was Tania going with Hugh to fetch the suits? Usually the groom and best man sort that themselves. Had she been intending to go with Toby to get them?'

'I think she always planned to go.' Heidi turned to Daisy. 'She had this fear about him picking up the wrong ones, didn't she?'

'Yeah. I hadn't realised it was Hugh who was taking her until Tania was back at the hotel again – without the suits – and Toby was yelling at her like a banshee.'

'You don't happen to know what he yelled?'

Daisy fiddled with a strand of hair between her fingers. 'It was a jumble of stuff. How stupid Hugh was, mostly. How he couldn't be trusted behind a wheel. How much the situation had cost him.'

'And he wanted to know why Tania had been with Hugh in the first place, now I think about it. Not that I recall her saying why.' Heidi's forehead furrowed as she thought back. 'We left them to it. Felt a bit awkward watching Toby shouting at her, didn't it, Daze?'

'Yeah,' Daisy agreed. 'At dinner that night, neither Toby nor Tania showed up. Hugh said they were having a bit of time on their own. We assumed they were making up after the slanging match.'

'A slanging match? That implies Tania was giving as good as she got.'

'Oh yes! Told him he should never have left her to go to work when it was their special week.' Heidi put her cup back on its saucer. 'Basically, she was accusing him of putting his career before her. Again.'

'Is that something Toby tended to do a lot, then?'

'Big time. It's another reason I don't rate him.' Daisy chewed at a red fingernail. 'When we saw Tania at breakfast the following day, she didn't want to talk about it. Said it was all sorted.'

'And was she okay in herself? Physically, after the crash?'

'She said she was okay, didn't she, Heidi?'

'Yes. Rubbed her ribs a bit, making me think maybe she was a bit bruised, but she seemed genuinely okay. Tania was excited, talking about—' tears welled in Daisy's eyes again '—about our spa day and the wedding and the shopping trip we were about to go on.'

Passing the younger woman a tissue, Maggie asked, 'You went shopping after breakfast on the day she died?'

'Yeah. Tania wanted to get a gift for Hugh for being best man.'

'I'm surprised Toby didn't want to do that.'

'I got the impression Toby had asked her to do it for him. He had planned to spend the day with Hugh – mend a few fences after what had happened, so it wasn't weird at the wedding.' Heidi moved her chair closer to Daisy's and put an arm around her shoulders. 'We went into Truro. Got Hugh some vintage port.'

Cursing herself for not asking Hugh what he had done on the day of the murder, Maggie ventured, 'And do you know what Toby and Hugh did?'

'They had a tour of Pocketful of Stones booked.'

'The distillery in Penzance?'

'Yeah. Toby has always been into his spirits, so Hugh booked a tour and tasting for a pre-wedding present.'

'Very nice too.' Maggie asked, 'Did they go on the tour?'

The girls looked blankly at each other before Heidi said, 'I assumed so, but I didn't ask . . . did you, Daze?'

'No. We didn't get back from Truro until it was almost time for Toby and Tania to go to The Mariner. Hugh wasn't around. I assumed the boys went as planned.'

Deciding to call the distillery to check, a new thought parked itself in Maggie's mind. *Do the police know about the crash? Surely they must* . . . She took a sip of her drink. 'I'm surprised Sergeant Peters didn't mention the crash to me last time I checked in with him.'

The women swapped an awkward glance. 'They didn't report it to the police.'

Maggie couldn't keep the surprise from her voice. 'How on earth did they get away with that?'

'Quiet road. No one about. Nobody injured, so there was no legal need to involve the police. Toby called a friend who runs the garage near his office. A pickup came to take the car away and the area was all cleaned up, and Hugh and Tania got back here before anyone was any the wiser.'

Letting out a low whistle, Maggie said, 'Can't be a quick thing to clear up – the moving of the damaged vehicle must take time for a start.'

Daisy agreed. 'If either of them had been seriously hurt, it would have been a different story.'

Maggie looked at each woman in turn as she said, 'The police need to be told now, though. Tania will have had a recent bruise from the seat belt – they might think it was from the fall.'

Heidi's hand came to her mouth. 'I hadn't thought.'

Daisy stood up. 'We should go and tell them.'

'But Hugh will get into trouble.' Heidi's eyes gave her feelings for Hugh away, a fact Maggie filed away, her idea that Heidi had fancied Toby now completely dead and buried. 'He might get arrested.'

'Do you know how the crash happened?'

'Tania said he was going a bit too fast. They'd been chatting and not slowed down for a bend that was more hairpin than either of them remembered. She said it all happened so fast; it was a bit of a blur.'

'I see.' Maggie got up. 'Thank you for talking to me. I think Daisy's right; you should go and speak to the police. Before I go, can I ask three more questions?'

'Shoot.'

'Can you think of anyone who'd want to hurt your friend? If she didn't fall, then if she was pushed by accident or deliberately shoved during an argument, someone must have been there to do that?'

'No idea.' Heidi looked at Daisy. 'Can you?'

'Nope.' Daisy's blotched eyes widened as she said, 'I wish the police would tell us what happened. What if she was stabbed or shot or something?'

'I can't answer that, but Mousehole is a small place; someone would have heard a gunshot. As to stabbing . . . I think they'd have been some gossip about that.' *And as the police didn't take Ryan's clothes away or search the bedsit for bloodstained items, and there was no blood on or near the harbour wall, I doubt she was stabbed.*

'Can I ask where you both were while Toby and Tania were at the pub?'

A shadow passed over Heidi's face. 'You can't think that . . .'

Holding her palm up, Maggie spoke fast. 'I promise, all I'm doing is getting a feel for where you all were.'

'Okay.' Heidi poured herself some more tea from the pot. 'Daisy and I had dinner in the hotel at half-seven.'

'Yeah.' Daisy picked up her phone and opened her photo gallery. 'Here, I took a pic of my dinner. My dad is a bit of a foodie; I like to send him photos of meals when they look good.'

'You found your phone, then?' Maggie studied the photograph of a particularly delicious-looking tagine.

'No, someone's either pinched it, or it got lost – my own fault. I left it in the spa with my changing bag, rather than putting it in the locker. I grabbed myself a cheap one from town earlier to keep me going until I get home to sort things out with my service provider.'

'But this photograph is from before you lost your phone.'

'I keep my photos on the cloud. I downloaded them to this one.'

'Sensible.' Maggie's pen hovered over her pad. 'And what did you do after you'd eaten?'

'I went to my room,' Daisy said. 'I was feeling a bit peopled-out.'

Heidi smiled at her friend. 'And I was feeling a bit weddinged-out. I ran a hot bath and stayed in it until it was tepid, then went to bed.'

'Thank you.' Maggie hooked her bag onto her shoulder. 'And lastly, could you tell me where Toby works, please?'

# Chapter Twenty-three

The wait for Inspector Houseman to return to the interview room had felt like an eternity. It hadn't mattered how many times Ryan had reasoned the situation through, he couldn't convince himself that, even if he wasn't wrongly charged with murder, he could rightly be charged with some sort of data protection infringement or, worse, stalking.

The only respite from worrying about being arrested for eavesdropping on Toby that Ryan's mind had given him was to think about his relationship with Bea.

*Her parents will never accept me now . . . not after two trips to be questioned by the police . . . and I don't suppose she'll be thrilled. Thank God she isn't here.*

The thought made Ryan gasp.

*Am I really glad she isn't here?*

When the door eventually opened, Ryan was relieved to have company just so his own mind would stop torturing him, even if it was in the shape of Sergeant Peters and Inspector Houseman. Both wore grave expressions, their previous lapses into friendliness completely absent.

A see-through evidence bag containing his phone was placed upon the table, next to Houseman's tablet.

'We've had a listen to your recording, Mr Stepney.'

*Back to using my surname . . .* Ryan winced. *That can't be good.*

'I'd like you to listen to it with us.'

Diane Houseman's eyes were fixed on Ryan's as she played the recording, not from the phone, but from her tablet, onto which the recording had been downloaded. The interview room filled with the sound of Toby's voice.

'. . . You said you could handle it! I wasn't planning on working today – as you well know. It's my stag do – at least it was! . . . What a fucking nightmare. The police want to talk to me later. God knows why – I wasn't there when she fell. You said this was a simple operation. One I wanted nothing to do with, but you insisted! . . . For goodness' sake! As if life wasn't complicated enough right now and . . . Hang on, the bus is here. I'll be there in half an hour – try not to let me down again before then!'

Ryan had to concentrate incredibly hard not to squirm in his seat as the recording was clicked off again.

Sergeant Peters crossed his arms as he asked, 'Do you have any idea who Mr Marrell was talking to, or any thoughts as to what this simple operation was?'

'No idea. Nor do I know where Toby was going on the bus, or what it was that he wanted nothing to do with.' Ryan reined in his impatience. 'Apart from seeing him talk to Tania in the pub, I'd never seen Toby before.'

The inspector sounded almost as tired as he was. 'And you made this recording because your work colleague, Maggie Tyson, has taken it upon herself to investigate Tania's death?'

Hoping Maggie would forgive him, but already picturing himself on the next available train to Birmingham when she asked Mr Robbins to sack him for disloyalty, Ryan closed his eyes. 'When you first spoke to me, you seemed convinced Tania had fallen or had an accident because she'd drunk too much – which she hadn't. And because I'd definitely drunk too much *and* was in the area shortly after Tania, you saw me as a witness or a suspect. Maggie didn't want me to be blamed for something I hadn't done.'

'Well, that didn't work out, did it.' Houseman folded her arms. 'Here you are – again.'

Ryan gulped. 'Maggie wanted to help.'

'Did she now?'

'Yes.' Ryan sighed. 'Please, how did Tania die?'

The inspector hesitated before she replied. 'She might just have fallen.'

'Fallen? Then why am I here? Why all this?'

'Two things, Mr Stepney. One, the way she landed – face upwards. If you fall or jump on purpose, you tend to fall face down. If you land face up, then . . .'

Ryan's words came out slowly. He felt sick as he imagined the horror Tania must have felt as gravity dragged her downwards. 'Then she must have been sat on the harbour wall with her back to the sea – not looking at the sea. Which suggests she was talking to someone.'

'Exactly.' Peters nodded. 'Why look inland when the harbour view is so stunning?'

'I swear I didn't push her. I didn't ever see her again after I left the pub!'

If the inspector noticed the panic in her suspect's voice, she didn't react to it. 'Secondly, Mr Stepney, you have a recording on your phone that casts suspicion on Tania's partner, Mr Marrell.'

'I . . .' Ryan stuttered, 'I told you, I was helping Maggie. She wanted to show you I was innocent by finding out things for you. She'll definitely tell you if she uncovers anything useful.'

Houseman turned sharply in her chair. 'Sergeant Peters, you grew up around here; how well do you know this Maggie at the chippy?'

David got to his feet. 'Could we have a word, please, Inspector? Outside.'

*

The taxi drew up outside a garage on Green Lane, in Marazion. Double-checking she had the correct address, Maggie got out of the car, taking her time to assess her surroundings.

Mount View Garage sat a few metres back off the pavement. It had a small forecourt in front of the main building. Above what she presumed would be the workshop was a white-painted, stone-walled flat. At first she thought it was residential, but as she walked along the pavement, Maggie saw a set of concrete steps running up the outside of the building, leading to a solid front door, upon which was a simple sign.

*Post for Marrell and Zimmerman to be left at the garage. Thank you.*

'Zimmerman? Rachel's surname?' Telling herself off for not having asked Hugh what Rachel's surname was, Maggie muttered, 'If they need a sign like that, it implies that there isn't always someone in the office to receive post.'

Remaining on the pavement outside of the premises, Maggie switched her attention to the forecourt that separated the garage from the road. On it, neatly lined up, were three vintage cars.

*This must be Toby's mate's garage.*

Checking the coast was clear, Maggie crept past the concrete steps and approached the back of the building. As she got closer, she could hear some sort of machinery whirring, telling her someone was at work. Taking a deep breath, she poked her head around the corner.

A person, clothed head to toe in dark green overalls, a helmet and visor in place, was running a polishing machine over a beautiful deep blue car. There was no one else in sight, but there was a once-beautiful blue sports car, with its bonnet concertinaed into a crush of splintered metal just outside the undercover working area.

*Toby's car.*

Ducking back out of view, telling herself to stop feeling like a criminal and to get on with doing what she'd set out to do before she had to get back to the shop, Maggie returned to the external stairs.

They were steep and made of concrete, and Maggie imagined they could be slippery in the rain or during the winter months. She instinctively rested a hand against the wall of the building as she climbed, wishing there was a rail to hold on to. She was rather alarmed to find herself short of breath when she reached the top. She was even more alarmed to see that the door, which had appeared to be closed, was slightly ajar.

*Don't panic, woman; it's a hot day, why wouldn't they want the door to be open!*

On closer inspection, Maggie saw this wasn't an ordinary door. It was thick, like a security door in a bank. Pulling herself together, she knocked. The sound disappeared into the reinforced surface, so she rang the doorbell to her right. No one answered.

With increasing unease, Maggie pulled the door open a little wider and called out, 'Mr Marrell? Hello . . .?'

There was no response.

Maggie hovered on the doorstep, uncertain. 'Mr Marrell, Miss Zimmerman?' The hairs on the back of her neck stood up as she took a few steps into the white-walled hallway, calling out again, 'Hello?'

On receiving no reply, she tiptoed cautiously forward into an office. She could just make out where dividing walls had once been positioned, marking out living areas and bedrooms in a flat. Now there was one large open space, with two black steel desks in the centre; neither was occupied. Maggie's breathing rasped in her throat as she forced herself not to run back to the door.

To her right, there was an open archway, through which Maggie could see a kettle and a collection of mugs. Shuffling around on the spot, she took in a row of filing cabinets which ran the length of the entire left-hand wall. In front of her, two doors were firmly shut. She guessed one would lead to a bathroom and one to either some sort of storage cupboard or possibly a meeting room in which to talk to clients.

Nothing appeared to be disturbed. Beyond the fact the front door was open, there was nothing to suggest a break-in.

*Maybe Toby or Rachel were here but left in a hurry for some reason, forgetting to close the door behind them?*

'Right.' Maggie spoke into the dry, conditioned air. 'I'll check behind those doors, have a quick peep at each desk, then leave.'

Dashing across the thickly carpeted floor, she pushed the nearest door open. She was confronted with a toilet and washbasin, and a shelf unit full of spare toilet rolls and cleaning supplies.

Exhaling in relief at not having found a pile of bodies or an unexploded bomb, Maggie told her overactive imagination off and closed the washroom door before moving to the next one. Levering down the door handle, she felt the door give a fraction, but it wouldn't open.

She tried again. The door juddered, but despite obviously not being locked, it wouldn't budge. Deciding something must be blocking it, Maggie put her shoulder to the wood and shoved harder. The door gave way for a split second but then quickly shut again.

*Is someone pushing back?*

Sweat broke out on Maggie's forehead as she leapt back. 'Hello! Is someone in there?'

There was no reply.

Forcing herself forward, she put her ear up to the door and listened.

Nothing.

All she could hear was the drum of her own heart beating and the hum of the air conditioning.

'For goodness' sake, woman, you're creating drama where there is none. Something's probably fallen over in there and is blocking the door.'

Resolving to do the sensible thing and let the police know she'd been there, Maggie reasoned that, as she'd come this far, she might as well keep going. Her pulse thudded in her neck as she sped towards the bigger of the two workstations that denoted the main part of the office.

Three monitors formed a backdrop to the first rectangular desk. There was a single keyboard centre stage, next to a wireless mouse, which was perched on top of a mat decorated with the logo *Mermaid Imports*.

Sitting in a large faux-leather swivel chair, Maggie reached for an open black A4 folder.

*This is the bigger of the two desks, so I'm guessing it must be Toby's.*

Scanning the top page of the open file before her, she saw a complex spreadsheet detailing goods to be imported – in this case from Agadir.

'Agadir . . . that's Morocco . . .' Looking a little closer, she ran a finger down a list of items – foot stool, occasional table, framed mirror. 'Furniture imports . . . Small items, easy to sell on.'

Flicking through the rest of the file, she found it to be full of similar spreadsheets concerning goods coming in from places she recognised as being in Morocco or Tunisia, and being landed at either Exeter airport or Plymouth docks, depending on their size. All the items of furniture had come via ship, while small picture frames, mirrors and a number of decorative trinket boxes had arrived via plane. Most of the imported items had been photographed, and these photos, showing exquisitely fashioned pieces, had been attached to each sheet, which, in turn, had an invoice stapled to it. All of them had 'paid' written across them in bold red handwriting.

Not entirely sure what she was hunting for, Maggie flipped over a few more pages. Every now and then there was a green cross drawn in the top right-hand corner of the invoice. Looking more closely, she worked out that the crosses were all drawn on the larger pieces of furniture, cupboards and chests of drawers, rather than stools or chairs.

*Probably means they needed to pay for extra space on the ship.*

Leaving the folder, Maggie's hand reached down to the two drawers built into the left side of the desk. She wasn't surprised to find them both locked.

On the right side of the desk, huddled next to the third monitor, was an accumulation of pots and old mugs, stuffed with pens – including a red one she assumed was used to mark the invoices as paid and a green one to provide the crosses – plus a stapler, rulers, paperclips, Post-it notes and other stationery supplies. Picking up the nearest pot, Maggie pulled out the Post-it notes and found a few receipts had been tucked amongst them. On closer inspection she could see they were for petrol purchases, all made at the supermarket between Marazion and Penzance.

A docking station, currently without a phone or tablet to charge, flashed a blue light on and off, showing it was ready and waiting for active service. A rather dusty landline phone was next to it. Behind them two books lay on their side. The top one, a guide to Morocco, well-thumbed and slightly tatty, sat above a leather-bound diary.

Opening the diary to that week, she saw that Rachel was, as Heidi had suggested, overseeing a shipment in Morocco. Further investigation showed her trips were regular monthly occurrences. Turning a few more pages, seeing that the diary only showed travel timings, Maggie was in the process of putting it back when the phone burst into life.

The abrupt ringing sound in the otherwise silent space made her heart race anew. Maggie peered around nervously, half expecting someone to come out of the kitchen area to take the call, but no one appeared.

A second later the answerphone clicked into life.

'Toby, where the hell are you? I've been waiting for ages.'

Maggie grabbed a Post-it note from the pot and scribbled down what she was hearing. The female voice cut through the quiet of the room.

'Why I couldn't meet you at the office, I don't know. It's not as if anyone is expecting you to be there.' There was the sound of an exasperated intake of breath, before the caller went on. 'We need to get the price for the next exchange sorted asap. If you don't call me today, I'll make the deal myself and take *all* the profit! Oh, and turn your bloody mobile back on!'

As the call ended, a shadow cast itself over the desk. Maggie only registered that she wasn't alone when a sharp thwack met the side of her head.

After that, the world went as black as Toby's metal desk.

# Chapter Twenty-four

'And this Mrs Tyson—'

'Miss.' Sergeant Peters interrupted as he sat back at the interview room table with Detective Houseman and Ryan.

'Miss Tyson, then.' Houseman looked from Peters to Ryan. 'She got you a job and found you somewhere to live, just like that?'

Ryan was tired. 'It was pure luck and good timing on my behalf. Mr Robbins needed staff just as I needed work and a home. I met Maggie, and it all came together.'

'Okay.' Houseman was sceptical. 'And you two already get on so well that she decided she'd investigate a crime – a *suspicious death* – to help you?'

Ryan laid both of his hands on the table. 'I know it sounds mad. And in all honesty, I've no idea why she is being so kind to me – but yes, that is what's happening.'

Sergeant Peters took over. 'Ryan, during the conversation I've just had with Detective Inspector Houseman outside of this room, I let her know that – as I'm sure you worked out for yourself earlier, Ryan – Miss Tyson and I go back a long way.'

'Maggie said you went to school together.'

'We did. So I know that she cared for her grandad and inherited his lifelong passion for puzzles and detective fiction. And here you are, Ryan, new on the scene, just when

Izzie—' he turned back to the inspector '—that's the daughter I mentioned outside . . .'

'Go on.'

Peters inclined his head before readdressing Ryan. 'So, just as Izzie, who is more or less your age, is away on her travels, you pop up to fill the gap in Maggie's life, giving her someone to look after. Then, on top of that, you give her the chance of a lifetime. The opportunity to play detective for real. She could get herself into trouble. Get hurt even.'

Seeing the serious expressions across the table, Ryan slumped back in his seat. 'I did tell her we should leave it to the police.'

'But you didn't, did you?' Houseman gestured to the bagged-up phone. 'You joined in.'

'Maggie's been kind to me.' Ryan suddenly decided he had nothing to lose by asking the question that had been nagging at him. 'The recording, what do you think? Toby wasn't supposed to be working, but there he was, going to work. That would have been a bit odd anyway, as it was during his pre-wedding stag break, but stuff does come up at work, so fair enough – but the day after his future wife was killed? What's so important that needs sorting when you're in shock or grieving or both?'

'Wanting to keep his mind occupied, maybe? Carrying on regardless, avoiding reality,' Peters suggested.

Ryan scanned through the notes he'd been making. '*Or*, whatever it was that Tania was wary of – the thing she didn't trust him over – the thing he'd been making secret phone calls about in the weeks prior to the wedding – maybe that was to do with his work? Maybe . . .'

'No.' Houseman's single word was as blunt as it was short. She gave Peters a stern stare of disapproval, before turning back to Ryan. 'This has got to stop. You and Maggie stick to serving chips and leave the police work to us. For all we know, this really was an accident – we can't prove it wasn't, and until we have spoken to Mr Marrell, we can't move this case forwards or sign it off as an awful mishap.'

'Okay.' Ryan lowered his head to the table.

Peters tapped a finger against the paper Ryan had written on. 'I agree with Inspector Houseman, Ryan, but I hope we aren't above asking if you have any theories as to what's been going on?'

Ryan dared not look at Houseman. Her disapproval might have been silent, but it was also tangible. 'I just wanted to keep busy – stop from worrying myself to death. And to help Maggie. She's been good to me.'

Ignoring the sniff from Houseman, Peters said, 'As you'll have gathered, I've spoken to Maggie since you were invited here to chat.'

'Is she okay?'

'She's worried about you. I caught up with her after she'd visited The Cabin Hotel, where she'd spoken to Mr Hugh Parkinson. The best man. Former best man.'

Ryan sat up straight. 'She's spoken to him?'

'She has.' Peters nodded, 'I'm sure Maggie will fill you in when you get home.'

'I can go?'

'You can.' Houseman tapped a finger on Ryan's notes. '*After* you've told us what you've been thinking about all this.'

'It's not much, really. Just theories.'

'Sometimes theories are all we need.' Peters smiled.

With a nervous cough, Ryan gripped the sheet of paper between his fingers. It felt as limp as he did after a night in the cells. 'It's just – well – I've been thinking about what Tania said about the row in the pub. If she was right, and it wasn't about cheating with another woman, then what was Toby keeping secret from her? What if it was something to do with his business?'

Houseman's voice rang out across the table, 'Let me guess: our would-be Miss Marple asked you to try and find the business premises so she could go and talk to Mr Marrell to find out what that secret was?'

'Something like that.'

'Right.' Houseman got to her feet. 'I'm ending this here. We will continue to look into Miss Stevens' death, but in all likelihood the coroner will record an open verdict or accidental death.'

'But . . .'

'Sergeant Peters will see you out. Your laptop and phone will be waiting for you at reception. *But* we might take them back at any time if the situation changes.'

Ryan was horrified. 'But I need . . .'

'And I need you to stop meddling. This isn't an episode of bloody *Scooby-Doo*! Go home, Mr Stepney. Go to work and do very little else, and let us do the investigating. The police are stretched enough without having our time wasted. Okay?'

'Okay.'

\*

It wasn't until Sergeant Peters had escorted him to the foyer of the police station that Ryan spoke. 'Thank you for listening to me.'

'No problem.' Sergeant Peters waved to the woman on reception as he keyed in the code that opened the outer doors, ready to release Ryan. 'In return, do me a favour and keep Maggie out of trouble.'

'I'll try.'

'That lacked conviction.'

Ryan gave an exhausted groan. 'I've not known Maggie long, but I know that she does her own thing.'

'Ain't that the truth.'

'I'm convinced Tania was killed. You are too, aren't you, Sergeant?'

'You know I can't answer that.'

'Hypothetically, then.'

Sergeant Peters couldn't help but grin. 'I can see why you get on with Maggie.'

'So?'

'It comes down to the angle of the fall.'

'The angle . . . Face up, you mean?'

'Face up and a little further out from the wall than you'd expect if she'd just dropped.'

'As if she'd been propelled by a shove?'

'You did not hear that from me.' The policeman hesitated before asking, 'Why is finding out the truth so important to you, Ryan? Beyond clearing your own name. If it's just to help Maggie, then . . .'

'It isn't.' Ryan was surprised by his sudden level of conviction. 'I had plenty of time to think in there, and the thing is – this is my chance as much as Maggie's.'

'Meaning?'

'She's always wondered if she had it in her to be an investigator. Now she can find out. Meanwhile, I've never known what I wanted to do, but this, it feels like something I could do. Something worthwhile.'

*And I'd like to prove to Bea that I'm every bit as clever as she is . . . and maybe, make my parents proud of me.*

'I see.'

An unpleasant thought flitted through Ryan's mind. 'Maggie wouldn't have carried on investigating on her own after talking to Hugh, would she?'

'Maggie's not stupid, Ryan.' Peters checked his watch. 'Anyway, it's gone four-thirty, she'll be setting up at the chippy.'

'Of course.' With a nod to the sergeant, Ryan stepped into the fresh air, desperate to get home and have a wash.

★

'Ryan!'

'Bea?'

'What the hell is going on?' Bea had her hands on her hips as she leapt off the same bench Maggie had waited on the last time he'd been taken to the station.

*But Maggie had been smiling.*

'What are you doing here?' Ryan was faintly aware he should be rushing into her arms, but shock at seeing his girlfriend, mingled with the humiliation of her seeing him stepping out of a police station, had robbed him of coherent thought.

'That Maggie woman emailed me. How did she get my email address?'

Ryan wiped sleep from his eyes. 'My laptop, I suppose. Why aren't you in Portugal?'

'Because Maggie *ordered* me to come here.'

'But how? I mean – surely the flights take time and . . .' A smile lit up Ryan's face. 'You got on a plane to see me when you knew I was in trouble.'

'Obviously! Luckily I was in Faro when the message arrived, so the airport was close.' Bea exhaled a puff of annoyance, before returning his smile. Lifting a hand to Ryan's fringe, she ruffled her fingers through it. 'Sorry I was grumpy. I was worried.'

'I'm glad you're here.' He wrapped his arms around her, only to be pushed away.

'Hell, you stink.'

'Sorry – it was hot in there, with no showers or clean clothes.' He took a step away to protect her nostrils. 'You were lucky to get a flight that got you here so fast.'

'Paolo has a private plane.'

'Oh. And Paolo is?'

'A friend who owns a plane. He's Moroccan. I told you.'

'No, you didn't, but never mind.' Ryan tried not to hate Paolo on principle. 'It was very kind of him. Thoughtful.'

'Unlike Maggie! Fancy demanding that I come here. It's not like it's a quick trip down the motorway.'

'I'm sure she didn't demand you came. She'd have just been telling you what had happened.' Ryan was beginning to wish Maggie had kept Bea out of it. His delight at seeing her soured as he saw how put out she was.

'She made me feel like I had no choice. Talk about playing the guilt card!' Bea examined his appearance from downwind. 'You need a haircut and a shave.'

Ryan stared at Bea in disbelief. 'Seriously? That's what you think is important right now?'

'You're scruffy!'

'Of course I'm scruffy!' Mentally taking some deep breaths, Ryan pointed back the way he'd come. 'I've just come out of the police station. I've been there for hours being questioned about the murder of a woman – a *murder*! Do you have *any* idea what that's like? Can you imagine how I feel right now?'

Bea opened her mouth, but Ryan kept talking.

'I met Tania once. *Once!* Then, suddenly, she was dead. I liked her. She was nice – someone who I thought might be a friend. *And* she was *your* friend. I didn't even know you still had friends here. Or that one of them was getting married! Not that you'd be able to tell. I mean, there's no sense of loss here, is there?'

'I came all this way to see you! And as for Tania,' Bea's voice quietened, 'it hasn't really sunk in.'

Ryan deflated slightly. 'Okay. Sorry . . . it's not been a nice few days.'

Linking her arm through his, Bea propelled Ryan towards the main road. 'Let's nip into the nearest clothes shop and get you dressed a bit better, then we'll have a nice meal in the nearest decent restaurant. That'll sort you out.'

'Are you insane? I want to go home. I want a shower and some kip. That's if Mr Robbins is alright about me missing the end of the shift. I might have to work.' Ryan pulled away.

'Hang on, how did you know where I was? Did the police call you?'

'Maggie said in her email.' Bea flicked some non-existent dirt from her fingernails. 'Bit of a busybody, that one. Bossy too.'

'She wouldn't have known I'd still be in there, though, not when she contacted you.'

'I asked her.' Bea looked as if she'd sucked a lemon. A facial expression that reminded Ryan rather too much of her mother. 'She put her email address in the message she sent me. I asked what jail you were in at lunchtime.'

'It wasn't jail; I was only being questioned.'

Bea wasn't listening. 'If I'd known you'd be let out so fast, I wouldn't have bothered coming. Can you imagine the expense . . . and I'll have to get back as well now. I've a good mind to send this Maggie the bill for the cost of travel.'

'You said your friend flew you over.'

'That's not the point!'

Ryan opened his mouth to argue but then closed it. When Bea was like this, any disagreement was pointless. Instead, he slipped his hand into hers. 'Let's go home.'

# Chapter Twenty-five

When he'd said home, Ryan had meant the chip shop. Bea, however, had other ideas, and now he was standing beneath the power shower in the flat he'd once thought they'd live in together.

Towelling himself dry with an ultra-soft bath sheet, Ryan said, 'I ought to let Maggie know I'm out; she'll be worried.'

'You said she'd be at work.'

'She'll have her phone in her apron pocket.'

Slipping her arms around his neck, a suggestive grin on her lips, Bea said, 'Why don't you let me help you forget about Maggie, murder and life for a little while?'

Very well aware that all that separated him from his girlfriend was a length of towel, Ryan was more than a little tempted, but a voice at the back of his head chose that moment to remind him how much Maggie had done for him. *And Bea hasn't been the best girlfriend lately . . . but it's been a while . . . and she's clearly up for it . . .* His stomach gave a low grumble, reminding him how long it had been since he last ate more than a soggy ham sandwich.

Gently pushing her away, Ryan continued to dry himself. 'I'd love that . . . I'd *really* love that—' he leant forward and kissed her pink lipsticked lips '—but first I need food, or my rumbling stomach will kill the mood.'

'Fair enough.' Bea kissed him once more, before heading to the door. 'I picked up some hoisin duck wraps on the way over. Still your favourite?'

'Definitely. Thank you.'

As he watched her go, Ryan was reminded of the girl he'd fallen in love with. She could be so kind.

*It's just a shame she's such a spoilt brat sometimes.*

\*

Seated at a brand-new pine table in the open-plan kitchen-diner, wearing Bea's fluffy fuchsia dressing gown, Ryan took a bite of his wrap. 'Delicious! So nice to have a change from chip butties.'

'I bet you've been having a few of those lately.'

'One or two.' Ignoring the disapproval in Bea's tone, Ryan pulled out his mobile. 'That's odd, Maggie hasn't replied to my message.'

'She'll be busy if she's working alone.'

Guilt nudged at Ryan as a yawn temporarily prevented him from chewing his wrap. 'I ought to be there.'

'If she's as nice as you claim, she'll understand.'

Disliking Bea's sarcastic tone, Ryan placed the part-eaten wrap back on his plate. 'Bea, you left me homeless. Maggie stepped in.'

'I never—'

Ryan interrupted. 'You can argue it any way you like, but you disappeared.' Perversely pleased to see how surprised Bea was that he was standing up for himself, Ryan sent another text to Maggie.

'Why are you putting so much faith in the woman from the chippy? Just because she got you a job and a place to stay, doesn't mean she's trustworthy. What do you know about her?'

Ryan ran a hand through his damp hair, sending it into tufty spikes. 'You've just got a downer on Maggie because she makes you feel bad.'

'She does not.'

'Come off it.' Ryan chewed the remainder of the wrap as he got to his feet. 'I'm going to the shop.'

'But we were going to . . .'

Ryan regarded Bea as if he was seeing her properly for the first time. 'If you think I can have sex with you while worrying about Maggie, then you are very much mistaken!'

Bea's blue eyes shone dangerously. 'What the hell is there to worry about? You were the one in trouble, and now you're alright.' Her expression abruptly softened again, and she reached out, tracing a fingertip across his cheek. 'Let's just go to bed; we can check on Maggie and the shop later.'

'No, Bea, we're going to check on Maggie *now*.'

\*

'What do you mean, she's not here?' Ryan took one look at Mr Robbins' round, scarred face and moderated his tone. 'It's six o'clock.'

'I'm aware of the time.' Mr Robbins grunted. 'She's not answering her phone.'

Ryan's insides did a backflip. 'Have you tried her house?'

'Needed here.'

'Of course. Yes.' Ryan bit his bottom lip. 'I'm sorry I'm late, I . . .'

'You were busy.' Mr Robbins wrapped a portion of chips for their latest customer.

*He doesn't want me to mention the police station in front of people. That's good.*

'I can start now, or I can go and . . .'

'Go and find her. Maggie's never late.'

Surprised at this blunt, but nonetheless obvious, concern for his member of staff, Ryan headed to the door. He was almost outside when Mr Robbins called after him, 'She was looking into things.'

'Understood.' Rushing outside, Ryan almost collided with Bea, who, having refused to set foot inside the shop, claiming the smell of chip fat cooking made her feel nauseous, was pacing along the pavement.

'What the hell's the panic?'

'She isn't here.'

'So what?'

'So what?' Ryan grabbed Bea's wrist and pulled her along with him towards her car. 'Maggie never misses work. Like, *never*. I need you to drive me to her house.'

With a sulky pout, Bea climbed into her Mazda. 'When did she become your responsibility?'

'From the moment she tried to help me after you pissed off to Lisbon, or wherever, without a word and I was falsely accused of murder.'

*

By the time they were in Maggie's home, Ryan could no longer remember what had attracted him to Bea beyond her Mediterranean good looks. And even those were fast losing their appeal as she leant against the door frame, her right hand twisting a lock of hair impatiently between her fingers. All she needed was to start chewing gum, and she'd be every inch the truculent American teenager.

Sifting through the notes on the dining room table, Ryan wasn't entirely sure what he was hunting for, but every instinct told him that Maggie had got in over her head.

'What are you doing?'

'I'm working out where she is.'

'If she's got herself into trouble, then it's her own fault. She should have left it to the police.'

Ryan glared across the room. 'If you can't say anything useful, I suggest you go. In fact, just go anyway.'

Striding to his side, Bea oozed panicked anger. 'I came all this way because I care about you!'

'Well, you've got a funny way of showing it!' Ryan returned his attention to the table. 'Her notebook's not here.'

Bea sighed. 'And that means what?'

'That she's taken it with her – so she must be investigating. But where?'

Giving in, Bea sat at the table, tugging the open map of the areas towards her. 'Where has she been so far?'

'Before I was taken into the station, she'd been to The Cabin Hotel.'

'That's where the hen party was.'

'The one *you* were invited to, yes.' Ryan kept his eyes averted from her, not wanting to have to repeat that she hadn't told him about the wedding, but the accusation hung in the air between them anyway.

'Does that mean Maggie has met my friends?'

'Heidi and Daisy – yes.' Ryan joined Bea in studying the map. 'They've checked out of the hotel now. They've gone to Heidi's home in . . .'

'Lamorna. Lamorna Manor.' Bea traced a painted fingernail across the map. 'How about Hugh and Toby? They were staying at The Cabin as well.'

'Sergeant Peters told me that Maggie spoke to Hugh at The Cabin.'

'But not Toby.'

'We don't know where he is.'

'She would want to talk to him, though, wouldn't she?' Bea ran her fingertip over the map, running it in a circle around the small town of Marazion. 'If she was intent on speaking to everyone who knew Tania, then common sense says she'd target Toby next.'

Deciding not to tell Bea about the recording he'd made, Ryan felt the knot of anxiety that had been forming in his stomach tighten. 'If she's discovered where he is.'

'You said she'd spoken to Hugh. He might have told her.'

'And she might have gone to talk to him – and now she's not turned up at work. We need to get to the hotel and ask Hugh where Toby works.'

'No, we don't.' Bea picked up a pen and drew a circle on the map. 'He works here.'

Ryan stared at her. 'Are you saying he'll be in Marazion?'

'I've no idea where he is. Sitting somewhere getting drunk, mourning his dead fiancée, probably. But his business is there.' She leant in closer to the map. '*Here*, to be precise. On Green Lane.'

Cursing his stupidity for not asking Bea where Toby worked in the first place, Ryan grabbed her hand. 'Come on, we're going there now.'

# Chapter Twenty-six

The triple vision she'd experienced on coming round was now just double vision.

Maggie's desire to throw up had passed, but she wasn't ready to move from Toby's desk chair as she heard a set of booted feet running up the stairs outside and through the hallway, only to be smothered by the deep pile carpet.

She tensed, wondering if her assailant had come to finish what they'd started, but she didn't have the energy to move. All she could do was hope that the phone number she'd blearily texted was the right one.

'Maggie?'

'David.' Lifting her head with exaggerated care, Maggie bit back a wince at the pain that shot through her head.

'No point in me reminding you that you promised not to investigate further, I suppose?'

Through gritted teeth she muttered, 'None whatsoever.'

'Thought not.' David lifted a hand to her head and gently parted her curls with his fingers.

'What are you doing?' Maggie brought her head up sharply at the unexpectedly intimate gesture, and instantly regretted it. 'Ouch.'

'Keep still, woman. I'm seeing how much damage you've done here.'

'*I've* done?!' Maggie growled. 'I hardly hit myself on the head.'

'If you hadn't been here...'

'Yeah, yeah. Alright. Point made.' Easing her back deeper into the leather chair, she looked at David properly. 'Thanks for coming. I wasn't sure you would.'

'You didn't think I'd ignore your cry for help, did you?'

Maggie immediately regretted her tone. 'I'm sorry, I put that badly. What I meant was, I wasn't sure you'd have the same phone number. I didn't want to call the station.'

David crouched on his haunches before her. 'I bet you didn't, but you know I'm going to have to report this, don't you.'

Maggie mumbled, 'Uh-huh.'

'As it happens, your timing was perfect. I'd just changed to go home.'

'Hence the jeans and T-shirt rather than uniform.'

'It's always a relief to get out of the work clothes, especially on a warm evening like this.' David tugged at his plain white T-shirt. 'At least you aren't bleeding everywhere.'

'You're all heart.'

'Aren't I just. You need to go to the hospital.'

'No, I don't. I just got a whack. I'm fine.'

'You have a lump on your head that is more grapefruit-sized than orange-sized and you're wincing every time you move. It's a miracle they didn't break the skin. Did you pass out? How's your vision?'

'Yes and fine.'

'Don't bullshit me, Maggie.'

'Okay, it's a bit blurred, but not like it was.'

'I'm going to call A&E and tell them we're on our way.'

'But...'

'But nothing.' David hooked an arm through hers. 'There are very few perks to being a policeman, but one is that I can call in a few favours and jump the queue with you.'

Maggie was horrified. 'You can't. Some people will have been waiting hours, and I'm just...'

David placed a hand under her chin and tilted her head back gently but firmly. When he spoke, his voice brooked no argument. 'Someone hit you on the head. Hard. You lost consciousness. That means hospital, no two ways about it. I am taking you to casualty and getting you examined. We may not have spoken properly for a long time, but I still care, and you are just going to have to put up with that.'

'Okay.' Maggie slipped her hand into his. 'Thank you.'

'And on the way, you are going to tell me what the bloody hell you were playing at breaking into someone's office.'

'I will. If you tell *me* why you didn't let me know you were back in the area.'

★

Ryan's seat belt was unbuckled, and his hand was on the passenger door handle, ready to jump out before Bea had brought her car to a halt.

As they'd turned into Green Lane, they'd been met with the sight of Maggie being escorted to a black Hyundai. It wasn't until Ryan was running towards his friend that he realised the man with her was Sergeant Peters.

'Maggie!'

David fished his car key from his pocket and gave Ryan a suspicious look. 'Ah, Mr Stepney. Did you know Maggie was coming here?'

'No.'

Maggie tutted. 'How could I have told Ryan? He was with you, being wrongly accused of murder.'

David let out a frustrated groan.

'What's happened?' Ryan took in the flash of pain in Maggie's eyes.

'Hit on the head.'

'Who by?'

'Don't know.'

'You should be in hospital.'

Peters opened the car door. 'That's where we're going.'

'I'll come too.'

Maggie tried to shake her head but stopped almost as soon as she'd started. 'Chip shop . . . serving . . .'

'Mr Robbins told me to find you. He was worried. He's running the shop on his own tonight.'

It was difficult to know who was the most surprised, Maggie or Sergeant Peters.

Ryan ran a hand through his damp hair as he asked Maggie, 'How did you know Toby worked here?'

'More to the point—' David's eyes narrowed '—how did *you* know to come here?'

Suddenly remembering he hadn't arrived alone, Ryan spun around to be confronted with the sight of Bea, leaning against the side of the car, her arms folded.

'Bea is a friend of Tania's. She knew that Toby worked here, and I guessed that Maggie would try and—'

'You told me your girlfriend was abroad.' David regarded Ryan with suspicion. 'Is anything you told myself and Inspector Houseman true? If it was all lies, then I strongly suggest you take up a career on the stage straight away.'

Blanching, Ryan spluttered, 'Of course it was true. All of it! Bea's here because Maggie told her I was in trouble. She flew back. I had no idea she was coming.'

'I didn't think she'd fly over,' Maggie mumbled. 'Assumed she'd just phone you.'

'Thank goodness she did, or I wouldn't have known where to find you! If Sergeant Peters hadn't come too, then you might still be in there.' Ryan looked at the garage behind them.

David eased Maggie into the back seat. 'This conversation can wait. Maggie should be at the hospital.'

Agreeing quickly, Ryan said, 'Let's go.'

'What about Bea?' Maggie managed as she slid the seat belt over her shoulder.

Ryan's mouth dropped open. *How can I have already forgotten about her?* By the time he'd turned round, Bea was back in her car, and the engine was on.

He pointed from Maggie to the car, in what he hoped was an 'I'm going with Maggie to the hospital' gesture. Ryan thought he saw Bea mouth something in response as she drew the car away from the kerb and drove off down the road, but he decided that he didn't want to know what it was.

'That was Bea, then,' Maggie murmured as Ryan sat next to her.

'Yeah.'

'Is she alright?'

'Pissed off.'

'I'm sorry.' Maggie fiddled with the clasp to her safety belt. 'I was worried about you and thought I should tell her what was happening.'

Ryan fixed his own seat belt in place. 'I'm glad you did. I think I needed to see her to get a few things straight in my head.'

'And are they? Straight in your head, I mean?'

'Yeah. Yeah, they are.'

\*

As Maggie slowly described her conversation with Hugh, followed by an account of her visit to Lamorna Manor, she was gripped by an overwhelming fatigue.

When she yawned for the third time, David increased his speed. 'Maggie, keep talking. No napping until the doctor has checked you over.'

Ryan leant forward as far as his seat belt would allow. 'Sergeant Peters is right, no sleeping while you have concussion.'

'I might not have . . .'

'Don't be daft, Maggie.' David clicked his indicator. 'Of course you're concussed. Keep awake by telling us what happened once you'd gone inside the office. An act which was unbelievably stupid and borderline illegal.'

'Borderline?' Ryan asked.

'Even if the door is open, if you don't have permission to go inside a property, you should not go in. But you *could* argue you were concerned for whoever might be in there.'

'I was,' Maggie whispered. 'I called out first, but when no one answered, I went in. After what had happened to Tania, I wondered if Toby . . .'

'After what happened to Tania, you should have called the police and stood well back.' David negotiated the turn into the hospital car park. 'We would have gone in to see if Toby was in trouble. You didn't need to.'

'Did you see who hit you?' Ryan gave Maggie a gentle shake as he saw her eyelids drooping.

'No. They came up from behind.'

David cleared his throat. 'Unlike with Tania.'

'You already told me that you suspect it was murder due to how she fell. Face up, rather than down.' Ryan kept his eyes on Maggie as he spoke. 'But that you can't prove it.'

'It's down to the coroner. If they think there isn't enough evidence to act, then that's that. You have to bear in mind that, in cases like this, it's incredibly hard to prove if she was pushed or fell. And without a strong motive to suggest why she'd have been killed . . .'

'But, if she was pushed hard by someone she was talking to and fell backwards . . .'

'Enough now, Maggie. You could be reading more into this than there is.' David turned left towards the hospital. 'You need to concentrate on getting better. I've only told you about the fact there's no evidence of murder – and actually, no real evidence of motive – to stop you hunting the information down and potentially getting yourself into more trouble. I shouldn't be saying anything at all! This stuff is confidential.'

Maggie tutted as Ryan asked, 'What were you doing before you were hit?'

Massaging her forehead, Maggie spoke quietly, each word an effort. 'When no one answered my call, I went inside. No one was there, but the aircon was on. It had the feel of a place where someone had popped out and would be back any minute.'

'I suppose someone could have just nipped to the shop.' Ryan remembered the corner shop he'd spotted as Bea had driven them along Green Lane. 'If you saw a person working in the garage, then it could be assumed that they'd keep an eye on things.'

'I wondered that, but the machine they were using was noisy. They wouldn't have heard anything.'

David shook his head. 'For God's sake! Why didn't you tell me someone was working downstairs when I found you? I could have gone to talk to them while we were there. Found out if they'd seen or heard anything.'

'Forgot.'

Ignoring the policeman's sigh, Ryan asked, 'Was the machine still noisy when you headed upstairs, Maggie? I mean, would Sergeant Peters have been able to hear it if the person you saw was still working when he arrived?'

Maggie thought, 'Possibly.'

David cursed. 'I didn't hear anything, but I should have looked – normally I would have, but—' he kept his eyes fixed firmly on the road; the unspoken hung in the air, '—I needed to get to Maggie to see if she was alright.'

Ryan moved the conversation on. 'Do you think it was Toby who'd been there, or his business partner?'

'Don't know, but there was a phone call – came through on the answerphone to the desk I was sat at. I'm guessing that was Toby's, but I can't be sure.'

'What was the message?' David slowed as he spotted a parking space. 'Male or female voice?'

'Female.' Maggie frowned. 'I wrote it down. Didn't you see the Post-it note on the desk?'

Turning off the engine, David shook his head. 'There was no note on the desk.'

'No note?' As the seriousness of the situation dawned on her, Maggie's shoulders trembled with the onset of shock. 'There was a folder open on the desk. My note was next to it. I was going to put it in my notebook when I got home and show you tomorrow and . . .' A fresh yawn broke through her speech. 'I feel awful.'

'There was no folder either, but never mind what happened in the office for now. I'll go and get a parking ticket, and Ryan, can you help Maggie inside? They're expecting her.'

\*

By the time Ryan had booked Maggie in and settled her into an incredibly uncomfortable plastic seat, David had called Houseman and filled her in on what had happened. Not mentioning the telling-off he'd received from his colleague about ignoring police protocol, failing to report the incident immediately and not having secured the scene, David sat down next to Maggie.

'You being attacked throws a different light on Tania's death. I'm going to have to leave. Will you take care of her, Ryan?'

'Sure.' He bit his lip. 'I ought to let Mr Robbins know what's happening.'

'I'll pop into the chip shop on the way to the station.'

The word 'station' brought Maggie back to herself. 'You've only just come off duty.'

'And now I'm back on.' He gave her a tight smile. 'You could have been killed. I want to know who hurt you. Houseman is already organising a guy from the forensics department to go over to the office. They'll need your prints for elimination.'

'Oh. Okay.'

'Is there anything else you can tell me before I go?' David dug his hands into his pockets. 'You'll have to give a full statement tomorrow.'

'Right.' Maggie licked her dry lips. 'At least you won't think Ryan has anything to do with all this now.'

Ryan, who'd already been feeling guilty at his relief that Maggie's attack had let him off the hook, reinforced David's question. 'Is there anything else Inspector Houseman should know, Maggie?'

'No.'

'Okay.' David got back to his feet.

He'd taken two steps away when Maggie called out, 'No, wait!'

David exchanged a worried glance with Ryan as they saw the flash of fear that had crossed their friend's face.

'I think there was someone behind the second white door.'

# Chapter Twenty-seven
## FRIDAY 13TH JUNE

Maggie rolled over, and the world swam into focus. Sunlight streamed in through the hospital ward's window, making her close her eyes again. Despite feeling as if she was recovering from the world's worst hangover, she hadn't wanted to stay in overnight, but the doctor had insisted.

Staring at the half-eaten remains of some toast and marmalade on the tray before her, Maggie realised she must have fallen asleep while eating breakfast. She groaned softly as her mind picked its way through her actions the previous afternoon. She knew that if Ryan had gone into the office alone, she'd have given him a lecture about being reckless.

Every bone in her body ached with an intense weariness.

*David didn't get the chance to tell me why he's not been in touch since he got back to Cornwall.*

To prevent herself from theorising about this, and to deflect the pain that thumped between her eyes, Maggie shut her eyes and tried to remember as much as possible about the folder she'd seen.

*Invoices. All paid. Red pen. Imports . . . but what was imported? Furniture . . . An occasional green cross . . .* The visuals she was creating in her head swam out of focus. She was just drifting back into sleep when a familiar voice made her open her eyes again.

'Morning, Maggie.' David pulled out a chair and sat down next to her.

'In uniform today, then.'

'On duty, ready to take your fingerprints, and expecting my colleague to come and question you as soon as they've found somewhere to park.'

'Oh.'

Having drawn the curtains around the bed, David undid a bag containing fingerprint equipment. 'The woman on reception tells me you'll be going home later today, as long as the doctor agrees after she's examined you.'

'Good.' A bit put out that they'd told him what they hadn't told her, Maggie sat up slowly. It wasn't until she was propped comfortably against her pillows that she remembered she was wearing a rather revealing hospital gown. She grabbed the bedclothes and pulled them up under her chin.

David's eyes told her he'd noticed, but he refrained from comment, instead saying, 'I hope this brush with a lunatic has brought an end to your little adventure into sleuthing.'

'Hardly a lunatic, more a—'

'Maggie!' David cut through her protest before it was fully formed and placed an ink pad on the bedside table. 'Ryan recorded the dead woman's fiancé at the bus stop, and you have been questioning Tania's friends. And look what has happened as a result.'

'If I hadn't, Ryan might still be a suspect.'

David rolled his eyes. 'For the final time, he was the last person to see her alive; we are duty bound to take that very seriously. It wasn't an excuse for you to start playing detective.'

'I wasn't playing, and it was only to help Ryan – and you!' Maggie remembered the thrill of excitement she'd felt when Heidi had assumed she was a private detective. 'Tania's friends would never have opened up to you like they did to me.'

'Maybe not.' David lifted her left hand, pressing one fingertip at a time against the ink block.

'The fact that Hugh crashed Toby's car would explain why Toby was using the bus when Ryan recorded him. What did you make of that, by the way?'

'I can see you're feeling better, then.'

'Just a headache. So, what *did* you make of it?' Maggie scowled, her mind flitting away from the unreported crash back to her visit to the office. 'I wish I could remember what I overheard on the answerphone.'

David sat back down again. 'We're taking the conversation Ryan recorded seriously. We are searching for Mr Marrell. When we find him, we'll be wanting some answers.'

'Good. I'd like to know what was so significant about that folder. It was just a load of paid invoices, so why would my attacker take it?'

'Maggie!'

'No, David, think about it for a minute. How many businesses use paper invoices these days?'

'That is a good question, and I will mention that to Houseman, but Maggie, a woman is dead, you have been hit over the head and Toby Marrell is missing – not officially, but no one seems to know where he is – which either suggests he's our killer or . . .'

'That he might be dead too?' Maggie closed her eyes, trying desperately to dispel the warmth from David's touch and remember what she'd heard before she'd been attacked.

'It's a possibility. Or he could be somewhere burying himself in work to try and escape his grief.'

Maggie mumbled into her glass of water, not wanting to make eye contact as she said, 'Possibly. Working hard is a good cure for heartbreak.'

'Well, you should know.'

'Let's not go there.'

'No, let's not.' David dropped her hand and wrote her name on the sheet of prints. 'You are sure you can't remember anything about who hit you?'

'Nothing. They either came in from outside or there was someone behind that white door. The office floor is thickly carpeted; I heard nothing.' She hesitated as David moved to the other side of the bed and pressed her right thumb against the inkpad. 'No, hang on a minute . . .'

'Maggie?'

'I heard you coming up the stairs . . . it was only when you got into the office that I couldn't hear you anymore, so I'd have heard someone else coming up the stairs.'

'Meaning they must have been in the cupboard.'

'It's a cupboard? Not an office?'

'Yes. I met the inspector there after I left you last night. I've no idea how someone could have been in there, though, Maggie. We had to almost batter the door down. A heap of folders was on the floor. A shelf had come off the wall and the contents were blocking the door.'

'Oh.' Maggie felt foolish. 'I could have sworn someone was pushing back against the door when I tried to open it.'

'That's what it felt like when I tried to get into the cupboard, but honestly, it was just a massive pile of old filing. The shelf was hanging onto the wall by one bent bracket. Looked like it had been like that a while. The whole cupboard was dusty and neglected.'

Maggie sighed as the ache in her head thudded harder. 'Odd to waste space like that.'

'True, but as you said, who uses paper files these days?'

'Touché.'

'We had a hunt for the folder you mentioned, but as one black A4 folder is very much like another . . .'

'Fair enough.'

'And there was no sign of the note of the recording you say you heard either.'

'I *did* hear it.'

'Okay, Maggie . . . I . . .' David stopped talking as a suited female figure came through the closed bed curtains and stood next to her colleague.

'Maggie Tyson, meet Detective Inspector Diane Houseman. She has some questions for you.'

Seeing the disapproval on the detective's face and recalling Ryan's detailed retelling of his experience in custody, Maggie mumbled, 'I'm sorry to have caused so much trouble.'

'I'm sure I don't have to tell you how much more serious this situation could have been, Miss Tyson.'

'Please, call me Maggie.'

'Maggie, then.' Houseman produced her tablet from her bag, ready to take notes. 'I'd like you to tell us what happened, from the beginning.'

'I went up the steps to the office. The door was open, so ...'

'No, Maggie. From the *very* beginning. From when you met Ryan Stepney.'

\*

As Houseman disappeared through the closed curtains, almost an hour later, Maggie understood precisely what Ryan had meant when he'd said he'd felt thoroughly told off by the detective.

'Is she always like that?'

'Yup.' David put his peaked hat on. 'And so she should be. Diane's very good at her job.'

'She doesn't like me.'

'She doesn't know you.' David got to his feet. 'She disapproves of what you've been up to, though. So do I, for that matter.'

'I told you; it was because ...'

'Because of Ryan. So you keep saying, but he's in the clear now.' David pulled back the curtain with a dramatic swoosh. 'I'll do you a deal. I won't suggest to Houseman that Ryan could have got from the police station to Toby's office in time to injure you, if you stop pretending to be one of those television detectives you're so fond of. Deal?'

\*

Ryan could feel Mr Robbins' eyes on his back as he moved around the chip shop. Although he'd covered for Maggie for short periods of time before and was getting used to how the place ran, this was the first time he was due to do an entire lunchtime shift on his own. Only now did he realise just how much Maggie did – and the last thing he needed was his employer watching every move he made.

'I can manage if you want to get back to . . .' Having no idea what it was Mr Robbins looked at all day, Ryan faltered.

'Haddock needs battering before the cod. Needs to sit in the mix longer for good batter.'

'I know. Maggie told me.'

'I'm too busy to help you.'

*Then don't!* 'It's okay, Mr Robbins, I'll manage. You go and do what you need to do.'

'The drinks fridge needs refilling.'

Ryan cast an eye in the direction of the fridge, which contained a choice of canned fizzy drinks, as well as a few cartons of orange or apple juice and bottles of water. 'I'll top it up between customers.'

'Hot day.'

*Well you do it then!* 'I'll be alright, Mr Robbins. I'm sure Maggie will be back later.'

'Tonight?'

'I don't know. I'll visit her after I've finished this shift.'

Mr Robbins grunted something Ryan didn't catch, before heading back to the solitary world he occupied with his tablet.

Finally left alone to get on with things, Ryan muttered an expletive as his mobile vibrated in his pocket. *Bea*.

**I came a hell of a long way to see you. If you don't come to the flat tonight, we're over.**

Ryan's fingertip hesitated over the phone screen for a minute.

Then he pressed delete.

*

Despite scrubbing at them twice in the hospital and again once she was home, the ink smudges on Maggie's fingertips refused to disappear.

'Perhaps it's just as well I'm not serving in the shop today.' As the seagull she'd been talking to through the kitchen window flew off, uncaring as to the state of her hands, Maggie checked the time. Her headache wasn't as bad as it had been, but it was affecting her concentration, and the hour until she was supposed to take the next round of painkillers felt an awfully long way off.

'This will pass. The doctor said I was fine, and at least Ryan can help Mr Robbins.' A smile broke through her discomfort as she recalled the note she'd found lodged on the coat rack inside her front door on her return.

*Hi Maggie. Go to bed! Don't worry about work. I'll manage with Mr R until you are better. Rest!! Will check on you later. Ryan.*

'I'm glad I gave him a key.' Moving slowly, she put on the kettle, announcing to the room at large. 'I'll make a coffee and then rest.'

Her intention to take her drink to the sofa and put on an episode of *Poirot*, however, was interrupted by the sight of the dining room table. Or, to be precise, the notes and map she'd made.

Massaging her forehead, she placed her mug on the table and sat down in front of the map of the area. It had been moved.

A shiver shot down her spine, and Maggie peered furtively around the room. Unsettled by the feeling that had come over her – that someone else had been there and maybe was still there now – she took some deep breaths and battled to think logically.

'The map has been moved because Ryan came here with Bea. He told me that. No one else is here now. It's just me.'

Disconcerted to find her hands were shaking, Maggie felt tears brimming. She angrily wiped them away. 'I'm fine. *Totally* fine.'

Leaving her cup where it was, Maggie headed to Izzie's bedroom. One glance at the empty single bed, complete with Horace, a purple teddy bear who was waiting patiently for his owner to return, and the cuddly shark she'd bought as a surprise for her daughter, was enough to tip the threat of tears into a waterfall of fatigue, discomfort and – although she'd never have admitted it – an overwhelming sense of being alone.

# Chapter Twenty-eight

Izzie stared at her mum in disbelief. 'I can't believe you did that!'

'You think I should have left well alone too?'

'No! I think you should keep going. And once you know who hit you on the head, tell me and I'll come over and hit them back! Bastard!'

The support of her only child almost set Maggie off into a renewed bout of tears, but she managed to hide it by rubbing her aching head. 'Thanks, love. Your support means a lot to me.'

'I've always said you'd make a good private detective. And I meant it.'

'Detective Houseman would not agree with you.'

'What's he like?' Leaning back against a white-painted wooden headboard, Izzie tucked her knees under her chin.

'She. Efficient, no nonsense, professional. Intolerant of amateurs.'

'That's no fun. I hoped they'd be a sympathetic aide – a Lestrade to your Holmes.'

Maggie giggled. 'Chances of that were always going to be slim.'

'At least I know what to buy you for Christmas.'

'Dare I ask?'

'Deerstalker hat – obvs!'

Maggie clenched the bear she was cuddling tighter as she asked, 'Does that mean you'll be here for Christmas, then?'

Izzie looked shocked. 'Absolutely. I said I'd be there, Mum.'

'Yes, yes, of course you did. Sorry. I'm not quite myself today.'

'Hardly surprising. Is that why you're in my room?' Izzie pointed towards her teddy bear. 'I hope Horace is treating you well.'

'He even brought me a mug of coffee.' Maggie raised her mug to the screen.

'Come on, Mum, why are you in with Horace?'

Sighing softly, Maggie confessed, 'I got a bit jumpy earlier – felt like I wasn't on my own in the house. Like someone might be hiding somewhere. I was alone, of course, but well . . . after all that happened, I needed to feel close to you for a while.'

'Oh, Mum.'

'I'm fine, really.' Maggie gave another brave smile. 'I'm glad you had time for a call, though.'

'I've always got time for you, Mum.'

Maggie chuckled. 'I'm supposed to say that sort of thing to you when you're having a bad day, not the other way around.'

'Works both ways.' Izzie hugged her knees tighter. 'I'm sorry I'm so far away.'

'As long as you're happy and having a good time, then how far away makes no difference.'

'But you're all on your own and—'

Maggie interrupted. This was exactly what she hadn't wanted. 'Come on, love, I didn't phone so you'd feel guilty about not being here. Anyway, I'm not totally alone. Ryan's been brilliant.'

Izzie's eyebrows rose. 'Is he still around? I thought Mr R would have scared him off by now.'

'Not so far. He's doing the lunchtime shift as we speak.'

'Brave!'

'Now I know what his girlfriend is like, I have to say, I think Ryan would be able to cope with most things.'

'Ohhh . . .' Izzie shuffled closer to the screen. 'What's she like? Spill, Mother, spill!'

'To be fair, I don't know her, but the way Bea's treated Ryan . . . Let's just say she hasn't endeared herself to me. I'm telling myself I shouldn't judge her until I've got to know her, but I've always had a few issues with poor little rich girls.'

Izzie pulled a face. 'I take it that Ryan isn't from the sort of family that her parents would approve of.'

'You've got it.' Maggie wavered. 'Actually, I'm being unfair. Bea did fly back from her holiday when I told her Ryan was in trouble.'

'Sod being fair, what do you really think?'

Maggie grinned. 'That Ryan was a pet project for her at uni – like *My Fair Lady* in reverse.'

'My Fair Lad.' Izzie chuckled.

'Exactly. But the reality of life has hit her, and him. Hopefully, Bea will go back to her tour of Portugal soon. Ryan deserves better.'

'Well, I'm glad he's been there for you.' Izzie paused. 'I think you should ask Ryan to move in with you until all this business is sorted.'

'Move in?'

'Yeah – keep up, Mum. Ryan could have my room – although you'd need to take care of Horace for me.' She waved at the teddy bear that was now sitting on her mum's lap. 'Perhaps he could sleep in with you while Ryan's there. I'd feel much happier knowing you weren't alone until Tania's killer's caught, and I'm sure Ryan'd like to escape Mr R's clutches for a while.'

Not at all sure Ryan would want to give up living in his bachelor pad, Maggie was glad Izzie had suggested it. 'I'll ask him.'

'Good.' Izzie relaxed back against her headboard.

'Actually, Ryan stayed the other day, but he slept on the sofa. I couldn't let him use your room without asking you first.'

'I wouldn't have minded, Mum, but thanks.' Izzie smiled. 'Poor guy, that sofa is so uncomfortable to lie on.'

'It needs replacing, but with me here on my own, I only remember it needs doing when I'm sat on it. As soon as I get up again, I forget!'

Izzie shook her head, sending a cascade of hair tumbling around her shoulders. 'When I'm home we'll go sofa shopping.'

'I'll get saving.'

'You need to set up as a proper detective agency, and then you'll be raking it in. New armchair *and* sofa!'

'As if!'

'So defeatist, Mother! Come on, tell me all about the case.'

'Izzie, I'm not investigating anymore. I promised the police I'd leave it to them.'

'Rubbish! You can't stop now! Tell me everything!'

\*

Ryan had half expected his knock on Maggie's front door to be ignored because she was fast asleep. But the door was soon swung open.

'Ryan. Why didn't you use the key?'

'I didn't like to – not with you home.'

'That's very considerate, but you can use it anytime. Just shout as you come in, so you don't make me jump.'

'Gotcha.'

'Anyway, your timing is perfect, I was about to put the kettle on. Cuppa?'

'Please.' He followed her into the hall. 'You look much better.'

'Nothing but a mild headache and hurt pride now.' Maggie headed to the kitchen. 'I've just called the distillery in town.'

'What for? And for that matter, what distillery?'

Clicking on the kettle, Maggie ran a hand over her forehead. 'Things that happened before I went to Toby's office have been slowly coming back to me. Heidi and Daisy said that on the day of the murder they went shopping with Tania, while Toby and Hugh went to the Pocketful of Stones distillery in Penzance – I wanted to make sure they actually went.'

'Why?' Ryan passed her two mugs from the cup rack. 'If it was before the murder?'

'Because Hugh said he didn't see Toby in person after the car crash, apart from in the foyer of the hotel before he and Tania went for their ill-fated meal at The Mariner.'

'You didn't believe him.'

'I was uncertain, but I was wrong to be suspicious in this case. The visit was cancelled, so Hugh wouldn't have seen Toby there.'

'I take it that Tania and co. did not know about the cancellation?' Ryan fetched the milk from the fridge.

'Heidi and Daisy talked as if the visit had taken place. Perhaps the men didn't want to upset Tania. The wedding was still on, and, as far as we know, Toby and Tania had made up after the crashed car issue. Why worry the bride unnecessarily?'

Ryan thought, before asking, 'How come the people at the distillery gave you private information like that?'

Maggie blushed. 'I pretended I was Hugh's mum wanting to know if there was a gin he'd liked above the others, with a mind to buying him some for his birthday.'

'Now, that is sneaky.'

Maggie's smile dimmed. 'It doesn't tell us anything other than Hugh and Toby didn't go to the distillery, though. I wish I could remember more about being in the office. I should have been paying more attention.'

'There's no way you could've known you were going to be hit on the head.'

'True, but I was trespassing while investigating a murder – honestly, I've seen enough detective shows to know how it goes. It was almost textbook cliché.' As she set about making their tea, she asked, 'Have you seen any more of the police?'

'No, thank goodness. It's bad enough having Mr Robbins breathing down my neck, without Peters and Houseman as well.'

Maggie looked surprised. 'Hasn't Mr Robbins been letting you get on with it on your own?'

'No. Every few minutes he was peering around the door, checking on me.'

'That's not like him.' Putting the mugs on the table, Maggie gestured for Ryan to join her. 'I wonder if it's you he's checking on.'

'Who else could it have been? I was the only one there.'

'No, I meant, could he have been popping in and out of the shop so often to make sure the police aren't watching the chippy?'

'Now you come to mention it, he did seem rather jumpy.' Ryan sat down. 'If that's the case, then what's he afraid of them discovering?'

'Probably nothing.' Maggie smiled. 'I've been chatting to Izzie. She remains convinced he's a crime baron.'

'Not hard to see why. He certainly looks the part.'

Maggie dipped her head to one side. 'Anyway, forget Mr Robbins, how are you?'

'Me? You're the one who was attacked.'

'And you're the one that spent a night in a cell and then had Bea to deal with.' Maggie paused, 'Sorry about that again. I was trying to help. You don't seem close to your parents, so . . .'

Seeing that Maggie was struggling with what to say, Ryan stepped in. 'It was a kind thing to do. And I'm glad you did it.'

'But Bea isn't glad, is she?'

'Not so that you'd notice.' His forehead creased. 'Rather than being concerned about me, she made a big deal of how lucky I was that she had a friend in the right place at the right time who was planning to fly here in his private plane anyway!'

'I wondered how she got here so fast.'

'She can be kind. She was nice to me once she'd stopped sulking, but well . . . when I was in the station, I realised I was glad she wasn't around. Can you imagine the fuss she'd have made? And if I wasn't wishing Bea was there supporting me then . . .'

Maggie gave Ryan a bolstering smile.

'If she hadn't turned up and been all "Bea" about the situation, I'd probably have convinced myself I only felt like that in the station because I was frightened, but now I've seen her, I know for sure. Bea isn't for me, and I'm not for her.'

Maggie picked up her tea, a flicker of sadness passing over her face. 'Does this mean you'll be leaving?'

'Leaving?'

'Going back to Birmingham.'

'No. I don't know.' Ryan stared at the table before them. 'I suppose, once the summer job at the chippy is over, I'll have to move on, but I'd quite like to stay and find out what happened to Tania.'

'Good.' The relief in Maggie's voice was obvious as she opened her notebook. 'Izzie and I have been chatting. We wondered – only if you want to – but the offer's there, so . . .'

'What offer?'

'You could stay here, in Izzie's room. I will quite understand if you'd rather not. It's nice to have your own space, and it's a good bedsit, and . . .'

'I'd love to.'

'Really?'

'Definitely.' Ryan gave her a shy smile. 'Working with Mr Robbins is one thing, but having to pass him in that flipping chair each time I go in and out . . . I know he has his campervan to kip in, but he doesn't leave until really late. He's always in the office when I go to bed and when I come down in the mornings. Sometimes I swear he sits there all night.'

'I wouldn't be surprised.' Maggie got up, grinning. 'Come and see Izzie's room – well, your room until she comes back.' She hesitated. 'I'll need her to have it when she's in the country. Will that be alright?'

'Totally.' Ryan followed her towards Izzie's room. 'You're sure Izzie doesn't mind?'

'It was her idea.'

'She probably doesn't want you to be on your own after what happened.'

Maggie confessed, 'That's true, but that isn't why I'm asking. I enjoy your company. It'd be nice to have you around.'

'Then – thank you. I'd really like to live here.' Ryan paused, before asking tentatively, 'How much rent will you charge? I am happy to pay, obviously, but—'

Maggie went to shake her head, but interrupted him instead. 'No rent.'

'But Maggie . . .'

'*No* rent. You'll be doing me a favour. I don't fancy being on my own right now.' Looking a little embarrassed, Maggie mumbled, 'Don't tell Sergeant Peters, but I was really freaked out in that office. I keep thinking someone will break in here, and . . .'

'They won't.' Ryan peered around the area, as if already checking for intruders.

Maggie added, 'And we get on well, so how about we take it in turns to buy the weekly food shop instead of rent money?'

'Are you absolutely sure?'

'One hundred per cent.'

'Then, thanks. That sounds perfect. I think I'll keep the bedsit on, though. That way, I'll have somewhere to go when Izzie's home, and we'll have somewhere we can do all this.'

'Do all what?'

'Investigate. There's room to pin the map to the wall and lay everything out on the bed. Plus, we'd have access to everything from work, and you can have your table back.'

'That's a great idea.' Maggie beamed. 'I can't wait to tell Izzie. She told me again today that I should start a detective agency.'

'It's a good idea. You have helped the police – albeit in a roundabout way.'

'*We* have – not just me.'

Ryan swigged down his coffee and stood up straight, experiencing a sense of purpose he hadn't felt in a very long time. 'I want to know who hurt you. In fact, I'm going to talk to the person at the garage right now – the one you saw working there. I want to know why they didn't help you.'

# Chapter Twenty-nine

'They'd never have heard anything over the machine they were using.' Maggie clutched her notebook to her chest.

'Possibly, but they might have seen someone hanging around.'

'True.' Maggie stood up. 'There's just time to get over there before we start work.'

'Oh, no you don't.' Ryan placed a hand on her shoulder and firmly pressed her back onto her seat. 'You're not working this evening, and you are resting here for the remainder of the afternoon.'

'I'm not. I'm fine. The doctor said so.'

'Maggie! You were hit on the head so hard that you had to stay in the hospital overnight. When the police arrest this person, they could go to prison for what they did to you alone, never mind the fact that they've murdered someone.'

'If it was the same person.'

'You think it might not be?'

'No idea, but I think we should keep all options open. I also think—' Maggie pushed her notebook into her handbag '—that two heads are better than one. I'm coming to the garage with you, because the last thing I need is to be sat here worrying about you going there alone!'

*

Ignoring the latest text to arrive from Bea asking to see him, Ryan climbed out of the taxi, grumbling, 'I'm saving up for a car. This is ridiculous.'

'Calling a cab isn't ideal for a quick getaway if we need one, that's for sure.' Maggie joined her young friend on the pavement.

As they stood outside Mount View Garage, the sunlight temporarily shrouded in cloud, the place had the same air of desertion as it had had before. The only sign that anything out of the ordinary had happened was a short length of police tape across the door at the top of the steps. A door which was firmly closed.

'If there's anyone here, then they'll be around the back.' Maggie strode forwards confidently. 'That's where the workshop is.'

Suddenly nervous, Ryan fought the rise of anxiety in his chest. 'I expect the police have already spoken to the people who work here.'

'I'm sure they have—' Maggie walked faster '—but they weren't the one hit on the head. It's not illegal to ask questions.'

\*

Unlike on her first visit to the garage, there was no sound of machinery in operation. Rounding the side of the building, Maggie slowed as they reached the spot where she'd previously peered around, unseen. 'The sports car that was all written off. It was over there.' She pointed to a spot a few metres from the closed workshop. 'It's not there now.'

'You think it was the one Hugh crashed.'

'I'm convinced of it.'

'Did you tell Sergeant Peters about seeing it?'

'No.' Maggie kept her eyes on the space where the ruined car had been. 'I forgot. Although, I suspect he'll think I withheld the information on purpose.'

'He seems to like you.'

'Ummm...' Maggie muttered, 'Inspector Houseman doesn't.'

'Nor me.' Ryan ran his gaze across the working space before them. 'She's probably just terribly professional and doesn't do liking or disliking when she's on duty.'

'Possibly.' Maggie took a step forwards.

Passing the car she'd seen being polished on her last visit and a recently arrived VW campervan, she aimed for the large double doors that, when open, would provide space in which to work. The sound of gulls cawing overhead was underscored by the faint hum of the sea and the rumble of traffic passing along Green Lane.

'It's quiet for a garage.' Ryan surveyed the scene. 'Whenever my dad takes his car in for a service, it's always buzzing. There's usually more work than the mechanics can handle. I know this is a town and not a city, but even so...'

Maggie couldn't help but agree. 'Perhaps they close on Fridays.'

Ryan's phone was already out of his pocket, and he tapped in their location, quickly bringing Mount View Garage up on Google Maps. 'Nope, says here they are open every day bar Sunday.'

'Do they have a website?'

'Yup.' Ryan was ahead of her. 'They specialise in vintage cars and campervans.'

'That would explain the van out the back and the car I saw being worked on. It also adds weight to my theory that the owner, or someone who works here, is the friend Toby called to remove his car after Hugh's crash.'

'Maybe Mr Robbins uses this place to service his campervan.'

'I'll ask him later.' Maggie moved past the closed metal shutter doors until they came to a reception-style office. Peering inside, she quickly stepped back, almost standing on Ryan's feet in the process. All the colour drained from her face. 'There's someone in there. A man.'

Whispering, Ryan said, 'Are you alright?'

'Yeah,' Maggie swallowed, making herself move forward. 'If I can't knock on the door and talk to a potential witness, then I might as well do what David tells me and stick to serving chips.'

★

The office was bigger than it had appeared to be from the outside. They were led inside by a fit-looking, fair-haired young man in a grey boiler suit, who offered them seats at his desk.

'How can I help? If it's a service or MOT you're after, I'm afraid I'm booked up until September.'

Maggie surveyed her surroundings. 'Business is booming, then.'

'Can't grumble. I've had to stop work on the actual mechanics to catch up on the paperwork today. If it *was* a service you were requiring . . .'

Ryan shook his head. 'No, thank you. We've not come about a vehicle.'

A cloud crossed the young man's face. 'Then, I'm not sure how I can help.'

Mindful of the abrupt change in the mechanic's demeanour, Maggie spoke fast. 'You will know of the incident that happened in the flat above here.'

'Of course. The police came.'

'I was the person who was attacked.'

His eyes widened. 'You were? Are you alright?'

'If I keep taking the paracetamol I am.' Maggie smiled. 'I wanted to apologise to you.'

'Apologise?'

Ryan glanced from Maggie to the mechanic, trying (and failing) to hide his surprise.

'I shouldn't have gone in upstairs when I saw the door to the office open. I should have come and asked you if you knew where Mr Marrell or Miss Zimmerman were, Mr . . .?'

'Taylor. Simon Taylor.' Pressing a few keys on the laptop in front of him, the mechanic closed the lid of his laptop. 'To be honest, Mrs . . .'

'Maggie, I'm just Maggie.'

'To be honest, Maggie, I probably wouldn't have noticed if you had come to see me. I was working on a rush job to take out a dent on a vintage car that was wanted as a wedding car tomorrow. I had the machine going and noise-cancelling headphones on. War could have broken out and I wouldn't have noticed.'

'I saw you before I noticed the office door was open upstairs, but I didn't like to disturb you in case I took you by surprise and you hurt yourself.'

'You came to the back of the garage?'

'Yes.'

'Uh-huh.' He picked up his mobile and swapped it from hand to hand. 'I hadn't realised. Sorry.'

'Not at all.'

Ryan stepped in. 'Did you see Mr Marrell yesterday?'

'I haven't seen him since his car was written off. He was cut up as all hell.' Simon got up and pointed to a small drink-making area at the side of the room. 'I'm parched. Cup of tea?'

Both guests nodded as Maggie said, 'Have you spoken to him since, then?'

'Toby called me on the Sunday.' Busying himself with the drinks, Simon said, 'I forget the date now.'

'Eighth of June.' Maggie went on. 'The day Toby's car was in a crash, and you came to tow it away.'

Simon visibly tensed as Ryan jumped in, 'My girlfriend was a friend of Tania's, so we heard about how Hugh crashed the car from her. She also said everyone is worried about Toby – no one seems to know where he is. Do you have any idea where he might be?'

Maggie was impressed with Ryan's white lie; maybe they were good detectives after all.

'Afraid not.' Simon relaxed as he poured boiling water into three mugs. 'Toby called me after the crash. He was in a right state.'

'Why call you and not the AA or RAC?'

'I've always looked after his car, so it was natural to call me. He works on my doorstep after all.' Simon rolled up his sleeves, revealing two muscular arms. 'He told me his friend Hugh had borrowed his car and smashed it into a hedge, which had been hiding a stone wall. Totally wrote it off. Bloody miracle no one was killed.' Using the wrong end of a dessert spoon to extract the teabags from each mug, he added, 'It's just as well no one else was involved, as Hugh wouldn't have wanted the police to question him about the crash.'

'Really?'

'Yeah. He lost his licence some time back. Dangerous driving.'

Maggie accepted her mug of tea. 'I was told that Hugh hadn't got a car of his own because he lived in London and it wasn't practical, not because he wasn't allowed to drive.'

'No one knew until Sunday. I only know because Toby told me about it on the drive back to the garage after I'd retrieved the car. He was furious – so was Tania. After the crash, Hugh had no choice but to tell her about his ban. She wanted to call the police there and then.'

Ryan flexed his long legs out under the desk. 'She wanted to report Hugh?'

'She did, but Toby didn't want that to happen, as it would have probably meant Hugh going to prison.' Simon sighed. 'Although, I doubt Toby would ever have let Hugh anywhere near his pride and joy if he'd known.'

'What was the car worth?'

'Just shy of eighty thousand pounds.'

'Wow!' Ryan's mouth dropped open. 'No wonder Toby and Hugh fell out.'

'Especially as Tania was in the car and could have been killed. Friend or not, I'd have been tempted to report Hugh anyway.' Maggie watched the mechanic carefully. 'I got the impression that Toby was as in love with his car as he was with his future wife.'

Simon turned back to the drink-making area and picked up the other two mugs. 'It's often the way with car enthusiasts. We can be guilty of putting them before our loved ones.'

Maggie tried to make her question sound casual. 'You think my feeling was right then? Toby did love his car more than Tania.'

'Not more, but possibly equally. I did regular mechanical checks for Toby – his was the sort of vehicle that needed looking after. We'd chat a bit when I did them, but only about cars. I know Toby had always wanted an E-Type Jag. He was so proud of that car. Had saved up for it since he learnt to drive, before then, even.'

'I don't know a great deal about cars. I'm assuming it was a sought-after model?'

'Collector's item. Indigo blue with beige leather and wire wheels. It hadn't got a scratch on it. She was perfect.' Retrieving a packet of ginger nuts from his desk drawer, Simon offered them across the desk. 'Heartbreaking. I had her towed to the scrapyard this morning.'

'How did Toby take that?'

'No idea. I mean, he knew that would have to happen, but I've not heard from him since I sent a text telling him that if he wanted to say goodbye to Sandy, he'd need to be here by seven this morning.'

'Sandy?' Ryan crunched into his biscuit.

'Toby's name for the car.'

'I see.' Maggie would never understand people who treated their cars like they were people. 'And Toby didn't come to see her off?'

'No. I've not seen him since he lost Sandy.' Simon blew across the top of his tea. 'Can I ask why you're so interested?'

Using the same line she'd used on Heidi and Daisy, Maggie said, 'We're helping the police find out what happened to Tania.'

'Ah, poor guy – losing both loves of his life in the space of two days.' He shook his head. 'Is that why you were upstairs yesterday?'

'I was searching for a clue as to where Toby might be. Would you say he had a routine at all?'

'Like I said to the sergeant last night, I didn't have anything to do with the office. They rent the space from me via direct debit every month, regular as clockwork. Unless Toby wanted to drool over a car I had for sale, or needed anything done to Sandy, he kept things separate.'

'You aren't friends, then?'

'We're friendly, like I said, but I'd say we are more acquaintances with a mutual love of cars than proper friends.'

Maggie nodded. 'What's Toby's co-worker like, Miss Zimmerman?'

'Rachel? Yeah, she's okay. Bit difficult. You know.'

'Not really, Mr Taylor.' Maggie took a swig of tea.

'Simon, please. Rachel – I'd say she was a bit . . . superior. A year or two older than Toby and very much the executive businesswoman. I've always wondered why she's here rather than living the life in London.'

'Not a local, then?' Ryan asked.

'No, but not from the Midlands like you. She speaks proper Queen's English – or should that be King's English now?'

Maggie smiled. 'What's her role in the company? The sign on the office door suggests that they're partners.'

'It's Toby's business, but I think Rachel considers herself a partner. He treats her like one. She does a lot of the travelling, meetings abroad and stuff.'

'Sourcing the furniture they are going to import, you mean?' Ryan asked.

'I think so. I've never actually asked. I believe she's away at the moment.'

'Would you say she was the face of the business, then?'

'I've never really thought about it.' The mobile on the desk rang, and Simon excused himself to take the call outside.

Ryan lowered his voice. 'Hugh hasn't got a driving licence.'

'Kept that quiet, didn't he?'

'Not surprising.' Ryan watched Simon as he continued to chat on the phone outside the office. 'Do you think the girls know?'

'Possibly not.' Maggie shrugged. 'They didn't say so when I asked about it. Just that there had been an accident and Toby had got it sorted.'

'If Tania had been killed in the crash, then I wouldn't have met her in the pub, and you wouldn't have been hit on the head.'

'A thought that makes me want to talk to Hugh again. What if he had intended for Tania to die then, and when that didn't happen, he tried again?' Maggie whispered as she got up. 'As soon as Simon's off the phone, we'll go. He's already been more helpful than I imagined he would be.'

'Likewise. You don't think he's involved?'

'If he is, I can't see how.' Maggie looked up at the mechanic as he returned to the office. 'We'll leave you in peace, Simon. Just one more question before we go. Did you tell the police about Hugh having lost his licence?'

Simon paled. 'No. No, I didn't. I promised Toby I wouldn't. Hugh is his best friend, after all.'

'But you told us?'

Rubbing an oil-stained hand across his face Simon said, 'I didn't feel good about not telling Sergeant Peters. In my opinion, Hugh shouldn't be allowed behind any sort of wheel ever again.'

# Chapter Thirty

'Let's get the bus back.' Maggie inhaled a lungful of sea air.

'Won't we be cutting it fine for prepping before opening the chippy if we don't get a cab?'

'We'll only be a few minutes late. With both of us working fast, we'll manage. I can't afford to keep getting cabs, and I doubt you can either. I'll text Mr Robbins and tell him we're on the way.' Maggie reached for her phone.

'Are you sure he won't mind?'

'Oh, he'll definitely mind, Ryan, but if he makes a fuss, I'll tell him it's in a good cause.'

'Good cause?'

'Keeping the police away from his chip shop.'

Ryan smiled. 'The more I think about it, the more I think Izzie is right. I don't mean about him being a mafia boss, but Mr Robbins definitely has the air of a man with a past he'd rather keep to himself.'

'Izzie was all for investigating him when she worked in the shop last summer, but I persuaded her not to.'

'Really?' Ryan was surprised. 'Aren't you dying to dive in to discover what he's up to?'

Maggie laughed. 'Mr Robbins is a rough old soul, but he's never unkind, and if I did uncover something unsavoury about him, what would happen to the chippy? What about my job – and your job too, now?'

'Good point.' Ryan stepped to the side to avoid a jogger passing on the pavement. 'I would like to know what he reads on that tablet all day, though.'

'I almost caught a glimpse of the screen once, but just as I was close enough to make things out, he folded the cover shut, and the mystery was preserved.'

Ryan chuckled. 'Perhaps it's nothing. Perhaps Mr Robbins simply enjoys a bit of subterfuge.'

'That wouldn't surprise me.' The glow of the sun warmed Maggie's face as they reached the bus stop, more therapeutic than any amount of painkillers. 'Talking of subterfuge, if you're alright with it, I might not stay to work this evening once we're set up.'

Ryan looked at her. 'You got a headache again?'

'No, but our esteemed employer doesn't know that, does he?'

The concern was evident in Ryan's voice as he asked, 'Are you sure you should be investigating on your own after what happened? In fact, shouldn't you just go home to bed?'

'I'll be fine.' Maggie gave Ryan a reassuring pat on the back as the bus drew up to the kerb. 'As I have a good excuse not to work this evening, I'd be foolish not to make use of it. I know it'll be busy, but Mr Robbins will help you. Plus, you have brownie points to accrue after your visit to a police cell.'

'Don't remind me!' Ryan shuddered as they boarded the bus and sat down. Lowering his voice, he murmured, 'Although the cell was cleaner than I imagined it might be. I was on my own in there, thank God, and there was no graffiti on the walls. All very sterile.'

'I've never had the pleasure.'

'Hopefully you never will.' Ryan checked to make sure none of the passengers were listening. 'What will you do this evening? Go through our notes and plan what we should do next?'

'Actually, I thought I'd go back to the hotel to talk to Hugh.'

'No.'

Maggie was taken aback by Ryan's blunt response. 'I really think . . .'

'Hugh wrote off Toby's car with Tania *in it*.'

'And I want to know why he was prepared to drive without a licence – especially with a passenger.'

'So do I, but you said it yourself just now – what if the reason for his reckless behaviour was that he had already decided to kill Tania for some reason?'

'I've been thinking about that – it's a non-starter as a method of murder. The car is a very unreliable choice of murder weapon.' Maggie stared out of the bus's window as she considered what Ryan was suggesting. 'Plus, he could have been killed himself.'

'What if there was a reason why he'd want to do that?' Ryan persisted. 'We know very little about any of these people.'

'Then it's about time we found out more.' Checking to make sure they weren't being overheard, she added, 'Hugh was not in a good place when I saw him. If he was thinking along those lines, he might have acted on it by now. Or, he might have been so shaken by the near miss with the car that he realised he didn't want to end it all but still needed to get rid of Tania.'

Ryan muttered quietly, 'If Hugh has decided he has nothing to lose, that makes him even more dangerous.'

'*If* he's the killer. He might not be. Plus, we don't know where Toby is. Hugh might have heard from him by now.'

Ryan repeated, 'I'm not happy about you going. Especially not alone.'

'Duly noted.'

As Ryan lapsed into silence, Maggie ventured, 'That was good thinking back there, you saying to Simon Taylor that you were connected to Hugh and crew via Bea.'

'I thought it would be wise to explain our knowledge about the case without showing how much we've been investigating.'

Maggie grinned. 'You're good at this.'

'So are you, but at the risk of sounding like the boring adult in this partnership, we need to be more careful. I can't stop thinking about how I felt when I saw Sergeant Peters helping you into his car. You were "all washed out", as my Gran would have said. You've been good to me ... I ...' Ryan stopped mid-sentence. 'If you'd been hit any harder ...'

Nausea swam in Maggie's stomach, but she battled it down. 'Bit of a baptism of fire. Miss Marple never had to deal with anything like that.'

'True.' Ryan sighed through his smile. 'But then, Miss Marple wasn't real.'

★

As soon as they turned the corner and saw the chippy in the distance, they knew something wasn't right.

'Why aren't the lights on?' Ryan sped up, with Maggie hot on his heels.

She was already fishing her shop key from her bag as they got to the door. Although there was ten minutes until opening time, there was no sign of Mr Robbins setting up the shop. 'The fryers should be on by now.'

'Has he ever opened late before?'

Maggie shook her head as she put her hand on the door. It was already unlocked. 'That's not good.'

'Did he reply to your text saying we might be a bit late?' Ryan entered the shop, half expecting someone to jump out on them as Maggie checked her phone.

'No. No, he didn't.'

'This feels wrong.' Ryan stopped just before the counter. All he could hear was the hum of the freezer and refrigerators and the beat of his own heart.

Maggie locked the door behind them, before calling out, 'Mr Robbins!'

When no reply came, Ryan put a hand on Maggie's arm. 'If someone who shouldn't be here is here, then we've just locked ourselves in with them.'

'Good. Then we'll find out who they are.' Maggie pushed her shoulders back. 'I'll go into the office first.'

'No, you will not.' Sounding braver than he felt, Ryan said, 'You don't need another bash on the head.'

Hesitating, Maggie whispered, 'Okay, we'll go together. Let's put the lights on.'

'Should we?'

'Of course we should. I never understand why they don't on the telly. So much easier when you can see what you're doing.'

As the overhead strip lights enhanced the late afternoon sunlight coming through the shop window, they went into the office.

'Oh.' Maggie stopped moving as they came face to face with Mr Robbins' orange chair.

It was empty.

'Where is he?'

'I've no idea, but in all the years I've worked here, he has never been absent during working hours. Not once. Not even a holiday.'

'Well, there's no one here.' Unease crept up Ryan's spine. 'What do we do?'

'I'm going to call his mobile, and you are going to get the fryers on.'

\*

Grateful that the first few customers through the doors were regulars, and so accepted with stoic grace that they'd have a twenty-minute wait if they wanted fish with their chips, Ryan and Maggie soon had the shop up and running.

Relieved that circumstances meant Maggie couldn't disappear to the hotel to find Hugh, Ryan watched her from the corner of his eye as they worked. While she was happily chatting to the customers, there was no doubt she wasn't her usual self. Every now and then, Maggie would wince with what he suspected was an intense headache. As the clock ticked towards half-past eight, and the flow of customers slowed, Ryan gestured towards the office door.

'I don't suppose the boss has replied to your message?'

'Nothing.' Maggie checked her mobile, which she'd left open near the sink, just in case Mr Robbins should ring.

'I think you should have a rest.' Ryan said as he saw Maggie attempt to stifle a yawn.

'I'm fine.'

Not convinced, he asked, 'When are you allowed your next painkillers?'

'About now, actually.'

Ryan adjusted the temperature on the fryers. 'Go through to the office and take them. You might as well put your feet up at the same time. It's quiet in here now. I can manage.'

'I know you can. You're a natural at this too.'

Unaccustomed to praise, Ryan felt a smile grow inside him and a blush form on his face. 'I like it. I hadn't seen a life as a chip server ahead of me, but I can think of worse jobs.' He turned to the giant chip pan. 'Although the smell can get a bit much.'

'Can't argue with that.' Maggie's grin dissolved. 'Do you think I should tell the police that Mr Robbins is missing?'

'I don't think he'd like that. Anyway, we don't know if he's missing. He could be in his campervan with a phone that needs charging.'

'True.' Maggie looked pained.

'Do you know where the campervan is?'

'Newlyn. At the edge of a bit of scrubland near the harbour. As far as I know, it's been in the same place for years.'

'If he isn't here by closing time, we'll go and see if he's okay.' Ryan took off his boater to let some air get to his hair.

'Good idea. He wouldn't want us fussing, but I'll never sleep if we don't check on him.' Maggie looked towards the office door. 'I had rather hoped we'd have the chance to nip up to your bedsit and consider how we might use it as our operations room.'

'Anyone ever told you that you are unstoppable?'

'Often.'

Pausing to serve two teenagers who came in for a cone of chips and a can of Coke apiece, Ryan decided he needed to take charge. 'Forget going to sit in the office for a bit; why don't you head up to the bedsit? The bed is made, and the sheets are clean. You could take a nap.'

'Clean sheets?' The surprise in Maggie's voice was obvious.

'I do tidy up sometimes, you know.'

'Is that so?'

Ryan laughed. 'I shoved almost everything into the washing machine as soon as I got back from Bea's flat. After being in the police cell, I felt a need for everything to be properly clean.'

'Makes sense.'

'Go on. Take a break. I promise to call if Mr Robbins comes back or if it gets busy.'

'I really wanted to go and talk to Hugh tonight. That young man has a lot of explaining to do.'

'He does, but he can explain tomorrow. Go on. The doctor said to rest, and you've done precious little of that since you were discharged.'

Maggie gave in gracefully. 'Thanks, Ryan.'

'No problem.'

Pleased that he'd been able to do something to help Maggie rather than the other way around, Ryan was about to batter the last couple of sausages of the night when the sound of feet running back down the bedsit stairs sent him flying to the office door.

'He's upstairs!'

Ryan frowned, his brain taking a few seconds to catch up with events. 'Mr Robbins is in the bedsit?'

'Spark out on your bed.'

'What?!'

Maggie sat down with a heavy thump in the orange chair. 'I think he's been knocked out.'

# Chapter Thirty-one

The sickening vulnerability that had come over Maggie on finding Mr Robbins lying on the bed, his arm hanging off the side, so soon after the attack she'd sustained, was making her shake.

*Was that meant for Ryan?*

Having checked he was breathing steadily and that there was no blood, her need to flee the scene had got the better of her; she'd left the bedsit three times faster than she'd gone into it. Then, picking up her mobile to call for an ambulance, Maggie had hesitated. An ambulance would automatically mean the police would be informed, and Mr Robbins would not thank her for that.

An image of Izzie came to mind, and, along with it, her conviction that Mr Robbins had a ne'er-do-well past. *Perhaps this is nothing to do with us ... maybe Mr Robbins' history has chosen this moment to catch up with him.*

Sitting in her boss's orange chair, Maggie listened to Ryan chatting to the customer. Guilt and fear swirled in her stomach. *No ... it would be too much of a coincidence for this not to relate to the case ... I shouldn't be dragging Ryan into this. I could have been killed, and so could Mr Robbins.*

Even as she had the thought, however, Maggie's usual common sense nudged her. *But we weren't. We could have been stabbed or bludgeoned to death ... These were warnings to leave things alone.*

Forcing herself to her feet, Maggie filled a glass with water from the office sink and threw a couple of painkillers down her throat.

*Mr Robbins is nothing like Ryan ... only someone who hasn't met Ryan or Mr Robbins could make that mistake.*

A new voice wafted in through the shop into the office, telling Maggie another customer had arrived to collect a late fish supper.

*Unless ... whoever it was didn't turn the light on, and Mr Robbins was asleep on the bed already ... The blackout curtains were down, so it was dark. All they'd have seen is a lump on the bed. It doesn't make sense ...*

Closing her eyes, Maggie tried to calm her mind.

*Anyone local could have known that Ryan works here, but how many people know that he rents upstairs?*

'Someone who didn't know that Mr Robbins camps out here virtually full time,' she muttered as she took a swig of water. 'But why was Mr Robbins upstairs?'

Ryan peered around the door. 'Are you talking to me, Maggie? Sorry, I couldn't hear you properly from the counter.'

'Talking to myself. Been trying to get things straight in my head.'

'Me too.' Ryan glanced over his shoulder to make sure no one had come through the open shop door. 'Why was Mr Robbins in my bedsit in the first place?'

'That's what I was wondering.'

'And,' Ryan removed his boater, 'how did whoever it was get in? The shop door is always locked when we're closed. Mr Robbins must have opened the door to them.'

'We don't know how long ago this happened. What if he was in the shop setting up for us with the door open? It's been a warm day, and it's always hot in there. He might have needed some air.'

'Possible,' Ryan did not look convinced, 'but Mr Robbins didn't answer when you texted to ask him to set up because we'd be late.'

'True. Although he might not have bothered to reply and got on with it. Or not looked at his phone.

'Either way, Mr Robbins let his attacker in, which means he knew them. I'm going to check he's alright. If he isn't showing signs of coming round, I'm going to call an ambulance and worry about whether he'd like that or not later.'

'Sensible.' Ryan swallowed. 'Whoever did this was after me, weren't they?'

'I suspect so. Someone wants us to leave well alone.'

Ryan gave a sardonic grin. 'Then, maybe we should put Inspector Houseman at the top of our suspect list.'

*

An hour later, Mr Robbins was back in his chair. Seeing him there made life feel less like it had been tilted off its axis.

When Maggie had gone back upstairs to check on him, she'd found her employer in the process of sitting up, one giant palm holding the back of his head, the other pushing himself upright.

Dashing to his aid, Maggie slipped her arm under his elbow. In all the years she'd worked for him, this was the first time they'd had any sort of physical contact. He was far lighter than she'd expected for such a heavily built man.

Mr Robbins, having refused the offer of professional medical assistance and the chance to stay where he was until the world stopped swimming before his eyes, had allowed himself to be guided down the narrow dark stairwell. The moment he was back in his office, however, he'd levered himself out of Maggie's care and plummeted into his seat.

It was only once the chippy had closed for the night, and he'd knocked back far more painkillers than Maggie considered advisable in one go, especially as he washed them down with a shot of whisky, that he spoke. His opening line took them both by surprise.

'Did you kill that girl, Ryan?'

'No!' Ryan practically shouted. After he regained composure, he continued, 'I didn't, Mr Robbins. I swear.'

'Someone thinks you did.'

'Or someone thinks Ryan knows who did and wants to keep him quiet.' Maggie levelled her gaze on her employer. 'Did you see who attacked you?'

'No.' Mr Robbins kept his eyes on Ryan. 'I don't think it was her anyway.'

'Her?' Maggie asked.

A chubby finger pointed at Ryan. 'His girlfriend.'

'Bea?' Ryan paled. 'Bea came here?'

'Searching for you. Said she was worried you were getting involved in things. Didn't think you could handle it.'

His face going from ghost-white to red with embarrassment, Ryan muttered, 'What the hell would Bea know about what I can handle?'

'Ryan.' Maggie caught his eye. 'Maybe she wanted to say goodbye before flying back to Portugal.'

'Gets Paolo to fly her back, you mean. What was I doing with a woman who has a friend with his own plane? I can't even afford my own car.'

Mr Robbins stopped rubbing his head and gave Ryan a shrewd stare. 'His own plane?'

'Yeah.'

'Interesting.'

When it was clear that their employer wasn't about to expand on that comment, Maggie asked, 'When did Bea arrive?'

'About half-three. Wanted to see you.'

'I wasn't here.'

'Obviously.' Mr Robbins' jowls shook as he regarded his temporary member of staff. 'I said she should come back later, but she was . . .'

'Determined?' Maggie suggested.

'Yeah. She wanted to wait upstairs. Insisted.'

'Bea's good at insisting.' Ryan shuffled from one foot to the other. 'Can I ask why you went up with her?'

'Don't like people I don't know on my property.'

'You let me rent the bedsit, and you didn't know me.'

Mr Robbins gesticulated towards Maggie. 'She said you were alright.'

Surprised by this open show of trust in his workforce, Maggie looked at Ryan, who continued, 'So you escorted Bea upstairs. She wouldn't want to knock you out. She'd never have the strength anyway.'

'Too weedy,' his employer agreed. 'When I said I wasn't going to leave a stranger on my property alone, she stomped off.' Mr Robbins reached out for the tablet on the table and switched it on. 'Thought I'd do the inventory while I was there. Landlord thing.'

'Right.' Ryan ventured, 'Did Bea say anything when she left?'

'That she'd come back later.'

'Which she didn't.' Ryan sighed.

Maggie took over the conversation. 'So, Bea left, and you started your inventory. That would explain why the front door was unlocked.'

Mr Robbins, his eyes now back on his tablet, even though it was only showing a screensaver of the sea, grumbled, 'I hadn't intended to be up there long.'

'What happened?'

'I'd finished the inventory.' He pulled a crumpled piece of paper from his pocket and put it on the table.

'Then?' Maggie coaxed.

'I was by the bed. The sun was streaming in, so I pulled the curtains shut, keep things cool. Bedsit can get very hot – Bastard! Head hurts too much to look at the screen.'

'Are you sure you don't want me to call an ambulance?' Maggie asked for the third time.

Her employer's unblinking stare answered that question.

'Then you should go home and rest.' Maggie picked up her phone. 'I can call a cab.'

'Got one.'

'Sorry?'

'Regular driver. I'll call him in a minute.'

Wondering how she hadn't known Mr Robbins had a regular cab driver, Maggie returned them to the point. 'You closed the curtains. Then what happened?'

'Went dark. Blackout curtains. I was about to leave, so wasn't bothered about turning on the lights.'

'You didn't hear anyone come in?'

'Door was open, and the carpet is soft.'

Ryan jumped in. 'The stairs are noisy, though.'

For the first time, Maggie and Ryan saw a flash of discomfort cross Mr Robbins' face. He raised a hand slowly to his right ear. 'Hearing not so good these days. Getting old.'

Unnerved by the flash of vulnerability on her employer's face, Maggie peered nervously around the room. The idea that anyone could creep up on the seemingly indestructible man in the chair without being heard was more than a little unsettling.

Knowing her boss would not appreciate sympathy, Maggie asked, 'Male or female?'

Mr Robbins' gruff demeanour had already returned. 'Guessing male. I'm not easy to topple.'

'Definitely not Bea doubling back, then.'

Ryan turned to Maggie. 'Bea would never do something like that.'

'From what little I know, I think Bea is capable of pretty much anything she puts her mind to.' Maggie returned her attention to Mr Robbins. 'Anything else you remember?'

'It happened not long after Bea left. Ten minutes, maybe. Saw nothing. All I remember is falling forwards, and then you arriving.'

Maggie chewed the inside of her cheek as she pictured how she'd found him. 'You should tell the police.'

'No police.'

'It was probably the same person who hurt me.'

This caused Mr Robbins to growl. 'I don't like the police.'

'But you like Maggie. It would help her.' Ryan pressed the point.

When Mr Robbins didn't reply, Maggie suggested, 'How about I call David Peters? You can talk to him unofficially first.'

'He'd make it official.'

'Possibly.' Maggie relented as both men regarded her as if she was nuts. 'Okay, probably.'

'I'll think about it.' Mr Robbins lifted a hand off the table and pointed a finger at his companions in turn. 'Neither of you tell anyone else about this. *Ever.* Understood?'

Maggie and Ryan nodded quickly.

'Good.' Mr Robbins ran a hand over his forehead. It was hard to tell if his lived-in expression was creased in pain or not.

'A random question, but do you have your campervan serviced at Mount View Garage?'

'Used to, Maggie. Not in years, though. It doesn't move anymore.'

'Do you know Simon Taylor, then?' Maggie asked.

'I knew his father – the boy I haven't seen since he was at school. Why?'

'Just curious.' Maggie paused. 'What I want to know is, why would anyone want to hurt you, Ryan? All this is obviously connected to Tania's death, so we can assume –

I think – that it was the same person who hurt me. So they must think I discovered something when I was in Marazion.'

'Or . . .' Ryan glanced at Maggie. 'Or, perhaps they're afraid that Tania told me something when we were in the pub. Something that I might have told you.'

'Maybe . . . it could even have been something that Tania didn't actually know – but the killer suspected she knew and wouldn't want anyone else to know.' Maggie spoke slowly. 'Like the fact that Toby's business isn't all it seems.'

'I can't find it listed online, and yet he can afford a car worth eighty grand,' Ryan said. 'I know import and export work can be lucrative, but his friends gave me the impression it's a small operation – just him and one co-worker.'

'So he's living above his means . . . I want to know how.'

'Assuming we're right about that. Simon said Toby had saved hard for the car.' Ryan chewed on his lip. 'Let's face it, we've only been guessing so far. We don't know anything for sure, do we?'

Mr Robbins snorted. 'Then it's about time you did.'

# Chapter Thirty-two
## Saturday 14th June

Ryan climbed out of the back of the car. 'Yesterday's bang on the head must have affected Mr Robbins more than I thought.'

'Because he volunteered to set up the chippy this lunchtime, so we have an extra half an hour to try and find out who hit him?'

'Yeah. Must have taken a hell of a whack to topple him onto my bed.' Ryan hid a shudder. He hadn't mentioned to Maggie that the knowledge that he had probably been the intended victim of the attack had seriously shaken him, but guessed she must have known as she'd insisted he move in with her immediately.

'He's a big bloke, but I bet he's got a headache this morning. I do wish he'd gone to the hospital, just to be on the safe side.'

'I bet he didn't go in case word got round – not good for his tough guy persona.' Ryan gave a half smile. 'Nice of him to lend us his driver. I didn't know he had one.'

'Nor did I.' Maggie mused, 'I'm not used to him being nice. He's never *not* nice – but being helpful is a new development.'

As they stood on the pavement outside The Cabin Hotel, Maggie watched the nondescript dark blue Citroën they'd arrived in cruise out of sight. 'The driver was the same chap that drove me to the hotel when you were at the police station. He looked a lot like Mr Robbins, didn't he?'

'The back of his head did. He was even less chatty than his employer.'

'His brother, maybe?'

'Sensible car for a criminal.'

'Come on, Ryan, we don't know he's a criminal.'

Ryan crossed his arms. 'Don't you think it's silly on the television when a detective has a really noticeable car? I don't mean Morse with his Jaguar – he's a policeman. He's not hiding his presence. But private detectives with cars that stand out a mile – it's daft.'

Maggie laughed. 'I suppose Lou Shakespeare has a bright red Mini with a private number plate in *Shakespeare & Hathaway*.'

'Exactly! And Magnum had a bright red Ferrari! Subtle – not!'

'I tell you what, if we ever do this professionally – as well as *always* turning the lights on at a crime scene – as soon as we can afford a car, we'll get a really boring one and avoid the colour red.'

Ryan chuckled. 'Or we could ask Mr Robbins to find us one.'

'Sounds like a plan.' Perching on the seawall behind them, Maggie nodded towards the hotel across the road and the reason for their visit. 'It would be useful if you could record our conversation so we can listen to it later.'

'No way.' Not meaning to be so blunt, Ryan hastily added, 'Not after last time – I'm amazed I was allowed my phone back. Houseman was not amused at us trying to help. She gave me a lecture about people's right to privacy.'

'Fair enough. I should have thought. Sorry, Ryan.'

'Not at all – recording things is a good idea, and if it was any other case I would, but . . .'

'Understood.' Maggie changed the subject. 'Any more ideas re Toby?'

'He's my number one suspect. Although, I've not discounted Hugh either.' Ryan dug his hands into his jeans pockets. 'But we know for a fact that Toby was angry with Tania in the restaurant for questioning him, and that now she's dead he's gone AWOL.'

'Okay, so let's take Toby's behaviour as our conversational angle with Hugh. On the surface we'll say we want to talk to him about Toby's business – I want to know if he's living beyond his means, or if he really did save up for that car.'

'While trying to find out if he had a personal motive to kill Tania.'

'I'd also like to see if Hugh's surprised that we're both up and about, rather than lying in hospital beds with bandaged heads.' Maggie pushed herself away from the wall. 'If all else fails, then at least they sell good coffee in the lounge.'

\*

Maggie spotted the oversized rucksack and matching sports bag on the floor near the stairway to the first floor only seconds before she saw the tall athletic man talking to the receptionist.

Nudging Ryan, she whispered, 'That's Hugh Parkinson. He's checking out.'

'What do we do?'

'We offer to buy him a latte before he goes. And I'd like you to chat to the waiter, Jack. He may well have seen or heard something helpful.' Maggie was striding across the brightly patterned carpet before Ryan could ask any more questions. 'Mr Parkinson, looks like we've just caught you.'

'Oh.' Hugh spun around in surprise. 'You're the lady who bought me a coffee. Maggie, isn't it?'

'That's right. This is my business partner, Ryan. We wondered if you could spare us a minute?'

'I've just checked out.' Hugh flapped an arm towards his luggage.

Maggie smiled. 'That's great. It must mean the police are happy for you to return to London.'

'Not exactly. I just didn't want to stay here on my own any longer.'

'Toby's not back yet, then?' Maggie enquired.

'No.' Hugh grunted as the receptionist passed him a printout of his bill. 'I really do need to leave, so . . .'

Maggie nodded towards the receipt in his hand. 'I understood the bill for this stay was on Toby?'

'It was supposed to be, but he's not here, so I've had to pay for everyone.'

'Ouch. That's not good.' Ryan added.

'The money isn't an issue. It's the principle of the thing.'

Not being able to imagine how such a large amount of money couldn't be an issue, Maggie noticed how tired Hugh was looking. 'How about a coffee? There have been a few developments in the case that you might like to know about.'

'Developments?' He raked a hand through his hair. 'The police haven't said anything.'

Maggie watched the door, as if expecting a squad car to pull up outside. 'I'm sure they'll be here to do so later, but as you won't be here . . .'

'Alright.' Hugh made a point of looking at his smartwatch. 'It'll have to be quick, though.'

'Got a train to catch?' Ryan asked.

Not answering, Hugh grabbed his luggage and strode into the coffee lounge, sitting down with a manner that was only just short of begrudging. 'These developments then, what are they?'

'Do you know where Toby is, Mr Parkinson?'

'That isn't a development; it's a question.'

'An important one,' Maggie stressed as the waiter approached the table. 'Hello again, Jack. Three lattes, please.'

As soon as the waiter had gone, Maggie added, 'The longer Toby is missing, the more the police will think he's guilty of murder, or they'll be increasingly concerned for his safety.'

Hugh paled. 'I get that they think he might have killed Tania – although I'm damn sure he didn't. But it hadn't crossed my mind that he might have been killed too.'

'Until the police know why Tania was murdered, they have to consider every possibility.'

'I suppose so.'

'And it's not a huge leap of the imagination to suggest that if Toby didn't kill Tania, then the real killer might want to keep him hidden away so the police think he's done a runner, keeping the focus off them.'

'You think he could have been kidnapped?'

Ryan said, 'Can't rule anything out. Have you seen him?'

Hugh glanced towards the counter, where Jack was making coffees. 'I've not seen or heard from Toby.'

'That doesn't worry you?' Maggie persisted.

Hugh shrugged. 'If it was out of character it would, but he does this every now and then. Anything that's hard to handle, he goes quiet. Especially if it's a situation that might be his fault or make him look bad.'

Maggie tilted her head to one side. 'Do you think Toby might have something to feel bad about?'

'Apart from having his heart broken?'

'You know what I mean.'

'I've told you before, I don't think he'd kill Tania.' Hugh sighed. 'I can't help. I truly don't know where he is.'

Ryan changed tack. 'Did you know that the police think Toby's office was broken into?'

'What?' Hugh's slouched position was abruptly replaced by a rigid back and a thrust-out chin. 'When?'

'We don't know,' Maggie admitted. 'There were no broken locks or windows. It's possible that either Toby or Rachel could have been there and forgotten to close the door behind them.'

Hugh stared at Maggie. 'What *exactly* is your role in all this?'

'We're helping the police investigate.'

Hugh crossed his arms over his chest. 'And you didn't think it polite to tell me that the last time we spoke?'

'At the time, that was not the case.' Maggie turned to Ryan. 'Jack has our coffees ready, why don't you help him bring them over?'

As soon as Ryan was gone, Maggie leant forward and whispered, as if sharing a secret with Hugh. 'Ryan was a suspect. He didn't do it, but as his girlfriend was a close friend of Tania's, I've agreed to help find out anything we can. The police are aware of what we're doing.'

Hugh turned to watch Ryan approach the bar. '*He's* a suspect.'

'*Was*. Past tense. Bea wants Ryan to find out what happened to her friend.'

'Bea! Bea is his girlfriend?' This time Hugh was even more incredulous, repeating in hissed disbelief. 'Bea is going out with *him*?!'

Not commenting on how Hugh made the word *he* sound like *that*, and having no idea if Ryan had told Bea that he considered their relationship over yet or not, Maggie reverted to the point of her visit. 'In the course of our enquiries, we have discovered that you should not have borrowed Toby's car to pick up the wedding suits. Is there anything you want to say about that?'

'Oh.'

'Any advance on "Oh"?' Maggie asked as Ryan sat back down, a tray of coffee in his hands.

Hugh remained silent until the drinks had been distributed. 'I've lost my licence.'

'How?' Ryan cradled his latte, looking at the man in the chair opposite him.

'Speeding.'

Maggie frowned. 'You must have been going at one hell of a lick to get all your points in one go.'

'I was caught speeding a few times – and then—' Hugh took a deep breath as he picked up his drink '—I was convicted of dangerous driving.'

'I see.'

'And before you ask, I wasn't drunk behind the wheel or anything. I just like going fast and got a bit carried away. No one was hurt, but, quite rightly, the police punished me. I was lucky not to be killed.'

'That suggests you got more than "a bit carried away". Can you elaborate?' Maggie flipped open her notebook.

'If you insist. I was driving along the A303 – past Stonehenge. There was no one else around and it's a nice open road, so I cranked it up a notch . . . too much, as it turned out. Flipped the car and hit a noticeboard advertising the Sarum services. Unfortunately for me, I was caught by a speed camera that had appeared since I'd last driven that way.'

'Good.' Maggie couldn't help feeling Hugh was very lucky to still have the use of all his limbs. 'I assume Toby was aware of your driving ban, but Tania wasn't?'

'You assume incorrectly.' Hugh snapped. 'Neither of them knew before all this. What I want to know is, how do *you* know?'

'We know because we were told,' Ryan stated. 'So, Toby *didn't* know about your driving ban before you totalled his car and endangered the life of his future wife; is that what you are saying?'

'Yes. That is what I'm saying.' Hugh glared at Ryan across the top of his coffee cup. 'I didn't want to tell him even then, but Tania was furious – threatened to tell the police.'

'And that would have meant prison for you.' Maggie saw fear flash in Hugh's eyes.

'Yes.'

'You realise that might now be a possibility. The police will find out about the crash.'

Hugh's hand shook as he raised his latte to his lips. 'You don't have to tell them.'

'I think we do.' Maggie spoke softly. 'Better still – *you* should tell them. Assuming Toby is found alive and well, he's bound to tell the police. If you tell them yourself, you'll be treated more leniently. Maybe a suspended sentence.'

'Please.' Hugh looked from Maggie to Ryan, his eyes pleading. 'Don't tell anyone.'

'The police *have* to be told.'

'I know, Maggie, but – what I mean is – I'll do what you say. *I'll* tell them, but I'd like to talk to Heidi and Daisy. Tell them myself first.'

Maggie considered this, before saying, 'If you answer any questions we ask you, then we will give you until the end of the day to tell the police. If you don't, we will tell them. Agreed?'

'Agreed.'

'So,' Maggie opened her notebook. 'Why couldn't Toby go with Tania to get the suits, as previously planned?'

Hugh was clearly surprised by the question. 'Work. Something had come up that he said couldn't be left until after the wedding and honeymoon.'

'And you have no idea what that something was?'

'Nope.'

'So, the obvious question: why didn't Tania drive? I'm assuming she was covered by Toby's insurance if they were about to get married.'

Hugh shuffled awkwardly. 'I ummm . . . I persuaded her that I should.'

'Despite being banned from driving?'

'Okay, I'm not proud of it.' Hugh picked at a fingernail as he confessed. 'I've always wanted to drive that car. Tania was getting stressed about getting everything done in time for the wedding – a situation not helped by Toby going into work during their stag and hen week – so I took my chance. I offered to drive so she could relax and order her thoughts about what she needed to do.'

Maggie gave him a hard stare before moving on. 'You were speeding through the lanes between here and where? Where were the suits being collected from?'

'A small wedding boutique in St Buryan.'

She hovered a pen over her notebook with the air of a secretary taking minutes at a meeting. 'How far had you gone before you crashed?'

'About two miles. There's a sharp bend just as the road narrows. It's a tiny side road. More of a lane, really.' His voice dropped to little more than a mutter. 'You couldn't see the wall. I could have sworn there were hedges along both sides.'

Hugh lapsed into silence for a few seconds, before continuing, his eyes now closed. 'Tania screamed so loud when we hit the wall – it was piercing. I was afraid to look at her at first, afraid to see if she was screaming in shock or out of pain.'

'How did you imagine you'd be able to keep the crash a secret from Toby?' Ryan asked.

Hugh's head shot round. 'I had no intention of doing so! Just the fact that . . .'

'That you were driving with neither a licence nor, presumably, insurance.' Maggie shook her head. 'You're a real prince, aren't you?'

'Yes, alright. I know! I'm a total bastard who nearly killed my best friend's girlfriend. I've got to live with that forever!' Hugh let out a heavy sigh. 'As soon as it had happened, I checked Tania was okay. Thankfully her screaming had just been from shock. Once she calmed down, I confessed about my lack of licence and asked her not to tell the police.'

'And she refused?'

'She had her phone out to call them, but I stopped her. Told her that, as no one was hurt, there was no need – not to mention that Toby wouldn't want them involved.'

Maggie's eyes flicked to Ryan's as she asked, 'Did Tania ask you why Toby wouldn't want the police notified?'

'Yes . . . Yes, she did.'

Silence hung in the air before Ryan coaxed, 'And did you tell her?'

'I couldn't. I don't know what it is he's up to, only that it isn't totally legit.'

*We were right; Toby's business isn't all it seems.* Maggie sipped her drink. 'So what did you say to Tania?'

'That she should ask Toby later about why he wouldn't want the accident reported, but that we should arrange to get the car sorted first.' Hugh sucked some latte foam off his lips. 'And, of course, I didn't really want the incident reported, because I'd . . .'

'Face a potential prison sentence for driving without a licence or insurance?'

'Yes.'

'So, you called Toby, and he appeared, with his friendly garage owner hot on his heels?' Ryan was pleased to see Hugh's astonishment at the mention of the mechanic.

'You know about the mechanic?'

'Know about him, met him, seen the smashed-up car.'

247

# Chapter Thirty-three

Maggie had rather liked Hugh the last time they'd met; now she felt she couldn't get away from him fast enough. 'What happened once Toby arrived at the scene?'

'He was almost in tears over that bloody car. Kept saying if I'd hit a hedge rather than a wall, everything would be alright, but now it might all be ruined.'

'*Might* be ruined?' Ryan blew across his coffee cup. 'Surely the car *was* ruined?'

Maggie turned to Hugh. 'And Tania? Did he make sure she was okay, or was it all about the car for him?'

'*Or* was he more interested in double-checking you hadn't called the police?' Ryan chipped in.

Hugh flicked a hair from his eyes. 'Whatever you two are thinking, Toby loved Tania. Even more than Sandy. That's what he called the car.'

'We know.' Maggie tapped her pen against her notebook. 'Once Sandy was in the mechanic's capable hands, what happened then?'

'Even though I'd pleaded with her not to, Tania told Toby about my lack of licence while Simon secured the car to the back of his truck.'

Maggie glanced at Ryan before turning back to Hugh. 'How did you know that the mechanic is called Simon?'

'You said that was his name.'

'No, we didn't.'

Hugh's eyes narrowed. 'Then Toby must have said when he introduced us at the crash site.'

'What happened next?'

'Tania got into the tow truck's cab with Simon and waited for Toby.'

'And Toby himself, what did he do?'

'Told me I wasn't his best man anymore.'

'But have you seen him since?' Maggie urged.

'Yes. Back at the hotel. In front of the girls, he acted as if all was normal between us, but the minute we were alone, he clammed up. Cut me dead.' Hugh put his cup down with a heavy thud. 'The last time I saw Toby was just before he and Tania headed to The Mariner for their final meal as an unmarried couple. I suppose that was the last time I saw Tania too.'

'How did they seem?'

'Fine. Happy. Smiling. Until they saw me sat in the reception. Then they stopped smiling and, without saying a word, left for their date.' Hugh got to his feet. 'I have to go.'

Ryan swiftly stood up too, his willowy height equal to Hugh's. 'When I met Tania in the pub, she'd just had a row with Toby. She told me that the argument had been about trust – that she felt she couldn't trust him, but she wasn't sure why. Can I assume that lack of trust came from you suggesting he wouldn't want the police involved after your crash?'

'I would guess that was it, but as I wasn't there, I can't be sure.' Hugh's chin jutted out in defiance. 'Toby went nuts when she tried to call the police.'

'Did you know about a surprise Toby claimed to be arranging for Tania?'

'Surprise?' Hugh pulled a face. 'No. Sorry.'

'Okay. So, back to the crash.' Maggie's pen hovered over her notepad. 'Tania wanted to call the police, despite being asked not to?'

'Yeah. At the time she wouldn't believe that they didn't need to be told. She had her phone out to press in the number, when Toby took it off her. It was only later on, when we were all back at the hotel, that she accepted we were right. Looked it up on Google once she'd calmed down, I suppose.'

Maggie frowned. 'Are you saying Toby ripped the phone away from her?'

'Not at all. Toby didn't act violently or anything. Just took the phone from her and said that getting the police involved wouldn't be helpful right now.'

'Tania didn't question that?'

'Oh, she did!' Hugh barked out a sharp laugh. 'But he said he'd explain later, and she should trust him. And, like I said, she admitted we were right later on, although she wasn't happy about Toby not wanting to report me for driving when I shouldn't have been.'

Maggie said, 'I'm surprised he stopped her.'

'I don't think he would have, if calling the police wasn't risky for him too.'

Ryan asked, 'And did he give Tania her phone back?'

Hugh frowned. 'I'm not sure. Now I think about it, Toby had it in his hand when he told me he and I were through as friends.'

'He must have given it back,' Ryan said, 'because she had it in the pub.'

'The more I know about Toby Marrell, the less I warm to him.' Maggie stood up as Hugh lifted up his luggage. 'The police will want to know everything you know about Toby. Including what work took him away from his stag week for a short while, and why he is keen to avoid them. I don't buy that you don't know why Toby wasn't available to collect the suits.'

'You can believe what you like, but I don't know what he was up to. I do know that he'd never have killed Tania. She was the only thing he loved beyond that bloody car.' Hugh's earlier bluster was gone as he met Maggie's unblinking eyes. 'He and I have been friends for so long – we've had arguments before. Big ones. And we've always been okay after a day or two. But this time I could have killed Tania in that car, and so he's washed his hands of me.' He lowered his eyes to the ground. 'And I can't say I blame him. Toby loved her.'

'And she loved him too.' Ryan confirmed. 'Despite the row I witnessed, Tania was sure the wedding would happen. But, she was also sure he was up to something. Have you *any* idea what that something was? It's important. Whatever it was could be the reason why Tania is dead. Could you even hazard a guess?'

'Like I've already said,' Hugh slumped back onto his seat, 'Toby told me he couldn't fetch the suits because he'd got himself into a situation he swears he regretted – I honestly had *no* idea what that situation was, beyond that it was connected to his work.'

'You know *where* he is, though, don't you?'

Hugh exhaled a gust of air. 'Look, Ryan, I don't *know* anything, but I suspect he's in Exeter.'

'Why Exeter?'

'Because he rents a flat there through the business. Rachel uses it more than Toby, but he stays there whenever he needs to oversee an early morning, late in the day or night-time arrival. Sorting customs forms and stuff.'

'So, Rachel Zimmerman might not be abroad? She might be in Exeter.' Maggie grabbed her phone. 'Have you told the police this?'

Hugh shook his head. 'It wouldn't be terribly helpful. Exeter's huge. I've no idea where the flat is.'

'Don't be so naive, Hugh. The police would be able to find the flat once they knew it existed!' Maggie looked him straight in the eye. 'I think you'd be very unwise to go back to London. Inspector Houseman will want to speak to you when she hears about our conversation.'

'I'm not going to London. Heidi has invited me to the manor.'

Remembering her hunch that Heidi had a crush on Hugh, Maggie added, 'Very kind of her, I'm sure.'

With a sharp tut, Hugh spun on his heels and stalked out of the hotel.

No sooner had he gone than Maggie scrolled through the contacts on her mobile. 'I have to tell David about this.'

'Are you really going to give Hugh until tonight before you report the crash?'

'I'm not sure. Come on.'

'Hang on a minute before you call the sergeant.' Ryan lowered his voice. 'Your idea of me asking Jack a few things while you spoke to Hugh paid off. He confirmed what Sergeant Peters told you about the CCTV – it doesn't cover the bedroom corridors, but it does cover the hall areas, bar, stairs and reception, so you'd be seen on camera going into the corridors that lead to all the bedrooms. It doesn't cover the dining area or the gardens – but it does cover the car park.'

'That means that those suspects that say they were in their rooms were telling the truth. The police are bound to have viewed the camera coverage and would have seen if someone wasn't going into the corridors to their rooms as they claimed. Unless they have seen something, and we just don't know about it.'

'Jack said the police haven't been back here yet. He lives in, so it's unlikely that he'd have missed them.'

'Interesting.'

'Not as interesting as the fact that Jack knows where Toby is going to be later today.'

'You're kidding!' Maggie was stunned. 'I think it's time we took a trip to the police station.'

# Chapter Thirty-four

Maggie threw a piece of battered fish into the fryer, the resulting spatter of fat only just missing her hands.

'You okay, Maggie?'

'I'm fuming.' She prodded the floating fish pieces. '"Meddling in things that don't concern you", indeed! Of course this concerns us. You were almost arrested for Tania's murder! You'd think the inspector would be grateful for our information. We didn't *have* to go to the station to tell them what we'd found out!'

'She accused me of acting as if I was meddling like in *Scooby-Doo* when I was in custody.' Ryan adjusted his boater. 'She's got no idea how much effort it took for me to go back inside the station after my last visit. I wish we'd just phoned Sergeant Peters.'

'Next time we've something to tell the police, that's what we'll do. I'll not be bothering with Houseman. At least David listens to our theories, even if he sometimes makes me feel as if I've been granted an audience with the King of England.' Maggie listened to the crackle of boiling fat. 'Thankfully we know they've acted on what we told them, although I feel like a cat on hot bricks. David said he'd call when there was news, but it's been three hours now.'

Thinking it highly unlikely that Sergeant Peters would keep his promise and let Maggie know what was happening, Ryan said, 'They had to get to Exeter. It's a long drive. They're probably not there yet, let alone found Toby. And even if they have, there'll be a lot to do before there's anything to report back.'

'I wish we could have gone too. If I had a car, I'd have driven to the airport myself and . . .'

'You can't drive.'

'I suppose we could've asked Mr Robbins if we could borrow his driver again.'

Ryan shook his head. 'You're still recovering from a bang on the head, plus we'd never be allowed past security without a pass or police authorisation.'

'But *we* did the work. *We* found out where Toby might be! Thanks to us, they now have a proper suspect who has gone on the run – well, sort of.'

Although he shared her frustration, Ryan injected a note of reason. 'It's annoying, but the fact is, we're needed here. We do have to work.'

'I suppose so.'

As Ryan turned the closed sign to open, he added, 'And we can't even be sure that what Jack told us was correct.'

'It would make sense, though. And it sort of coincided with Hugh's idea that Toby might be staying in the firm's flat.' Maggie placed a piece of fish in the warmer, ready to be sold. 'I just hope Jack heard correctly, and it was Exeter airport the consignment was coming into.'

Ryan washed his hands in preparation for another evening of serving fish and chips. 'Let's recap what Jack said. Toby was alone, talking into his mobile in the reception area. He appeared to be begrudgingly agreeing to meet an incoming consignment of goods.'

Maggie prodded the cooking fish. 'Jack was convinced it was Exeter airport he heard mentioned, and that it was this evening Toby had to be there.'

'I wish we knew who Jack overheard Toby talking to.' Ryan added a handful of mayonnaise sachets to a box on the counter. 'And, of course, things could have changed.'

'What do you mean?' Maggie's eyes narrowed.

'I was thinking about the timeline of all this. Jack overheard Toby on the phone *before* he and Tania went to the pub. *Before* Tania was killed. What if, after he'd lost his fiancée, Toby cancelled everything? I tend to believe Hugh about Toby being heartbroken. Whatever he was supposed to be doing in Exeter, Toby could've changed his mind.'

'You think Toby might *not* have gone to the airport. That he'd have changed his plans because he was bereft.'

'If it was me, I'd have gone to ground – well, to bed probably – and hidden from the world.'

*If Bea had been taken from me like Tania was taken from Toby, would I have felt bereft? Once maybe ... but now ...*

'But,' Maggie interjected, 'you said he didn't seem grief-stricken when you saw him, and both Heidi and Daisy told me Toby wasn't that upset.'

'I've been thinking about that. If Toby was worried about what was going on, this situation Hugh said he'd found himself in might have overridden his grief while he was on the phone.'

'Possible. Daisy didn't seem that fond of Toby, maybe she just said he wasn't upset to make him look bad.'

'Heidi said he wasn't upset too, though, didn't she?'

'Fair point.'

Drying his hands, Ryan reasoned, 'If Hugh's telling the truth, and Toby wanted to avoid the police for whatever reason, Toby will have worked out there's a high chance they'll search for him at the airport. He could have done a total runner. Be literally anywhere.'

'Or we could be completely wrong, and whatever Toby's doing isn't connected to his work at all.' Maggie immediately backtracked. 'No, I'm convinced this situation is connected to Toby's work; otherwise why would whoever hit me take the folder of invoices?'

'Importing furniture isn't illegal.'

'No—' Maggie stood very still '—but importing drugs is. What if he's smuggling drugs in with the furniture?'

A sinking feeling hit Ryan's gut. 'You said he'd done drugs at uni.'

'According to Hugh, he did.'

'Do we believe Hugh, though?' Ryan was quiet for a moment before adding, 'There's a huge leap between taking a few drugs as a student and dealing in them as an adult.'

Maggie was about to answer Ryan's question about Hugh when a customer came in, followed by three more. It was only once the shop was empty again that she said, 'I take your point about the drugs.'

'I knew several people who dabbled at uni, but not one of them moved into dealing. Too damn dangerous for a start. And anyway, we don't even know if Hugh was telling the truth about Toby taking drugs when he was a student.'

'I'm not sure I'd trust Hugh about anything, but I can't see why he'd lie about Toby's time at university.'

'Nor me. How long are you going to give it before you call Sergeant Peters to tell him about Hugh's driving ban?'

'I said I give him until the end of the day, so I suppose that means midnight.'

'You're going to keep your word on that, then?'

'I have to; otherwise I'm no better than he is.' Maggie stared at the hands of the fish-shaped clock ticking round to eight o'clock. 'If David hasn't called me by nine, I'm going to phone him. Even if we have been wrong about everything, I need to know what's going on.'

'Would he tell you?' Ryan wasn't so sure. 'I know you and Sergeant Peters have an understanding, but . . .'

Maggie looked away. 'We don't have an understanding, Ryan, we've just known each other a long time.'

Feeling as if he'd accidentally trespassed into Maggie's private life, Ryan mumbled, 'Either way, the same can't be said for us and Houseman. She'll probably want to arrest us for wasting police time if we send them on a wild goose chase.'

'That's true. We'd best not suggest there's a drugs angle, then. Drugs are a big deal, and we have no proof, just theories, guesswork and the word of a man we can't trust. Hugh's the only one who's mentioned drugs in connection with Toby – maybe he made that up to distract us.' Maggie deflated as she stared at her mobile. 'I've really got nothing to say to David, have I? If we keep the drugs theory to ourselves, we've got nothing new.'

'We've helped the police already by telling them what Jack overheard. We just need to wait.'

'I suppose so.' Maggie slipped her phone back into her apron pocket. 'How about you get us a cuppa? Mr Robbins will be gagging for his evening tea by now. Who knows, a bit of caffeine might get us thinking clearer.'

\*

'Darren.'

'I beg your pardon?' Maggie's forehead creased as Ryan passed her a mug of tea.

'I asked Mr Robbins the name of his driver. It's Darren.'

Maggie smiled. 'You're getting braver.'

'Not really, I was scared stiff. But I did also ask him who Darren was and how come he employed a driver. All I got was a grunted thanks for his tea and an enquiry as to how busy it was in here.'

'Mr Robbins maintains his "man of mystery" image.' Maggie chuckled as she checked the status of the chips in the fryer. 'Talking of mysterious people, I was thinking, we don't know anything about Toby's business partner, Rachel Zimmerman, do we?'

'Simon gave the impression she's a bit of a cold fish.'

Maggie agreed. 'She's part of Toby's everyday life, but no one's really mentioned her.'

'Her past history with Hugh means that she wasn't invited to the wedding, so there'd be no reason for her to be around, or even considered as part of the group.'

'Hugh said she was a bit of a player when it came to relationships. Maybe Rachel was playing with Toby after all.'

'Or maybe she wanted to, and he said no.'

'When I mentioned Rachel to Heidi and Daisy, the atmosphere went frosty. I don't think any of them like her.'

'That's not a motive for murder, though, is it?'

'I suppose if not being liked by your ex's friends was a motive, there'd be a murder a minute.' Maggie let out a sharp exhalation of air. 'Unless . . . unless it wasn't premeditated. Just a row that went wrong and ended in Rachel and Tania arguing over Toby – or over the future of Toby's business, perhaps – which ended in Rachel pushing Tania so hard she toppled off the harbour wall.'

Ryan shrugged, but Maggie was warming to her theme. 'It was a woman's voice I heard on the answerphone in the office when I was hit on the head.'

'And you think it was Rachel?'

'Who else could it have been? It's so annoying that I can't remember exactly what she said.' Maggie sighed. 'How can I help solve this if I can't even be sure what I heard?'

'Don't beat yourself up. You've helped the police plenty.'

'*We've* helped them, Ryan – not just me.'

'Do you think Jack overheard Toby talking about Exeter airport because he was, in fact, planning to skip the country?'

'If he was, he's a fool. Running away permanently would make him appear even guiltier than going missing for a while, and for all I've heard about him, I don't see him as an idiot.'

Ryan agreed. 'Tania wasn't the sort of woman who would have fallen for a fool. At least, she didn't come across that way.'

'Tomorrow we'll go and talk to the girls again.'

Ryan looked surprised. 'What for? Surely the police will have found Toby at the airport and arrested him by then.'

'If he's there.'

Ryan nodded. 'If he's there.'

Pulling a face, Maggie asked, 'Gut instinct, Ryan: do you think Toby murdered Tania?'

'No. Everything we've heard has told us that Toby loved Tania – but he is the only one we've encountered with a clear motive.'

'Because we're assuming that she discovered whatever he's up to.'

'She might not have, though. Toby hadn't told her anything by the time he stormed out.'

'Everything fits it being him, but I can't stop this nagging doubt at the back of my mind telling me it's all a bit neat.' Maggie watched as the hands of the clock ticked closer to half-past eight. 'If you were up to something criminal, and Bea found out, would you kill her to keep her quiet, or would you trust that she loved you enough to say nothing?'

'Bea would sing like a canary if there was something in it for her.'

'Sorry. Bad example.' Maggie grimaced. 'But, what if whoever killed Tania believed she knew something – something they couldn't risk her knowing?'

'That's possible, and it fits with what we thought about why you were knocked out – because you knew what Tania had told me . . . and you were digging about for information.'

'Hugh has a motive – wanting to keep out of prison after crashing the car. Tania was the only one threatening to tell the police.'

Ryan nodded. 'And maybe Rachel has one too, assuming she's involved in whatever this dodgy side to his work is.'

'I wish we could talk to her.' Maggie was about to theorise further when Harry ambled in. 'Evening, Harry. Your usual?'

'That'll be perfect, me 'ansum.' Harry beamed at Maggie. 'You cracked the case yet?'

'And what makes you think I'd be trying to do that?'

'Cos you got yourself bashed on the head when you were poking around that office in Marazion.'

'How on earth . . .?' Ryan began, but a sharp glance from Maggie stopped his words in their tracks.

'Hell of an imagination you have there, Harry.' Maggie scooped some chips into a cardboard holder.

'It's all over Penzance, lass.'

'Then someone should mop it up.' Maggie added a piece of fish on top of the chips. 'You know better than to listen to gossip, Harry.'

'Normally, yes, but I know you, Maggie Tyson. You're like a dog with a bone once you've got a puzzle between your teeth.'

As she took his money, Maggie asked, 'How are you anyway, Harry?'

The old man chuckled. 'Fair enough, lass. I'll drop the subject. And I'm fair enough in myself as well, thanks.' He tapped his leg. 'Despite the aches and pains.'

'See you in the library next time,' Maggie said as Harry picked up his supper.

'I'll tell you about what I saw the night that girl died when we're puzzling over your latest crossword then, shall I? Or would you rather I told you now?'

Maggie rolled her eyes. 'You're an old tease, Harry, you know that, don't you?'

'I know, but there aren't many pleasures left to an old man. We must take them where we can find them.'

Ryan opened a new box of wooden chip forks. 'What did you see, Harry?'

'The girl. Tania, wasn't it? The evening she died.'

'Have you told the police?' Maggie was tempted to turn the shop sign to closed so they could be sure they weren't interrupted, but didn't think Mr Robbins would be too pleased with that idea.

'Only realised my mistake tonight.' He sighed. 'I get my evenings a bit muddled these days. Every night is the same. Dinner, the news, a crossword, a quiz show, then failing to sleep. I get insomnia something terrible. Thought I'd tell you as I was coming here anyway, and then you could tell your old friend for me, Maggie.'

'Old friend?' Ryan quizzed. 'You mean Sergeant Peters?'

'Hasn't Maggie told you? They were . . .'

Stopping Harry's next words in their path, Maggie held up a palm. 'Which evenings have you got muddled up? What exactly have you remembered, Harry?'

# Chapter Thirty-five

Ryan opened the curtains in the bedsit and peered out across the harbour. The twinkling lights from the boats coming in and out, as trawlers returned from a fishing trip or left to try their luck against the waves, gave out a comforting glow. Whatever had happened there, just a few short days ago, life was now carrying on as before. The police cordons were gone, and the only sign that anything untoward had happened were the bunches of flowers propped against the harbour wall: tributes from the local people in memory of a girl lost so young.

Picking up his rucksack, Ryan stuffed it with enough clothes to see him through a week at Maggie's house. Grateful that he didn't have to sleep in a bed where his boss had been assaulted, Ryan slung his bag over his shoulder, flicked off the light and headed down the stairs.

*

David Peters was waiting outside Maggie's house as they approached. They could see him shifting his weight from foot to foot, impatience oozing from his stance.

'He got here fast.'

Maggie quickened her pace, and Ryan had to jog to keep up with her. 'Slow down a bit, he might not be able to tell us much.'

'I know, but if we ask him the right questions, we can work out what he hasn't said.'

'You're sneaky, you are.'

David came forward to meet them before they reached Maggie's front door. 'What have you found out?'

'In a second.' Maggie fumbled her keys from her handbag. 'Did you find Toby at the airport?'

'You know I can't tell you that.'

'You were acting on information we found for you! Of course you can tell us.'

David followed Maggie into the house. 'More than my job's worth. In fact, those were Houseman's exact words when I told her that the tip-off about Toby potentially being in Exeter came from you two.'

Noting that David knew where he was going as they moved through the house, Ryan grumbled, 'That sounds about right.'

The sergeant gave him a wry look as they reached the dining room table. 'You didn't take a shine to my boss, did you?'

'You could say that.' Ryan threw down his rucksack. 'I'll go and put the kettle on.'

David gave Ryan a searching look. 'Shouldn't you ask Maggie first? It's her house.'

Maggie stepped in. 'A pot of tea for three sounds like a great idea, thanks, Ryan.' As her new lodger disappeared through the door into the kitchen, she turned to David. 'He's staying here now. Better than living with the constant smell of chip fat.'

'And Izzie doesn't mind?'

'She isn't here – but no, she doesn't mind.'

'How is she?' David pulled out a dining room chair and sat down.

'Staying in New Zealand for a few months. Working at an Outward Bound place.'

'And you're okay with that?'

'I'd rather not talk about it, if you don't mind.'

With a nod of acceptance, David picked up a piece of paper on which Maggie had drawn a rough map of the route from The Mariner to the harbour wall. 'You're not going to drop this detective thing, are you?'

This time it was Maggie who avoided answering the question. Instead, she asked, 'Do you still have sugar in your tea? I'll have to tell Ryan to bring some in.'

'I gave it up.' He patted his stomach. 'The uniform trousers were getting a bit snug.'

'That reminds me.' Maggie called through to Ryan, 'If you have a rummage in the cupboard over the kettle, you'll find some biscuits.'

'You think biscuits will help my trousers fit better?'

'No, but they'll make my brain work better. If you don't want a biscuit, then don't eat one.'

Taken aback by her caustic tone, David poured some milk into his mug. 'You said you had something else to tell me.'

'One of our customers told us they saw something on the night Tania died, but they didn't want to bother the police.'

David groaned. 'Why do people do that? We are here to be bothered. It's a potential murder, for goodness' sake!'

'You're admitting that now, then? That it wasn't a fall?'

'Potential murder, I said. Until the coroner rules, we're keeping an open mind.'

'Vacant, I'd have said,' Ryan mumbled as he returned, brandishing a packet of Hobnobs. 'When I was being interviewed, Inspector Houseman made it crystal clear she wasn't interested in listening to amateurs.'

'Her hands are tied by the rules. If we listened to every—'

'Make your mind up,' Maggie interrupted. 'Either you want to hear from the public if they have information, or you don't.'

'You know that what you and Ryan are doing is very different from a member of the public seeing or hearing something helpful.'

'I believe we have been proactive and very helpful – or would you rather we hadn't told you what Jack overheard?'

Exasperated, David spoke through clamped lips. 'Maggie, please, tell me what you've found out.'

'*After* you've told us what happened at the airport.' Maggie passed David a biscuit. 'Eat it. Live a little.'

Crunching into the oat biscuit, sending crumbs flying across the table in the process, David regarded the two people opposite him. 'In other words, you're telling me nothing until I tell you what you want to know. That's blackmail. Worse, it's blackmailing a policeman.'

Maggie took a biscuit for herself and dunked it into her tea. 'Do we have a deal?'

'The best I can do is listen to what new information you have, and then – *if* I think it will help us move forward – I will give you a basic outline of what happened in Exeter.'

Moving the biscuit packet out of David's reach, Maggie conceded, 'I suppose we can agree to that, but no more biscuits until we hear what we want to know.'

'You drive a hard bargain, Maggie Tyson.'

'True.' Maggie settled back in her seat. 'On the night that Tania was killed, we know that she left the pub at half-past ten, and that when Ryan went down to the harbour thirty minutes later, she wasn't there.'

Ryan chipped in, 'And Inspector Houseman suggested that the pathology report said that she died in that half hour, rather than going somewhere else and returning later.'

David looked back at the plan he'd seen earlier. 'You've plotted out the walk we suspect Tania took from the pub to the harbour.'

'As I'm sure you have.' Maggie traced a fingertip over the plan, from The Mariner, along the road, towards the place where Tania must have sat before her fall. 'There aren't many places where anything secretive could have happened.'

'And yet your customer saw something previously unreported.'

'Yes, at least, something that Ryan and I were unaware of. You may already know, of course.'

Blowing out a short breath of air, David said, 'For God's sake, Maggie, just tell me.'

'That evening, late, Harry had a splitting headache, so he decided to go for a walk.'

David sat forward and picked up his mug. 'Harry who?'

'It doesn't matter yet.' Ryan continued to tell Harry's story. 'He was getting some fresh air at around half-ten; thought the sea air might clear his head before he tried to sleep. He had reached the gift shop on South Cliff, when he needed to rest, so he propped himself up in the doorway.'

'Effectively hiding him in the shadows.' Maggie took over telling the story. 'Tania passed him. He doesn't think she saw him, as she was intent on whatever was on her mobile phone screen.'

David shrugged. 'That is hardly unusual.'

'She was texting.'

'You're sure?'

'Harry was.' Ryan asked, 'Did you find Tania's phone?'

'No. We assumed it was washed away, sank in the sand, or . . .'

'Was taken by her attacker?'

'It's an option.' David rested his elbows on the table. 'We tried to ring it, but we got no response.'

Maggie's eyes narrowed. 'Is that what you were after when you searched Ryan's bedsit? The phone?'

'It was on our radar.' He turned to Ryan. 'Any idea who she might have been messaging?'

'I'd guess Toby, seeing as they'd just rowed.' Ryan stirred a teaspoon through his tea, watching the liquid swirl in the cup. 'Personally, I'd have wanted to clear the air and be reassured that the wedding wasn't off.'

'That would make sense, but perhaps . . . well, if it had been me,' Maggie suggested, 'I wouldn't have contacted the person I'd been rowing with; I'd have wanted to talk to a friend. Have a moan and find a shoulder to cry on.'

'One of Tania's friends, then.' David sipped his tea.

'One of her best friends, which means Heidi, Daisy or Bea.' Ryan pulled one of the other maps they had open on the table towards them. 'Bea would have told me if it had been her. We should go to Lamorna Manor tomorrow and see what Heidi and Daisy have to say for themselves.'

David lowered his mug back to the table. 'Correction. *I* should go to the manor and talk to them after I've spoken to this Harry bloke. You two will leave well alone.'

Ignoring him, Maggie said, 'Tania stopped walking so she could type something as she passed Harry, moving on as soon as – presumably – whatever she'd written was sent. He said she went towards the harbour. Sadly, however, he never saw her again, deciding he was too tired to do more than hobble back home.'

'Hobble?'

'Harry uses a walking stick. He's elderly. You keep up your part of the bargain, and I'll give you his details.'

David was stern. 'This is important, Maggie. I need to talk to him. I want to know what made your customer suddenly remember this anyway.'

'You're doubting his story?'

'Old man, lonely maybe. Wants a bit of limelight, so makes up a story – a bit late in the day – about seeing a girl of the right sort of age in the right place. Probably just fancies a bit of attention.'

Maggie was furious on Harry's behalf. 'He would never do that!'

'Then why didn't he come forward earlier?'

'He got his nights mixed up. Thought he'd gone for this stroll the night before he did, but tonight he realised his mistake.'

'And what makes you think he's got his evenings correct this time?'

'Because he's not daft. He was watching his favourite quiz show – don't ask me which, I don't know. Anyway, the announcer said that after a few evening schedule changes, the show would be back to its usual time slot next week. That's when he noticed that he'd gone for his walk on the Saturday, not the Friday.'

'Umm. He could still be wrong about it being Tania. Either way, he should have come to us and not you.'

'Perhaps he thought you'd see he was old and dismiss him out of hand!'

'I would never . . .'

'You just did!' Ryan was almost as cross as Maggie.

'I was being practical. The older we get, the less reliable our eyesight and . . .'

'Bollocks to that!' Ryan gripped his teacup. 'If Harry says he only just remembered, then that's what happened.'

'Are you two really willing to withhold any information even if that might, potentially, delay finding Tania's killer?'

Maggie scribbled a name and address onto a piece of paper and slammed it onto the table. 'We have been trying to share things with you, but . . .'

'Okay, point taken.' David took the offered note. 'Thank you. It might not have been Tania, though. Harry could have seen someone else. The photograph of her in the local paper wasn't great as she'd recently had her hair cut for the wedding; her parents had yet to take a photograph of her new haircut.'

'Fair enough. It's possible Harry was wrong about who he saw. But if he was, then there was another woman down on the harbour that night wearing a velvet cap at about the time Tania died.'

'A velvet cap?'

'Yeah. I'd forgotten until Harry said, when Tania left the pub, she put a hat on, a velvet cap. Once it was on, you couldn't see her hair. I'm sorry, Sergeant, I'd honestly forgotten.'

'It happens.' David swigged down his tea. 'Can you recall the colour of the hat?'

'Blue.' Ryan probed, 'I get that you can't tell us much about your investigation, but can you at least say whether you've found Toby?'

'And if so,' Maggie added, 'is he alive or dead?'

His phone already in his hand to call his boss, David got to his feet. 'After your tip-off, I called the Customs team in Exeter. They confirmed that Toby was meant to be there to meet a consignment of trinket boxes from Morocco. He didn't show. And before you ask, no, he was not at the flat the business rents in Exeter – nor was his business partner. We do not know where either of them are at this time.'

Maggie let out a low whistle. 'Thank you.'

'What's the address of the flat in Exeter?' Ryan asked.

'Don't push your luck.' David grinned. 'We only found it because it's the address the import desk have for Mermaid Imports. And yes, I will tell you if we find Toby or Rachel, but only to stop you pestering me!'

'Thanks, David.' Maggie smiled. 'Be kind to Harry.'

'As if I wouldn't be. Oh, and you did not hear any of the information I may have accidentally given you from me.'

'Understood.' Maggie got up as her guest headed to the front door. 'There's something else. It's probably nothing, but I think Heidi has a crush on the best man.'

'Interesting.' David's eyes met Maggie's, but they didn't smile. A second later he was at the front door. 'For your own good – both of you – do *not* go looking for Toby or go up to Lamorna Manor to talk to the others involved in this case again.'

'Sorry, David, I didn't quite hear that.' Maggie winked at Ryan. 'Forgive me not seeing you out; got lots to do.'

269

# Chapter Thirty-six

'You didn't tell him about Hugh's driving ban.'

'It isn't midnight yet. I'll give Hugh the full day – fair's fair.' Maggie threw her notebook back into her bag.

'Where are you going?'

'Lamorna Manor. Do you want to come as well?'

'But it'll be gone eleven at night before we get there! No one will be up.'

'I bet they will be. But if they're not, we'll wake them up.'

'I thought you said we'd talk to the girls again tomorrow?' Ryan scooped his phone and house keys off the table as Maggie charged towards the door.

'I did, but things have changed. For one, Toby wasn't in Exeter, so where is he?'

Picking up on Maggie's urgent tone, Ryan peered out of the living-room window just as a blue Citroën parked up outside. 'Mr Robbins' driver is here. When did you call Darren?'

'While you were in the loo, after David left.'

'Blimey, you move fast.'

'I can't shift the feeling that time's short. Plus, I've got a nagging sense that we've missed something.'

'Missed what?' Ryan asked as Maggie bundled him out of the house and locked up behind them.

'I've no idea, but I'm sure Toby didn't kill Tania.' Maggie climbed into the car. 'Everything we've learnt about Toby suggests he'd be too proud to go running after her once they'd had any sort of argument. He'd expect her to chase after him.'

'Agreed.'

Maggie fastened her seat belt. 'When I spoke to Heidi and Daisy, they said that Toby didn't like being made to feel as if he was in the wrong, even when he was – in fact, *especially* when he was!'

'When we were in the pub, Tania told me Toby said he was going back to the hotel when he stormed off. He'd want her to know where he was so she could say sorry, so I bet that's exactly where he went.'

Maggie agreed. 'Waiting for her to grovel and massage his ego.'

Ryan stared out of the window; the stunning vista of the Cornish coastline was hidden by the thickening dark of night. Instead, the memory of Hugh telling them how Toby was involved in something he couldn't get out of loomed large in his mind. 'If Toby wasn't at the airport or the flat, then where the hell is he?'

'Not a clue.' Maggie pulled out her notebook as the car slowed to stop at some traffic lights and quickly wrote a list of everyone's names. 'Let's go back to basics and forget about everything except the murder. It's all got horribly complicated, but to understand this, we need to keep it simple.'

'Okay.' Ryan switched on his phone's torch function so Maggie could see to write.

'Where was everyone – or where did everyone claim to be – at the time of Tania's murder?'

'Hugh said he was in his hotel room.'

Maggie put a tick next to Hugh's name. 'And, thanks to Jack, we know that the CCTV will show him going through the door from the communal areas into the bedroom corridors, so that would be an easily disproved alibi.'

'Same goes for Daisy and Heidi, then.' Ryan looked at the open notebook. 'Heidi said she was in the bath, and Daisy said she was in her room.'

Maggie counted on her fingers. 'So that's three of the chief suspects accounted for.'

'And Toby too.'

'Toby? I know we don't think he did it, but it would be good to have proof of his whereabouts so . . .'

Ryan finished Maggie's sentence for her. 'So, the CCTV would also show him entering the corridor towards his room.'

'It's so obvious.' Maggie smacked her palm against her head. 'If he came back here after their row in the pub, it would be so easy to prove.'

Ryan frowned. 'Which means that maybe he *didn't* come back . . . The police checked the CCTV – if they saw Toby going into the corridor that led to his room, then they wouldn't be so keen to track him down . . . would they?'

Maggie looked out of the window as the night sky dulled the seascape. 'Unless . . . hang on . . . what did David say about wanting to find Toby? Did he actually say they wanted to talk to Toby about Tania's murder?'

'I'm not sure – no . . . no, not specifically.'

'So, what *did* he want to talk to Toby about? Maybe it was something else.'

'It has to be about his business – the thing that was causing trust issues with Tania.' Maggie flicked through a few pages in her notebook. 'What if the police already suspected Toby of something before Tania died?'

'Wouldn't Sergeant Peters have told you?'

'More than his job's worth – isn't that what he said, Ryan?'

'He did. So, maybe there were drugs hidden in furniture imports after all. Maybe Mermaid Imports have been on their radar for a while.'

'O . . . kay, we're in danger of inventing crimes to suit us now. We might be right, but we could also be well off.'

Maggie doodled a circle on the paper. 'If we discount Hugh, Daisy and Heidi because they can't be in two places at once, who does that leave, apart from Toby?'

'No one. Well, I suppose there's Simon.'

'I hadn't forgotten our handy mechanic friend, but I can't see how he's involved.'

'Friend . . .' Ryan mused, 'Simon said Toby wasn't so much a friend as an acquaintance. Yet, Simon knew Heidi and Daisy by name, and he seemed quite comfortable talking about Hugh and Tania.'

'They were at the crash site. Hugh said Toby introduced him to Simon there.'

'Yes, but—' Ryan stretched out his legs '—now I think about it, he used their names like they were familiar, not like he was talking about people he'd met in the line of work.'

'You think Simon is friends with all of them?'

'It's a thought. Even if he isn't, I bet he knows more than he's letting on about what Toby is up to.'

'Probably.' Maggie sucked on the end of her pen. 'But short of applying thumbscrews to make Simon talk . . . And don't forget, Toby pays him rent for the office. There's no way he'd want to risk losing that income by sharing Toby's secrets – if Simon even knows what they are.'

Ryan pulled a face. 'I'm not so sure. There's always someone who wants to rent an office.'

'In the past, maybe,' Maggie said, 'but these days, when so many people work from home, and so little is committed to paper—' She abruptly stopped talking.

'What is it?'

'The folder. I commented to David at the time about how odd it was to keep paper invoices these days.'

'You mean the one that went missing?'

'Why take it? What was so important about that file?'

'We'd need to ask Rachel, but as she's in Morocco . . .'

Ryan met Maggie's eyes as they spoke in unison. 'But is she?'

Leaning forwards towards their driver, Maggie said, 'Darren, change of plan. We're going to The Cabin Hotel.'

As the car slowed to turn right instead of carrying straight on to Lamorna, Ryan asked, 'Why are we going back there?'

'Because before we talk to Tania's friends again, I want to see a few things for myself.'

\*

'This is really good of you, Jack.'

Maggie followed the waiter as they crossed from the bar to the main stairway.

'You only just caught me. I knock off at eleven. I was destined for a quick shower and an episode of *Only Murders in the Building*.'

'I love that series!' Ryan grinned.

'Me too. It's my third rewatch.'

Maggie looked blank. '*Only Murders in the* . . . what?'

Ryan stopped dead as they crossed the plush carpet towards the reception desk. 'Seriously? Are you telling me there's a crime drama that you haven't seen?'

Jack smiled. 'It's amazing. You've got Disney Plus, right?'

'I haven't even got Netflix.'

'That explains it.' Looking as though the concept of not having two of the most popular streaming services was beyond him, Jack produced a plan of the hotel from under the counter.

'This shows the fire escapes. There's one on the back of every hotel bedroom door.' He took a red pen from a pot on the desk and drew a circle around a room on the second floor. 'This was Miss Stevens' room. Her future husband's room was on the ground floor, here. Next to his was Mr Parkinson's bedroom.'

Maggie scribbled room numbers and floors in her book. 'So the men were on the ground floor, and the women on the second floor, with a floor in-between.'

'That was how it was supposed to be.' Jack checked to make sure no one was watching him giving out confidential information. 'However, we had a late block booking of a bigger party who wanted to all be together. We asked the Marrell party if they'd mind moving one of their rooms to the lower floor. So Miss Makepeace was moved from the second floor to the ground floor.'

'Daisy was in a room next to Toby?'

Jack tapped the plan. 'Yes, it went Hugh, Toby, Daisy.'

'While Heidi was upstairs with Tania?'

'Miss Spenser-Davies was next door to Miss Stevens on the second floor.' Jack confirmed. 'We were lucky that one member of the party withdrew at the last minute. Miss Makepeace was happy to take the room on the ground floor, so the party I mentioned could be together upstairs.'

Assuming that room had been meant for Bea, Ryan asked, 'Do you work on reception as well, Jack? I mean, why would a waiter know all this?'

'I do a bit of everything. I'm studying hospitality and hotel management. It's an apprenticeship degree – so I have a finger in all the pies here.' He paused. 'If anyone finds out I'm helping you like this, that'll be my career down the drain.'

'They won't hear it from us,' Maggie assured him. 'One more question, then we'll let you get going. Was there another room booked, or another guest expected with Tania and Toby's party? A Rachel Zimmerman?'

'Not to my knowledge. I can check for you, though.'

'Thank you.'

'My pleasure; this sleuthing is fun.' Jack winked as he ran the name Zimmerman through the computer. 'No. We've not had a guest of that name here. Although, I can't promise they haven't been through the door. People visit for coffee, dinner or to use the spa – or to visit guests.'

Maggie nodded thoughtfully. 'Thanks Jack, you've been a star.'

'Before I go, would you like to see Mr Marrell's bedroom? He hasn't checked out yet, but nor has he been back to the hotel. The police have asked us all to look out for him, so I'm sure I'd have heard if he had.'

'You are every private detective's dream,' Maggie said as Jack produced a keycard from a locked drawer and strode purposefully in the opposite direction to the bar and coffee lounge, down a narrow corridor which, although well lit, felt shadowy and a touch claustrophobic.

As they followed Jack, Ryan found himself glancing upwards, towards the CCTV covering the foyer. Just looking at it made him feel like a criminal.

# Chapter Thirty-seven

Once they were safely in Toby's room, the door shut behind them, Maggie expressed her thanks. 'This is above and beyond, Jack, thank you. We'll just have a quick mooch round; I don't want to get you into trouble.'

'It should be okay. We show future guests around sometimes, usually people wanting to make block bookings for wedding guests or the like.' Jack stood by the door, his foot against it just in case anyone should try to come in. 'As Toby's in Exeter, I can't imagine we'll be interrupted.'

Not confiding that Toby's whereabouts remained unknown, Maggie and Ryan stood next to each other in the centre of the room and surveyed the space. Signs of Toby's occupation were sparse. An open suitcase on an armchair near the window suggested he'd been in the process of packing, or unpacking, when he left. When Maggie went through to the ensuite bathroom, it was devoid of all occupation – there was no toothbrush, no shaving equipment, no deodorant – nothing but the lingering aroma of what she guessed was an expensive aftershave clinging stubbornly to the towels.

Ryan turned to Jack. 'I don't suppose you saw him check in?'

'I didn't, sorry.'

'No problem, I just wondered how much Toby brought with him.'

'All I know is that the wedding party had a lot of luggage. The porters were moaning about it. Saying how glad they were that some of the rooms were on the ground floor.'

'I guess they'd have a lot of stuff as they were having their stag and hen week here, plus, the guests were staying here the night of the wedding itself. Maggie recalled a wedding she'd been to years ago. 'There's always a tendency to take more than you need to a wedding, just in case.'

'In case of what?' Ryan asked as he peered in the wardrobe.

'In case a shirt gets stained, a hem gets ripped or a shoe heel breaks, or the summer becomes winter overnight. Usual stuff.'

'If you say so.' Ryan perused the row of largely empty hangers. 'His suit is here – and a few changes of shirt, but not much else.'

Maggie joined Ryan. 'His wedding suit never got collected. At least, I'm assuming it didn't.'

'This looks like a normal business suit.' Ryan frowned. 'If he'd intended to go to Exeter, then wouldn't he have worn that? David said he was expected there, and it was a work thing, so he'd need to be smart.'

'A man like Toby would have more than one suit.'

'Yes, of course,' Ryan conceded.

'It's a point, though, isn't it? At the time of the crash, they didn't know there wouldn't be a wedding. Presumably someone else would have fetched the groom's outfit at some point.'

'It definitely isn't in here.' Ryan paused, then spoke suddenly. 'Maybe Hugh has it. When my friend Stephen was best man for his brother, he had to care for the suits and various other things.'

'And, as we know, Hugh had some ground to make up with both Tania and Toby; he might have got a cab and gone to fetch them the next day. Something else to ask Hugh about when we get to the manor.'

'It's not really relevant, though, is it?'

'Possibly not. I just think that the more we know about the situation as a whole, the better.' Circling to the side of the king-size bed, admiring the tasteful cream duvet that matched the curtains and lampshades, Maggie realised she had no idea what she was searching for.

Moving to the desk and chair positioned in the bay window, she took in the untouched hotel notepaper and pen, and the phone that would summon room service in an instant. Pulling open the single slim drawer beneath it, she was greeted by a copy of the Gideon Bible, a brochure about the local area and a folder full of emergency contact details, restaurant recommendations and the Wi-Fi code.

Behind her, she could hear Ryan opening and closing the drawers of the bedside cabinets, one each side of the bed.

'There's nothing on the left side, Maggie, so presumably that was Tania's side of the bed if she slept in here. Only a couple of sets of underwear and two T-shirts on Toby's side.'

'And there's no sign of any other luggage, so he must have packed a bag with his toiletries and a few clothes to take with him.'

Looking up from the desk, Maggie was faced with a view of the garden. A trickle of anticipation, like she was on the edge of something, made her fingers tingle. Not sure what it was, and not wanting to move in case the sensation went away, Maggie asked Jack, 'Daisy and Hugh had rooms either side – are they the same as this one?'

'Exactly the same, yes.' Jack joined Maggie at the window, gesturing to the right as he spoke. 'Oh, except that Daisy's room doesn't have a bay window, as it's the end room on the floor.'

Maggie shimmied around the desk, easing herself between it and the window. 'The side windows open, but the middle one doesn't.'

'That's right,' Jack confirmed. 'It's the same in the one Mr Parkinson had.'

'But Daisy's is different. How did her windows work?'

'There's only one large window that opens, just off to the right side of the room, then there are two smaller windows, which can't be opened.'

Ryan and Maggie looked at each other, both having the same thought at the same time. It was Ryan who spoke first.

'The windows are big. Would it be possible to climb out of them and into the garden?'

'I suppose so, but it'd be a big step up, and a bit of a drop down the other side.'

Maggie chewed the inside of her cheek. 'All of the people involved here are young and fit. I'm neither, but I could get out of here if I really wanted to.'

'And the garden isn't covered by CCTV?' Ryan turned to Jack.

'No. No, it isn't.'

'Where do the gardens come out? It's too dark to see much right now.' Maggie was just able to see the well-kept flowerbed beneath the window and beyond to the start of a lawn.

'The car park is to the left. That's the way out.'

'But if you didn't go left, if you went forwards or to the right?'

'Right, and you'd hit a brick wall – a high one.' Jack moved closer to the window. 'No way could anyone get over it. But if you went straight ahead, you'd get to the main road and sea. You'd need to walk over some flowerbeds, but you could get out that way.'

'And, if it was dark, unless anyone else was in the garden, you wouldn't be seen.' Maggie muttered to herself as she imagined a figure climbing out of the window and creeping across the lawn. 'Even if someone else was looking out of a window, in the dark it wouldn't have been too difficult to remain unseen.'

'And CCTV would miss you.' Ryan reiterated his point.

'Which means that neither Hugh nor Toby – if he was here – nor Daisy have alibis anymore.'

'Or Heidi,' the waiter added.

Maggie and Ryan spun round to Jack.

'Curiosity got the better of me.' He shrugged unapologetically, 'I watched the CCTV about an hour ago. I hoped you'd come back so I could tell you that, at seven o'clock the evening of the murder, Heidi came down here and entered the corridor that led to her friends' rooms.'

'Did she now?' Maggie's eyes narrowed.

'Going to see Daisy?' Ryan suggested.

'I bet it was Hugh. I'm convinced she likes him more than as a friend.'

'We can't be sure it wasn't Daisy.'

'I know, but the girls had no reason not to tell us about visiting each other's rooms. Anyway, I've got a gut instinct about this.'

'If you're right, then I wonder why Hugh didn't mention it.' Ryan looked out of the window again. 'Did he say nothing because he didn't know she'd been here, because he was out at the time? Or because he wanted to keep being with Heidi a secret?'

'If it was as early as seven, Heidi could have been and gone again by the time of the murder.'

Jack shook his head. 'There's no sign of her coming out of the corridor again until the following morning.'

Ryan frowned. 'When we spoke to Hugh, he said he'd been invited to the manor by Heidi. He didn't seem too thrilled about it. Like, maybe he didn't want to see her.'

'So he did . . . I assumed he didn't want to stay local and await his inevitable arrest, but perhaps it was Heidi he was avoiding and not prison.' Maggie gave an internal sigh. 'What we have here could be as simple as a classic case of horny bloke sleeps with besotted girl and then dumps her – possibly without bothering to tell her first.'

Ryan's cheeks coloured. 'You can't know that.'

'That's a bit judgey,' Jack said.

'Quite possibly,' Maggie admitted. 'Well, okay, perhaps it was the other way around. Perhaps we are jumping to conclusions and they simply met as friends. Either way, I'd bet that Heidi and Hugh were together and didn't tell anyone.' She turned to Jack. 'The police must have also come to this conclusion. They'll have seen the camera footage.'

'They have copies of all the camera footage for the entirety of the group's stay, so I'd be surprised if not,' Jack confirmed.

'Although, David looked surprised when I told him my suspicions about Heidi and Hugh being a couple.'

'Heidi might not have been going to see Hugh at all.' Ryan mused. 'She could have been sneaking out to meet Tania at the harbour.'

'Heidi's bedroom was on a higher floor, so she couldn't have—' Maggie abruptly stopped talking. 'We've just established she might have gone into Hugh's room. What if she snuck out of his window? What if she and Hugh are in this together?'

'Or she could have gone into Daisy's room – they could be in this together.'

'Why would they be, though, Ryan?' Jack was looking doubtful.

'I've no idea.' Ryan took a last sweeping look around the room. 'If Tania stayed in here sometimes, I would have expected there to be a few telltale signs, but there's absolutely nothing to say she was ever here.'

'Good point.' Maggie followed Ryan's eyeline back to the bed. 'The night of her death was supposed to be their last night together before they became a married couple, so surely there'd be something, even if it was just a toothbrush.'

'Unless he went to her room. Or perhaps Mr Marrell couldn't stand to have anything of hers around after her death. Too upsetting.' Jack volunteered. 'Or maybe, she simply didn't leave anything in here.'

'True.' Maggie agreed.

'Unfortunately, I can't show you Tania's room as the police have closed it off. The other related rooms have new guests in them.' Jack checked the time on his watch. 'Actually, we should go. I've pushed my luck having the master key for this long already.'

'You've been brilliant. Thank you.'

'My pleasure. If you ever need a helpful pair of eyes in the future, just shout.'

\*

As they reached the outside world, Ryan wasn't surprised when Maggie turned into the garden.

'I want to see how easy it would be to get through those bedroom windows and out into the garden. Climbing up out of the window from the inside would be straightforward enough, but jumping down to the ground may not have been so easy, and then they'd have had to get back inside later. Especially at night when it's pitch black.'

Ryan checked to make sure they weren't being watched, feeling like a criminal himself as they crept into the dark, weaving between a group of unoccupied picnic tables and benches on a patio that divided the garden from the car park. Then, moving onto the lawned area, they peered up at the hotel's main building.

'If someone did climb out of one of those downstairs windows, and so avoided the CCTV in the stairs, reception or the lift, then it wouldn't have been too hard to stay undetected this late at night.'

Ryan moved forwards, getting closer to the side of the hotel. 'I reckon that's almost a metre drop. It's higher on the inside – the flowerbeds have been built up, so there wouldn't have been much of a fall.'

'Making it a bit easier to climb back inside if the window was left open.'

'Easier still—' Ryan turned to Maggie '—if there was someone in the room, ready to let you back in again.'

'Come on.' Maggie sidled to the edge of the lawn. 'Let's see how easy it is to get to the road without going through the car park.'

Creeping forwards, Ryan and Maggie soon left the lawn and pushed their way through a packed bed of well-established shrubs, before stepping over a low brick wall and, just like that, found themselves on the pavement that ran alongside the road back into the heart of Mousehole.

'That was ridiculously easy.' Maggie waved along the road to Darren, who spotted them at once.

As Mr Robbins' driver sparked the car's engine into life, Maggie glanced behind them. 'Anyone could get into the garden without much hassle. In the day it might raise an eyebrow, but at night, when there's no one about, who'd be looking?'

Ryan opened the car door. 'So much for crossing suspects off the list. Now every single one of them is back on it again.'

# Chapter Thirty-eight

Despite the lateness of the hour, Ryan had been surprised when Maggie had asked Darren to drive them home, rather than take them to Lamorna. He couldn't help being a little relieved, though. He hadn't relished explaining why they wanted to get everyone out of bed to talk about their friend's death. Besides, now they knew that Heidi, Toby, Hugh and Daisy all had the opportunity – even if their motives were unclear – to have killed the future Mrs Marrell, some thinking time was welcome.

Ryan was less surprised when Maggie asked Darren to come back to pick them up the following morning. Although the hour of day she'd requested made him pause for thought.

'I can't imagine anyone at the manor being up and dressed at eight in the morning.'

'I'm sure they won't be.' Maggie plonked herself down at the dining room table and placed her notebook in front of her. 'That's not where I think we should go first.'

'Then, where . . .?'

'The garage. It opens at eight in the morning, so Simon should be there by the time we arrive.'

'Why do you want to see him again?'

'In all honesty, I'm not sure – it's just a feeling. I'm hoping by the morning I'll have worked it out.'

Ryan watched in silence while Maggie scribbled furiously on a fresh page. Not wanting to interrupt her flow, he opened his phone and stared at the screen. A text from Bea confronted him. Another one.

He hadn't told Maggie about the texts from Bea, either demanding to know why he was avoiding her or asking to see him, because he didn't want to hear her opinion about them. The latest message echoed the five that had gone before, but this one had a hint of urgency about it.

**I leave tomorrow night. This is your last chance Ryan. Call me!**

His finger hovered over the reply button, but then he lowered his hand again. What else was there to say? She was leaving, and it was for the best. For both of them. Ryan wasn't sure if he was disappointed or relieved.

*Although, we didn't really end things ...* A yawn escaped his mouth, making Maggie look up. 'You should go to bed.'

'So should you. It's just gone midnight.'

'You're right. I'm not sure I'm thinking straight anyway.'

'Breakfast meeting at seven to discuss what to say when we get to Lamorna?' Ryan tore his eyes away from his phone screen. 'I'm assuming we're going there after Marazion, and before work?'

'Absolutely.'

# Sunday 15th June

Ryan's mobile burst into life as Darren, silent as ever, pulled the blue Citroën up against the side of the road opposite the Mount View Garage.

Watching him dismiss the call, Maggie asked, 'You alright, Ryan?'

'Sure. Getting a lot of spam calls.'

Not convinced, Maggie undid her seat belt as she leant forward to speak to Darren. 'We won't be long.'

The large bald head nodded without turning round.

Brushing herself down, Maggie took a deep breath. 'Are you ready for this?'

'I have no idea.' Ryan looked at the garage. There was no sign of life – at least, not from where they stood by the road, but their previous visit had told them that wasn't unusual. 'The police tape's still across the entrance to the flat.'

Maggie put a hand to the back of her head as the memory of her visit to that flat surfaced. 'Are you okay with what we're going to say?'

'Yep. Been rehearsing in my head all the way here. I feel like a kid trying to remember lines for a school play.' Ryan sounded more confident than he looked. 'Let's hope, after all our planning, that Simon is here.'

\*

The mechanic, while surprised to see them, did not appear concerned by Maggie and Ryan's arrival.

'Hello. Did you forget to ask me something?'

Relieved to have such a friendly welcome, Maggie said, 'Just one thing, it's come to our attention that you saw Toby once more after the crash.'

'Did I?'

'You told us that you invited Toby to come back and see his car before it was scrapped.'

'I did, yes.'

'You also said he didn't come – but I've been thinking about that. It doesn't sit right with everything you said about his devotion to that car.'

'And yet, he didn't come.'

'Or he didn't come when you were here.' Maggie pointed to a security camera on the back of the garage wall, looking out over the workshop and its surrounds. 'Would you mind if we watched the footage for the night before Sandy was taken away, please?'

'If you want.'

'And, we've one other question – it's about Rachel Zimmerman . . .'

★

Darren was turning into something of a godsend.

When Maggie and Ryan returned to the car, they found two takeout coffees waiting for them and a bag of doughnuts on the back seat.

'Mr Robbins said to keep you fuelled.'

Maggie and Ryan stared at each other in shock, partly from the realisation that Darren had a voice, and partly from this unexpected evidence of their employer's capacity to be considerate.

'Thank you.' Maggie opened the bag of treats and selected a heavily sugared ring doughnut. 'Darren, I wondered – how long have you worked for Mr Robbins?'

'We go way back.'
'How far . . .'
'Way back. I'll drive; you enjoy your doughnuts.'

★

As a taciturn Darren pulled the car into a layby at the bottom of the driveway to Lamorna Manor, Maggie found herself wishing that Izzie was there.

She knew they were close to the answer. She could feel it. She also felt more alive than she had in years. But, at the same time, she was anxious. Her gut instinct was telling her that it was sensible not to drive right up to the house, as it gave them the element of surprise, while her nerves told her that if they'd driven up, they'd have a quicker means of exit if things went wrong.

Ryan drew his phone from his pocket. 'You want me to make the call, or do you want to do it?'

'I'll do it,' Maggie said as they began to walk along the driveway towards where, just out of sight, she knew the house to be. 'While I speak to David, you should reply to Bea. It *is* Bea that keeps messaging and calling, isn't it?'

Staring at his trainers, Ryan mumbled, 'I've nothing to say to her.'

'You look like a teenager who's just been told off.' Maggie resisted the urge to hug her friend as she pressed David's number on her phone screen. 'I'm sure there are things to say. You and Bea were together a while.'

'*Were*, but we aren't now.'

'Does Bea know that?'

'Well . . .'

Maggie put a hand on his arm. 'Feel free to tell me to butt out, but Bea strikes me as someone who wouldn't take being left easily. Have you told her it's over, properly, and in person?'

'No.' Ryan blushed a deep pink. 'I don't want to row with her. It's so obvious we weren't meant to be. I was a fool to ever think otherwise.'

'Yet, she flew all the way here to see you when you were in trouble.'

'Suppose so.'

'You'll feel better once you've spoken to her and drawn a line . . .' Maggie's phone burst into life. '. . . David, it's Maggie . . . I wondered if you'd be interested in an information swap . . . Good. It's about Toby and his vintage car . . .'

\*

The enticing aroma of a cooked breakfast met their nostrils as the front door opened. A young woman with spiked hair, wearing jeans, a T-shirt and a full-length apron, regarded them with blatant curiosity.

'Can I help you?'

Having expected a butler at the very least, Maggie was a little taken aback as she said, 'Yes please; we'd like to speak to Miss Spenser-Davies and her friends.'

A heavily pencilled eyebrow rose in response to the request. 'Only Daisy is up, but the scent of bacon and eggs usually fetches them down.' She stepped back to let the unexpected guests in.

'You with the police?'

'Associated to, rather than with.' Maggie smiled.

'Thought so.' She shut the door behind them. 'I'm Monika. Come and have a cuppa while you're waiting.'

Exchanging a glance of surprise, having expected to be either turned away or made to explain themselves fully on the doorstep, Ryan and Maggie followed Monika into the kitchen.

'This is beautiful.' Maggie admired the old but functional dressers, large oak tables and a sparklingly clean set of Belfast sinks.

Monika chuckled. 'It's all very pretty, but you should try standing on these stone slabs all day! The sooner they put some easy-clean lino on the floor, the better, as far as I'm concerned, whether it's in keeping with the period of the house or not.'

Ryan and Maggie immediately looked down and made sympathetic noises about the situation, while also noting the thick-soled trainers Monika wore on her feet, which, they assumed, counteracted the very problem she was complaining about.

'There's coffee in that pot, and tea in that one.' Monika motioned towards a table beneath a window. 'Milk is in the fridge. If you don't mind helping yourselves, I'll go and rattle a few doorknobs and tell the loungers that you're here.'

'Loungers?' Ryan asked.

'My employers aren't bad people. They might fancy themselves as the lord and lady of the manor sometimes, but they work hard up in London. Both Mr and Mrs Spenser-Davies have management positions in the City. Financial stuff – I've never asked doing what. Their daughter and her friends, however – they wouldn't know hard work if it bit them on the butt. I work; *they* lounge.' Monika gave a friendly wink as she disappeared through the open doorway.

'Now *she*, I was *not* expecting. I think she's rather fabulous.' Maggie poured herself a coffee, before asking Ryan if he'd like one too.

'Thanks. I'll grab the milk.' Ryan replied, tugging open the stiffly sealed fridge door. 'Wow, Monika might not look like your average housekeeper, but boy is she organised.' He stood to the side to show Maggie the perfectly organised contents of the refrigerator, a myriad of labelled tubs, from cottage cheese to smoked salmon, grated parmesan, steak chunks and chicken wings.

'That,' Maggie let out a low whistle as she came to Ryan's side, 'is Tupperware on a grand scale.'

'Gran would be so proud. When I was a kid, she had rows of tubs like these on her kitchen shelves for cereal and stuff.'

Moments later, a smiling Monika returned. 'They'll be down in a minute. I can't say they were thrilled to know you were here.'

'I can imagine.' Ryan blew across his milky coffee.

'Can I ask you a question, would you mind?' Maggie leant back against the nearest sink.

'Sure.'

'When did Hugh arrive?'

'About the same time as Bea and Paolo.'

'Bea's here?' Ryan's face drained of colour. 'Bea *and* Paolo?'

Seeing the confused hurt flash across her friend's face, Maggie asked, 'Is Paolo a friend of everyone here or just Bea?'

'Everyone, I think.' Monika shrugged. 'He flies for Toby sometimes. They're old uni friends, I think.'

'And he's here *with* Bea?'

'Yeah.' Monika regarded Ryan in such a way that Maggie was sure she'd picked up on the subtext. 'They arrived at the same time.'

Ryan didn't have the time to reply, as Heidi strode through the kitchen door.

'Oh, it's you.' She looked at Maggie, her annoyance at the unannounced arrivals at odds with her good manners. 'How can I help?'

'I'm sorry to arrive so early and without warning.' Maggie gave Heidi her biggest smile. 'Please pass on my apologies to your parents.'

'Mummy and Daddy aren't here. They're travelling.'

'How lovely.' Maggie waved a hand towards Ryan. 'This is Ryan, my associate. The police are aware that we're here. We have a few more questions concerning Tania. Would it be okay for us to speak to you and your friends?'

Heidi made no comment but stared at Ryan, her voice hollow. 'You're the one who broke Bea's heart.'

'Seriously?!' Ryan cried. 'That is what Bea is saying? Unbelievable.'

Not wanting their investigation to be derailed by romantic strife, Maggie cleared her throat. 'I'm sure Bea's view on the situation is rather different to Ryan's, Heidi, but for now, can we concentrate on why we are here? Perhaps Bea and Ryan can have a little chat before we leave?'

'If Bea wants to.' Heidi glared at Ryan, before swinging round and walking out of the kitchen. 'You'd better come this way.'

# Chapter Thirty-nine

Following on Heidi's heels, Ryan and Maggie found themselves in a grand dining room.

*I can see what Monika meant about the family playing at being nobility!*

The dining table before them was laid out with all manner of warming plates. Each domed dish had custody of one element of a traditional English fry-up. Set for eight, the table currently had five people seated around it.

Having left Maggie and Ryan standing at the end of the room, Heidi had sat at the head of the table and immediately poured herself a cup of steaming hot coffee from a nearby pot. To her right, Daisy picked at a croissant with one hand, while fiddling with the pendant that hung around her neck with the other. Hugh, on Heidi's other side, began to plough through a heavily loaded plate of bacon, sausage and beans, as though he hadn't eaten in decades.

It was the figure next to Daisy that held Ryan's attention. He could feel the tension radiating off Bea as she cupped one hand around her coffee cup and the other around the hand of the man sitting next to her.

*I've been worried about how to tell Bea it's over, and she's been seeing someone else all along.*

The pilot, unlike everyone else in the room, beamed brightly at the unexpected guests. Paolo's white teeth were so perfect that Ryan found himself wondering how much it cost to keep them that way. His flawless dark skin added to his appearance of contentment and self-confidence.

Heidi broke the silence. 'So, here we are. What do you want that brings you here so early?'

'A few questions.' Ryan tried to disguise his apprehension.

'And why should we answer them?' Bea turned her glare from Ryan to Maggie. 'You say you're with the police, but you're not, are you?'

'They are aware we're here.'

Bea pursed her plump lips. 'But are they? I wonder.'

Daisy concentrated on the demolition of her croissant. 'What do you mean, Bea?'

'I mean, these two are no more working with the police than I am. They work in a fish and chip shop.'

Hugh's fork clattered against his plate. 'Is Bea right?'

'Of course I'm right!'

'Maggie, Ryan, I think you should leave.' Hugh gripped the side of the table with both hands. 'Now.'

Maggie stood her ground. 'As I said, the police are aware that we are here. We've been helping them. If you would like this fact verified, then feel free to call Sergeant Peters. You all have his number.'

'Why the hell would any of us have—?'

Bea's indignant enquiry was cut short as Ryan pulled out one of the unoccupied chairs and sat down. 'If you'd been here, Bea, with your friends when they needed you, you would know that the sergeant gave everyone his card in case they remembered anything about the night Tania died.'

Bea's face turned a deep scarlet, matching the enamel necklace that hung around her neck. 'It was the chance of a lifetime. I . . .'

'No, it wasn't.' Ryan's tone was unusually sharp. 'Your parents are rich, and your mother's family is in Portugal, so you could go there whenever you liked. So why now?'

Heidi and Daisy glanced at each other as the truth of what Ryan was saying sank in. It was Paolo, however, who spoke first, in an educated accent that seemed somewhat at odds with his clipped English.

'You jump to conclusions.'

Maggie responded before Ryan could. 'If we are making incorrect assumptions, then perhaps you could enlighten us.'

'My pleasure, Mag-ee.' Picking his teacup up, his little finger stuck out to the side in a manner that made him look rather fake – a man trying too hard to fit into the titled set – Paolo fixed his large brown eyes on Maggie. 'It was my fault. I had to fly to Agadir that day; it made sense for Be-trice to come with me then and not next month as planned.'

Bea shot Paolo a devastating scowl as Ryan crossed his arms over his chest. 'So you were always going to go travelling with him, then? You failed to mention that when you asked me to move into your flat and live with you forever.'

'Be-trice?' Paolo swivelled his entire frame around in his chair. 'You intended to live with this . . . man?'

'No. I just . . .'

'Keeping our options open, were we? If Paolo wasn't all you'd hoped, then there I was to fall back on, and vice versa.' Ryan was relieved to find the blush he'd been expecting to suffuse his cheeks didn't come. Instead, he found himself in icy control. 'I can end any thoughts you have in that direction right now. We are done.'

'Ryan, I . . .'

Amazed at how calm he felt, Ryan took in Bea's guilty expression. 'Now I'm no longer your pet project, you can stop lying to me, and to your friends here, and tell us what it was that made you go abroad when you did, rather than wait until after your friend's wedding? And before you say it's because that's the only chance you would get to do such a trip, then please remember that we all know that you could have gone at any time you liked.'

'Bea?' Heidi picked up a honey pot, and, for a split second, Ryan thought she was going to throw it at her friend. The slight wince Bea gave made him wonder if she'd thought the same. 'Tania had your dress ready. You even confirmed your size for the shoes only a week before the wedding.'

'I know. I'm sorry, it's just . . .' Bea had the good grace to look uncomfortable.

'Just what?'

'Alright, Ryan.' Bea gave an overly dramatic sigh. 'I was running away. I'm not proud of it, but I got scared, and I knew Paolo was flying for Toby just before the wedding, so I asked for a ride.'

Ryan felt his cheeks flame with heat. 'Scared about what, exactly?'

'Us, okay? Us. It got so serious, and I wasn't . . . I don't . . .'

Maggie placed a hand lightly on Ryan's arm as she said, 'You panicked about commitment, saw a way out, and took it.'

'In a nutshell.' Bea swallowed.

'But the flat and moving to Cornwall and . . . it was all your idea.'

'I know.'

'And Paolo?'

'I've been seeing him too – on and off. I'm sorry, Ryan, you and I would never have worked.'

'So why did you fly back when Maggie emailed you? Why lie about how you felt?'

Bea shrugged. 'I wanted to be sure I'd made the right decision.'

'Unbelievable!' Ryan clamped his lips together, not trusting himself to say more.

Paolo, seemingly oblivious to the tension, said, 'Bea explained about flying over. I'm glad she was nice to you.'

'She wanted to sleep with me!'

The Moroccan sniggered. 'She would not do that. She was just boosting your ego.' He grinned wider as he turned to Heidi. 'Bea wouldn't have missed the wedding. I'd have got her here and then taken her back again. Easy.'

'Easy?' Ryan blew the word out in disbelief.

Thankfully, Monika arrived back in the room at that point, breaking the tension as Maggie cleared her throat. 'Heidi, the dining table is laid for eight, but there are only five of you. I know your parents are away, so who are the other spaces for?'

'No one.'

'Really? Then why . . .?'

'It's a question of the look of the thing. You wouldn't understand.'

'You mean, it's sometimes seen as unlucky or untidy to lay an odd number of places at a table, so if, for example, you were only expecting five for breakfast, you would lay a place for six – an even number of places. That sort of thing?'

'Yes, that sort of thing.'

'But you have *three* empty seats. Why ask Monika to lay the table for eight?' Maggie turned to the housekeeper. 'Do you always lay for eight, or does it depend on the day?'

'I do what I'm asked to do. But you're right about the even numbers. I always lay for two if only one is expected, four if three are here. It looks nicer.'

Maggie looked around appreciatively at the tidy surroundings. Everything was neat and pleasing on the eye. 'So you would know how many were expected for breakfast each morning, so as not to over- or under-cook. I'm assuming you would be told this the evening before?'

'Yes. Usually by six o'clock.' Monika sounded less certain now, her eyes darting to Heidi.

'Can you tell me how many people you were expecting to feed today?'

'Today, I wasn't sure. Heidi said there might be two extra guests. I don't think she meant you, though.'

'Then who do you think she meant?'

'I don't know.'

Maggie tilted her head towards Heidi. 'You already have a sixth guest staying here, don't you, Miss Spenser-Davies, and you are expecting a seventh. Mr Simon Taylor.'

'How on earth did you . . .?' Bea's response died on her lips when she saw Heidi's icy glare across the table. 'Oh, sorry.'

Heidi blew out a gust of frustration. 'Yes, Simon is due later.'

Maggie levelled her gaze on Hugh. 'He wasn't just introduced to you for the first time when you crashed the car. Simon is your friend.'

Hugh visibly swallowed, but he said nothing.

Maggie kept her eyes fixed on Hugh. 'And Toby is here now. Yes?'

'He . . .'

'Perhaps you could fetch him, Hugh?'

'Maggie, he isn't . . .'

'I think it would be a really good idea if we spoke to him before the police arrive. And they will be arriving. As will Simon, quite soon now.'

Daisy put down the teacup she'd been holding with a sharp clatter. 'That's where you're wrong. Simon isn't due until lunchtime.'

'So he *is* part of this friendship group – we were right about that.'

'A friend of the boys.' Heidi glared at Maggie. 'It's really none of your business who Toby and Hugh know.'

'I see.' Maggie checked her watch. It was almost a quarter to nine. 'I think you'll find Simon will be here at nine-thirty.'

No one at the table moved. It was as if not one of them dared to look at the others in case their expressions gave them away.

The silence that followed was mercifully broken by the vibration of Maggie's phone.

'That was a text from the police. Don't you think it would be for the best if you gave Toby the chance to come down and get his side of things out in the open before they arrive?'

# Chapter Forty

'Toby is here? Has been staying *here*?' Monika was not impressed. 'The police think he killed Tania, and you've been harbouring him!'

'Monika, it's not like that!' Heidi was on her feet, looking panicked in the face of her housekeeper's wrath.

'That's exactly what it is like!' Monika moderated her tone, but her annoyance remained clear. 'Him being here secretly would explain a few things! I was beginning to think I was going mad.'

'Food going missing?' Ryan asked.

'Uh-huh. A slice of ham here, a piece of cake there. I thought I'd miscounted, misportioned. Things I simply do not do. But, I see now, there was a mouse – a big one.'

'Monika—' Heidi gave her housekeeper a desperate smile '—I didn't think it fair to tell you. After all, the police are involved. I didn't want to get you into trouble.'

'You'd rather I think I'm losing my marbles!'

'Monika! Don't forget your place!' Heidi's sharp rebuke made Ryan feel embarrassed, but it did not have the same effect on Monika.

'I do *not* take kindly to being taken for a fool, Miss Spenser-Davies. I suggest you work out what to tell your parents about this before I do.' She turned to Maggie and Ryan, the swift nature of her movement making the pendant at her throat bounce against her jumper. 'If you'll excuse me, I have work to do. And a lot to think about.'

As Monika left, Maggie slid her phone across to Ryan so he could read the text message she'd received.

**Houseman isn't going for it. Sorry Maggie. Do yourself and Ryan a favour and keep out of it. Don't go to the manor. If you've already gone, get out before you're arrested for interfering or something worse!**

Speaking quickly, hoping the knowledge that help wasn't coming didn't show on his face, Ryan asked, 'Which one of you got word to Toby that we were here and that he should stay in his room?'

Bea wasted no time in putting herself in the clear. 'Well, it wasn't me. I didn't know he was here.'

'Really?' Ryan wasn't sure he'd ever believe another word she said.

'It's true,' Daisy said. 'Bea didn't know. Neither did Paolo.'

'And you? When did you know, Miss Makepeace?' Remembering how wrong-footed he'd felt in the police station when he'd suddenly been addressed by his surname, Ryan was gratified to see the same tactic working on Daisy.

'Not until yesterday.'

Maggie addressed Heidi, 'And you?'

'Also yesterday.'

'This is your home. Are you honestly telling me you haven't noticed that he's been here all this time?'

'I became aware of him being here.' Heidi pulled herself upright. 'I would appreciate you not labelling me a liar.'

'You haven't lied, but you have been very clever with your choice of words. I applaud you for that.' Maggie sipped some coffee before turning to Hugh. 'So, when did you make Heidi aware that Toby was hiding out here?'

'I refute the implication that . . .'

'For goodness' sake! One of your friends is dead!' Maggie yelled. 'Several days have passed since Toby was last seen, since Ryan last saw him at the bus stop outside of The Cabin Hotel. Has he been here the whole time?'

'I don't know.' Hugh exchanged a hasty glance with Heidi, before carrying on. 'But I advised him that this might be a safe place for a while two days after Tania died. I haven't asked him when he got here. I only arrived myself last night, as you both know.'

'So, Toby knows the house and grounds well enough to get in unseen? He knows how to get to the kitchen for food and such?'

Hugh gave a silent inclination of his head.

'And you were alright with that, were you, Heidi?' Ryan asked, as all the eyes in the room focused on their hostess.

'As I said, I was unaware of this, but I wasn't surprised when I heard. Toby has been visiting on and off here since we were children. He knows the house and grounds well.'

Ryan wasn't sure he believed Heidi had been unaware of Toby's presence all along, but decided to accept their hostess's claim for the time being. 'Why did you keep your girlfriend in the dark, Hugh?'

'Girlfriend?' Daisy's head shot up from where she'd been staring at her plate of wasted food. 'Don't be ridiculous. Hugh and Heidi aren't . . .' Her voice faded as she saw the look in her friend's eyes. 'Oh my God . . . you are, aren't you? Well, thanks a million for telling me! Not! Best friends, huh – I don't think so!'

Daisy was on her feet and had stormed from the room before anyone could stop her. Ryan stood to follow the redhead, but Maggie shook her head. 'Let her go. She needs to let off steam.'

'Daisy always did behave like a twelve-year-old,' Bea sniped before giving Heidi a shrewd stare. 'You finally got what you wanted, then.'

'Bea, I . . .' Heidi let out a heavy sigh. 'We didn't think this was a good time to tell people we were together. Initially we didn't want to steal Toby and Tania's thunder over the stag and hen week and the wedding, and then . . . well, after what's happened, it felt in poor taste to . . .'

'Announce your engagement?'

'Alright, yes. We're engaged.' Heidi glared daggers at Maggie. 'How did you know? I've deliberately not worn my ring to keep it secret.'

'I guessed. Going out together isn't a thunder stealer, but a new engagement and another wedding to plan – that's big stuff.'

Seeing the flash of envy in Bea's green eyes, Ryan asked Hugh, 'Did Toby know?'

'Not until after Tania had died. I told him when I suggested he come here.'

'To lie low.'

'To give himself some breathing space.'

Ryan crossed his arms. 'He knew the police wanted to speak to him – and so did you. Why hide him when you knew it made him look guilty?'

Hugh muttered, 'That's his story to tell, not mine.'

'Then, if you could go and fetch him, I'd very much like to hear that story.' Maggie took a sip of her coffee.

'I can't. He left this morning.'

'How convenient.' Maggie pulled her notebook from her bag. The simple gesture acted like a magnet for everyone's eyeline; they all watched her turn the pages as she spoke. 'Previously, Hugh, you told us that you hadn't seen Toby since you argued. That he cut you dead after the accident, and that he didn't say anything to you when you saw him and Tania prior to their trip to the pub.'

'And that was the truth.'

'Apart from the fact that you've seen him here.'

'I hadn't seen him when I spoke to you the first time.'

Maggie held her nerve. 'But you had spoken to him on the phone. Lies of omission are still lies, Mr Parkinson.'

'Why did Toby feel the need to lie low here?' Ryan coaxed. 'We don't believe he killed his fiancée, so what reason has he to hide?'

Paolo leant forward. 'At last, someone with eyes. I too see he would not do this. He love her.'

Slightly rocked by support from such an unexpected source, Ryan went on. 'We knew that Tania was beginning to wonder if she could trust Toby. We know from you, Hugh, that Toby was involved in something he was uneasy about, and we've good reason to believe that something was connected to his work.'

The mention of Toby's work made Maggie rub the back of her head as she added, 'A recent visit to his office confirmed that suspicion.'

'When I last saw Toby, he was on his way to meet someone connected to his business.' Ryan tried to watch everyone's reaction at once. 'Rachel Zimmerman, perhaps.'

Neither Hugh, Heidi nor Bea's faces moved a muscle, but Paolo was clearly working from a different script to everyone else.

'Oh, she is not liked. Good job Daisy's not here. She hates her.'

Heidi's tut was out-drama-ed by Bea's rolling eyes. 'Really, Paolo, do you have to be so transparent? Daisy's dislike of Rachel is not relevant here, and she would not like you airing her dirty laundry in public.'

'Her dirty laundry?'

Ryan translated, 'She means Daisy prefers her secrets and feelings to be kept private.'

'It is no secret.' Paolo puffed. 'Rachel is a difficult person. I think she is okay, but I have to work with her – the others, they have no time. They can't cope with her . . . umm . . . forcefulness.'

'You fly for Mermaid Imports?'

'Sometimes, when the cargo is small. I fly over often anyway. I'm cheaper than the main airports.'

'I bet you are,' Ryan mumbled to himself, before asking, 'And where do you fly from? Where is your base?'

'Agadir.'

'And is that where your home is – in Morocco, I mean?'

'Part time. I fly there often, but I divide my time between here and there.'

'Here, as in Cornwall?' Maggie took over from where Ryan had left off.

'I live near the airport in St Just.'

Maggie scribbled in her notebook before asking, 'Would it be fair to say that, when you fly things in for Toby and Rachel, His Majesty's Revenue and Customs might not always be in the know?'

Paolo sat up straight, finally cottoning on to the 'shut up now' looks Bea had been giving him for the last few minutes. 'The United Kingdom and Morocco have a long-standing trade agreement. It is all perfectly acceptable.'

'And always legal?'

'I do what I am paid to do.'

'Which airports do you fly into in the UK?' Maggie's pen hovered over her notebook.

'Exeter often, sometimes Bournemouth, but my plane is small, so usually Land's End Airport.'

'Thank you, Paolo.' Maggie smiled. 'I'm sure the airports will have records of your visits, yes?'

'They will.'

'And this time, when you flew Bea in so she could see Ryan, where did you land, and did you have any cargo with you?'

'No cargo. Was just Bea. We land locally.'

'And you picked her up from which airport?' Ryan asked.

'I told you, Agadir. You should listen.'

Ryan spoke slowly. 'You didn't fly her here from Faro airport?'

'Faro? No, she was with me in . . .'

Bea let out a low groan. 'I can explain, Ryan. I . . .'

'You were in Morocco, with . . .' He shook his head sharply. 'Were you *ever* in Portugal?'

'Not this time, no.'

'You lied about where you were so you could cheat on me.' Aware of every set of eyes in the room on him, Ryan forced himself to remain outwardly calm. 'Right now we have more important things to think about.'

Maggie waited for a brief nod from Ryan, before she turned to Heidi, noting the exotic necklace she wore, as she said, 'None of you liked Rachel – was that because she was simply not someone who you connected with, or was there a reason for this dislike? I understand that she was at university with Toby?'

Hugh provided the answer. 'As you are already aware, Maggie, Rachel broke my heart. It's a hobby of hers, reeling people in and then hurting them.'

Ryan couldn't resist scowling at Bea. 'Popular hobby around here.'

Maggie was still looking at Hugh. 'And yet, Toby, your best friend, employed Rachel as his business partner.'

'She's very good at her job.'

'She must be.'

'Anyway, she was only technically a partner – it wasn't official. Toby had already got Mermaid up and running at uni. In his first year, actually. He almost left so he could work on it full time, but his parents wanted him to get his degree, so he stayed. Rachel joined him a year or so later. She liked to be referred to as his partner, but on paper, she wasn't.'

'Would she have been eventually, do you think?'

'Probably.'

Maggie was about to ask another question when the clock on the mantel struck nine-thirty.

'It's half-past nine.' Accusation shone in Heidi's eyes. 'You said Simon would be here by now, and he isn't. Nor are the police. They aren't coming, are they?'

'No.' Maggie closed her notebook with a thump.

'Bea was right! You're nothing to do with them, are you!' Heidi looked fit to explode as she hissed, 'You conned us! Turning up, asking a heap of personal questions with no right at all! I think you should both leave. Now.'

Maggie stood up, gesturing for Ryan to follow suit. 'Thank you for the coffee. I'm sorry we interrupted your breakfast.'

Heidi got up. 'I won't see you out. Thanks to you, I've a best friend to go and appease.'

# Chapter Forty-one

'Now what do we do?' Ryan peered out of the car's back window as Darren drove them away from the manor's driveway and back through Lamorna village.

'We find Toby.'

'But how? We were sure he was at the manor, but . . .'

'And we were right – but then Bea and Paolo arrived. The significant part of that, I suspect, being Paolo.'

'You aren't kidding.' Ryan's eyes might have been on the view through the car window, but all he saw was Paolo's handsome face.

'No, I mean . . .'

'I know what you mean – you mean the fact that Paolo flies for Mermaid Imports.'

'Umm . . .' Maggie flicked the pages of her notebook through her fingers. 'I wonder if he does?'

'But he said . . .'

'He said he worked for Mermaid Imports, Ryan.'

'Toby's firm.'

'Mermaid Imports *is* Toby's firm, but what if Rachel wanted more of a stake in the business? What if Paolo really flies for Rachel? What if she was blackmailing Toby? You know, make me the senior partner, even if just for appearances' sake, or I'll expose what you're up to. Assuming she knows what that is.'

'You might be onto something. I wish we knew more about her.' Maggie paused. 'I'm an idiot.'

'You really aren't.'

'I am – I didn't ask when Toby left the manor, or when Hugh or any of the others last saw him at the manor.'

'Surely he left when one of them got word we'd arrived.'

'That was the implication. We even helped them make it seem like that with our questions.' Maggie frowned. 'But what if he'd already gone? What if he left when Bea and Paolo arrived?'

Ryan groaned. 'We didn't ask what time they got there either, did we?'

'I'm sorry about Bea.'

'I don't want to think about it.'

'Fair enough.' Maggie swept her hands through her mass of curls. 'Why did I ever think I could do this detecting lark? That's two basic questions I didn't think of – who knows what else I failed to ask!'

'I was there too, and I didn't think of those things either.' Ryan took his phone from his pocket. 'But I can get an answer to one of those questions.'

'You're calling Bea? I'd have thought she was the last person you'd want to talk to.'

'Desperate times and all that. Anyway, it's the quickest way to find out what we need to know.'

'Thanks, Ryan.' Maggie watched the landscape change through the window. 'Now, I think we should be good citizens and go to the police station. Could you take us into Penzance, please, Darren? We've just got time to annoy Inspector Houseman before heading to work.'

\*

Maggie knew David was feeling awkward. From the expression on his face, you'd never have known, but the way his right foot was rubbing the back of his left leg as he listened to his boss vent her frustration told her all she needed to know. It was an involuntary gesture she recalled from when he felt uncomfortable in his youth. Maggie didn't need to look at Ryan to know he'd be feeling awkward too – the poor boy seemed to live in a state of awkwardness.

*If Bea told Ryan the truth on the phone, and she and Paolo only arrived at the manor house late last night, then Toby hasn't been gone long. Logically, therefore, he must either be in a local hotel or hostel, at his parents' home or ...*

The sound of silence brought Maggie back to the moment. She knew she'd zoned out as Detective Inspector Houseman laid out her views on amateurs potentially messing up crime scenes and murder investigations in very blunt terms, and now everyone was staring at her expectantly.

'I'm waiting for an answer, Miss Tyson.'

Maggie considered bluffing, but Houseman was no fool, and she didn't deserve to be treated like one. 'Forgive me, but I stopped listening about ten seconds into you telling us off.'

'You stopped listening?' Houseman couldn't have been more surprised if Maggie had told her there was a bomb in her handbag.

'I thought my time would be better spent thinking.' Maggie picked her bag off the desk in the police station's reception area. 'If you aren't interested in hearing what Ryan and I have discovered, then we'll be on our way.'

'But you shouldn't have been out collecting information!'

'A point you've made very clear, Detective Inspector. What baffles me is why you haven't been out doing the same thing?'

'Because we don't need to! The coroner has yet to rule cause of death – and when he does, it's highly likely it will be death by misadventure. If that isn't the case, and it is ruled as suspicious, then Miss Stevens' fiancé is the most likely culprit. Until we find him – which *we* will do without you sending us on another expensive wild goose chase – we are busy with other matters.'

'And you'll be looking for him where? I understand from one of their friends that the house he and Tania were due to move into wouldn't be free until after their honeymoon, and, until now, he's been living with his parents in Sennen.'

Ryan glanced nervously at Houseman as Maggie relayed what Bea had begrudgingly told him on the phone.

'He is not in Sennen.' The detective took a long, slow intake of breath. 'And if I discover that you've been bothering his mum and dad, I will have you arrested for harassment.'

Maggie took no notice of Houseman's warning tone. 'I'm assuming you have wholly discounted that one of Toby's friends or his business partner – who, if you are interested, might not have been his business partner but merely an associate or employee – could have been involved?'

'We have discounted nothing.' David lowered his right foot to the floor, intervening before Maggie got herself arrested for wasting police time. 'Come on, you know we have procedures to follow.'

'I do, and I respect them, but not listening to members of the public when they come in with information is not a procedure; it is incompetence.'

Ryan suddenly found his voice. 'No wonder Harry was reticent about coming to you. Did you talk to him about the girl he saw, or did you dismiss him as a muddled old man?'

'I spoke to him.' David uncrossed his arms. 'I went to see him just after I—'

'That's enough, Sergeant Peters.' Houseman gave her colleague a look of pure poison. 'Now, if you'll excuse us, I think we've wasted enough time here.'

Houseman had buzzed her way back into the heart of the police station before anyone else had moved.

'I think you annoyed her.' David chuckled. 'Doesn't take much.'

Maggie shook her head. 'I thought you said she was a good detective.'

'She is. Just gets a bit fed up with people thinking they can do her job better than she can.'

'We never claimed that.'

'No, you did something far worse – you have been *proving* that you can. Thing is, you have no barriers. No rules. We have guidelines and procedures; they slow things down to a frustrating level. She'd love to be able to just barge up to people's homes and ask questions without reason.'

'I can believe it.' Maggie nodded. 'We really do have information you might find helpful, David.'

'Okay, I'll calm things down here and then meet you for a coffee over the road during my break. You know the café around the corner?'

'Very well,' Ryan grumbled. 'It's where Maggie took me after you tried to make me out to be a murderer.'

★

Maggie and Ryan had eaten a slice of cake each and were making serious headway into their pot of tea by the time David arrived. The wait hadn't been a problem, for while adding considerably to their daily calorie intake, they went over everything they'd learnt and tried to make sense of what they didn't yet understand.

'Sorry, I couldn't get away any faster.' As David sat down, his uniform swapped for jeans and a T-shirt, he called to the waitress behind the counter. 'Usual, Tina love.'

'You're a frequent flyer here?' Maggie watched as Tina moved around the counter, gathering up a sausage roll and a mug of tea.

'Every day, including Sundays when I'm on shift, since I got back to Cornwall.' David shrugged. 'Saves me having to worry about making a packed lunch – and I can't stand the canteen. Coming here gets me out of the station at least once a day.'

Ryan's forehead furrowed. 'But you must go out every day, walking your beat and so on.'

'Ah lad, those were the days. It's more a whip around the block in a police car now, or going out when called to a crime scene. A bobby walking the streets is a luxury the taxpayer can no longer afford.'

Maggie tutted as she referred to the new raft of notes she and Ryan had made. 'Are you ready to listen to us?'

'I am, but I can't guarantee I'll be able to do anything about it. If I had a higher rank or was in CID, then maybe. But as it is . . .'

'It's alright, I get it.' Maggie kept her eyes on her notes. 'Just to reassure you – or, so you can reassure your boss – we aren't doing this for any kind of reward or to be featured in the papers, or anything like that. We just want to help.'

'Okay. So, tell me everything.'

'First thing this morning we paid a call on the Mount View Garage and spoke to Simon Taylor. We asked him a few questions which then led us to Lamorna Manor, where we believed we could find Toby Marrell. Which is why we asked you to join us at the manor.'

David put down the sausage roll that had been halfway to his mouth. 'You never said that Toby was there! You said that you wanted an exchange of information. If we'd known that . . .'

Maggie was already shaking her head. 'As it turned out, we'd just missed him, so it's fortunate you dismissed us out of hand. I can imagine Detective Houseman's face if we'd got her to come to another place to apprehend her lead suspect, and he wasn't there.'

'Indeed.' David paused. 'But if you think *I* dismissed you out of hand, then—'

'Anyway,' Ryan cut in as he stirred his tea, 'Toby didn't kill Tania, Sergeant.'

'Oh, the irony! Weren't you the ones who went on and on about how a partner would be the most likely suspect in a murder?'

'David, you know full well it was murder!' Maggie spoke fast. 'And yes, partners are the most likely suspects, just not in this case.'

'Are you two ever going to get to the point? I've only got half an hour, then I need to put the uniform back on.' David bit into his sausage roll.

'Then we'll be brief.' Maggie spoke quietly, so as not to alert the other customers. 'During our visit to Simon Taylor this morning, he admitted that Toby had been to the garage recently, despite previously claiming he hadn't seen him.'

'This wasn't actually a lie.' Ryan took over. 'Simon hadn't *physically* seen Toby, but he had spotted Toby on the garage's security camera. The fact he'd watched the CCTV confirmed what we'd been thinking. Simon *expected* Toby to come.'

David wasn't impressed. 'But Toby works there, Maggie, so what's so unusual about that?'

'Toby works upstairs in the office. He has no need to go into the garage workshop area. However, he is a lover of cars, especially vintage cars, and he'd just lost his pride and joy – Sandy, his Jag. Simon told us he didn't come to say goodbye to her before she was scrapped, which we thought odd, as he treated that car as if it was the love of his life. In fact, a few people said he loved the car as much as he loved Tania.'

David sat back in his chair. 'So, he returned to say goodbye to the car. So what?'

'When I spoke to Hugh, he said that after the crash Toby was ranting and raving. This you might expect, as his future wife could have been killed, but Hugh said that Toby kept saying that if he'd hit a hedge and not a wall, things would have been okay, but now might be ruined. This morning I worked out why that sounded a bit odd to me.'

'Go on.'

'It was the word *might* – *might* be ruined. Surely, it *was* ruined – his car was undriveable.'

Ryan passed David his phone. 'This is grainy, but when Simon showed us the recorded footage of Toby – reluctantly, I should say – I recorded it. Here.'

As Ryan pressed play, all three of them sat in silence, watching a shape that Simon had assured them was Toby, under the cover of darkness, a torch in hand, creep into the garage yard to try to open what would have once been the glove box on the passenger side of his car. 'He can't get to it. He's giving it a good go though – too concertinaed.'

David glanced up at Maggie. 'What was in there, do you think?'

'Something small. Something worth coming back for. Something he wasn't supposed to have.'

'And maybe, something too valuable to leave to the scrap merchants.' Ryan lifted his eyes from his teacup. 'Did your colleagues find anything in Exeter? Anything that could have been smuggled inside the consignment from Morocco?'

'No, but—'

'But if we accept that Tania was murdered—' Maggie interrupted '—and if the murder and the smuggling are connected, then they wouldn't have been stupid enough to bring in anything until the investigation into her death had concluded and the coroner made their ruling. Until then, there was always a chance you'd be watching.'

'If it had been drugs, I think we'd have found something.' David played a crumb of pastry through his fingers. 'We had dogs with us. Standard procedure at an airport, and there was no sign of any narcotics. If there had been drugs at any time in the containers they use for transporting goods

– which are reused again and again – there'd have been some reaction from the dogs. But there was nothing.'

'Good.' Maggie felt relieved. 'I didn't want this to be about drugs. But I do think Mermaid Imports are moving more than just furniture. Something that they would prefer not to pay customs duty on.'

'And I bet that Paolo is up to his neck in it,' Ryan grumbled.

'Paolo.' Maggie froze.

'Are you alright?' David reached a hand out towards her, but quickly withdrew it again.

'The folder.'

Ryan's eyes narrowed. 'The one that was taken when you were attacked?'

'It was full of invoices. Old-school paper ones . . .'

'Which we considered odd.' David caught Maggie's eye. 'Paper records in this day and age isn't something we associate with new businesses, especially those run by members of the younger generation.'

'But—' Maggie closed her eyes '—perhaps it isn't so strange. Think about it. Paper can be destroyed. It's much harder to delete computer records these days; there's always something left after deletion. Always a ghost in the machine.'

'But why have records at all?' Ryan asked. 'Safer to have no paper trail.'

Silently acknowledging Ryan's point, David didn't speak. He could see Maggie was thinking.

'The invoices I saw, I swear they seemed ordinary. All were marked paid. But every now and then one had a small green cross in the corner. I thought it might mean something but wasn't sure what. It felt like a puzzle – a code. One I couldn't crack. But now . . . what if it was . . . ?'

'Paolo!' Ryan spoke the word with venom.

'Exactly.'

'Exactly *what*, or who?' David was getting impatient.

Maggie leant across the table, her whisper urgent. 'Paolo said he flew in small pieces for Mermaid Imports, usually to Land's End airport. What if his imports were the ones marked by the green crosses?'

'Or, what if the green crosses marked consignments that had a little extra hidden within them?' Ryan suggested. 'What's small enough to be hidden in trinket boxes and in picture frame packaging?'

'Rare stamps or coins?' David pondered. 'Gemstones? Diamonds?'

Ryan shrugged. 'That's heavy-duty stuff – diamonds especially. Would Toby be mixed up in that?'

Maggie answered before David could. 'Toby might not be, but Rachel could be. Or maybe it's simpler than that. Maybe it's just a case of them cutting corners, not smuggling high-value stuff, but avoiding some costs.'

'Duty-dodging?'

'Yes.' An image of the three women they'd seen that morning flashed through her mind. 'Pendants.'

'Pardon?' Ryan exchanged a blank look with the sergeant.

'The women all wore pendants this morning. All similar in style. I didn't think about it at the time, but what if they all came from the same place?'

'Paolo, you mean?'

'Paolo via Toby.

'Or Rachel?'

Maggie nodded. 'I'm not convinced she's abroad. If she was here, she'd have motive to kill Tania. Plus, she could well have been the woman Harry saw texting near the harbour; not Tania but Rachel . . . Assuming they look alike, that is.'

'Okay – that's it.' Fed up with observing the two-way conversation before him, David got to his feet. 'One: Rachel *is* in Morocco. We checked – she flew out the day before Tania died, and there is no record of her returning, so Harry did *not* see her. I've spoken to him, and I think it was Tania he spotted. Two: who the hell is Paolo? And three: we've found *no* evidence of smuggling *at all*. There was nothing dodgy about the trinkets that arrived in Exeter, apart from the fact that Toby didn't arrive to collect them. So whether the girls were all wearing pendants or not this morning has nothing whatsoever to do with anything. Now, I must get back to work!'

'But logic suggests they wouldn't smuggle every time. That would be stupid, and they don't strike me as stupid people.'

David glared pointedly at Maggie. 'Oh, and four: will you *please* just stop all this! *If* the coroner rules there has been a murder, we will find Toby and arrest him. If we have any reason to suspect Toby or this Rachel Zimmerman are up to something dodgy, we *will* arrest them for that *if* we can find proof. And that will be that. Sometimes life is boringly straightforward. I do wish you two would stop making it so complicated.'

# Chapter Forty-two

Maggie put a hand on David's arm. 'Please, stay for a moment longer.'

'Maggie . . .'

'Just to tell us what you plan to do now.'

David sat down again with a resigned sigh. 'I'll tell Houseman everything you've told me. Then I'll patiently wait while she gives me a bollocking. Once her pride has died down, I'll see what action she wants to take.'

'Is that all?'

'As I was trying to say, nothing you have told me has any proof to back it up.'

'But—'

'Toby was at the manor, but he isn't now. He did visit the garage, and he *might* have a business partner who is up to something – the sort of something we can report to Customs, who can watch out for her and this Paolo chap on our behalf.' David got back to his feet, holding up a palm as he saw Maggie ready to protest. 'I am taking what you are saying seriously. Please don't do anything until you've heard from me.'

'There's something else.'

'What?' David groaned.

'Despite claims that Simon was only friends with Toby and Hugh, we didn't buy that Simon didn't know the girls that well. So, when we saw Simon earlier, I asked him if he had a partner. I thought that maybe he was going out with one of the girls – that he was connected with the group in another way – via a relationship.'

'And?'

'And we were right . . . in a way . . .'

*

Ryan waited until Sergeant Peters had gone through the door and walked past the café's window in the direction of the station before he said, 'What are we going to do next?'

'We're going to go to work.'

'Oh yes! I'd forgotten about the chip shop!'

Maggie chuckled. 'Don't let Mr Robbins hear you say that.'

Ryan flexed his arms out over his head, almost touching the café ceiling. 'Feels a bit of an anticlimax, leaving it all to the police now.'

Maggie grinned. 'Don't you worry. We're not done yet.'

'We aren't?'

'You heard David. The police have rules to follow. Procedures. They take time, and my gut tells me we don't have time, so, after work, we're going to do what the police can't.'

'Which is what?'

'Sneak around a bit.'

*

'Darren will take you.'

Maggie knew better than to argue with Mr Robbins.

'Thank you, a lift at this time of night would be welcome. He should stay in the car. He looks a bit . . . well, we don't want to provoke trouble.'

Her boss nodded, his jowls wobbling in the process. 'Darren will have his phone ready. If you need help, you call him. Yes?'

'If we need help, we will call the police.'

'Darren first, police second. Darren will be closer.'

Unable to argue with his logic, Maggie thanked Mr Robbins again, silently hoping that there would be no need for Darren and his hefty fists to get her and Ryan out of trouble.

*

Ryan's heart pounded as he opened the passenger door and stared up at the night sky, which shrouded Marazion in darkness. As if in tune with the nature of their enquiry, the sky was devoid of stars, blanketed instead with an ominous cloud cover.

'Are you sure he'll be here?'

'No, but I'm sure this is where I'd go if I was him. It's the perfect place. It's hidden from the main road, and there's a sofa to sleep on. He can't go home or to his parents; he's already run from the manor, and his office has been taped off by the police. Where else is there?' Maggie leant forward to Darren. 'We'll shout if we need you.'

The driver produced a newspaper from beneath his chair and settled down to read with the air of a man used to waiting.

As Maggie joined Ryan in front of the Mount View Garage, he whispered, 'Do you think Simon will be here too?'

'Unlikely. It's half-ten at night. Anyway, I doubt Simon knows he has an overnight guest.'

Adrenaline shot through Ryan's system as, mobile phone torches held out before them, they passed the stairs up to Mermaid Imports' office and made their way around the side of the garage.

The faint glow of a single light came from within.

Maggie mouthed, 'There's someone there.'

'Toby?'

Neither Maggie nor Ryan knew how to proceed.

*Do we knock on the door? Walk on in? Shout out that we're here and risk him running?* Checking over his shoulder,

Ryan muttered, 'We can't just stand here, he'll get spooked. We must be throwing shadows.'

Maggie agreed, shoved her shoulders back and put her hand on the door. 'Here goes nothing.'

Unsurprisingly, the door was locked, so she knocked hard on the glass. 'Toby! Please let us in. My name is Maggie, and I'm here with my friend Ryan. We know you didn't kill Tania. We want to help.'

There was a heavy silence. The only sign that she'd been heard was the abrupt switching off of the light within.

'Toby, please. We really are on your side. But the police are convinced you're involved. We can help you.' Maggie pushed her point home. 'They'll find you eventually. What have you got to lose by talking to us?'

Nothing happened.

Ryan was about to speak, when a shuffling sound from within stopped the words forming in his throat. The outline of a man was forming on the other side of the frosted glass door. The scrape of a key in the lock was followed by the door opening a fraction.

'You the two that Hugh told me about? From the chippy?'

'That's us.' Maggie smiled encouragingly. 'We really do want to help you.'

'Why?'

'Because,' Ryan replied, 'I met Tania once, and I liked her.'

Toby opened the door wider. 'I've never seen you before. How come you knew Tania?'

'She sat with me in the pub after you stormed out.'

'Oh.' Toby lowered his head.

'Can we come in?' Maggie wrapped her arms around her.

Walking back inside without a word, Toby left the door open by way of invitation. 'How did you know I was here? I haven't told anyone.'

'A guess.' Maggie followed him through to the office they'd sat in with Simon that morning. A coat had been rolled up to make a pillow on the sofa at the back of the room. 'I take it that not even Simon knows you're here?'

'No. I only got here an hour ago.'

'Why did you leave the manor?'

Toby appeared to be caught between surprise and fear. 'You know I've been there?'

'That was our first guess.' Maggie sat on a desk chair as Toby perched on the edge of the sofa. 'We must have missed you by only a few hours.'

Next to Maggie, Ryan regarded the man who he'd last seen at the bus stop. All signs of arrogance were gone. This was someone whose self-assurance had been wiped from him, to be replaced by fear and grief.

Toby clasped his hands together. 'Was Tania very angry with me when you saw her?'

'Sad, not angry. You were the angry one. I got the impression she didn't understand why you were so cross.'

'I wasn't. Not really. Just frustrated. I wanted to tell her, but . . .'

'But if you'd told her, you'd have implicated her in a crime, and you didn't want to do that.'

If Toby had been surprised before, now he was stunned. 'How did you . . . ?'

Maggie took her notebook from her bag and held it up by way of explanation. 'It was the only way all the puzzle pieces fitted together. Although, I'll admit, I'm missing a few bits of sky.'

'Pardon?'

Maggie clarified, 'I just meant I'm not sure I have all the pieces of this puzzle in the correct order, but you could help with that. Help catch Tania's killer.'

'How?'

'Do you have a recent photo of Tania? The one in the paper had her old hairstyle.'

Toby immediately opened the photo gallery on his phone. 'Here.'

'That's a nice one. Tania, Heidi and Daisy.'

Toby sniffed hard, his eyes suddenly red with the effort of holding back tears. 'That was taken in the lobby of the hotel before everything went wrong.'

'Could I have a copy, please? There's a potential witness I'd like to show it to.'

'There is?'

'A friend of ours saw a woman on her way to the harbour the night Tania died.'

'You need a photo to show him, to see if it was Tania?'

'Exactly.' As Ryan read out his mobile number to Toby so he could forward the picture, Maggie said, 'Forgive me, but it's been mentioned by more than one person that you haven't appeared to be upset by Tania's death.'

Wiping a hand over his eyes, Toby muttered, 'I can't even begin— I suppose I can't believe she's gone. And with everything else that's happened. I've been so scared.'

'"Everything else" being things connected with Mermaid Imports?'

Toby nodded mutely, silent tears flowing down his cheeks.

Maggie spoke gently. 'We're pretty sure we know what it was that sparked all this. Or should I say, who it was?'

Toby licked his lips nervously. 'I've not said anything to anyone, so how could you know what this is all about?'

'By paying attention.' Maggie ran a hand over the back of her head. 'Plus a bit of poking our noses in where they weren't wanted.'

'Oh.'

Maggie gripped her notebook. 'How long has Rachel been secretly importing jewellery?'

Toby's entire frame went rigid. 'How the hell did you know about that?'

'I began to suspect that your business was involved in smuggling a little while after I'd seen inside your office. The folder on the desk – some of the invoices were marked with green crosses. They had to stand for something, but I wasn't sure what. Ryan suggested that the crosses might refer to furniture that had been used to smuggle smaller goods into the country without bothering the taxman. When I saw the women at the manor this morning all wearing pendants, each striking and a little exotic, Moroccan perhaps, I saw Ryan was probably right.'

'The pendants were legal imports. Presents for their roles in the wedding. But—' Toby gulped '—there was one for Tania too. A locket. Beautiful, like her. It was supposed to be a surprise. It was so valuable that it would have needed declaring separately at customs.'

'And Rachel suggested hiding it in some furniture?'

Toby tucked his hands in his jeans pockets. 'A one-off, she said. I jumped at it. The wedding was cripplingly expensive and . . .' He rapidly ran out of steam. 'I swear I didn't know Rachel was already bringing in things illegally.'

'Do you know how long she's been doing this?' Ryan asked.

'At first she said it was only since I asked her to pick up the locket for Tania and some nice jewellery for her attendants, and something for Monika for all her hard work with the catering arrangements. But then she admitted it had been going on for a while – she wouldn't say how long.'

'From the very beginning?' Ryan ventured.

'Maybe.'

'The green crosses,' Maggie asked, 'we were right about those?'

'Yes. In the past Rachel claimed the crosses showed which invoice payments she'd double-checked. Recently, I learnt otherwise.' Toby looked exhausted. 'I just wanted something extra special for Tania. A present for our wedding day. Rachel has a better eye than mine when it comes to that sort of thing. It made sense to ask her to find something.' Toby raked his hands through his hair. 'If I hadn't asked her to do that, then I might never have found out.'

Ryan nodded slowly. 'So, the surprise that Tania had decided you were making up was real. It had been the jewellery?'

'Yes. Like I said, I thought I was suggesting a one-off additional shipment to come over with the furniture. Rachel told me that if we slipped the gifts inside the furniture, we would skip having to pay any duty. I should never have agreed, but she has a way of being very persuasive. And I thought, why not? We pay loads in taxes already. What's the harm? I had no idea this was a regular thing; that she was already bringing things in and selling them on in Devon before returning to Cornwall.'

'I see.' Maggie said. 'We discovered you had some furniture coming in this week. The police were waiting in Exeter for you. They searched the package but found nothing.'

'Nothing to find. She isn't stupid. Once news of Tania's death reached her, Rachel pulled the plug.' Although, I'd be very surprised if she didn't start things up again once everything dies down.'

'You *really* didn't know about Rachel's extra enterprise beforehand?' Ryan was incredulous.

'No. She did it so easily – and was so calm about bringing it all in under the radar that I got to thinking . . . and I started to ask questions. Started to look through our paper records. Came to the same conclusion as you about those crosses, Maggie.' He sighed. 'I wish I'd kept my mouth shut. If I had, then Tania would be alive, and I wouldn't be hiding like a coward!'

Maggie paused, before saying, 'You think Rachel killed your fiancée?'

'As a warning to me to keep my mouth shut. Yes.' Toby's eyes welled with tears.

Ryan, whose opinion of Toby was shifting fast, said, 'Rachel was in Morocco when Tania died.'

'Says who? Flights to and from Morocco are regular and cheap – and they don't take long. She could have hopped over and hopped back. No problem. Especially if Paolo brought her in.'

Maggie shivered slightly.

'Maggie?' Ryan was worried. 'You okay?'

'Yes. At least, I think so.' She looked up at Toby. 'Why doesn't your business have a website? We couldn't find any online presence. You must need to advertise for clients sometimes.'

'No need. We have all the clients we can handle.'

'That's a bit odd.' Ryan frowned.

'Maybe, but Rachel liked to keep things manageable.' Toby winced. 'At least, that's what she said. Now I'm wondering if it was just to keep us off the radar.'

'But isn't it *your* business, not hers?' Maggie watched Toby carefully.

'Umm, yeah. The thing is, she's quite forceful, and we always have loads of work. I can't believe how stupid I've been. I've let her pretty much manage the place for months – I thought she was being nice. Taking on the lion's share of the burden while I had a wedding to organise. But in the last few weeks it's become obvious that she intended to take over my company.'

As a dullness came over Toby's eyes, Maggie asked, 'When did you last see Rachel?'

'In person, about three weeks ago. Via Zoom two days after Tania died.'

*So, when Ryan heard Toby say he'd see her in thirty minutes when he was sitting at the bus stop, it wasn't for an in-person chat; it was for a Zoom call . . .* 'Toby, I need you to make a phone call to Lamorna Manor.'

# Chapter Forty-three

Once Toby had made the call Maggie had requested, she made a phone call of her own to Mr Robbins, asking if he would mind a temporary tenant in the bedsit.

Having then summoned Darren to the garage, who escorted a worn-out Toby to the relative safety of the fish and chip shop's bedsit, Maggie sat down on the sofa.

Ryan asked, 'What did Sergeant Peters say?'

'That if I'm right, and something happens tonight, we should call 999, but that he'd much rather we stopped playing detective and went home.'

'Which we are not going to do.'

'Not now we've got this far, no.' Maggie massaged some of the tension from her shoulders. 'At least we know that Toby will be safe with Mr Robbins.'

'Surely he'll be settled in his campervan by now?'

'Darren will pick him up on the way to the chippy. Toby will either feel extra safe or extra intimidated, sat in the car with those two.'

Ryan gave a wry smile. 'Do you think you should tell David we've seen Toby?'

'Not yet.' Maggie felt nerves flutter in her stomach. 'I have the feeling that, right now, the police chasing Toby will muddy the waters.'

'You know who killed her, don't you?'

'Let's just say I've narrowed it down to two suspects.'

A look of frustration passed over Ryan's face. 'I've been everywhere with you, Maggie, and I don't know who hurt Tania.'

'I suspect you do.'

Ryan sat quietly, his eyes widening as he began to think. 'But do we have any proof?'

'None.' Maggie drummed her fingers against Simon's desk. 'And as Inspector Houseman has made it clear she's not interested unless we have information typed up in triplicate and wrapped in a neat bow, then I am not inclined to share what I know until I can show her that this isn't just a game we're playing.'

'Houseman? Or is it Sergeant Peters you are keen to impress?'

'I'm not trying to impress anyone. Come on. The cab I've called to take us to Lamorna will be here in a minute.'

'Okay.' Ryan stood up. 'But first I must have a pee; otherwise I'll be watching out for trouble without being able to concentrate on anything other than how much I need to go to the loo.'

\*

Flattening her back against the hallway wall, Maggie hoped the shadows were deep enough to hide them as she and Ryan waited. Although they couldn't see the entrance to the manor's downstairs bedroom from where they waited, Maggie was sure they'd hear anyone approach.

After what felt like forever, the echo of faint footsteps made them look at each other.

Maggie put a restraining hand on Ryan's arm and mouthed. 'Trainers. I'd guess that's Simon arriving to answer Toby's summons.'

A moment later, Ryan nudged Maggie's arm and mouthed, 'Someone else is coming.'

'That'll be—' Maggie's jaw dropped open as David appeared by their side. 'Bloody hell, you gave me the fright of my life. Did Monika let you in?'

'Yes, now be quiet,' David muttered. 'A car pulled up the drive just after I ran in here.'

'Did they see you?' Ryan asked.

'No. I hid my car round the back. But if you don't shush, then all this Secret Squirrel bollocks is going to be for nothing!'

Hoping Monika's loyalty to the household didn't cause her to give them away, Maggie tensed as another set of footsteps – moving hastily, but with exaggerated care – approached.

The bedroom door opened and closed.

Maggie counted to ten, then eased herself away from the wall. As one, she and her companions crept forwards.

\*

Simon's face was creased with anger, until he saw Maggie open the door. Then it morphed into confusion.

'What are you doing here?'

'We've come to speak to you.'

Ryan stepped into the room, leaving David in the shadow of the hallway. 'Toby said you'd be here.'

A flicker of uncertainty crossed Simon's eyes. 'He phoned to say he was here.'

'So you thought you'd come and greet him?' Ryan asked.

'Yes. He seemed in a state.'

Maggie nodded. 'I'd be in a state if I were him. His fiancée is dead, and his favourite thing in all the world, his car, has been destroyed along with, potentially, his business and his good name.'

'His business?' Simon's voice faltered. 'What do you mean?'

'You know what I mean.' Maggie stared at Simon as she and Ryan moved further into the small bedroom that Toby

331

had been occupying until so recently. 'Why don't you sit down? Ryan and I have some questions for you.'

'You've asked me enough questions. Where's Toby? I'm worried about him.'

David stepped into the room, his breadth blocking the door, barring the exit. 'You don't have to answer their questions, but you do have to answer mine, and the first of them is, how did you get in here in the middle of the night? You don't live here. Do you have a key?'

'Toby gave me one, for emergencies.'

'Toby did?' Ryan's eyes narrowed. 'Toby gave you a key to a house he doesn't live in. I can just about accept that he had a key, as he was staying here so recently, but why would he give it to you? You claimed that he was an acquaintance, not a friend.'

'You'll have to ask him.'

David continued to watch the mechanic. 'I will do that.'

Simon perched on the edge of the single bed. 'He said he'd be here. Maybe he's in another room.'

'He is, but not here.'

'Then, where . . .?'

'He's safe.' Maggie exchanged a quick glance with David, who gave her an almost imperceptible wink of reassurance as she went on. 'Simon, you came here because Toby called you. Said he wanted to give himself up to the police, but you persuaded him to talk things through first. Isn't that right?'

'No, he . . .'

'We were with him at the time—' Maggie brandished her phone '—and we recorded the call.'

Simon paled. 'You might have recorded Toby's half of the conversation, but not mine.'

'True, but he told us what you said. He has no reason to lie to us by this point.'

'Has he been arrested?' Simon swallowed.

'Not *yet*.' David put enough emphasis on the word yet, to make it clear that was still a possibility.

Simon mumbled, 'I didn't kill Tania.'

'No one said you did. But you and your—' Maggie was interrupted by the sound of running feet outside the room and then the door flying open.

'What is the meaning of this?' Heidi, wrapped in a silk dressing gown and matching slippers, stormed into the room.

'Ah, Miss Spenser-Davies.' David sounded commanding. 'Your timing is perfect. Perhaps you could wake your guests and ask them to assemble in the dining room. Oh, and I should say that Constable Harker is already in there. I'd hate for someone lurking in the shadows to make any of you jump.'

As the two friends, shepherded along by Ryan, reluctantly did as they were told, Maggie turned to David, unable to contain her smile. 'Assemble in the dining room? I thought I was the detective fiction fan.'

'Takes one to know one.'

*

Roused from their beds, Heidi, Hugh and Daisy appeared in their nightwear. Patterned silk and satin in Heidi and Daisy's case, boxers and a white T-shirt in Hugh's.

A worried-looking Hugh and a furious Heidi, hand in hand, leant against the sideboard that, in only a few hours' time, would be groaning under the weight of various cooked breakfast choices. Monika, meanwhile, appeared more curious about Simon's presence than annoyed about having to attend to such late callers, while Daisy, wiping sleep from her eyes, slumped onto the nearest chair.

Maggie stood with Ryan by the door that connected the hall to the kitchen and back bedroom, so recently used by Toby and which, she imagined, had once been used by a scullery maid. Constable Harker had moved to stand in front of the door to the main stairway and, therefore, the front door.

Heidi broke the tense silence. 'Are you going to tell me why you have brought Simon here and what is so important that it couldn't wait until morning?'

'We did not bring Simon here,' Ryan answered quickly. 'Where are Bea and Paolo?'

'They left this afternoon.'

'Left to go where?' David asked.

'Bea to her parents, and Paolo back to Morocco.'

Perversely pleased that Bea hadn't flown back with Paolo, Ryan remained silent as Sergeant Peters addressed the group.

'I will speak to them later. For now, Maggie has something to say. Perhaps you would all like to follow Miss Makepeace's example and sit down.'

'I don't need to be invited to sit in my own home.' Heidi bristled.

'Then stay standing.'

There was a begrudging pulling out of chairs as the small group of friends sat anyway. Maggie and Ryan followed suit, but David and Constable Harker remained on their feet, blocking the exits.

Before Maggie could launch into the statement she'd been rehearsing in her head ever since they'd climbed into the car and driven to the manor, Hugh asked, 'Did you find Toby?'

'We did.' Ryan nodded.

'I've been worried about him. Is he alright?'

'Considering what he's been through, then yes, he's alright.'

'Where is he?' Daisy was staring blankly at the cream tablecloth.

'He's safe.' Ryan had a mental image of Mr Robbins sitting in his orange plastic seat at the foot of the stairs, while Toby lay on the bed upstairs.

'Good.' Hugh looked satisfied as he said, 'I know it's a frightful cheek of me to ask, as this isn't my home, but would it be alright if we all had a coffee or something? I suddenly need caffeine.'

# Chapter Forty-four

Although it had done nothing to ease the nerves that were attacking Maggie's stomach, the cup of hot chocolate she now cradled (Monika had refused to produce real coffee at that time of night) was providing a welcome source of comfort as she finally spoke to the assembled group.

'Hugh, I take it that Heidi is now aware of your driving ban?' As Heidi inclined her head, Maggie swapped her focus to Hugh. 'You didn't tell the police about it.'

'No. I was going to, but . . .'

Heidi put a protective arm across Hugh. 'I can't see why you need to bring that up.'

Maggie moved her eyes to a suddenly pale Heidi. 'I'm bringing it up because if your boyfriend hadn't crashed the car, then I don't think I'd have got to the bottom of this.'

'Bottom of Tania's death?' Daisy's eyes widened. 'Really? You've worked out what happened?'

'With Ryan's help.'

Daisy gave Hugh a suspicious look. 'What driving ban?'

Hugh sighed. 'I was caught driving dangerously a while back. Had my licence revoked. I shouldn't have been driving Toby's car, but Tania needed the suits for the wedding, and well . . . the chance to drive Sandy was so tempting . . .' He looked up at Maggie. 'I assume you told the police?'

'I did.'

'I thought you would. I just wish I'd never . . .'

As Hugh's words petered out, Ryan filled in the rest of the story. 'As you all know, Tania was in the car when Hugh crashed it. Luckily no one was hurt, but the car was written off. After this, Toby wouldn't talk to Hugh. We assumed this was because Tania could have been killed. We have since learnt that was only part of the reason for his anger.'

'I imagine he was furious that Hugh had lied to him.' Monika was not impressed. 'Whenever Mr Marrell visited, he drove here. He loved that car.'

Hugh blanched. 'He was fuming. And rightly so. I should never have got behind the wheel. But I honestly thought . . .'

'I'm not sure you thought beyond yourself in that moment.' Maggie shook her head. 'I'm sure Sergeant Peters here will be talking to you about your driving offences later. For now, however, we should be oddly grateful to you. Toby was furious about the loss of his car, and that you lied to him, and that you could have killed his bride. But there was something else as well. He was afraid.'

'Afraid of what?' Heidi asked.

Maggie lifted her hot chocolate to her lips, taking a sip before saying, 'Let me take you back to the night Tania died. As you know, Ryan met Tania in The Mariner after she and Toby had rowed.'

Ryan took up the reins. 'I saw Tania and Toby arguing as they ate their desserts. I couldn't hear what it was about, but afterwards, Tania joined me at my table. It was busy, and there was nowhere else for her to sit.

'We got talking, and I discovered that Tania was having trust issues with Toby. At the time I wondered if he was having an affair, but Tania discounted this, and we soon did too.'

As Ryan picked up his mug, Maggie took over. 'It was when we began to look into Toby's business that we realised he had, accidentally, found himself involved in something he didn't want to be involved in.'

'Like what?' Hugh asked.

'You said, when we spoke at the hotel, that Toby and you had fallen out before, but never for long. This time, however, you were concerned he wasn't going to come round.'

'That's right. He did, though.'

'Did he explain why he'd been so angry?'

'He didn't need to. It's obvious. I destroyed his car and could have done the same to Tania. What other reason could there have been?'

'Because, in Sandy's glove compartment, Toby had hidden a gift for Tania. A very expensive gift. One it was now impossible to retrieve.' Maggie turned to Simon. 'Isn't that right, Mr Taylor?'

Simon nodded. 'I didn't know what was in there, but Toby came back late at night. He was clearly trying to get into the glove box – but it was pointless. Anything inside would have been crushed, along with the bonnet of the car.'

Monika played with her mug in her palms. 'Is Toby alright?'

'He's okay. Shaken, but okay.' David said as he left his vigil by the door and came to sit next to Maggie as she went on.

'So, first we have a smashed car, with something of value in the bonnet that Toby is desperate to get out. Not only that, but we have an overheard conversation between Toby and someone – presumably a work colleague. This conversation was about an issue so serious that Toby had to go to work only hours after his fiancée had been killed. This made us want to look more closely at Toby's working life.'

Simon shuffled in his chair. 'Hence your visit to the office I rent to him.'

'Precisely. A visit which left me in need of hospital treatment.'

'What?' Heidi sat up straighter. 'Are you alright?'

'I am now, thank you.' Maggie switched her attention to Daisy. 'When we met in Heidi's garden, I told you that Ryan had been with Tania at the pub. You asked me if Tania had been moaning to him about Toby. I considered it an innocent enough inquiry at the time. But it wasn't, was it? You were gauging what might have been said, trying to find out if Tania had said anything damning to Ryan, and if Ryan, in turn, had passed that information onto me.'

Daisy faltered. 'No. I only meant that . . . well, we told you that we didn't rate Toby.'

'And yet he was allowed to hide out here.'

'We didn't know that until he was already here.' Daisy protested. 'I doubt it would've crossed his mind to ask first. He always needs to have his own way.'

'I remember you saying.' Maggie gave a soft smile. 'You rather overstated that fact.'

'All he cared about was his bloody car.' Daisy twirled a strand of hair around her fingers.

'So you've said.' Maggie moved them back to the point. 'When I first spoke to you, I didn't tell you what Ryan had discussed with Tania in the pub, and it would have been too obvious if you'd asked me exactly what Tania had said to him.'

Heidi frowned. 'Why is that a problem?'

'For you, it isn't, but for Daisy it was vital information.' Maggie shifted on her seat so she was directly facing the redhead. 'You weren't sure what had been said or what I knew, so you had to act. You had to assume I was aware of what had been going on with Toby's business and felt the need to do something that would frighten me into silence. That something being to have me hit over the head.'

David moved closer to Daisy. 'Maggie could have been killed.'

'I could have, but not by Daisy. In this case, she was simply the messenger.'

Heidi's forehead furrowed in confusion. 'Daze?'

When her friend didn't reply but just stared silently at Maggie, Heidi inched her chair closer to Hugh.

'Nothing to say, Daisy?' Ryan asked.

'I have plenty to say, but it wouldn't be constructive.'

'I'm sure it would be interesting, though.'

'I didn't attack anyone.'

As Daisy glared at the policeman, Maggie changed tack, asking the room at large, 'What can any of you tell me about Rachel Zimmerman?'

'Toby's business partner?' Monika asked.

'Partner, associate, colleague – no one seems sure about her actual role. We got to wondering exactly who worked for whom. So Ryan made some enquiries at Companies House.'

Hugh frowned. 'That bitch didn't take his business from Toby, did she?'

Maggie saw a flash of the same hurt in Hugh's eyes as she'd witnessed when he'd told her of his past relationship with Rachel. 'If she did, it wasn't official. Mermaid Imports is registered in the name of Toby Marrell. However, we've spoken to Toby, and he wasn't sure how much longer that would be the case.'

'How do you mean?' Simon asked.

'I mean, that Miss Zimmerman was putting pressure on him to sign the business over to her.'

'Cow!' Daisy growled. 'She always was greedy. Can't stand anyone having what she wants.'

Ryan commented. 'This morning, Paolo hinted that there was no love lost between you and Rachel, Daisy.'

'She picks people up, uses them and then spits them out.' Daisy dipped her head towards Hugh. 'She did that to you, didn't she?

'And to you.' Maggie watched carefully to see Daisy's reaction. 'Hugh told us Rachel left him for someone else. And that someone was you, wasn't it?'

Daisy shook her head. 'Don't be ridiculous.'

Observing everyone's silent, stunned gaze move from her to Daisy, Maggie went on. 'How long was it between you learning that Tania might have confided in Ryan and you calling Rachel?'

'I did no such—'

David interrupted. 'It is standard procedure in a suspicious death case to view the phone records of all involved. You've called an overseas number several times over the past week. An overseas number in Morocco.'

'Yes, I've spoken to Paolo.'

'Perhaps, but Paolo has been in England for a few days. Why would you call his Moroccan number while he was here? And before you say you didn't know he was back, don't bother. We know you knew he was here.'

'So what?'

'Are you denying you had a relationship with Rachel?'

A loaded silence cloaked the room, eventually broken by Hugh.

'*You're* the one she cheated on me with?'

Daisy sighed. 'It was a long time ago. It was stupid, and I was ashamed of my behaviour towards you. It was over before it began. I'm sorry, Hugh.'

When Hugh didn't reply, David nudged Maggie to continue.

'As I was saying, Daisy informed Rachel that Tania had shared her suspicions about what Toby might have been up to with Ryan.'

'Why would she do that?' Heidi asked.

'Because she's still in love with her.'

'I most certainly am not.'

Leaving Daisy's fervent claim for a moment, Maggie continued. 'Shortly afterwards, there were two orchestrated attacks on myself and Mr Robbins – not attacks that were meant to kill – but warnings.'

'What happened to you, Maggie?' Heidi held her breath as she waited for a reply.

'I was hit over the head. Hard. While I was reading some paperwork in Toby's office. Paperwork I now know Toby himself had been reading in an attempt to see the depth of Rachel's deception.' Maggie turned to David. 'The office hadn't been broken into; it was Toby. He left in a hurry. It was as simple as that. He wasn't thinking straight and simply forgot to lock up.'

'Thinking straight can go to pot when you lose the person you love,' David muttered as he looked at Maggie.

'None of you appear to be thinking straight.' Daisy folded her hands over her chest, as if giving herself a reassuring hug. 'If you think I could have hit anyone, then you're insane.'

'We didn't say you did.' Ryan shook his head. 'Rachel's latest lover could have, though. She does seem to get through them.'

'What latest lover?' Heidi looked at Hugh, who shrugged, cluelessly.

'Who hit you, Maggie?' Monika was now observing Daisy with open suspicion.

'Simon.'

The mechanic stiffened, his jaw set, his mouth firmly shut.

'Daisy might just have had the strength to knock me out, but no way could she have wielded a blow that would render Mr Robbins unconscious; not that he was the target.'

'That was me.' Ryan fixed an accusing eye on Simon. 'But in the dark of the bedsit, you just hit out at the only figure you saw.'

Simon remained silent.

'But why would Simon . . .?' Heidi gaped at the mechanic for a second, before she added, 'Oh, I see . . . because you are Rachel's latest partner.'

'Victim, more like. She has a way of making people do what she wants.' Daisy growled with distaste. 'How long has she had you in her clutches, then?'

'Longer than anyone else she's ever been with!' Simon's lips dripped venom as he glowered at Daisy.

Maggie observed the mechanic carefully for a moment. I assume you took the note I'd written about the phone call

I overheard. I'd like to know where you were hiding while I was in Toby's office. Hiding places aren't in plentiful supply, and I would have heard you come up the stairs.'

Simon locked his dark eyes on hers, his previous friendliness gone.

'I suggest you answer the question, Mr Taylor.' David gestured to Constable Harker to move around the room and stand behind Simon's seat.

'I'm not saying anything without a solicitor.'

'Very wise.' Sergeant Peters turned to Harker. 'Please take Mr Taylor to the station and arrange for a solicitor to visit.'

As Simon was escorted from the room, handcuffs now in place, Heidi was distraught. 'I can't believe he's a killer. I let him into my home.'

'And I can't believe he's been dating Rachel! I took him for a chap with more sense than that.' Hugh took hold of Heidi's hand.

Maggie said, 'He's a fool who has been manipulated. But I don't think he's ever murdered anyone.'

Hugh clasped Heidi's palm tighter. 'But that means it has to have been . . .'

'Rachel.' Daisy broke in. 'It must have been her. We all know she's more than capable.'

'She's in Morocco.' Heidi shook her head.

'She is now, but it doesn't take long to fly from Morocco to the UK and back again. It is perfectly feasible that she flew out officially, nipped back with Paolo, or another private pilot, killed Tania, and then flew back again. No one would be any the wiser.'

Heidi drew in a sharp breath. 'But why? Tania wouldn't have hurt a fly.'

Maggie answered before Daisy could. 'Because Rachel was afraid that Toby had told Tania about the additional business enterprise she was involved in and had, by default, got Toby involved in.'

'Doing what?' Daisy asked.

Maggie put a hand to her own necklace as she said, 'You all had some lovely pendants on earlier. Presents, I believe?'

'Gifts from Toby and Tania for being bridesmaids, yes.' Heidi touched her neck, where the necklace would have been.

'Moroccan jewellery. It's gorgeous, and not that expensive from the markets of Marrakesh and similar. However, you can also buy extremely expensive, stunningly beautiful and very saleable jewellery there.'

'What are you saying?' Heidi asked. 'That Rachel was selling jewellery as well as furniture?'

'She was and has been, without Toby's knowledge, for some time. Without paying customs duty.'

'Smuggling?'

'Precisely.'

'Don't be daft. Rachel's many things, but she isn't that stupid.' Daisy wasn't having any of it.

Maggie's eyes narrowed. 'You just claimed Rachel was capable of murder; now you're telling us she's not that stupid.'

'I was referring to her smuggling.' Daisy's cheeks blazed almost as red as her hair. 'How on earth could anyone pull something like that off anyway?'

'By being very careful and making sure she was usually the one overseeing the flights and receiving the deliveries at the airport.' Ryan placed his hands flat on the table. 'And she was careful. Right up until she tried to include Toby in her enterprise. Rachel misjudged him. Thought that, as we've heard before, he was all about himself, all about not caring providing he was alright. But, although Toby admitted to us that he could be like that, he loved Tania – and when Rachel caught him in her web of deceit, he wasn't as supportive as she'd assumed he'd be.'

Maggie drained the rest of her hot chocolate before adding to what Ryan had said. 'To prevent Toby from going to the police, she threatened to make it look as if he was the one behind the smuggling, saying she'd take his business from him if he didn't do what she wanted. When Toby began to hunt through the office paperwork for evidence of her crime. He went through a folder of invoices – some had been marked with a green cross. Rachel had previously told him they were marks to show she'd double-checked that the invoices were paid – that the money had gone through. But if that had been true, then surely every invoice would have had a green cross on it. Toby came to the conclusion that the crosses marked consignments which had a little extra something hidden within them. He told Rachel he was going to go to the police, but that he'd give her until after his honeymoon to give up what she was doing. If she did that, he'd say nothing to the police.'

'I bet she wasn't for persuading.' Hugh sighed, 'Rachel doesn't like being told what to do.'

Heidi frowned, 'No wonder Toby didn't seem that upset over Tania – he's probably been so scared that Rachel will get him arrested, that he hasn't had a chance to let things sink in.'

'He's certainly had a lot to deal with lately.'

'Umm.' Daisy leant forward a fraction. 'Are you saying that Rachel flew over here, in secret, just to kill Tania and frighten Toby into saying nothing?'

'No. Rachel is in Morocco just as everyone claimed.' Maggie placed her mug back on the table. 'I'm saying *you* killed Tania.'

A terrible silence descended as every pair of eyes landed on Daisy.

'But she was one of my best friends!'

'She was, but you still loved Rachel. You wanted to show her how much. Wanted to prove your love in a way no one else would. While Simon believed himself and Rachel to be so mutually in love that he was willing to assault two people for her, he drew the line at murder. Finally, here was your chance. *You'd* do what she wanted – *you'd* be loyal to the end and win her back from him.'

Heidi's face paled. 'Daze?'

Avoiding her friend's face, Daisy glared at Maggie. 'You have no evidence to prove that at all. In fact, as I was in the hotel, there's no way I could have been down by the harbour.'

'Tania sent you a text after the row with Toby.'

'Rubbish. Tania's mobile went missing, washed out to sea or stolen, probably. No one knows what messages she did or didn't send.'

Breaking his silence, David said, 'We know, because we have your phones. Your old one – which was found in the spa a couple of hours ago – stuffed down the side of a large stack of towel bales. You said you'd lost it. Then, you got a new pay-as-you-go one just a few days ago. We have that too.'

Daisy stared at Sergeant Peters in horror as she saw him hold up both her phones, each safely deposited in its own see-through evidence bag.

'You had no right to take my things!'

'This is a murder enquiry.' He nodded at the first phone. 'This is your original phone – not lost, but carefully stowed away, ready to be collected when this was all over.'

Not giving Daisy the chance to reply, Maggie flicked through her notebook. 'I was surprised that you hadn't deleted the texts between you and Rachel. Quite explicit, some of them; on your side at least. Rachel told you she was dating Simon. She assured you – as the texts you exchanged show – that she was using him as a means to an end, that it meant nothing – but if that was the case, why date him for so long? It has been six months, according to Simon. You must have been beginning to panic. To think that *you* were the one she was using.'

'Well, I . . .'

'You were cocky enough to believe we'd never look at you as a murderer. That we'd never believe one of Tania's best friends could have done such a thing. Plus, you wanted proof to show Rachel how far you'd go for her in the hope that she'd take you back.' Maggie read from her notebook. 'At thirty-five minutes past ten on the night she died, Tania sent you a text saying she'd had a row with Toby about all the secrets he'd been keeping and that she was getting some fresh air by the harbour. You replied, saying she should stay there, and you'd come and make sure she was alright.'

'I . . .'

'One of the locals saw Tania texting. For a while I thought he'd seen whoever had attacked her, but no, thanks to a photo Toby gave us of Tania in her last days of life, we've been able to confirm that it was her he saw as she paused in her walk to the harbour to message you.'

'You received a text from Tania, climbed out of the window of your downstairs room at the hotel, crossed the garden, thus avoiding all CCTV cameras, and went to find Tania. What happened? Did she cry? Was she worried about Toby having another woman?'

Daisy's expression changed in an instant. Gone was the pretence of caring; instead, hard lines of determination etched her face. 'Toby's a fool. If he'd just let Rachel use his furniture to bring in the jewellery, then none of this would have happened.'

'Tania had no idea about it.' Ryan shook his head.

'I had to be sure. For Rachel's sake. But Tania wouldn't tell me what Toby had said. Said it was private – I couldn't take the chance. I didn't want . . . We'd only just got back together.'

'You were together again, then? As a couple.'

An odd smile came to Daisy's face. 'Yes, she said I was the only one, that she'd made a mistake in leaving me, that she was just using Simon as he was handy to have around, and—'

Maggie interrupted. 'Rachel was using everyone. You *and* Simon included.'

'No way. She'd never do that to me.' Daisy agitatedly pushed a strand of hair from her face. 'If Toby had reported Rachel then ...'

'She would go to prison, and you'd never have the chance to live happily ever after with her. Not that that would have happened.' Maggie watched as David produced a pair of handcuffs from his pocket. 'And now you'll go to prison too. You never know, you might get lucky and be in the same one as Rachel.'

# Chapter Forty-five

Standing outside the manor house, the dark of the night wrapping around her, Maggie yanked up the zip of her coat. 'David, how did you know where we were?'

'Ryan called me from the garage's bathroom before you left for the manor. He's a sensible lad.'

'I'm glad you finally think so.'

'I know you're sore that I had to take him in for questioning, but it's my job.'

Maggie nodded. 'I know. Sorry.'

'No problem.'

'Thanks for coming.'

David gave her a sad smile. 'You didn't think I wouldn't, did you?'

'You only came because Ryan phoned you.'

'My shoes were already on, and I was on my way to talk to Mr Robbins to find out where you were. I knew you'd have told him.'

'Oh.' Maggie shivered in the dark of the night as she watched a police car drive Daisy away. 'That was scary – exciting, but scary.'

'Go home, Maggie. We'll need to talk to you soon, get it all written up properly, but for now, find Ryan, and get some sleep.'

# Monday 16th June

Maggie was amazed she'd slept, but the sheer rush of the previous evening had wiped her out. Now, having found a similarly refreshed Ryan already up and making coffee, they were soon on their way to the bedsit over the chippy to tell Toby what had happened. On their arrival, however, they found that David had beaten them to it.

Toby looked shell-shocked as he said, 'I've just had a call from Sergeant Peters. Simon has confessed to the assaults. Apparently, during both attacks, he had the foresight to come up each set of stairs without shoes on.'

Ryan looked down at his own feet. 'Socks wouldn't have made a noise.'

Maggie automatically ran a hand across the back of her head. 'It's no wonder I didn't hear him.'

Toby sighed. 'What will happen to Daisy?'

'She'll be formally questioned, but the evidence of the phone records and her past relationship with Rachel seem quite damning.'

'I can't believe she pushed Tania off the wall.'

'Perhaps she didn't mean to,' Ryan suggested. 'Perhaps it was a row that went wrong.'

Maggie shook her head. 'At no point did she claim it was an accident. She wanted to impress Rachel.'

'Has Rachel been arrested too?'

'Not yet, but she will be. The police also have some questions to ask Paolo, and Hugh will be taken in for questioning about driving while banned.'

'Oh God.' Toby cradled his head in his hands. 'That only leaves Heidi, and she's so in love with Hugh I doubt she'll even speak to me again. I've lost my wife and all my friends in one go.'

Ryan muttered, 'I'm so sorry.'

'You've no need to be. If it hadn't been for you two, I would probably have been blamed for Tania's death.' Toby got to his feet. 'Do you think Daisy meant to frame me?'

'I think so. After all, everyone knows that the most likely suspect in a murder is the deceased's partner.'

★

Four hours later, their lunchtime shift complete, Maggie unwrapped two parcels of fish and chips and passed one to Ryan.

As they sat, side by side, their legs stretched out before them on Mousehole's tiny beach, Ryan said, 'I feel as if we ought to be celebrating, but I can't help feeling sorry for Toby and Heidi.'

Maggie chewed as she spoke. 'I know what you mean, but it still feels good. We helped catch a killer and broke up a smuggling racket.'

'I suppose we did.'

They ate a few more chips, watching the gentle ebb and flow of the waves before Ryan asked, 'What did Izzie say when you told her?'

'That she was very proud of me, and that I was right to keep busy while she was away. Keep my mind off her being so far away.'

'Sounds sensible.' Ryan broke some batter off his cod. 'I could do with my mind being taken off things too. Bea really took me for a mug.'

'What a group of friends! Manipulative and then some.'

'Do you think Bea knew that Paolo was smuggling things into the UK?'

'I doubt it.'

Ryan thought for a while, before asking, 'Should we do it again, then? Properly?'

'Properly?'

'Well, you're the one who's always wanted to be a private detective.'

'You mean, do what Izzie's always told me to do and set up a detective agency?' Maggie found herself grinning.

'Yeah. Why not? I've searched online, and there isn't one this end of Cornwall, and well, while I think we should keep working in the shop, I'd like to be busier too – take my mind off being played by Bea for one.'

'Keep both of us from moping by setting up a detective agency?'

'Yup.' Ryan got up and picked up a nearby piece of driftwood, using the end to write in the sand.

*The Fish and Chip Shop Detective Agency*

'How perfect!' Maggie clapped. 'Let's do it!'

'It's time for The Fish and Chip Shop Detective Agency to start trading.'

Ryan sat back down. 'And the first thing we are going to do is start saving for a car. But not . . .'

'A red one!'

Maggie and Ryan sealed the deal with a chink of their Coke cans and a promise to always turn the lights on at a crime scene.

**RAISING READERS**
Books Build Bright Futures

Dear Reader,

We'd love your attention for one more page to tell you about the crisis in children's reading, and what we can all do.

Studies have shown that reading for fun is the **single biggest predictor of a child's future life chances** – more than family circumstance, parents' educational background or income. It improves academic results, mental health, wealth, communication skills, ambition and happiness.[1]

The number of children reading for fun is in rapid decline. Young people have a lot of competition for their time. In 2024, 1 in 10 children and young people in the UK aged 5 to 18 did not own a single book at home.[2]

Hachette works extensively with schools, libraries and literacy charities, but here are some ways we can all raise more readers:

- Reading to children for just 10 minutes a day makes a difference
- Don't give up if children aren't regular readers – there will be books for them!
- Visit bookshops and libraries to get recommendations
- Encourage them to listen to audiobooks
- Support school libraries
- Give books as gifts

There's a lot more information about how to encourage children to read on our website: **www.RaisingReaders.co.uk**

Thank you for reading.

hachette UK

---

[1] OECD, '21st-Century Readers: Developing Literacy Skills in a Digital World', 2021, https://www.oecd.org/en/publications/21st-century-readers_a83d84cb-en.html

[2] National Literacy Trust, 'Book Ownership in 2024', November 2024, https://literacytrust.org.uk/research-services/research-reports/book-ownership-in-2024

# Acknowledgements

First, I must thank my very own 'Ryan', who helped me form the initial concept for The Fish and Chip Shop Detectives – and for letting me bounce countless ideas off him as I plotted and planned this novel.

Special thanks must go to Hodder & Stoughton for taking a chance on me and my detectives – Maggie and Ryan – and to my editor, Audrey Linton, for being so enthusiastic about my new Cornish adventures. An extra thank you must go to my agent, Kiran, of Keane Kataria, for her help, valued input, kind guidance, and for offering my work to Hodder in the first place.

Finally, to my Cornish grandparents – gone but never forgotten – whose home in Penzance kept me, my brother and my parents visiting year after year. Little did I know, as I played on Marazion beach, or bought rock in the Buccaneer gift shop, that I was storing up experiences that would serve me well so many years later.